WHEN YOUR BEAUTY *IS* THE BEAST

Fairytale Anthology #1

www.YeOldeDragonBooks.com

Ye Olde Dragon Books
P.O. Box 30802
Middleburg Hts., OH 44130

www.YeOldeDragonBooks.com

2OldeDragons@gmail.com

ISBN 13: 978-1-952345-37-1

Published in the United States of America
Publication Date: May 1, 2021

Table of Contents

Foreword

It all began in 2019 in a little restaurant in St. Louis. We were attending the Realm Makers Conference. Michelle Levigne and I had a very long lunch, partly because we got carried away with plots and characters and all the projects we had whirling around in our brains. And partly because we had a waitress who ran in circles and simply would **not** bring us our check! Our forty-five-minute lunch break stretched to two hours. We missed one whole session in the afternoon while the waitress continued to blow us off for a table of about twelve people who decided at the last minute to insist on separate checks. But we came away from that luncheon talking about forming our own cooperative to get our many projects into print. We needed editors, formatting skills, networking, and between the two of us, we had the skills and the contacts to get the job done. We kicked it around for another six to eight months, and Michelle kept ending her emails with: "...are you regretting this yet?"

I have never regretted it! We each fulfill what the other needs, and our partnership works. Living two states apart is a challenge, but we compensate with several emails a day and the occasional phone call. Our main goal was to publish our own books. But we also wanted to give something back to those who had been our biggest support system, the Realm Makers group.

For both of us, Realm Makers has been a tribe to call Home, a group of crazy writers who gather once a year to celebrate new books, cry a few tears over failed projects, dust off scraped egos and gain the courage to try again. We both started with the first Realm Makers Conference in St. Louis in 2013 with about eighty science fiction and fantasy writers, the orphans and outcasts of the Christian literary world. Now Realm Makers has a roster of thousands of members, a presence on Facebook, and a shiny new website for daily interaction called the RealmSphere.

Young and old, writers have found their niche with these crazy, geeky, fandom-loving folks. They come from all over the United States and from as far away as Great Britain, New Zealand, Japan, and Australia. Maybe more countries, but those are the ones I've met personally. They come to the annual banquet as elves, dwarves, fairies, hobbits, Avengers, Dr. Who's many incarnations, and any number of other fantasy creatures, occasionally even cartoon characters. They are the hardest working, most dedicated, most loving and generous people on the planet. Michelle and I feel a debt of gratitude to them for their collective support over the past several years.

We decided to open not just one but two anthologies every year to allow our friends and allies to participate. (Expect the next one around Halloween!) Then we added a couple of writers I met long before Realm Makers. They fit well with this crazy bunch. Stir the batter. Voila!

Well, if we thought we were giving back to our community, I'm afraid we were mistaken. These amazing writers turned the tables on us and we are in their debt. Our friends and colleagues have amazed us by writing the most astounding stories I've ever read! You are holding in your hands a truly mind-blowing collection of stories. We threw out the idea of a Beauty and the Beast retelling—with a twist. Beauty IS the beast in some way, shape or form. Surprise us.

Wow. Did they ever!

We have humor, pathos, action, and even a touch of horror. (And some stories that we just could not resist, even if they strayed a little close to the "classic" fairytale.) What our friends sent us were gifts, one right after another, and it has been a privilege beyond compare to assemble this book. With every story, I've marveled at these talented people. I consider it an honor and a blessing—one I hope will be repeated many times in the years to come.

To my "partner in crime", I'm glad we had that lunch, Michelle. It was worth missing a session. This has been a blast!

To everyone who contributed to this collection, thank you so much. You've blessed me with your stories, and challenged me to be a better writer and a better editor. You ROCK!

To everyone who reads this book… well, to quote a popular movie, "You're in for one wild ride!"

Enjoy.

Deborah Cullins Smith
March 2021

Foreword Redux

<Cue: Evil Laughter>

First off, kudos and enormous gratitude to my partner in crime, who carried the hero's portion of the task of this first anthology. She sent out the invitations, maintained contact with our authors and sent friendly nudges and did the initial reading and the vast (we're talking 96.55555555 %) majority of the editing.

(This is the AA moment, where I confess I have this mental disease of taking on dang too many projects ...)

Thank you, Deborah, for making this lovely, fun, amazing volume possible. I promise I'll do a bigger share of the heavy lifting on the next ... dozen or so.

Yeah, we're gonna have FUN with this little series of anthologies. Basically, faerie tale spin-offs and rip-offs in the spring, and classic movie monster "tributes" in the fall. Look for Wolfman stories in the fall ... (check out the back page if you're interested in more information)

There's not much else I need to say. Deborah took care of it, relating our history and the mega-thanks to the gutsy people who took a chance on us. You guys are awesome. I had such fun reading through all the stories as I did the formatting.

Thank you, everyone who has bought this fun collection of "Hey, what if ..." You're gonna have fun. We hope you laugh and shiver and maybe sniffle a little, gasp, grin, and stop and say, "Hmm..."

Ready?
Set?
Go!

Michelle L. Levigne
March 2021

AFTER HAPPILY EVER

Kristiana Sfirlea

It isn't easy being a marriage counselor to fairy tale couples.

Polyphonte maintained her neutral expression as she watched the argument unfold between the couple sitting on the couch. Beauty and the Beast. This was their third session, and already Poly recognized that most of their issues were tales as old as time.

"He never cleans the sink after he shaves!" Belle exclaimed. "It was bad enough when he used to shed, but now every day I have to wipe down a sink full of stubble—"

"Something you wouldn't *have* to do if you hadn't *insisted* on cutting the servants' hours," Beast—otherwise known as Adam—broke in.

"We were working them too hard. They never had any time off!"

"And now *I* don't have any time off from your complaining! What does it matter if there's stubble in the sink? Who cares? It's not like we ever have guests over. You're too busy with your nose in a book. We don't even go out to town anymore!"

Belle looked down at her folded hands. "You knew who I was when you married me."

Adam, as usual, gave into his temper. "I thought the only reason you stayed inside so much was because you were my prisoner! I didn't realize that marrying you would make me *yours*."

Both sets of eyes snapped to Poly, each pleading with her to take their side. It was a comically common occurrence in sessions like these. In her two years working as a counselor for After Happily Ever Services, she'd seen nearly every couple in the book—as in, any fairy tale book you can get your hands on. They came, always, by recommendation. "Polyphonte saved our marriage!" Cinderella would say, and the next thing you know, her schedule was booked through the next six months.

Never mind what her credentials must look like to the average passerby. A thirty-year-old blonde, fresh in her career, with no love life of which to speak—what could *she* know about fixing marriages?

Well, she knew one thing: a good marriage counselor never

picks sides. They look down the middle for a compromise.

"I have a thought." Poly pushed her round glasses up the bridge of her nose. "Adam, it sounds to me like you're feeling as though Belle is purposefully ignoring your social needs. And Belle, it sounds to me like you're feeling as though your home and safe spaces are being disrespected. I'm not saying that either of you are doing this on purpose. Very few couples I see are actually *trying* to make each other miserable, if you can believe it. But it's important for all of us to understand where the other is coming from. Now here's my thought. What if you had a gathering at your palace? Something that would allow Adam the chance to visit with friends and Belle the opportunity to show off your beautiful home."

Belle perked up. "Like a ball?"

"Well," Poly backpedaled, "a ball is a rather *large* gathering, but—"

"A ball is a wonderful idea!" Adam's smile lit up the room like a thousand lanterns. "How did we not think of it?"

"Organizing a ball can be a stressful experience," Poly reminded them. "For your marriage's sake, perhaps a smaller—"

But Adam's smile was so bright it was blinding, and Belle's eyes glowed with glass slippers and elegant gowns and endless chocolate fondue. There was no going back now. The party planning spirit had them possessed.

"We'll host it at the end of the month," Belle announced excitedly. "Oh, you have to come, Polyphonte! Say you'll come. We couldn't do it without you!"

Poly thought of the stack of fairy tale books piled on her bedside table at home. Her "homework," as she called it. If there was one lesson she'd learned from those time-tested stories, it was that balls changed people's lives. The question was, did she want her life changed?

"I'll think about it," she said.

~~~~~

Lunch break found Polyphonte at her favorite place in town: Honey Bear's Bakery. She went inside and spotted the owner, her dear friend Bruin, handing out samples near the register. Bruin was a mammoth of a man. Built like a bear, some would say, but it was more than that. He *was* a bear. A werebear, to be precise. Some called it a curse—Bruin called it his life's calling. An unfortunate camping trip in his youth had resulted in a considerable growth spurt,
~~~~~

impressive facial hair, and an all-consuming taste for honey. Since that day, he could pound dough faster than five bakers, make hairnets look as good as a queen's barrettes, and dazzle the dullest of taste buds with his honey baked goods.

Not to mention, Bruin was Honey Bear's Bakery's very own mascot. Customers adored his transformation into an apron-wearing grizzly bear who padded between lines, letting anyone who dared stroke his brown, fuzzy fur.

Poly would've liked to bury her face in that fur today and hide from the world, but she forced a smile on her face as she approached her friend. "What's cookin', Bruin?"

"Just my world-famous honey breakfast cakes." He offered her the sample plate with a gentlemanly bow. "Care to taste?"

"They sound delicious, but I think I'll stick with tea and honey today."

Bruin's smiling eyes turned squinty. Appraising. "Something's wrong."

"What?" Poly gave a high-pitched laugh. "No, it's not. I'm fine. Really."

"You never refuse free samples unless something's the matter."

"Maybe I had a big breakfast," she mumbled.

Bruin put down his samples with the decisive *clank* of plate against counter. "Get your tea and pick a table. I'll be there shortly."

A few minutes later, cup of tea in hand, Poly sat down at a table for two. Bruin folded his massive frame into the chair across from her, and not for the first time, she felt like one of her very own clients under his gentle gaze.

"So." She averted her stare. Blew on her tea. "I had a session with Beauty and the Beast today, and they're having a ball."

Bruin bit into a honey breakfast cake. "Going that well, is it?"

"No, I mean a *literal* ball. With gowns and guests and catering. They'll probably come to you."

"Excellent! I love serving royalty."

"I thought you said they were your worst customers. Always complaining that something's too dry or too sweet?"

"They *are* my worst customers," he ceded, "but they're also my most satisfying. If I can get a picky princess to like my honey cakes, I know I've made it. Plus, they could use the sweetening. Just like you."

Poly flicked a sugar cube at him. "I'm perfectly sweet!"

He caught the cube in his teeth and crunched. "And I take full credit for that. Now, what's wrong with Beauty and the Beast having a ball? Are you not invited?"

She stirred her tea gloomily. "No, I'm invited."

Bruin seemed to tick off potential problems in his head. "Do you not have a dress?"

"I have a dress."

"Transportation?"

"No magic pumpkins necessary."

"A fairy godmother?"

Poly raised an eyebrow.

"How about a date?" he said.

She cleared her throat. Took a sip of tea. Prayed her discomfort wasn't written all over her face.

Bruin read her easily. "You shouldn't worry about a date. You might meet someone there."

And there it was. Her problem.

"But what if I don't *want* to meet someone there?" Poly blurted. Immediately, she wished she could take it back before he jumped to the wrong conclusion.

Too late. He'd made the leap. "Is there someone you *want* to go with?"

Poly sighed, taking off her glasses and polishing them on her sleeve. "Owl Girl" the kids at school (Bruin included) used to call her. True, her round spectacles did give her an owlish look, but she took the nickname to mean that she was wise despite her youth. A confidence that had followed her into her career—until this moment. What would Bruin say if he knew the truth about her? That in a world obsessed with finding their perfect, fairy tale match, she had zero interest in romance? That she laughed inside every time a well-meaning client looked at her with a pitying gaze and insisted she'd "find the right man soon"? That as a teenager, she'd dreamed of joining the Artemis Convent for Girls, if only to escape the widespread notion that singleness meant lovelessness and loneliness?

What would people say about a marriage counselor that had no desire to get married?

"No, there isn't anyone I'd like to go with," Poly said and winced inwardly at the brief flash of disappointment on Bruin's face. "The truth is...the truth is I don't want to go to the ball at all. Royal balls are half the reason I have a job. Couples meet, they dance, they fall in love in the span of sixty seconds, get married, then show up on my doorstep wondering what 'true love' really is."

"And you're afraid that's what will happen to you?" Bruin asked.

Is *that* what she was afraid of? That this mysterious law of attraction would set its sights on her and force her to fall in love with someone against her will? She shivered. "Maybe."

Bruin threw his head back and laughed. "Listen to me, Owl Girl. You are the last person on the planet to fall for that fairy tale fluff. Go to the ball. Wear a pretty dress. Eat lots of honey cakes and save me a dance. No falling in love necessary."

Poly smiled. "You really mean that?" A burden lifted off her stomach, and she eyed his plate of pastries hungrily.

He passed her one on a napkin and patted her hand as she took it. "What are friends for?"

~~~~~

Polyphonte was good at her job, but she wasn't *this* good.

Belle sat with her legs draped across Adam's lap, cuddled close. He twirled a piece of her hair lovingly around his finger. They stared adoringly into each other's eyes.

"So…" Poly said. "How are things going?"

"Amazing," Belle sighed.

"Sublime," Adam agreed.

They kissed.

Poly cleared her throat after a moment, and they broke apart. "How are plans for the ball coming along? Not too stressful I take it?"

"Oh, it was stressful," Adam replied. "Way too stressful. We were arguing about everything, weren't we, honey?"

Belle nodded. "Literally everything. The color scheme, the catering, the guests…"

"And what changed?" Poly prompted.

"We just…realized how much we loved each other." Belle nuzzled Adam's shoulder. "Didn't we, sweetheart?"

"Yes, we did, my Beauty." He reached down and booped her nose.

Booped her nose. *Booped* her nose. The surefire sign of a love spell.

Oh, no they *didn't*.
~~~~~

Poly looked sternly down her nose. "You went to Aphrodite's Acupuncture, didn't you?"

Aphrodite's Acupuncture—the bane of After Happily Ever Services' existence. How many faithful clients had she lost, in a moment of weakness, to Aphrodite's tawdry love spells? How many hardworking couples had thrown away everything in exchange for imitation affection? And how many of them spent their life savings buying endless, love-dunked needles to save their marriages?

At least Beauty and the Beast had the decency to look sheepish.

"We were just arguing so much," Belle said meekly. "How were we supposed to plan a ball when we couldn't agree on anything?"

Poly took in a deep breath to maintain composure. "Which is why I suggested that a ball would be too big of a gathering for this exercise. This was supposed to be an opportunity in learning how to put each other's interests above your own."

"I know, I know, we made a mistake and that's why we had to go to Aphrodite's. But it was a one-time deal," Adam assured her. "We'll never go back again."

That's what they all said.

"I think that's enough for today's session." Poly closed her notebook and stood. "I'm taking an early lunch."

Not at Honey Bear's Bakery. No, ma'am. Aphrodite's Acupuncture had poisoned her clients for the last time! She was going to have words with the owner.

~~~~~

Polyphonte faced the heart-shaped double doors of Aphrodite's Acupuncture. Gritting her teeth, she marched right through.

Inside, the waiting room was all red velvet couches and black satin pillows. A woman of shocking beauty sat at the front desk. She got up at Poly's arrival with a smile as dazzling as it was deceiving.

"Well, well, well," Aphrodite crooned. "If it isn't the little Owl Girl. And what brings you to my humble establishment? Surely you aren't here for our services. Or have you finally decided to do something about your nonexistent love life?"

Poly put on her most clinical smile. "Hello to you too, Aphrodite. May I speak with you in private? It concerns…mutual clients of ours."

Aphrodite's smile widened. "I think I know to whom you are referring. Follow me."

She took Poly to an office in the back. It was occupied by a young
~~~~~

man, bare-chested and sculpted as if from stone.

"Polyphonte, meet my son, Eros," Aphrodite said, gesturing to the boy. "He's training to be an acupuncturist. Perhaps you can be his next practice patient."

Hard pass. "No, thank you." Poly took a seat at the desk.

Aphrodite slid gracefully into the seat across from her. "This is about Beauty and the Beast, is it not?"

"Yes."

"You're upset because they chose my services over yours."

"That isn't quite why I'm here."

"You're unhappy because my services have done—in a single session no less—what After Happily Ever Services has failed spectacularly to do over the course of several weeks?"

Poly swallowed back a jagged retort. It left her throat raw with restraint. "That's not why I'm here, either."

Aphrodite steepled her elegant fingers. "Tell me, my dear. Who has the happier customers—me or you? Whose clients come back joyfully, week after week, under no compulsion except the desire for a happy marriage?"

"No compulsion? They're under a spell!"

"And what is love if not a spell? You don't suspect some sort of sorcery in the way your fairy tale couples 'fall in love' in the span of a single ball?"

"Falling in love is the easy part. Staying together is the real magic. And that requires honest work, not instant gratification."

Aphrodite laughed. "Such wise words from someone who has never been in love herself. Tell me, Polyphonte, are you afraid? Do you see the miserable messes your clients find themselves in, and it steers you away from any thoughts of marriage? No? No, I think it's something else. Something entirely more pitiable. I think you are broken. Yes, there is something wrong with you, and it must be fixed. No one should get away with forsaking love. Love keeps us young, my dear." She picked up a hand mirror on her desk and admired her reflection. Booped its nose. "The way you're going, you'll die a shriveled old maid before you've ever even lived. And how does that make you feel?"

The irony of the phrase was not lost on Poly. "Like I don't owe you an explanation for the way I live my life. And the only explanation I want from you is the antidote to your love spell."

"Oh, is that all you came for?" Aphrodite waved a hand in front of her face like the question was no more bothersome than a lazy fly. "Well, why didn't you say so sooner? I'm required by law to give the antidote after every administration of my love potion."

"Love *poison*, you mean," Poly snapped.

"Potion, poison." Aphrodite shrugged delicately. "Whatever makes you more comfortable. And we want you to be *most* comfortable, don't we, Eros?"

In a flash, the boy grabbed Poly, pinning her body tightly to the chair. Poly shrieked, struggling against his strong arms.

"Now, now, there's no need for dramatics, my dear." Aphrodite opened a drawer of her desk and withdrew a small, thin needle and a vial of pink liquid. She dipped the needle expertly into the serum and tapped off the excess. "This won't hurt a bit."

Poly jerked against her human bonds, but Eros held firm. "Why are you doing this?" she cried.

"Because." Aphrodite leaned in close to her face. "You are an insult to love, you and everything you represent."

"You don't know what love is!"

"I know everything I need to, and so will you after I insert this needle. Once I do, you will fall in love with the first man you lay eyes on." Aphrodite lifted Poly's sleeve and pushed the needle into the meat of her forearm. It went in with a dull ache.

She withdrew the needle.

"That's—that's it?" Poly panted.

"That's it," Eros confirmed in a smooth, sultry voice.

Poly immediately shut her eyes, refusing to look at him. He chuckled in her ear.

"Now what's the antidote?" she demanded.

Aphrodite intoned with just a touch of melodrama:

"Find the one embittered not
By the effects a curse has wrought
Accept from them a gift of peace
And you will find your love has ceased
But once the spell of love is broken
Never again can it be awoken"

~~~~~

Polyphonte ducked her head low as she dodged through crowds on the way to Honey Bear's Bakery. The ground was a blur beneath her feet; she'd taken her glasses off. Can't fall in love with a man if
~~~~~

you can't see him, right? Or that was her working theory.

"Find the one embittered not, by the effects a curse has wrought." Who else could she go to but Bruin? He treated his werebear curse like it was the best thing that ever happened to him! Surely he could whip up whatever a "gift of peace" was and give it to Beauty and the Beast—and to her, or she'd never be able to look at a man again.

Poly stumbled blindly into the bakery and felt her way over to the counter. "I need to speak with Bruin," she told the cashier without looking up. "Please tell him it's urgent."

"Too urgent to try my new honey almond bear claws?"

Poly looked up instinctively at the sound of her friend's voice. She met the smudges that were his forest brown eyes.

The most amazing, the most sumptuous, the most intoxicating eye smudges she'd ever seen. Oh, that those glorious orbs would never leave her blurry sight!

She fumbled with her glasses for a better look.

Bruin's forehead crinkled in a frown, and Poly's heart nearly broke from emotion. She wanted to kiss those furrows away! What did he have to frown about when they were together?

"Are you okay?" he asked her. "You look kind of..."

"Happy?" Poly sighed. She took his plate of samples and placed them on the counter, then grabbed his hands in hers. "Because that's what I am. I'm the happiest I've ever been!"

Bruin peeled his fingers gingerly from her grip. "I was going to say drunk, and don't listen to what the cool kids tell you, the two are not synonymous."

"The only thing I'm drunk on is love!" she cried and threw her arms around him.

"Okay." He patted her back. "Something is definitely wrong here."

"If our love is wrong, I will gladly be wrong for the rest of my days!"

"If our *what* now?" Bruin pushed her away, gently but firmly. "Poly, what has gotten into you?"

"The only thing I'm into is *you*." She booped his nose.

Said nose wrinkled in distaste. "Love spell," he said. "Did you have a run-in with Aphrodite?"

Poly twirled a lock of hair coyly around her finger. "Maaaybe."

"Tell me what happened."

"Why do you want to know?"

"Because you came here to tell me. Didn't you?"

Oh, *fine*. He had a point. "Beauty and the Beast are under a love spell from Aphrodite's Acupuncture, which completely nullifies their marriage counseling, so I went there to find out the antidote. But apparently Aphrodite will only tell you the antidote after she administers the love potion, so she and her son Eros gave it to me. Against my will, it's true, but now that I have it, I'm—"

"The happiest you've ever been. I know." Bruin shook his head. "What's the antidote?"

Poly frowned. "Why should I tell you, my love? Don't you like me this way?"

"Not in the least, and neither would you if you were in your right mind. This isn't you, Poly. It's the opposite of everything you stand for. You *help* couples who find themselves in situations like these. Now let me help you."

Tears welled in her eyes. "Why are you doing this, Bruin? Why aren't you supporting me? I thought we were friends."

Bruin smiled wryly. "And I thought you wanted to be *more* than friends. Tell me the antidote."

"No."

"Be wise, Owl Girl. Tell me the antidote."

"No!"

"Tell me!" he roared and transfigured before her eyes. Muscles bulged and brown fur burst from his skin. His mouth lengthened into a snout, and his teeth sharpened into fangs. There was the crackles and pops of reshaping bones. When it was all over, he towered over her, a fully-grown grizzly bear wearing an apron.

The bear cleared his throat. "Please," he added, his voice deep and rumbly.

If Bruin thought changing into his beast form would deter her love for him, he underestimated the depth of her affection. Poly gazed up at his beastly face adoringly. "Will you come to the ball with me?"

He exhaled slowly. "If I say yes, will you tell me the antidote?"

Hmm. That seemed like a fair trade. "Yes."

"Then it's a deal. So let's hear it."

"Fine," Poly huffed. "It goes like this:

"Find the one embittered not
By the effects a curse has wrought

Accept from them a gift of peace
And you will find your love has ceased
But once the spell of love is broken
Never again can it be awoken"

Bruin was quiet for a long moment. Then he nodded his head and said, "See you at the ball."

~~~~~

"My, my, Polyphonte, might I say, you look positively ravishing tonight."

Polyphonte turned at the sound of Aphrodite's voice. The woman's striking figure cut a path down the ballroom, and she came Poly's way, a smug sashay to her hips.

Poly blinked. "What are *you* doing here?"

Aphrodite tossed her luxurious hair. "Despite what Beauty and the Beast may have told you during their session, they're pleased with the results of my treatment. Inviting me to their ball was a show of gratitude."

More like *attitude*. What were Belle and Adam thinking, inviting someone of Aphrodite's reputation to their ball? Wasn't Poly enough for them?

Was she?

She shook the thought away. "You ought to be ashamed of yourself. You and your work."

"Me? I'm not the one whose job it is to give out love advice while having no personal experience on the matter. Well, until now. I'm sure you've found your special someone, haven't you?"

Poly's cheeks filled with heat. She scanned the ballroom of beautiful guests for Bruin's tall, handsome head. Where *was* he? He'd said they'd meet at the ball, but the festivities had begun and there was no sign of him. Being separated for so long was making her anxious. How could his heart stand for them to be apart?

"It's a dazzling feeling, isn't it?" Aphrodite crooned, a triumphant gleam in her eye. "Being in love. Think of everything you've missed out on all these years. I helped you become *whole*, my dear. Just remember that, and you'll be thanking me soon enough." She tapped one of Poly's blushing cheeks and accepted an invitation to dance from an attractive stranger. They whirled away onto the dance floor, leaving Poly alone.

All alone.
~~~~~

She watched the couples step and twirl in perfect synchronization. Once upon a time, her heart would have leapt to see such unity and purpose on display, like a marriage put to music. Never desiring it herself, yet always admiring it in others. But now, replacing that joy, a sick feeling wove its way around her insides, pulling tight like a knot. Where was Bruin? Why wasn't he dancing with her? Was he avoiding her?

"Polyphonte!" Belle appeared and took Poly by the arms, spinning her out of her thoughts in a merry circle. "You made it! Oh, thank goodness. We've been looking for you."

Standing at her shoulder, Adam nodded. "Bruin wants to see us in the kitchens. He says he has something for us."

Bruin? Bruin was here and wanted to see her? A smile split Poly's face. "Lead the way!"

They followed a bustle of waiters to the kitchens where the werebear himself was counting cookies on a silver platter.

He smiled at their approach. "Thank you for coming. I thought you might like to try one of my honey cookies. It's a new recipe, and I wanted my hosts' approval before sending them out to the guests. Plus, even the best balls can be stressful, and cookies always sweeten the mood." Bruin offered them the platter.

How sweet! How thoughtful. How—

A line from the antidote came to Poly's mind like a slap to the face. *"Accept from them a gift of peace, and you will find your love has ceased."*

"Don't!" she shrieked and smacked Belle and Adam's hands away. "He's trying to break our love spells."

"Isn't that what you want?" Bruin countered her. "That's why you went to Aphrodite's in the first place. To break their love spell. For goodness' sake, you had a love spell put on yourself just to find out the antidote!"

"Is this true?" Adam asked her quietly.

Poly hesitated. Cast her gaze on the floor and nodded. "I wanted to help you. I thought I could, but now I'm not so sure. Aphrodite's right—what do I know about love? Maybe I shouldn't be a marriage counselor. Maybe the only way to a happily ever after *is* a love spell."

"Oh, Poly." Belle took her hands, and she looked up. "Why do you think every couple in the kingdom knows your name? It isn't because of your experience with happily ever afters. It's your commitment to after happily evers. We can get all the advice about love and relationships from our married friends, but what they can't offer us is a new perspective. You are a happy, healthy, single woman, and you are able to see our situations in ways that no one else can. Your outlook and opinions are not only valued and appreciated—they are absolutely essential."

"And we're going to prove it to you." Adam reached for the platter of cookies. He took one for himself and gave another to Belle, and they each bit into them. In an instant, their dewey-eyed expressions evaporated like morning mist.

Adam turned to his wife. There was tenderness in his eyes—*real* tenderness. "It isn't always easy living with you. And I know I'm not always easy to live with, either. But the truth is, I love you and I want to make this work. No matter what it takes."

Belle reached up and kissed his cheek. "Me, too, my love. Me, too." They laced hands and looked at Poly expectantly. "Your turn," they said in unison.

Bruin held out a cookie. It was in the shape of an owl. "I made this one specially for you."

Poly recognized the impulse of the love spell that made her want to throw her arms around his neck and kiss him. But she also recognized something else inside: the love for her friend that had always been there, deep and true and comforting. One emotion screamed for her attention. The other quieted her heart with peace. A gift of peace, just like this cookie.

She reached for it and paused. "Before I do this, I have to ask you something. Do you have feelings for me?"

Bruin watched her closely for a moment. Then he answered. "Yes."

"And you still want me to take this cookie? You know how the antidote goes: *'But once the spell of love is broken, never again can it be awoken.'* This love spell only works once. If you break it, you're giving up your only chance at having a romance with me. You know that, don't you? Once the spell is broken, you'll be my friend and nothing more."

"The Poly I know and love won't see it like that. She doesn't see friendships and romance as something 'more' or 'less.' Just different. And you know what? I'm okay with that. Because more than anything, I just want to be part of your life, whatever that looks like."

A thousand impulses cried for Poly's attention, but she only gave in to one. Poly grabbed the owl cookie and stuffed it into her mouth. Sweet, blessed clarity filled her mind, shooing away any remains of the love spell. She let out a sigh of relief, spraying crumbs in Bruin's direction.

"Oops," she giggled and swallowed. "Sorry."

Bruin handed her a napkin. "How are you feeling?"

"Like I'm about to hug you in a very long, very platonic way."

"I think I can handle that."

Poly squeezed him tight. "Thank you," she whispered and let go. "Now can we all agree to never have anything to do with Aphrodite's Acupuncture ever again?"

"Didn't I see her out on the dance floor?" Bruin said. "Whose big idea was it to invite her to the ball?"

Belle and Adam glanced guiltily at each other. "Never again," they promised.

"I don't know where she gets off telling people about love," Bruin scoffed. "The only person she's in love with is herself."

In love with…herself. *Wait a minute.* "Bruin!" Poly cried, grabbing his arm. "You're absolutely right! When I was in her office, she was admiring her reflection in a mirror and she—she *booped* its nose! I think she used a love potion on herself. And we know how to break it. Grab those cookies, and come on!"

They found Aphrodite idling by a table, sipping her champagne with a complacent smile on her face. She saw Poly, Bruin, Belle and Adam coming her way, and her smile deepened. "If it isn't my favorite clients. And who is your handsome companion, Poly?"

Poly hooked her arm through Bruin's. "Someone I care about very much. Aphrodite, you told me that one day I'd be thanking you for what you did to me, and you were right. I've learned so much about myself and the people around me. I know more about love today than I did yesterday, and if that isn't the best way to live life, I don't know what is. And it's all thanks to you."

"As a token of our gratitude," Bruin announced, "we want to offer you the first taste of tonight's sweetest delicacies. Might I suggest the heart-shaped one?"

Aphrodite admired the silver platter of cookies. "You're too kind." She selected the heart-shaped one and took a guileless bite.

Her expression changed from smug satisfaction to pure panic.

"Give me that!" Aphrodite snarled, snatching the platter of cookies from Bruin. She dumped the sweets on the floor and stared at herself in the platter's silvery reflection. "What have you done?

What have you done?"

With a cry like a wounded buffalo, Aphrodite smashed her champagne glass on the table and charged at Poly with the jagged end. Bruin let out a bearish roar and transformed, meeting the angry woman mid-charge and pinning her to the floor. He crouched over her in full bear-form and roared again in her face, coating it in spittle.

"To the dungeon with her!" shouted Adam, and the ballroom of guests cheered.

Poly doubted that any of them had a clue what was going on, but what's a royal ball without at least one person being sent to the dungeon? Guards appeared and led Aphrodite away in shackles.

"Aren't you glad you decided to come to the ball?" Bruin rumbled, grinning down at Poly with his massive bear teeth.

Poly grinned back. "Wouldn't have missed this for the world." She took his paw. "Now you owe me a dance."

The band struck up a slow song, and Poly leaned into his furry shoulder. She spotted Belle and Adam dancing nearby, their movements a touch out of step but getting better by the second. Beauty and the Beast, braving their problems together. An after happily ever indeed.

Poly looked up at her own beast. Her dearest friend. Maybe theirs wasn't a love story that caused teenage girls to swoon or provided fodder for the greatest ballads of the town troubadour. But maybe it didn't have to be. Maybe fairy tales looked different for different people, but their endings were the same: love, commitment, and the magic of staying together.

And they all lived after happily ever.

END

SKIN DEEP

Stoney M. Setzer

"And you say you haven't seen or heard from Michelle all day?" I asked.

"Not since late yesterday afternoon," Carla replied. "And they haven't seen her at the gym where she works. Nobody else has, either. But I thought that somebody had to be missing for forty-eight hours before you could file a missing persons report."

"Old TV cliche. If you think somebody is missing and endangered, you don't have to wait that long. Besides that, I'm family. Even if we really did have to wait forty-eight hours to officially file a missing persons report, you know I can start unofficially looking. Not like we have a major crime wave going here."

"Thank you." Carla sniffed. Mom embraced her tightly and gave me one of her patented looks, the one that always made me feel like a kid, one she was trying to coax into doing the right thing without actually saying a word.

Mom reached over for a tissue and then leaned in close. "Okay, honey, take a deep breath. Dane needs to ask you some more questions, so I need you to be strong, all right?"

Carla nodded, doing her best to compose herself. Since Michelle was my only niece and the closest thing I had ever had to a child of my own, I needed a minute myself to mentally shift gears, to think less like a brother and an uncle and more like a sheriff.

"All right, did Michelle ever take off without telling you? Is this the first time she's ever done anything like this?"

Carla shrugged. "Well, she's twenty-three, and she doesn't live in my house anymore, so I don't guess she has to check in with me...but no, never. Even if it was spur of the moment, she'd at least break off a text so I wouldn't...well, worry."

"So you don't think she and a couple of her friends might have taken a spur of the moment road trip or anything of that nature."

"On a Tuesday?" Mom asked incredulously. Another Lorraine Carter special, the one that always made me feel like a kid who just broke the living room window after being told not to play ball in the house.

"And I already know you've checked her house." Carla and her late husband had owned a rental house on the same block, with their backyards adjacent to each other. When Michelle turned twenty-one, they had basically signed the place over to her.

"Yeah. Nothing amiss, unless you count her usual sloppiness."

"But no signs of struggle?"

"Nope."

There was a sound on the roof of the house. We all glanced upward, but we didn't hear it again. Maybe it was squirrels or cats or something.

"Did she have any enemies?"

Now both Mom and Carla gave me a look. "Does half the town count?" Carla asked.

I had walked right into that one. "Well, if you could narrow it down a little bit beyond that, that would be great."

She shrugged. "You know yourself how it was with her. People liked *looking* at her, but they didn't like *her*. I guess you could start with any girl who ever competed against her in a beauty pageant, or any guy she ever turned down for a date without being particularly nice about it. Throw in any woman who ever got tired of her husband or boyfriend gawking at her."

"All right." That really was half the town, especially that last part. Problem was, they were the wrong sort of enemies. By that, I mean the kind of people who would dislike her enough to want to see her taken down a notch or two, but not enough to drive them to violence. Humiliation, not harm. Not unless she had actually started fooling around with somebody else's man, which seemed highly unlikely. Michelle dated here and there, but she was picky, and she had been raised better than to play homewrecker.

I went through the rest of the procedural questions and said my good-byes. As I stepped out the front door, I could have sworn I glimpsed something out of the corner of my eye. I stopped and took a good look around, but I couldn't see anything. Shrugging it off, I assumed it was just my imagination.

Well, we all know what happens when we assume.

~~~~~

A little background on my niece, one Michelle Tomlinson.

Everybody who knew her could agree on two things. The first
~~~~~

was that she really was beautiful. Nobody with eyesight good enough to hold a driver's license would deny that. Five-foot-nine, wavy brunette locks that flowed past her shoulders, hourglass figure, and near-perfect facial features, complete with a "beauty mark" on one cheek. If anyone wanted to argue that she wasn't the most beautiful woman in the area, she could produce any number of crowns from years of local beauty pageants to prove otherwise—and knowing her, she probably would have.

That brings me to the other thing. Pretty much anyone who had ever met Michelle would tell you that her beauty only ran skin deep. As in the old saying: *Beauty is only skin deep, but ugly goes clear to the bone.* Michelle's problem was that she *knew* she was beautiful. It went to her head and stayed there, then spilled over into how she treated other people. That's where the ugly part comes in.

A lot of people have wondered why she didn't move away from here after graduation, try to go someplace bigger and break into modeling or acting. Well, she does model—she's on billboards everywhere in the tri-county area, endorsing everything from tire stores to veterinary clinics to pharmacies. As for why she didn't go someplace bigger, she claimed that it was because she didn't want to get caught up in the party lifestyle and the substance abuse that went with it, and that she didn't want to get pressured to do any risqué modeling jobs that would make her daddy roll over in his grave.

I'm not calling her a liar, not necessarily. Those reasons are true enough as far as they went. However, it's my job to know people, so I have my own theory.

"Sheriff? You there?"

I pressed the talk button. "Yeah, I'm here."

"You anywhere near the Magnolia Heights subdivision?"

I did a double-take. That's where Carla lived, where I had just left. "Yeah, not far at all. What's up?"

"Got a weird report over at the corner of Magnolia and Willow. Go check it out."

Only a couple of blocks away from Carla's house, and I had just pulled out of the neighborhood, going the other direction. Still, how could I miss something that close?

I put on my flashers and hauled tail back into the neighborhood. Mom was just stepping out onto Carla's porch as I raced past. By that point, I could already see the disturbance that dispatch had called about.

Somebody was standing on the roof of the Fitzgerald house. From this distance, it was clear to see that it wasn't Richard Fitzgerald trying to clean out his gutters. This figure had long hair, white with some black streaks, and its skin was a weird grayish color I had never seen before. A crowd was beginning to form around the house. Most of the people were crowding in, with the exception of a heavyset old woman watching the scene unfold from across the street.

I jumped out of the car and ran over as best I could with one bad knee. Looking up, I noticed that the person on the roof was a female. A female who might have given the Bride of Frankenstein a run for her money, but female nevertheless. Her legs were crouched as if she had thoughts of jumping off the roof, but scared of how she might land.

Was that what we heard on the roof? Or what I saw out of the corner of my eye?

Then she looked at me. Even in her distorted features, I read a reaction of horror. She screamed and ran toward the other end of the roof. A big oak tree was on that side of the house, with one limb ending just a few feet away. She took a running jump and barely grabbed the limb in time to avoid disaster.

A squirrel or a cat might do that, look as if they were about to fall, and then still be able to recover and scamper up into the tree. Unfortunately for her, she weighed more than any squirrel or cat. The branch snapped immediately, sending her to the ground with a wail and a thud.

"Dispatch! I need an ambulance in Magnolia Heights, on the double!" I barked into my radio as I rushed over to see about her.

Fortunately, she didn't seem to be badly injured, minus the funny angle at which one foot jutted out at the ankle. A bad sprain, maybe a fracture. Either way, she was in pain and making no effort to put any weight on that leg. For the first time, I got a good look at her face. Her nose was like that of a pig, one eye was bigger than the other, and her teeth had a sickening black tint. That grayish skin looked more like scales on closer examination.

However, what really caught my eye was the mole on her left cheek. A beauty mark—one that looked mighty familiar.

"Uncle Dane?" she said, her voice full of desperation. "Help me!"

~~~~~
~~~~~

"But it doesn't make any sense!" Carla cried.

"Oh, I agree with you, Sis. One hundred percent. The problem is, that doesn't seem to matter very much."

Mom and Carla had met me at the hospital, where they had taken the beastly-looking female. That's how I was thinking of her at that point, though I didn't voice it. In my head, I had to call her something, and I still couldn't quite bring myself to call her Michelle.

A young man stepped out of the room and faced us. His photo ID proclaimed his name to be Braxton. "Well, I can tell you that she didn't break anything. Her ankle is severely sprained, but not broken. It could have been a lot worse."

I nodded. "All right. What about...the rest of it?"

Braxton shuddered visibly. "That part, I have no explanation for. Her vitals are all normal, so internally, she seems perfectly, well...normal."

"But you don't know what happened to her face or her skin?"

"No idea." He looked at me skeptically. "Sheriff, do you really mean to tell me that's the Ego Queen in there?"

I'll never forget the look on my sister's face. The derogatory nickname obviously didn't sit well with her, but there was something else there. Something else in her eyes said that, for better or worse, she knew Michelle had earned that moniker. Chances were that this nurse or intern or whatever he was had been among the many whom Michelle had shot down over the years. That must have made for an interesting examination just now.

"That's what we intend to find out," I answered noncommittally. Although I tried to keep my voice calm, there must have been something in my eye. Braxton backed away quickly, the way you might try to distance yourself from a snarling Doberman.

"Are you two ready to go in there?" I asked.

"Yes and no," Mom admitted, but Carla was already walking in.

"Uh, I'm sorry, but there are really only supposed to be two visitors at a time in there," Braxton said nervously.

Mom rolled her eyes. "I'll go sit out in the lobby, then. I'm sure you probably want to ask her some questions."

"Thanks, Mom."

Carla was already sitting beside the beastly female's bed, but she had yet to reach out to her. It didn't take a genius to see that she didn't know just what to do.

The patient had tears streaming down her face. "Mom? Uncle

Dane? I don't know what's happening...."

"Us either," Carla replied, rather noncommittally.

I stepped up. "Do you mind if we ask you some questions?"

She looked up at me, and I tried hard to hide my revulsion. Imagine if you sat a group of cartoonists together in a room and assigned each of them a facial feature, with instructions to draw it to look as hideous as possible. Then, suppose you put their finished products together like puzzle pieces. No face should be that outlandishly ugly.

"What kind of questions?" The voice was Michelle's, all right.

I took a deep breath. Since I hadn't discussed my plan with Carla, I could only hope that she picked up on it and decided to play ball. "What's your date of birth?" I asked.

Those ghastly eyes widened, and I can't even begin to describe the expression on the rest of her face, but Michelle gave me the correct answer.

Carla glanced at me for just a second before turning her attention back to the girl. "That little beagle you had back when you were in kindergarten—what was its name?"

Between the two of us, we must have asked twenty or more questions like that, questions that only the real Michelle would know. With each correct answer—and they were all correct—the reality became harder to ignore. Somehow, this was Michelle.

"Are you convinced now?" Michelle demanded. Each correct answer had been given with less and less patience. Her fear wasn't completely gone, but that haughty streak Braxton had referenced was beginning to show through. Of course, that was just more positive proof of her identity.

I looked at my younger sister. "Good enough for you?"

Her lip trembling, Carla nodded and squeezed her daughter's hand. She tried to say something, but only tears came out. A second later, Michelle was sobbing as well, a strange sight indeed. You don't expect to see tears from a face that looks like something out of an old-school horror movie.

I stood there for an awkward moment or two before I cleared my throat. "Michelle, I need to ask you some more questions."

"*More* questions?"

"Not the same kind as before. We need to find out...."

"What happened to me? How I wound up like this?" Michelle asked sarcastically. "Let me go ahead and cut through all the crap for you, Uncle Dane. I have no earthly idea!"

Carla patted her hand. "Baby, your uncle is only trying to help you. You might not know everything that happened, but you can tell him everything you know."

After a moment, Michelle nodded. "Okay, fine."

"Do you remember when this happened?" I asked.

"This morning. I woke up, went to the bathroom, looked in the mirror—and saw this." She gestured at her face.

"And when you went to bed last night, you looked...?"

"Normal."

"Did anything unusual happen last night? Or any time yesterday, for that matter?"

Michelle had this habit of biting her lip when she was deep in thought. She was doing it now, a bizarre sight with her current face. "Yeah, but I'm afraid to tell you about it."

"Why are you afraid to tell us?" Carla said, squeezing her hand again.

"Because it doesn't make sense, Mom. You're both going to think I'm crazy on top of everything else." She bit her lip again, and I resisted the urge to look away. "But the thing is, there's no other explanation...."

"It's okay, Michelle. Just tell us and let Uncle Dane be the judge."

Michelle looked at the ceiling. "I guess it all started when I came home from work that afternoon and found that big package sitting on the front porch."

I looked up. "What kind of big package?"

"Long, wide, and flat. I took it inside and opened it up. Turned out to be a mirror."

Carla and I exchanged a look. If there was one person who had enough mirrors and didn't need another, it was Michelle. Only a carnival funhouse had more mirrors than she did, and none of hers were of the "trick" variety.

"But I didn't order a new one," Michelle said quickly, anticipating the question. "It just came. Not that it was a big deal...that frame was beautiful, the most gorgeous mirror frame I've ever seen."

"Any idea who it came from?" I asked.

"None. There was a card, but it didn't have anybody's name on it. Just a message."

"What did the message say?"

She chuckled and shook her head. "Craziest junk I've ever read. One side said, *Beauty is only skin deep.* The other side said, *This is the most accurate mirror in the world. Say, "Show me myself," then take one look at your reflection, and you will see yourself as you really are."*

I asked her to repeat the message so I could take it down accurately. She complied, but she wasn't happy about having to repeat herself. Once I got it down, I asked, "Did you try it?"

"No, not right away. I set the mirror up in my bedroom, in a corner, and then I went to the gym to teach my evening class. It was after nine o'clock before I came home to stay, and later than that when I tried it."

"And then what?" Carla asked, trying to hide her impatience. She wasn't in law enforcement, so she wasn't used to having to coax information out of somebody a little bit at a time. Not that I wouldn't have loved to get to the bottom line faster myself, but I was used to it.

"I stood in front of it, I said the words, and then the mirror got all hazy for a minute. Then, when it cleared up, I saw—*this.*" Michelle's voice cracked, and she pointed to her face.

"Your face, as it is now, in the reflection."

"Yes!" Michelle snapped. "So I went to the bathroom, looked in that mirror. Everything was normal there. I went around the whole house, looking. Every other mirror looked right except for that one."

"What did you do with the mirror?" I asked.

"I covered it up with a blanket. I thought about smashing the thing, but I didn't want to have to clean all that up. Then, there's that whole thing about seven years of bad luck. Not that I'm really superstitious, but that mirror already had me freaked out a little anyway, so I didn't want to take any chances, you know?"

"Understandable," I said. Not a complete lie, but not completely truthful either.

"I figured I'd just try to see if somebody with a truck would help me haul the thing off. Problem is, I woke up the next morning, and *every* mirror was showing the same reflection. Of this." She pointed to her face again.

"So you just went to sleep like normal, and woke up like that."

"Yeah." Her tone was softening ever so slightly.

"Where were you when I was in your house looking for you?" Carla asked.

"Hiding in the attic. I didn't want you to see me like this, and the attic was the only thing I could think of."

"But the ladder wasn't pulled down."

Michelle looked down. "I ran outside, and then I just kind of—jumped."

"Jumped?" Carla demanded.

"Like what you were trying to do on the Fitzgeralds' roof?" I asked.

"Yeah. It's...weird. I just thought about doing it, and there I was. It was like that changed along with my face."

"Do you have any idea who might have sent it to you?"

"No, sir."

"Did you keep the packaging that the mirror came in?"

"Yeah, just because it's so big and I'd have to get help hauling it off too."

I looked her in the eye, doing my best to ignore the rest of her face and remind myself that was still my only niece, somewhere under there. "Do you care if I go into your house and take a look at it?"

"But Uncle Dane, what if something happens to you?" It was the first time in a long time I had heard her express a legitimate concern for someone else, other than maybe her mother and grandmother. Maybe. It caught me a little off guard, but I didn't let it show.

"Don't worry. I won't ask that mirror to show me anything."

~~~~~

"You're thinking something," Mom said.

"I suppose I am."

"Can you elaborate?"

We had left Carla at the hospital with Michelle. Although her injury wasn't that serious, the doctors wanted to run tests to see if they could figure out what happened to her face. I had a feeling it wouldn't do much good, but it probably wouldn't hurt anything, either. I wanted another set of eyes with me, and Carla wasn't ready to leave her child, so now Mom was sitting in the patrol car with me.

"I'm thinking this is Sardis. We shouldn't be any more than a little pinpoint just east of the Mississippi state line, but instead we're the weirdest town in Tennessee, maybe even the whole Southeast. No violent crime to speak of, but we corner the market on the bizarre."

"Son, you're not telling me anything I don't already know." Mom looked out the window, fidgeting. I expected as much.
~~~~~

"We've got one single mom and her two nineteen-year-old twins who are one hundred percent convinced some kind of boogeyman is gonna get them if they venture more than a mile and a half beyond their yard. Not one mile, not two, but specifically a mile and a half. The mom almost had to quit a good-paying job in Memphis over it—would have, if not for teleworking."

"Yeah, and the mom and the sister both claim that going beyond that is how the brother got to be—well, you know." She tapped the side of her head. "From high school salutatorian to the mind of a kindergartener, overnight."

"And no other explanation except their wild story. Then we've got an older couple, absolute teetotalers 364 days a year, who without fail get drunk as skunks every Arbor Day, to the point that I usually have to run them in. They're the only reason I even know when Arbor Day is. Ask them why they do that, and not only do they clam up, but they look like they've seen a ghost."

"I know."

"My point is, living in a place like Sardis, and then this happens to Michelle, it really gets your mind running in directions you'd rather not have to explore."

"Yeah." One simple word, but Mom's tone of voice spoke volumes. She was right; I hadn't said anything that she hadn't already thought about.

That was the whole reason I wanted her to come along, and I think that was the reason she agreed. She seemed to know more about the weirdness factor in Sardis than anyone else I knew.

~~~~~

Carla had insinuated that Michelle was a sloppy housekeeper, but it wasn't all that bad. No pile of dirty dishes, no overflowing trash cans, no weird smells. Granted, her bed hadn't been made, and there was a good bit of clutter on top of her dresser, but that was it—more disheveled than dirty.

None of that earned more than a cursory glance from me. I was more interested in the full-length mirror standing in one corner of her bedroom, covered by a blanket, and in the packaging that Michelle had left leaning against another wall.

I grabbed the blanket and pulled it off the mirror. The image in the glass was dark, as if reflecting a room where the lights were off—despite the fact that we had turned on the lights as we entered. My reflection and Mom's were visible, but there were just shadowy
~~~~~

outlines with no real detail.

"What do you make of it?" I asked.

"That carving on the frame. I've seen it before, but I can't remember where."

Stepping over, I examined the packaging. I really didn't expect to see a return address, but there it was: 542 Glyburn Road, Sardis, TN. I pointed it out to Mom. "Looks like somebody wasn't too shy about letting people know who sent it."

"That used to be Jackie Hornsby's old house. I think her daughter and granddaughter live there now," Mom said. She was trying to keep up a poker face, but her eyes were giving her away.

"You know her?"

Mom nodded stiffly. "You got your phone on you? I don't."

"Yes, ma'am. Why?"

"Call your sister. Put it on speaker phone, and then have her do the same. I need to ask Michelle some questions."

I had plenty of questions, but I complied, figuring I'd have my answers soon enough. Once I had Carla on the line, Mom leaned over. "Michelle? This is Grandma. We're at your house, and I need to ask you some questions."

"Yes, ma'am?"

"Does the name Hornsby mean anything to you?"

"No, not really." If she was trying to hide her impatience, she wasn't doing a great job of it.

Mom appeared to be lost in thought. "Who did Val marry again...what about Owens? Does that last name ring a bell?"

Even through the speaker phone connection, I could hear Michelle hiss like a cat. "Yeah. Angela Owens."

I cut in. "All right, who's she?"

"Little blonde heifer who was on that last catalog photo shoot with me. Can't stand her." From there, Michelle called this Angela a name—one that a lot of people in Sardis would have said was the pot calling the kettle black.

"Listen to me," Mom said. "We're about to come pick you up, and we're going to take a little drive. It's important."

As she hung up, I protested. "Mom, the doctors may not be done yet, and Michelle's ankle…."

"It's important," Mom repeated, going to her no-argument tone.

~~~~~

"I don't want to do this," Michelle griped as we helped her into
~~~~~

Carla's car.

"Sometimes we have to do things we don't want to do," Mom replied without looking at her.

Fortunately, the hospital didn't give me too much flack about going ahead and checking her out. It probably would have been a different story if it had been anybody else, but the badge carries its privileges.

I mentioned earlier that I had my own theory about why Michelle had wanted to stay in Sardis. Now is probably as good a time as any to share it.

For all her beauty, for all her accolades it has earned her and all the heads she has turned, I've always secretly suspected Michelle has some self-doubt issues. Secretly, because most people would say I'm crazy, but hear me out. If she went to a bigger city, she'd have more competition—other beautiful women besides her, all vying for the same attention, the same modeling jobs. In a big city, she'd run the risk of being overshadowed, perhaps even overlooked. Sardis was just the right size to let her be a big fish in a small pond. Michelle never was good at sharing the spotlight.

That's what I thought about when Michelle mentioned "a little blonde heifer"—anybody trying to steal her spotlight was automatically her enemy. The name Angela Owens didn't mean much to me, but Mom thought it was significant. So we were all on our way to the Owens house, with Carla driving Michelle in her car, right behind us.

Our destination sat just beyond the city limits, on some pretty decent acreage and well off the main road. The house was at least sixty years old, maybe older, but somebody had done a fair job of keeping it up. I doubted that it could have looked much better when it was brand new.

Beside me, Mom was murmuring something under her breath. I glanced over and saw that she had her head bowed—praying. Fine by me, but if my mother felt the need to seek out divine assistance before we arrived, I couldn't help feeling a little nervous.

We parked in front of the house and got out. Almost immediately a middle-aged lady stepped out of the house. She was tiny and looked like a strong wind might carry her across the state line. As soon as she saw us, her gaze fell on Michelle, struggling to maneuver on her new crutches. However, her face showed no revulsion or horror, just a little smug smirk. That expression was enough to catch my eye.

I disliked this lady right off the bat, but I knew my badge meant I had to conduct myself professionally. "Mrs. Owens, I'm Sheriff Carter. Forgive for bothering you, but...."

The woman ignored me and turned her attention to Mom. "Why, hello, Ms. Lorraine."

"Hello, Val." There was no warmth in Mom's tone.

"I suppose you're here because you think I had something to do with that." Val nodded toward Michelle.

"Well, didn't you?"

Carla, Michelle, and I looked at each other. All of us had grown up hearing the weird stories of Sardis, and being sheriff, I had witnessed more than they had, but not as much as Mom. However, this was the first time any of us had been directly involved in the weirdness. That was not nearly as disconcerting as seeing that this wasn't Mom's first run-in with this Val Owens. They had history, and I couldn't help but be consumed with morbid curiosity.

Val chuckled. "You flatter me, Ms. Lorraine, you really do."

"Forgive me if I don't quite feel up to playing cat and mouse with you, Val. Now talk to me. What do you know about Michelle's face?"

"So you think I had something to do with that?" Val pointed at Michelle.

"Didn't you?" Mom countered.

Val smirked before looking back inside her house. "Angela! Come out here on the porch for a minute!"

"No!"

"I'm not asking you. I'm telling you."

"No! I don't want to!"

"That doesn't matter! Now get your butt out here!"

Angela finally trudged out onto the porch. Given Michelle's attitude toward her, I expected to see somebody around her age, maybe a year or two younger, with a beauty to rival hers. From the neck down, I suppose I was right, but it was hard to pay much attention to that. Whatever Angela's face had been before, it had been transmogrified to match Michelle's—a mirror image, no pun intended. The only difference was her silver hair had blonde streaks. Based on Michelle's hair, I could only assume Angela had been a blonde before this.

Val stood there with her hands on her hips. "Hopefully this

proves I didn't have anything to do with what happened to your Michelle—unless, of course, you believe I'm capable of doing something like that to my own daughter."

Michelle had walked all the way up to the porch, and Angela had come down the steps. They looked at each other in astonishment. After a moment, Michelle asked, "You too?"

"That's what it looks like, isn't it?" Angela snapped. Michelle had used that tone countless times, but she winced at being on the receiving end.

"Did...did somebody send you a mirror?"

Even under her distorted features, Angela's surprise was evident. "Yeah, they did. You too?"

Michelle nodded. "Yep."

I stepped forward. "Uh, Angela, do you happen to remember the return address on that mirror?"

"No. Why would I have looked at that?"

Angela and Michelle had more in common than I thought. "Do you still have the packaging?"

She motioned toward the porch. "Right up there. Help yourself, Sheriff."

Val brought the packaging over to the porch rail and handed it to me before I reached the steps. I wondered if she had a problem with me coming up onto her porch, but I didn't pursue it. The return address jumped out at me. "Michelle, this is your address," I announced. "And her mirror had this as its return address."

"Why would both of you get a package from the other one's address? How is that even possible?" Carla asked.

"Not that big of a deal, really," I said. "Anybody can put any return address down, and it doesn't mean a thing."

"Sounds to me like you've both made an enemy," Val remarked.

"What do you mean by enemy?" I asked.

She shrugged. "Somebody who sees them as two peas in a pod, outer beauties who are ugly on the inside. Somebody who figures that they both needed to be taken down a peg or two."

"Any ideas who that might be?"

"You'd have to ask them."

I turned toward Michelle and Angela. "All right, ladies, any thoughts? Anybody you might have both ticked off?" The look they gave me spurred me to add, "Anybody specific?"

They conferred in lowered voices for a moment, and I couldn't help thinking this might be the first real conversation that they had ever shared. After a moment, they both looked up and shook their heads.

"We can't narrow it down," Michelle lamented, a tear running down her disfigured cheek. "There's...there's been too many."

I can't say that I was terribly surprised. Even though I didn't know Angela at all, I knew Michelle, knew too much about how she treated people. It didn't take too much to see that Angela was cut from the same cloth. Still, we were back at square one, and it was a punch to the gut.

"Now what do we do?" Carla asked.

I looked from Mom to Val. "Any ideas?"

They both shook their heads, but then I heard a voice behind me. "Are you open to a little outside help?"

I turned around to see an old woman walking toward us from a 1957 Chevy parked on the side of the road. She looked familiar, and after a moment I had it. When I had responded to the call about Michelle on the roof of the house, this lady had been the one standing by herself across the street. She was short and stout, creating the illusion that she was as wide as she was tall.

"Are you open to a little outside help?" she repeated.

"Hazel Dell! I might have known!" Val exclaimed.

"You mean you know something about this, Mrs. Dell?" Mom demanded.

"I take it you ladies know each other?" I asked, even though the answer was obvious. They clearly had history together, it was just a matter of what.

Mrs. Dell smirked. "I guess you could say that."

Mom stepped past me to confront the newcomer. "Did you have anything to do with all this?"

"I didn't cause it, but I think I might have your solution," Mrs. Dell replied. She turned away from Mom to face Michelle and Angela. "Do you ladies think you'd be interested?"

"Yes, ma'am, please!" Michelle replied.

"Yeah, tell us! Come on!" Angela chimed in. "Out with it!"

Carla grabbed my arm. "Dane, what's going on here?"

"We live in the weirdest town in the Southeast," I whispered back. To Mrs. Dell, I asked, "What do you know about what happened to them?"

"Well, Sheriff, I can tell you that I've seen something like this one other time, years ago. Somebody with means has decided that these two young beauties were horribly ugly on the inside. But there is a way back. A real beauty treatment, if you will."

I had always known that this town was weird, but this was a different level of bizarre. "What do you mean?"

The old lady looked from Michelle to Angela. "Are you young ladies interested?"

"Yes, ma'am," Michelle replied, her voice choked with emotion.

"No, we could care less!" Angela barked sardonically. "Of course we want to know!"

Mrs. Dell reached into her purse and pulled out a small vial that looked like a tiny bottle of expensive perfume. "The only problem is that I've only got enough antidote for one of you. One of you is going to have to let the other one have it."

"Say what?" Angela demanded. "You've got to be kidding!"

"There's not enough to share?" Michelle asked.

"Sorry. Half a dose won't do any good at all. You two are going to have to make a choice somehow."

Angela spun around and faced Michelle. "I want it! You've had your turn at modeling! Let somebody else have a shot at it!"

"But I need it, too!"

"Who's got a brighter future, Michelle? Me or you? You've had plenty of time in the spotlight! It's my turn now!"

For a minute, Michelle just stood there, trembling with emotion. Biting her lip again, really going at it now. After a moment, she looked at us. "Is this anything like how I used to act?"

Carla sighed. "I'm afraid so, dear."

Michelle looked at the ground for a long time before looking back up. "All right. Mrs. Dell, you...you can give it to Angela."

"And why is that, dear?" Mrs. Dell asked.

"That note on that mirror. About it showing me my true self. I've been ugly on the inside for far too long. I'd rather change that."

"Very well." Mrs. Dell walked over and handed the little vial to Angela. "Drink it."

Angela practically ripped the cap off of the vial and chugged it down. She stood there for a moment. "Nothing's happening!" she protested.

"Oh, I wouldn't be too sure about that," Mrs. Dell said sweetly. "Look at Michelle."

Before our eyes, Michelle's face was changing. Her skin began to clear up, and her nose was beginning to reshape itself. In under sixty seconds, she looked like she had once before.

"What's wrong?" she asked, looking at all of us. "Is something else happening to me?"

Carla ran up and hugged her, followed by Mom. "You're back," Carla said.

"What about me?" Angela screeched. "That was supposed to be for me!"

"Be quiet, Angela!" Val commanded. Angela screamed and jumped, landing on the roof easily. I guess that's how Michelle's leap must have looked, and if I hadn't seen it, I wouldn't have believed it.

Val was glaring at Mrs. Dell. "I know what happened. A pretty nasty trick, Mrs. Dell."

Mrs. Dell shook her head and chuckled. "Oh no, Val, not a trick. A test."

"How long will I stay this way?" Angela screamed. She kicked the roof in frustration.

"That part is up to you, my dear." Mrs. Dell turned her attention to Michelle. "My dear, I hope you remember this day for a long time. Something about you has to change, either inside or outside. You get to choose which."

"Yes, ma'am," Michelle said through her tears. "But...what about that mirror?"

"Well, my dear, you can do almost anything you want with it. You can cover it up, turn it to face the wall, or stick it in your attic. However, you have to maintain possession of it...as a memento of what you learned today."

Michelle looked as if she wanted to question that directive, but she thought better of it. "Yes, ma'am."

"Good, good. Well, in that case, I suppose I must be going." Mrs. Dell waddled back toward her car.

I stepped forward. "Mrs. Dell, is it?"

She turned and smiled. "Yes, Sheriff?"

"I...well, we appreciate your intervention and all, but this is all very unusual. I have some questions...."

The heavy-set lady chuckled. "Why, yes, I'm sure you do. But today isn't going to be the day for them, I'm afraid."

"Ma'am, as an officer of the law, I'm afraid I must insist...."

"Have I broken any laws, Sheriff? I didn't do this. I thought all I did was help."

"Well, I…."

"Let her go, son," Mom interrupted. "She hasn't done anything wrong."

"Wanna bet?" Angela grumbled, but nobody paid her any attention.

"Yeah, you'd better let her walk," Val added, with a grudging edge to her voice. "I'm sure your paths will cross again before it's all said and done."

I wanted to press the issue, but something in my gut told me I'd better listen to my elders this time. "All right, fine. Thank you, Mrs. Dell."

"You're welcome." She drove off without another word.

Somehow, I knew that Val was right. My instincts told me that I hadn't seen the last of Mrs. Dell, but for now, I did my best to put it aside.

For now.

END

GASTON AND THE BEAST

C.S. Wachter

The table wobbles. The screech of its legs against the rough floor pierces my comforting peace.

No. I will not lie. I have learned my lesson and must not twist the truth. The table beneath my cheek shifts about a foot, forcing me out of my alcohol-induced, nightly stupor. I raise my head and pry open one crusty eyelid. My eyeball bounces around the room. No, not literally, figuratively of course. I'm not an idiot.

They are dancing again. And singing. The floor trembles from the stomping and jumping. I truly hate the singing; it sets my pounding head to rattling. Oh, it wasn't always that way. There was a time when I led the singing. A time when the whole town looked up to me. And I don't mean because I am taller than everyone else here. No. Three years ago, I was a different man, respected, admired, sought after by all the beauties in the village … except her. Belle.

The fingers of both hands curl like claws, my untrimmed nails gouging the soft pine plank that serves as a tabletop. New gouges join their myriad kin in a crosshatch pattern of light and dark as Belle laughs. She tosses her head, oblivious to the spectacle she and that beast who now wears the guise of a prince are making. Even Maurice, crazy old fool, flings the hat off his head exposing a halo of spidery hair and dances on a table.

"Enough." The word erupts in a soft growl. Unable to take the senseless frivolity and hypocrisy any longer, I push up from my seat, teeth grinding at the burning torment searing its way up my spine. Visions of my fall that fateful night—the pain, the fear, the ominous darkness—permeate my mind, sinister and final. Like death. I should have died; at first, I thought I had died. Then the blistering pain came, followed by days and nights of fever and nightmares. Groaning, I succumb to the agony and collapse back onto the rickety chair, trapped and trembling at the rage I cannot release.

The murky dregs at the bottom of the mug call to me. I down the remains of the dark brown ale and lick out clear droplets from the bottom of a shot glass, then wave to the tavern owner to bring me more. He stares without response. It only takes the promise of violence in my eyes for him to relent. Shaking his head, he brings me a pitcher and a bottle.

"Go on home, Gaston. Stop doing this to yerself."

With a flick of my wrist, he scuttles away like the frightened rabbit he is. His advice and pity sour my stomach. I may not be the huntsman I was before my fall but I'm still the best hunter within a hundred leagues of this pathetic little village. I uncork the bottle and fill the shot glass, sloshing a puddle of liquid onto the table as I pour.

It is oblivion that I seek. And yet ... despite my desire to remain aloof from other patrons, my gaze is drawn to the cloaked figure sitting in the darkened corner opposite mine. I toss down the contents of the glass, its welcome burn coats my throat and crashes into my stomach. Reaching for the bottle again, I stop, my gaze drawn to the stranger. We don't get many outsiders in Coques.

An outsized cloak with the hood pulled far over the face do an admirable job of hiding the visitor's features, but the long-fingered, finely boned hands wrapped around the mug of ale give me pause. Not just a stranger, but a female alone. Odd. Very odd.

The fire flickers and in the trembling glow that permeates the shadows, I detect eyes focused on Belle and her husband.

Without warning, the woman's gaze lands on me. I pull in a breath. There is something in those golden eyes that sends a prickling of fear through me. In one swift, graceful movement, the feminine hand releases the mug, disappears within the folds of the cloak, then reappears and tosses coins upon the table. Swirling gray tweed blocks my sight as the figure rises and slips past the dancers toward the exit. A moment later, she is gone. One peculiar thought circles within my mind as I stare at the closing door: whomever she was, she had small feet clad in heavy boots.

I reach for the bottle but then stop myself and turn the shot glass over. The room closes in on me. I must get away. Muttering a curse, I down my ale and rise. Grabbing my coat, I wrap it around me, fasten one button, and, clutching my walking stick, hobble out into the breezy dark of midnight.

A full moon casts beams of silver light on the uneven, cobblestone street. Alone, I leave behind the noisy revelry and make my way out of Coques. The brisk autumn wind chills my chest. I pull in the flaps of my coat and fasten the remaining buttons. My head clears as I draw deep breaths in and huff them out. Step, tap, gasp, step, step, tap, wheeze. The damaged bones in my back voice their complaint in waves of pain. A full half-hour later, the dark form of my mansion appears, rising above the surrounding shrubbery like a phantom climbing out from its earth-bound grave.

Dim, flickering lights appear in two of the lower story windows. Evidence of a crackling fire in the great room, set by a servant in advance of my arrival. I quicken my pace, eager to shed my coat and bask in the fire's warmth.

For the second time this night, a prickling of fear filters through me as a spectral howl rides the wind, imbuing the air with a sense of danger. Hunter that I am, I cannot stop the shiver that sends me shuffling toward my front door. A second cry soon follows, then another. By the time I slam the door shut behind me, sweat beads my temples and dribbles down the center of my back. Whatever beast hunted tonight was unknown to me. A predator I hoped never to meet.

~~~~~

A week has passed. As is my custom, I frequented the tavern nightly. Each evening, I hoped to see the mystery woman again. Why, I cannot say. My mind began inventing stories centered around her; who she is, why she had come to Coques, why she hadn't returned. I imagined her as beautiful. More beautiful than Belle. Where Belle is slight and pretty, my mind pictured the stranger as tall and regal. But it was all meaningless drivel. She hadn't returned. Probably would never return.

The tavern is quiet. Belle, her prince, and their crowd of sycophants are noticeably absent. The aroma of roasting venison sets my stomach to growling and I signal my need to the owner. He smiles. Probably pleased that I have ordered food and not just drink. The money-grubbing busybody.

Scanning the large, open room, I sigh. Though I detest the singing and dancing whenever Belle and the prince are in attendance, I find myself missing them tonight.

After the enigmatic woman looked into my eyes the night of the howling, I had found a rare clarity to my thoughts. It lasted until two days ago when the emptiness of my broken state sent me seeking solace in the bottle again. She wasn't coming back. I admitted it to myself. And why that mattered to me, I had no inkling. I never saw her face. Or heard her voice. Only saw those singular golden eyes that touched my spirit in some inexplicable way. No. She's gone and
~~~~~

good riddance.

The door opens, swinging wide and slamming into the wall with a loud thump. Startled, I look up. A blast of wind circles through the room, flinging dead and drying leaves before it, sending them into corners where they will lie until they are swept away. I avert my face and raise an arm to protect my eye.

As things settle in the calm after the door shuts, I focus on the cloaked form walking across the floor from the entryway toward the back of the room. A moment later, the woman settles into the chair she had occupied the other night.

An unfamiliar warmth creeps up my chest and invades my mind. The need for oxygen forces me to pull in the breath I had held from the moment I'd seen *her*.

Useless. It is all useless. I cannot resist. Her presence draws me like a moth to flame. Old, almost extinct pride exerts its power, holds me in my seat. I am Gaston. The great hunter. The pride of Coques. Who is she? She who hides behind a hood.

My fingers trace the scar that runs from my scalp, through the ruin of my left eye, and down my cheek. Another reminder of my fall. She may hide beneath her cloak, but I am the one who should hide. A beast. Hideous. No! I am Gaston! I will … what? What will I do?

I pull in a deep breath, wrap my fingers around my blackthorn cane, push upright, and straighten my back the best I can. Though my smile was described as handsome in the past, in recent years, it has been likened to a grimace. I plaster one on and attempt to walk in a casual manner past the crackling fire to the lone table sitting in the shadows beyond the hearth.

She doesn't speak as I approach, but her heated gaze rests upon me. I do not ask permission but lower my body onto the chair opposite her as her eyes narrow and follow my actions. I catch the movement as her mouth flattens into a stern line.

All else is forgotten when she reaches up and slips the dark hood from her head, revealing long, wavy chestnut hair that glimmers with golden highlights in the glow of the flickering firelight. My heart thumps a rapid rhythm. Before me now sits a young woman whose beauty leaves me speechless. I open my mouth to speak, but it hangs useless. My mind has shut down. An arrow has pierced the heart of the great hunter Gaston and I am defenseless against its power.

The chuckle starts low in her throat, reminding me of a growl. A curious mix of attraction and fear churns within me at the sound. She chuckles again, this time louder, and heat rises up through me, landing in my face. I fear I am blushing.

"You should think about closing your mouth and, perhaps, breathing."

Her voice, unexpectedly low and husky, causes my eye to widen. Such a voice seems at odds with her finely boned, oval face and full lips. Oh, those lips. They call to me. Their soft siren song commands me to touch them with my own.

Her lips turn up in a smile and, yet again, I am taken by surprise. Tiny, canine teeth peek out from behind those perfect lips. Her words sink in and I catch my breath and close my mouth.

"You are different than I expected."

I blink. "You expected me?"

Her laughter again laces the air. "Of course. Who has not heard of the great hunter Gaston?"

"You ... you've heard of me?"

I almost miss her next words as my eye focuses on those pale lips. I blink and she stops speaking. Her look tells me she noticed my lapse. I swallow and ask, "Who are you? I ... I ... what is your name?"

She hesitates and in the quiet, wood pops within the fire. Bugs, I think, it's bugs that cause the popping noise. I halt that line of thought, redirecting my attention back to our words as I await her reply.

"Ransome," she murmurs. "My name is Ransome."

Her eyes meet mine, a challenge written there. The question flits through my mind, why? Why would she challenge me?

"I heard about your fall. And yet, here you are. Do you still hunt?"

Her question brings my thoughts to a stumbling halt. How could she ask such a question? She couldn't miss the ruin of my face, my inability to walk without my cane, my—I must admit it—drunken state.

"No, my lady. I can no longer hunt without help. Help. Yes, there was a time I had help. After the fall. My old friend, Lefou. Without his help I would have indeed died. But he deserted me not long after."

My thoughts turn dark as I recall his departure. My anger and drinking drove him away. I never thought to seek him out. It was he who abandoned me, not the other way around. He could have come back at any time, but he has not.

Quiet descends upon us once again as Ransome turns her gaze to the fire. Her kindness does not go unnoticed.

"I haven't eaten yet. Would you join me?"

I meet her questioning eyes, my one good eye twitching. I nod, the desire to get to know Ransome better growing stronger within me.

We talk until the owner chases us from the tavern, claiming he needs to close.

I had never met a woman, or man for that matter, who understood me like Ransome. We fell into a pattern of meeting evenings for dinner and drinks and conversation that persisted over the next few weeks. I felt as if I had been given new life.

~~~~~

I stare into the flames, watching with disinterest as they devour a massive log in the fireplace. I suspect pops and sizzles would permeate the air were it not for the noise. The tavern is full tonight. Belle, her prince, and a group of revelers from the castle fill the air with laughter and song. In the past, their joy would have depressed and angered me, driven me to drink more deeply in my need to reach an insulating level of numb. Tonight, I allow it to roll off me like rain from a well-oiled slicker.

The thump of the door against the wall draws my attention. A tall form enters; not the one for whom I wait but a blonde man wearing a frock coat. He is familiar but I cannot recall his name, one of the many denizens of the castle.

Drumming my fingers on the table in a steady pattern, I wait, my thoughts wandering. Tomorrow night's full moon will mark thirty days since I first saw Ransome, sitting here, alone. Just like tonight. But so much has changed in the past month.

My fingers curl into the smooth material of the cravat at my neck, clean and well tied, a fine forest green. The bottle sits before me, untouched. As if with a will of its own, my hand wanders up to my face. Tracing the scar that mars my features, I grimace; but pride swells within me as my fingers find my clean-shaven chin and strong, manly jaw.

Ransome is late tonight. Each time the door opens, my eye is drawn to it. My breath rushes out in relief when she appears. She hesitates, her gaze meeting mine, but then shifting to focus on the
~~~~~

prince. After another quick glance in my direction, she walks over to where Belle and her *Princely Beast* are laughing at something Maurice has just said.

My heart falters. Is he the reason she is here? Will she choose him like Belle did?

After a few words I cannot hear, Maurice moves down a seat and Ransome takes the chair next to the prince.

Nausea climbs upward from my stomach, constricting and bitter. I growl deep within my throat and reach for the bottle. I don't bother to pour a glass but pull the cork and gulp enough liquid to send a ball of fire down my throat, into my chest, and all the way to my stomach where it lands with a burning fury. My focus narrows as if I am watching through a tunnel as Ransome and the beastly prince converse, their expressions intense.

I drink deeply, the familiar numbness setting in. Though I try to look away, my efforts are useless. I scan the room, feigning disinterest, only to have my eye return and lock on Ransome. Belle reaches over and rests a hand on Ransome's arm, a look of compassion flitting across her face.

What is happening? Why is Ransome there and not sitting across from me, pulling me out of myself?

In time, Ransome pushes upright, the prince rising at her side. He pulls her in for a hug. It takes every ounce of willpower I possess to not charge across the room and pick up where I left off the night of my fall. She looks up into his now handsome face and says a few more words before turning away and walking toward me, her shoulders hunched, her steps slow. Her glorious hair falls loosely, blocking my view of her expression. But I can tell from her posture, she is pained about something. What did that beast say to her?

I rise out of my seat as Ransome approaches. She lifts her head. Tears mar her pale cheeks. My anger runs hotter, my control lost as the numbness vanishes behind a wall of hatred. He did that; he made her cry. Seeing red, all I want to do is kill the beast. But as I move to pass Ransome, she shifts to block my way. Her fine-boned hand slips up to my chest, stopping me and holding me transfixed.

She blinks, moisture from her eyes coating her thick lashes. "No. Please, Gaston, sit. I need you to be with me now. Please?"

Anger sears through me, the need for violence rising in its wake. Ransome steps even closer, her face bare inches from mine. Her hand moves upward to cup my scarred cheek, her eyes impale me with their need. Though I have stared into those reddish-gold orbs often in the last month, it is only now that I see the otherness there. A shiver races through me, dispelling the anger, chilling the burning need within me. I nod and, without looking, reach back, find my chair, and drop back into it.

Ransome sits across from me. Her hands tremble as she reaches for the bottle and a glass, pours out a hefty tumbler, and gulps it down in one swig. She doesn't speak, just stares at her hands, watching her fingers shift the small glass back and forth. The minutes drag by. When I can stand it no longer, I open my mouth and hot words pour out.

"It was all a lie, the time you spent with me. The things you said. You only used me so you didn't have to be alone while you waited to talk to *him*. You came here to meet him, not me."

Her eyes lift, sorrow laden, they meet mine. "Yes." The word is quiet, almost whispered. "Yes, Gaston. I did come here for him. But then I met you. I've never known anyone like you. The way you understand me and my love of the hunt. I never expected to feel what I feel when I look at you."

I snicker. "What, revulsion? I carry no illusions. I am aware of not only my physical scars, but my ruined reputation. I am no longer the hunter I was. Do not lie to me any longer. Go. Go, if you must. Join the beastly prince. Leave me alone."

She drops her gaze and shakes her head, tears once again tracing her cheeks. "No. Please. You do not understand. He cannot help me. I thought he could, but … no."

We sit in a cocoon of silence as the party continues in the room beyond us. Ransome pulls in a loud breath, lifts her focus to me, and squares her shoulders. "Meet me tomorrow evening at the hour before moonrise. Hunt with me."

Anger flares briefly in the pit of my stomach, but Ransome's expression of need stifles it. And yet, she asks for that which I can no longer do. Why would she do that to me?

"You ask me to hunt with you, why? You know my physical limitations."

"There is something you need to understand."

I shake my head, but the truth rests in my eye. I cannot deny her.

In an instant, her sorrow evaporates, and a confident smile lifts the corners of her lips. The flickering light of the fire again flashes on small, sharp, far too white teeth. "You cannot deny me this. I see it on your face. I ask you because with me you will be fine ... more than fine, my handsome hunter. I will await you in front of your mansion. Tomorrow, my love."

She does not give me time to answer but, with a flurry of movement, leans in and kisses my ruined cheek. Oh, the sudden warmth that infuses my face!

Another smile emerges, and with a flick of her cape, she leaves the table and hurries to the door. Shock holds me captive as Ransome vanishes into the night. A bolt of lightning flashes in my mind. Her words. Their meaning. "My love." And that kiss. A confident smile lifts the corners of my lips.

~~~~~

A lightness I had not experienced in years fills me. It is near to sundown. Dressed in clothing I have not worn since my fall, I wait in the foyer, my gaze eagerly searching the woods beyond my manicured lawn. A strange thought occurs to me. Why would I seek Ransome in the woods rather than on the road? I dismiss the thought and pull at the hem of my loose-fitting forest green brocade vest. When I had last worn it, the buttons at my chest strained to hold together. Now, the material hangs on my thinner frame.

Ransome's face hovers before me and her words from last night play tag with the doubts in my mind. She called me her love. She kissed my scar. I shake off the daydream and again scan the woods. A movement of branches and underbrush draw my eye. She is there. At the edge of the shadows. I must not keep her waiting.

"Avent, my jacket."

My manservant helps me into the maroon jacket and comes in front of me to fasten the buttons. I wave him away. Though my fingers fumble, I fasten the buttons. Straightening upright, I debate between taking my cane or my walking stick. Grasping the taller and heavier stick, I heft it before me. "Yes."

"Will there be anything else, sir?" Avent asks.

"No, Avent. Do not wait up for me. I will return late."

A cool breeze caresses my face as I descend the steps from my front door and hurry across the lawn. The chill sends a shiver through me. Autumn is well underway and though a few trees remain a deep, tired shade of green, most sport vibrant shades of orange or red. The acrid aroma of dead oak leaves drifts through the air, their stiff remains crunching under my feet as I venture into the thick woods where I had seen Ransome.
~~~~~

The angled light of the setting sun throws moving patterns of shadow and light beneath the wind-tossed branches of old-growth trees. My heart thumps to a faster rhythm when I catch sight of her standing next to the immense bole of a copper beech, her tweed cloak pulled tightly around her, the hood up.

She waves, then turns and stalks deeper into the forest. I follow, my walking stick thumping in an awkward pattern through the tangle of scrub. Several times, Ransome pulls up and waits for me before starting forward again, not allowing me to get close enough to talk. Thick underbrush gives way to sparce growth as we move beneath the heavier canopy. Walking easier, I increase my speed. Soon we reach a familiar opening. A fire blazes at its center and Ransome has stopped just beyond the flames.

She waves toward a log set next to the fire. Though worn and insect riddled, I recognize it. I had dragged the thing over and placed it there a week before coming face to face with the beast. Lowering my stiff body to sit, I stop, straighten, and look to Ransome.

"Please sit. I ..." She pushes the hood from her head, revealing her unbound hair, then nods toward the log. "Yes. That is your gun. Please sit." She turns toward where the sun has disappeared beyond the trees. "I don't have much time and there is much you need to know."

Ransome turns back and drops to sit on the ground in front of me. I hesitate a moment but then take a seat on the log, my hand resting on the barrel of the weapon which had been my favorite, the one I thought I had lost three years ago.

"Where did you find this?"

"That is not important now." She glances over her shoulder again, but then returns her gaze to me. I open my mouth, the question still pressing for an answer. She raises her hand, palm toward me. I clamp my mouth closed. Her message is clear. She needs to speak, and I must be silent. Though it goes against my nature, I cannot deny Ransome. I nod my acquiescence.

Ransome chews her lower lip; her sharp teeth seem even longer and sharper in the flickering half-light. She pulls in a deep breath, lets it out.

"I didn't plan to fall in love when I came here. You are right. I came to meet with the prince. I needed his help." She shakes her head. "But he couldn't help me. What happened to him was unique to him. My ... *situation* ... is different. I cannot be helped."

Her eyes seek out my own, hers glowing with a supernatural light, my sole eye widening at the impact of her gaze.

"I retrieved your gun so you could help me, my handsome hunter. You, Gaston, the manliest hunter in the land. Only you had the strength and courage to try to kill the beastly prince. And ... only you can kill me."

My thoughts reel at the words. I must have misheard. But no. Ransome stares at me, the meaning clear in her glowing eyes.

"Moonrise will be upon us soon, my love. You must do this for me. I trust you. My heart weeps that we will never have the chance to explore our love more fully, but I am the beast you must kill now. And this time, you must succeed."

Exhaling a hiss, Ransome flings off her cloak, pulls off her boots, pushes up onto her feet, and begins pacing beyond the fire. My mind tilts, her words and actions make no sense. Struggling to reconcile her demand with the pleasure I feel watching her pace, I trace her actions. Her graceful movements stir my imagination, they are almost cat-like, her tread silent upon the leaf-strewn ground. Almost like a predator ... no, not *like* a predator.

She *is* a predator. Graceful. Lethal. The thought fixes firmly in my mind. How could I not see it before? The hideous beast hidden behind the beauty. My fingers wrap around the stock of my gun. Ransome seems unaware of my actions. She continues to pace, mumbling under her breath.

All that I lost three years ago can be regained. My reputation, my honor restored. Pushing up onto my feet and standing with straight back, I check the gun. Ransome had prepared for this moment. It is ready. But am I? My focus shifts to Ransome and every instinct comes alive, crashing into my feelings for the beauty who entered my life a scant month ago.

The first feeble rays of the full moon filter through the trees, reaching out like claws toward Ransome, snatching her from me. They touch her back as she watches me, her expression one of profound sorrow as she mouths the words, *thank you*. A tremor takes her. Her eyes gleam brighter. Her face distorts, growing longer. A snout appears, fur-covered and sporting large canine incisors. Seams rip and clothing drops away as the tiny, human form morphs into a seven-foot-tall, fur-clad werewolf. It drops to stand on four, huge paws. A monster. A beast.

The moment of glory I have waited for my entire life brings a broad smile. Gaston the hunter is back. I raise the gun and take aim. Finally, all is right. Until I see her eyes. Ransome's eyes. A groan slips out from between my clenched teeth. The beast before me is Ransome. I cannot kill the beauty I love.

The werewolf releases a deep, throaty growl before turning and loping away. I bow my head, unwilling and unable to face the truth. A band of iron constricts my chest.

Time slips by but I continue to stand, unmoving and numb beyond imagining. A shiver races through me. The night has turned cold. Without thought, I scan the tiny hollow. A small pile of wood catches my eye. My back protesting the effort, I gather a few pieces of tinder and feed the dying fire. Once the kindling is burning well, I add a couple logs. I sit and stare at the licking flames, my heart turning to darkened embers as I wait.

~~~~~

A rustling to my side pulls me awake. I grab my gun and study the shadows, alert for any threat. Seconds tick by. No sound nor movement. I shiver and wrap my arms around my torso.

The fire, nothing more than glowing coals, does little to warm my trembling body. The need to feed it in the dawn chill presses on me. Setting the gun on the log, I rise and make my way back to the diminished wood pile.

Within minutes, a steady blaze coaxes me to reach out icy hands toward its flickering warmth. My front toasty, I turn to warm my back.

She stands in the shadows. We freeze in place, she and I. Though the darkness hides it, I know she is naked … shivering.

Her cloak, a crumbled lump of gray tweed on the ground near me, draws my attention. Keeping my movements slow and unthreatening, I walk to it, scoop it up, and hold it out to Ransome. She stares without moving.

A tingle races up my crooked spine and I shift my gaze to look away from Ransome, hoping she doesn't disappear. The material is snatched from my hand. I give her another minute to cover herself then turn to face Ransome.

The hurt look on her face almost undoes me, but I have made my decision. Sometime during the night, I chose my course of action.

"Why?" Her word comes out in a harsh whisper. "I am a beast. You are a hunter. Why did you not kill me? I wanted it to be you. I knew now what I didn't know before; that you would honor my
~~~~~

death and end my suffering. You weren't an uncaring stranger. So, why? Why would you not do that for me?"

Four steps bring me to Ransome. Four steps to change my life forever. I now understand. Fame and glory are fleeting. I have learned what Belle had known all along, to look past the outside and into the heart of a person.

Ransome steps back but I am too close, my arms reach around her and pull her into me. A huff of shock sounds from her but I pull her even closer. Her head tilts back and the shock on her face causes me to smile. But only for a second. The smile vanishes as I lower my lips to hers. Her hesitation lasts only a second before the kiss becomes mutual.

Our future is uncertain, with the promises of danger, difficulties, and strange adventures. But at this moment, there is one thing of which I am certain: I, Gaston the hunter, have been tamed by the love of the most beautiful beast of all.

END

ROCKY MOUNTAIN PARADISE
Lyndon Perry

"They say this town's not big enough for the both of us, but pards, let me tell you how it's gonna be. We're gonna live peaceably in this ol' watering hole from here on out. No more shootin', no more robbin', and no more gamblin'.

"Well, I suppose a little gamblin' would be all right every now and then.

"But the carousin' each month that sets us one against another has got to stop! You hired me as marshal, and by gunnysack, I aim to marshal.

"Why all the rules and changes, you ask? Well, times change, don't they? And the law eventually settles over every frontier town; this here Rocky Mountain City ain't no different.

"And besides, us beauties and beasts have got to learn to live together, or we'll just end up huntin' each other 'til extinction.

"Don'tcha remember that's how it used to be? Some twenty years back, when they came a'wandering into these here parts? Thought they'd found paradise, they did. These beautiful lower slopes of them magnificent mountains. The rivers, the valleys, the trees. The wild game and fish.

"They came in peace, I tell you. But a lot of us wouldn't have it. We were downright beastly about it, in fact. It's how we got our name.

"Now don't you argue. I remember! Don'tcha recall how it all unfolded? I sure as shootin' do.

"Mebbe now that Boot Hill's gotten kinda full with the kith and kin of both our sides, y'all are ready to listen!

"After listenin' for a spell, I'm prayin' we'll all do what's right. And come together."

~~~~~

With the breaking sun at their backs, streaking slivers of gold pointing westward across the expansive prairie, the wagon train of settlers caught their first glimpse of the Rocky Mountains. The snowy peaks glinted back the morning light and, like a beacon, commanded
~~~~~

the travelers hitherwards.

The sight took the Beauties' breath away.

"She's still a far piece off, but my Lord, the illumined feast of those mighty hills makes my heart beat so."

That remark from Zevi Rand, the leader of the forty-one settlers who had left Independence, Missouri, earlier that spring in search of a mountain paradise they could call their own.

Zevi's wife, Yilva said, "See how the sun sparkles off those distant peaks? It's a beckoning sign from heaven above. Our new home is just ahead, friends. Our prayers have been answered."

"Praise the Lord," responded the travelers near enough to hear. Murmurs of 'Amen' echoed among the rest of the faithful.

A generation ago, their small sect left the troubled village of Dolphus on the edge of Germany's Black Forest and came to America. The children, now adults, were about to fulfill their parents' dreams of settling in a new world where they could pursue peace and harmony with man and nature.

Such a path was called the Way of Beauty in their beliefs, and its adherents were commonly known by that descriptor as well.

Beauties.

Not that they were perfect. Far from it. But Zevi and Yilva and the other six Elders tried their best to follow the Way and lead their small congregation toward holiness.

"Will we finally find a place to call our own, Zev?" asked Lucas Night, quietly. He and his wife Dora were the youngest of the Elders, and he struggled with his faith every now and then. "A lot more pilgrims on the trail than I expected. I wonder if there will be any room for us at all when we arrive."

Zev called to the rest of the small colony to prepare to move out. He then answered his friend with an assuring nod.

"Most of those other folks are heading on through the mountains to Oregon. Rest assured, Luke, the Lord has ordained for us a beautiful valley in which to settle."

This seemed to satisfy the young man who left to hitch up his team of oxen and help his wife and children load up their weathered Conestoga.

Within a short time, all the campfires were extinguished, all the children were accounted for, and the morning prayers were said.

Zev smiled, pointed west and, with a hearty *hi-ya!*, took up the reins and guided his massive beasts, and the rest of the Beauties in his charge, toward their future.

~~~~~

The Beauties arrived in Rocky Mountain City on a late summer day, 1848. It wasn't much of a city. In fact, it was barely a small town, struggling for survival on a diluvian plain in the shadow of some foothills that rolled upwards toward distant majestic peaks.

A cold rushing stream, fed year 'round by mountain springs and ice melt, provided the town with fresh water. The thunderous rapids also hinted at the presence of alpine valleys further back toward its source, vales and meadows lush with life, both plant and animal. It was to one of those hidden glens the weary travelers were heading, or so they prayed.

"We'll stop for supplies and continue on our way in a few days," Zev announced to the pilgrims under his care. "We don't want no trouble."

The sun was moving westward and the mountain shadows had reached out to blanket the small town in twilight. A few of the settlers looked at the rising moon in the east and muttered to one another, shaking their heads. The sooner they left this intrusive outcropping of civilization, the better.

A lanky man with long limbs and fidgety hands ran out to meet the wagon train before they got too close. He took off his hat, revealing a shock of black hair, and waved it in front of him as if to warn them off. The gesture belied his welcoming words.

"Greetings, travelers," he said with a nervous smile. "I'm Mayor Thomas Braswell. I assume you all are just passing through?"

"A pleasure, Mayor. I'm Zevi Rand, and yes, we're simply passing through. Thought we'd camp upriver a bit. Just a night or two to restock and such. Then we'll be on our way."

The mayor spun his hat in his hands, then motioned it northward. "You know the pass to Oregon is that-away some fifty miles. Probably best if you leave in the morning. Getting late in the season to cross them Rockies."

Zev glanced at his wife and she smiled back reassuringly.

"We're not heading to Oregon," Zev said, his tan face aglow with anticipation. "Our plans are to settle further up in those yonder hills. Find a peaceful place where we won't bother anyone."

"You all Mormons? 'Cause we don't want no Mormons 'round here, Mister."

"No, we're not—"
~~~~~

"Still open country, isn't it," demanded Luke, joining the conversation. "Makes no difference if we're religious or not."

Zev placed a placating hand on his friend's arm and turned to the mayor. "We're not Mormons. Just travelers looking for a place to call home. We'll provide for most of our own needs, so we won't be visiting... What's the name of this town?"

"Rocky Mountain City," Braswell said with pride.

"...well, we won't be visiting Rocky Mountain City very often. How does that sound?"

The mayor stole a look back at the small crowd that had gathered some hundred yards behind him, seemingly protecting the half dozen shanties that made up the town.

He bit his lip and said, "It's a mighty hard country, friend. There's Injuns and grizzlies and wolves...."

Braswell trailed off. Zevi nodded. The two men looked at each other in silence, each waiting for the other to speak.

Finally, the mayor sighed. Lowering his voice, "I can't stop you, of course. But just take care wherever you end up. Our townsfolk don't take too kindly to strangers."

The mayor plastered a grim smile on his face, indicating their interview was over.

Zev gave instructions for the small colony to skirt the town and set up camp closer to the foothills. He nodded again to the town's representative and the man made his way back to the safety of the waiting assembly. They stood there, as stark and bleak as the handful of rough wooden buildings they guarded.

When the colony was tucked in for the night, campfires blazing, Luke and his wife, Dora, along with two other Elder couples, approached Zev and Yilva. The eight of them settled themselves around a warm fire, their demeanors subdued.

"I don't have a good feeling about this town," Luke began. "They obviously don't want us here."

"We'd more than double their population if we stayed," Dora said. "They feel threatened is all." The other wives nodded.

Yilva smiled. "Rest assured, my friends, we'll find our own paradise far enough away from these strangers so as to not cause them any worry."

The rest murmured their agreement.

"Hello the camp," came a voice from out of the darkness.

The four couples stood, looked at each other and peered into the chilly night.

"Hello, Stranger. The camp is open. Step to the fire and warm yourself."

"Mighty hospitable of you," said the voice, which, the camp soon saw, belonged to a young man of about twenty years of age. He held out his hand in greeting.

The small party was struck dumb for a moment by the newcomer's overt friendliness. Yilva nudged her husband and Zev reached out, accepting the handshake.

"What brings you out this way," the camp's leader asked. "Not to be rude, but the reception we received this afternoon wasn't exactly what we'd call warm."

"Don't I know it! Sorry about that, and my pa sends his apologies as well."

"You mean the mayor?" Luke asked.

"Who, Braswell? No, he's not my— Oh! Sorry. Where's my manners? Name's Leverich. Chad Leverich. And my pa goes by Red. He owns the dry goods store, and, well, he's askin' if you'll be needin' any provisions."

"So you come at night. How very thoughtful of you." Luke huffed and shook his head.

Chad looked down at his feet. "Not proud of it, but you'd not be welcome in town. My pa wouldn't want you goin' without supplies, though."

"And miss an opportunity to fleece the latest passersby?"

"That's enough, Luke," Zev said. He motioned for the young man to sit down and they all got settled back around the fire. "We do need to restock. Yilva can provide you with a list of items. We're mighty grateful for your father's overture."

"Me and Pa just wanna make a livin' and figure it's best policy to be friendly to everybody." He sat a moment, staring into the flickering flames. "I heard you folks are thinkin' about settlin' in one of the valleys up river?"

Another Elder, David Leloup, responded. "That's right. You see a problem with that? From the town's perspective, that is?"

"I don't reckon so," Chad replied. "Plenty of room hereabouts. If you follow this ol' stream, the Timberline River we call it, and then take the north branch about five miles in, you'll come to some mighty fine country."

"Unclaimed?" asked Ana, David's wife.

"Oh, some friendly Injuns and a few trappers make their way through the area from time to time, but they won't bother you. Like I said, there's enough space for everybody in these here mountains."

So the matter was decided. Just before noon the next day, the small colony, provisioned and eager, blazed a trail along the Timberline to their new home. It was late afternoon when they first set eyes on the hidden valley, and they wept with joy.

The sun had been playing peek-a-see with the excited travelers for hours, skipping behind huge clouds of cotton one moment, showering them with rays of warmth the next. After they'd followed a mountain pass into a long vale, the sky finally cleared and the sun lit up the length of the glen for all to behold.

Families jumped from their wagons in awestruck wonder.

A clear mountain stream ran through the valley, separating the open land into two flower-filled meadows. Stands of quakies, cottonwoods, willows, and maples ran along the sloping hills on either side of the widened dale.

Deer were coming out to graze. Birds were chirping their evening songs. Trout were jumping for insects up and down the stream.

Husbands hugged their wives and children ran gaily through the colorful field.

The Beauties had found their paradise.

~~~~~

Mayor Braswell ambled into Red's Dry Good Store about a week after the wagon train had departed upriver. He took off his hat and watched as the owner, Lester 'Red' Leverich, stocked shelves.

"Red, you got a moment?"

"Seein' as how there's no one here but you an' me, Thomas, I 'spose I do."

The owner continued arranging items behind the counter. He eventually stopped his work, wiped his hands on his store apron, and faced the mayor. He raised an eyebrow expectantly.

Braswell cleared his throat and fingered the brim of his hat, then began spinning it in his hands. He put the black felt hat back on his head, then swept it off again.

"Look here, Leverich, I've got a message from the town council and you're not making it easy on me."

"I'm all ears, Mayor. I'm not the one stoppin' you from talkin'."

"All right, then. The council doesn't look very highly on you
~~~~~

selling to those settlers."

"Uh-huh."

The two men stared at each other.

The mayor coughed and said, "That's the message. They'd prefer you not supply those Mormons again."

"They're not Mormons, Thomas. Even if they were, that would be my business, to provision 'em or not."

Red's son, Chad, entered from the back of the store. "Wagon's loaded, Pa. I can hitch up a team and take it up to them Beauties after lunch."

Braswell's eyes went wide. He harrumphed and shook his head in disgust.

Red sighed and said, "The council can't tell a man how to make a living, Mayor." Turning to his boy, "That would fine, son. If you can't make it back afore sunset, jus' spend the night at their camp."

The mayor turned to go, but stopped before reaching the door. "Chad, what did you call them people again?"

"The settlers? They call themselves Beauties. Has to do with their religion, the path of beauty or somethin' like that."

Braswell huffed once more and was about to leave when Rusty Morgan, excited and breathless, burst into the store. His sides were heaving and he bent over double for a moment, hands on his knees.

"Mayor! Glad I caught you." He nodded briefly at Red and Chad. "You all won't believe what I saw last night. I mean, it was the biggest durn thing I ever did see. And I clipped it, for sure I did. I know'd it."

"Slow down," Braswell said. "Now what's all this? You shoot a grizzly? Is it close to town?"

"No, not some bear. A timber wolf! Biggest one ever, I reckon. Was huntin' up the north branch of the Timberline, had my Hawken flintlock ready, and I hit it. The beast went howling into the night and was gone afore I could reload."

"We haven't had a wolf pack in these parts for some time," Red noted. "Mountain men cleared out the upper valleys years ago."

"You didn't kill it then?" asked Chad.

"No, but I musta wounded it purty bad. Mebbe it loped off somewhere to die. I only come back to town to get Dusty. We're gonna track it and bring it back for everyone to see."

"Well, you and your brother best be careful," Braswell said. "If there's a wolf pack movin' in, the town council will want to know about it."

Rusty left as quickly as he came and the mayor followed him out the door, but not before he said to the father and son proprietors, "Keep in mind the wishes of the council, Red."

"I wish the council would kiss my behind," Red said after the mayor had gone. Chad merely chuckled and grabbed a couple of horehound candies from a big jar on the countertop before his dad could swat his hand away.

~~~~~

The Beauties were in a somber mood when Chad drove his two mules leading a wagonload of supplies to the outskirts of their camp. It was mid-afternoon and the late summer sun was shining bright, but the forty-some settlers were not reflecting any of its warmth toward the intruder.

"If you're here to sell us more goods, you can just turn that wagon back around." This from Elder David Leloup, who broke away from the cluster at the center of their makeshift compound. The hostility in his voice was unrestrained.

Taken aback, Chad said, "Well, no sir. This here's the rest of your order from when you first came through town. Is Yilva here? She's the one who gave me the list. We didn't have all the items last week..."

He looked at the women and men standing a ways off. They were murmuring quietly and shaking their heads. As they milled about, Chad caught a glimpse of what looked like someone lying on the ground, on a blanket. A woman was kneeling beside the still form, rocking back and forth, hands over her mouth.

"Is something wrong over there? Is someone hurt?"

Leloup didn't answer, but he did wave toward the group, beckoning.

After a moment, Yilva emerged from among the pilgrims, calling out as she approached, "David, it's all right. Chad is a friend."

"Well, he best be long gone by sundown," the Elder muttered before returning to stand vigil with the others.

To Yilva, Chad asked, "Is someone sick yonder? I can get Ol' Ma Tucker from town to come up. She ain't no reg'lar doctor, but she knows her herbs and tonics and such. Mebbe she can help."

At that moment, the kneeling woman let out such a keening that Chad had to clamp both hands over his ears. Yilva rushed back to her friends, and the young man followed warily.
~~~~~

As the crowd parted to let their leader through, he saw the supine figure shudder and jerk, the spasms creating a rippling effect up and down its frame. One would have thought it a man's body upon initial observation, but with every convulsion, the mass changed form, first human then...beast!

At last, the seizures stopped and the hairy, brutish figure transformed one last time into the shape of Lucas Night. The man was dead, it was plain for all to see.

"What in tarnation!" Chad cried before he could stop himself.

With a roar, Leloup turned and ran toward the unwelcome visitor, arms wide, hands like claws, ready to grapple and maim and kill. Chad shrank back, unable to defend himself except to raise his forearms in fear and trembling.

"David! No!"

The voice was Zevi Rand's. It brooked no disagreement and the enraged Elder stopped just before administering a slashing blow onto the helpless human.

"David, it wasn't this man's fault. We'll see justice done, but blind vengeance is not the way."

Zev approached to where Chad was cowering low. Leloup towered over him, breathing heavily. Slowly, the Elder withdrew from the quaking townsman. He started back toward the others, saw the tear-streaked face of the woman kneeling next to the dead form, and balked. Suddenly, he cried out and fled, dashing across the field, ripping at his shirt, throwing it aside, bounding, wailing, cursing, until he disappeared into the thick woods at the edge of the valley.

The men and women who had traveled so long and so far to find peace sobbed quietly; and then began tending to Luke's body and to the heart and soul of his widow.

Zev nodded toward the scene. "That's Dora, David's sister. Luke is...was David's brother-in-law."

"What happened?"

Zev gazed down the valley as the mountain shadows stretched eastward. After a moment, he said, "A hunting accident, probably the best way to describe it."

"Yeah, but, I mean...what did I just see? What happened to Luke's body? He...he looked like...I couldn't be imaginin' things, could I?"

The leader of the Beauties closed his eyes, bowed his head, and sighed. "It's what's going to happen that has me worried," he said at last. "Soon everyone's imagination will be running wild. And as the rumors spread, so will the hate. So will the killing."

"I don't understand."

"Neither do we, Chad. Neither do we."

Chad wrinkled his forehead in confusion, suspecting that Zev was referring to some other concern altogether outside his own experience. He wasn't wrong.

~~~~~

They made him leave as soon as all the supplies had been unloaded from the wagon. It was late in the day and the settlers couldn't conceal their urgency to see him off.

Even Zev seemed worried about the lateness of his visit. He accompanied his goodbyes with these parting words: "Best forget what you saw here today, son."

Chad pondered that, and what he'd seen, as he watched a big, bright moon, just past full, crest the horizon. Before reaching town, he thought he heard the howls of wolves echo among the foothills.

When asked by his pa if everything went well with the settlers, he was noncommittal and went straight to bed.

The next morning, he was awakened by shouts outside. Within moments, the residents of Rocky Mountain City were streaming from their stores and homes into the main street of their small town. Chad and Red angled their way to the front of the pack.

"Rusty's dead," came the cry. "My brother's dead!"

Dusty Morgan, anguish on his face, and his brother's bloody and mutilated body in his arms, walked and wailed up and down the street, petitioning the growing crowd for a hearing.

"They sent 'em, I tell ya! Those damned fanatics. I saw them send the wolf that kilt my brother!"

Mayor Braswell, in the act of pulling on his suspenders, shirt still untucked, rushed to Dusty and tried to placate the hysterical young man.

He called to a couple of townspeople gawking at the scene. "Jack, Elmore, come take Rusty...Rusty's body. Now Dusty, you...you let go and you tell me what happened."

As Dusty cried, the men gently extracted the body of his brother from his arms and carried the dead man away.

Braswell said again, "What happened, son?"

"Them Mormons or whatever the hell they are, they brought them wolves, I tell you. We ain't had wolves in these parts since who
~~~~~

knows when, but Rusty, he shot one the other night and he come to get me so we's can track it and bring back the pelt to show you all, but when we got up there last night there was howlin' and, and screamin' and all sorts of ungodly noises, and then we saw a man point and all a'sudden a wolf comes tearin' straight toward us. Rusty got a shot off, but it musta missed, and then that damned beast caught Rusty's throat and my God...."

Dusty broke down then and collapsed to the ground. Everyone stood, silent, staring. Even the air was still, accepting the grave solemnity of the moment.

Chad stepped forward, thinking to comfort his peer. He knew Dusty and his heart hurt for the grieving brother.

But Braswell motioned to him and his father.

"It's those settlers, I tell you. You shouldn't have helped them. Isn't that what the town council decided? You should have sent them on their way down the Oregon Trail. We don't need no religious cult in these here mountains. Who knows what types of wild beasts they'll unleash upon us?"

Red responded, "If there are wolves up river, their arrival has nothin' to do with these newcomers. How can you even think such a thing?"

"Strange timing, though, you have to admit!" someone yelled from the crowd.

"That's right!" shouted another. "I've got goats missing from my pen. I betcha some wolf took 'em in the night. Maybe them settlers arranged it!"

"Honestly!" Red shouted back. "You can't blame these folks for missing goats!"

But Chad wasn't so sure, and he silently backed his way through the agitated mob.

Within a matter of minutes, he was saddling up his roan and blazing a trail up the Timberline. An hour later he was at the Beauties' camp. He took in the scene before him.

David Leloup was nursing an injury to his shoulder; his sister Dora was attending him. The other pilgrims were scattered about, busy with their morning chores. For all the world it looked like what it appeared to be: a group of regular folks trying to establish a routine for living in a new world.

Zev and Yilva waved and made their way over to their new friend. Chad stayed astride his horse.

"You intend to stay here in this valley and establish a home?" Chad asked, his voice even.

The two leaders nodded. A few others stopped what they were doing to listen in.

"Yes, we do," Zev replied. "We didn't come a few thousand miles to pack up at the first sign of trouble."

The young man thought about that.

It was the same with him and his pa. When Chad's mother had died of consumption shortly after they'd arrived in Rocky Mountain City, they'd dug in with grit and determination. This was their home now, and by gum they were going to continue on.

"Is that right?" he asked, just to make certain.

"That's right," Zev said.

Chad pursed his lips. "Then you best tell me 'bout these past couple a'nights." He let his meaning sink in. "'Cause I aim to know what kinda trouble we might be getting' ourselves into."

When the two Elders blinked and hesitated, he got down from his horse and continued.

"I think it's only fair. If I'm gonna be the one to help y'all establish yourselves in this new paradise, you might as well tell me your whole story, right from the beginning."

Yilva and Zev glanced back at the families under their care, nodded to each other in agreement, and proceeded to do just that.

~~~~~

Marshal Chad Leverich finished telling the story, reminding the townsfolk of those early days when the Beauties first arrived in their fair city.

"The fightin' and the killin' went on from there," he said. "Seemed like ev'ry month, when the moon was full, there was some 'huntin' accident', if you get my meaning."

The crowd that had gathered in front of the new marshal's office chuckled uneasily. They'd all come that morning to hear out the new lawman. It was 1868, and the town council finally saw fit to hire their first man with a star.

"Now, I don't need to recount ev'ry tragedy that happened, we all went through it. Mayor Braswell dead and gone. Elder Leloup missing for years now.

"'Course, we haven't always been at each other's throats. We've learned over the years that to go along we got to get along. A few of them Beauties grew up and came to work in town. A few of you
~~~~~

townsfolk moved into them upper valleys.

"But there was always an underlyin' enmity between us, which inevitably led to tragedy. And like I said, times have changed. We've got to change. We're gonna put a stop to the fightin' once and for all. That's why you hired me."

Dusty Morgan raised his hand and asked if he could have a say. Chad nodded. "Come on up, Dusty. Tell us what's on yer mind."

The middle-aged man made his way to the front of the crowd. He stepped on the boardwalk, leaned himself against the hitching rail.

"I had hate in my heart for years. You all know'd it. When most of us finally figur'd out the truth about them Beauties, we added fear to our hate. That's a potent combination. Somethin' not easily cured. Made us like the beasts we thought they were."

He paused a moment, then motioned for someone in the crowd to join him at the rail.

"But when me an' Dora met a few years back, we talked it out, and the fear and anger just sorta seeped out of me."

He pulled Dora close to his side. "We been seein' each other in secret for quite some time now, though you've prolly heard rumors. Anyways, her children are grow'd, and we're gonna get married as soon as practicable."

A few gasps were heard and Dusty shuffled his feet while he waited for the crowd to settle back into silence.

"Well. That's all I've got to say."

He took Dora by the hand and the crowd parted, letting them go their way. It was no accident that one side of the group was made up of Beauties and the other side were all townies.

Chad stepped forward and said, "They ain't the only ones, neither. Zev and Yilva are here and can vouch for that. A number of 'secret' relationships are developin' between our two groups. The only question is, are we gonna acknowledge it public'ly?"

The marshal ran his gaze over the eighty odd citizens of Rocky Mountain City. He concluded his speech with a question.

"Are we fin'ly gonna to come together as one community?"

Folks were silent for a spell, soaking it all in. Then side conversations erupted. The murmurs rose and fell until it seemed like a consensus was reached.

Slowly, a few of the younger Beauties, who were but children when they'd arrived and took up residence in their idyllic valley, made the first move.

They approached the divide that separated them from their rivals, hands extended. The silent moment stretched out interminably, until one by one the townsfolk responded in kind. Within the space of a few heartbeats there were handshakes and hugs, smiles and laughter, as well as tears of confession and joy.

Chad caught the grateful nods of his friends, Yilva and Zevi Rand. It had been twenty years since he'd promised to help establish them all in these beautiful mountains.

He smiled back, acknowledging their thanks. It looked like everyone had finally made it to their Rocky Mountain paradise.

END

BETWEEN DOG AND WOLF

Carla Hoch and Lisa Godfrees

"Your beast will eat anything." Reggie's belly shakes with laughter, and the buttons of his too-small khaki shirt hold on for dear life.

She doesn't respond right away. Can't. She's too exposed, standing with her arms up, feet shoulder width apart, face forward, like every weekday morning of the past eight years. It's never gotten easier, being looked at so closely. Even when the security guard is a dear friend.

Reggie steps back, then gestures at her foot with his wand.

She looks down at her Channel ballet flat. A single furrow creases the topaz toe of her shoe. "Oh, you've got to be kidding me."

"That dog is going to eat you whole one day."

"Well, that would be a Herculean effort on his part." She unzips her purse and opens it wide. "He's only got one tooth left."

"One?" Reggie takes a cursory glance inside her bag. "What happened to the other two?"

She reaches inside her purse and pulls out a glasses case. Its end is marred by punctures.

Reggie guffaws and adjusts his glasses. "Probably needed to chew on something to take his mind off having a lady name."

"*Jewel* is not a lady name." She drops the case into her purse and pulls out a small paper bag. The top is folded over and secured with a gold sticker. "Jewels are genderless."

Reggie takes the cookie and smiles. His obsidian cheeks push his glasses up. "The Mrs. will kill me for this."

"Lucky for you, sir, this is keto."

"What kind of *toe?*" Reggie looks at it suspiciously. "You trying to kill me?"

"I would never kill you." She winks as she adjusts her purse on her shoulder. "Well, not on purpose anyway. Besides, if I killed you, who would eat my horrible Thanksgiving casseroles?"

"No one," Reggie assures her. "Except Reggie, Jr. Now, he'd eat your horrible cooking forever if you just gave him a chance."

She rolls her eyes, straightens his Chief of Security badge, then bids Reggie a good morning.

"Kinda ironic that Jewel has lost about all his pearly whites," he calls after her. "A jewel-less Jewel."

"Pearls aren't jewels," she responds as she walks across the foyer's marble floor.

She catches the elevator doors before they shut. "Don't forget—today's the fifth, Reggie."

A man waiting to be scanned through security complains about the delay. Reggie looks down with a side-eye and the man quiets.

"So?" Reggie calls to her.

"Isn't that your anniversary?"

Even from a distance she can see white all the way around Reggie's eyes. She laughs and holds a hand up. "Come see me," she calls out. "I have the perfect thing for Mae."

"Be down in fi—"

The elevator doors shut. She leans against the wall, away from the shining brass doors, and presses the button marked "B." It glows emerald, and she sinks into the earth.

~~~~~

The doors of the elevator open to Higgins. It's unlike her boss to lie in wait for her. He says her name three times, punctuating each syllable with a clap of his hands.

It's too much, too early. She reaches for the "Close Doors" button.

"No, no, *mademoiselle*," Higgins protests, "you must come to my office *tout de suite*!"

"Higgins—"

"*I-know.*" He claps in beat with the words. "*I-know.*"

Generally, she can handle his clapping, but not before nine. And not without coffee.

"This is *très important*. Please indulge me. I wouldn't ask were it not important, and as I said, it is *très-im-por-tant*." He again claps with the syllables of the words. "That means, *ve-ry-im-por-tant*."

She sighs and exits the elevator with a tight-lipped smile. He knows not to meet with her until she's gotten at least an hour of work under her belt. Two hours, if he wants her to agree to whatever job he has for her.

Outside the door of Higgins's office, two plain-clothes strangers stand sentry, still as bookends.
~~~~~

Odd. No arrivals were scheduled for this morning on the calendar.

Inside the office, she finds two men in business suits. Higgins follows on her heels and closes the door behind him.

Though a master jeweler himself, Higgins is also a Francophile hoarder who fancies all things gauche. His office is a cacophony of kitsch and crushed velvet in jewel tones. She appreciates that irony, along with his inexhaustible *joie de vivre*. She appreciates it far more in the afternoon. Late afternoon.

The shorter of the two businessmen has thick, obsidian hair, veined with a silver that accents his aquamarine eyes. A garnet tie pin of no less than two carats skewers his tie. She tries not to stare at it.

The second mountain of a man is bald and wears dark glasses. He stands head and shoulders above the first and faces the wall ahead of him. She wonders if he is blinded by the room or simply wishing he were.

Higgins rubs his hands together excitedly, then gestures toward her. "Gentleman, this is the lovely lady you've heard so much about. The Queen of Copy herself."

Her nostrils flare. She hates when he calls her that.

Turning the right side of her face away from their clients, she nods at the men in greeting.

"This is Sergei Yahontov." Higgins gestures to the man with the tie bling.

He bows his head at Higgins's introduction. "It is a pleasure," he says in a thick Russian accent.

She pulls her hair over the right side of her face and shoots Higgins a furtive look. He winks in return.

The door behind her opens and Reggie saunters in. He smiles at the room in greeting.

Higgins claps his hands, giving her such a start her purse falls off her shoulder.

"Now that we're all here, shall we?" Somehow, Higgins manages not to clap any words, although his voice reaches to a new level of exuberance.

The larger man steps from behind Sergei and places a metal briefcase on Higgins's desk. The handcuffs connecting the case to the bodyguard's wrist create a discordant jangle. Sergei removes his phone from his pocket, dials a number, then holds the screen close to the lock of the briefcase. It opens with a sharp *click.*

Eggcrate foam lines the hard case and embraces a white satin bag. From it, Sergei takes a rectangular, lacquer box and places it on the desk. He waves his hand, and the larger man removes the briefcase.

Higgins's hands are at his mouth, and there are tears in his eyes. Reggie steps next to Higgins, opposite the Russians, and leans forward. The excitement in the air is palpable, even to her, though she doesn't know what the box is meant to contain.

Sergei holds out a pair of white gloves to them.

"The lady should have the honor." Higgins gestures to her, then takes a handkerchief from his pocket and wipes his nose.

Hesitantly, she grits her teeth and accepts the gloves from Sergei. Higgins knows she hates being the center of attention like this. If she's lucky, a monster will emerge from the box and devour her whole. It would be far less painful than her current circumstance.

She reaches for the box, and Higgins inhales a sharp breath. Reggie stretches out his neck for a look. Even Sergei and his companion go still.

The hinged lid opens with a soft creak.

Inside is… indescribable.

She pulls her hands away. The lid snaps shut with a *crack,* and the room tilts beneath her. She stumbles backward and falls onto a bergère chair. Its citrine velvet shushes under her.

~~~~~

The cool glass of water feels good against her forehead. Reggie urges her to take another drink. She nods, still unable to speak, and takes a sip.

Sergei accepted no apologies for her stupor. In fact, he said it gave him greater faith in her. "Clearly, she understands the miracle before her."

Higgins returns to the office after seeing Sergei out. He sits behind his desk, puts his elbows on the rich mahogany, and rests his chin on his clasped hands. He smiles at her. "How are we doing, *mademoiselle?*"

She wipes away the tears that cascade over her scarred face, then shakes her head at the piece that is so much more than a necklace.

Higgins clears his throat, then quietly claps his hands twice. "*O-kay.*"

"The replica is to tour Europe in December," he explains. "That
~~~~~

gives us enough time to create any stones we need in the lab. But I think we have plenty of red spinel." He turns the box toward himself and looks at the piece over the top of his glasses. "Where did they find so many pigeon blood rubies?"

After another sip of water, she finds her voice. "How?"

She covers her mouth, stifling unexpected emotions. Why this was stirring up such a reaction in her she didn't know. Maybe it was the beauty of the work—one artist feeling the work of another. Maybe it was because she understood how much of the artist's soul had to go into a piece so labor intensive. Or maybe it was because, for the first time in her life, she'd found something that did not disappoint.

"A servant of the Romanovs secreted the necklace away before the Bolsheviks took over the Winter Palace. She took it to a monastery, which gave it to another monastery, which gave it to another, and so on until it came to rest in Spinalonga, Greece. There it was placed in a box and buried in the middle of a leper colony." Higgins pauses to laugh then claps quietly with the words "*Af-ter-all,* who in their right mind would go looking for anything in a leper colony?"

"Well, clearly someone was not in their right mind, because here the thing is." Reggie crosses his arms over his chest. "Something doesn't feel right. I don't like this."

Higgins holds up his hands. "It *was* a leper colony. It no longer is. Not since about 1960."

"They all die?" Reggie asks.

Higgins shrugs. "Legend is they were all healed." He raises his brows and gestures with his head toward the necklace.

"What are you... wait. You saying this thing healed them?" Reggie shakes his head. "Don't like it. Nope. You don't need to touch that thing, miss ma'am."

She smiles and chuckles through her nose. "It's okay, Reggie. I touched the Hope Diamond and lived." She sets the glass of water on the side table and reaches for the necklace.

"Well, now, wait a minute." Higgins pulls the box back away from her. "You have to wear gloves for this one." He holds his hands up to hush her protest. "I know. I know. You like to be able to touch the work. But Sergei gave strict instructions. Gloves one hundred percent of the time. It should not come into contact with bare skin." He shifts in his seat then straightens his lapel. "*No-ex-cep-tions.*"

"Because..." She leans in for the answer.

"He is the client, and that is that. We will not betray his trust, and clearly, he does trust us. He's only left one security guard to monitor this process." Higgins gestures to the corner of the room.

She and Reggie startle at the man standing behind them.

Reggie instinctively reaches for the gun that was on his waistband until he retired. "Have you been there the whole time?"

"He doesn't speak English, Reginald. Why Sergei left us with such a situation, I'm not sure."

The bald guard and Reggie stare at one another an uncomfortable number of moments. Slowly, Reggie turns away from the man.

"Don't touch this thing with your bare hands," Reggie says to her. "I don't like it. I don't like old Rasputin back here—"

The room quiets at a sound, and the three Americans stare at the Russian.

Reggie points with his thumb over his shoulder. "He just *hiss* at us?" He turns square to the man. "I don't know how it is in Russia, but in New York City, you don't hiss—"

"Let's just get back to our work here, shall we, Reginald?"

Reggie and the Russian continue their face off.

They're all being ridiculous. She reaches out and touches Reggie's arm. "It's okay, Reggie."

He looks down at her hand. "I don't like it," Reggie whispers.

"It's just a piece of jewelry," she tells him, although it is clearly so much more.

"Right, well then, when do you think we can start on this?" Higgins wiggles his fingers in the air.

She sits tall in her chair. "I understand that the client requests the use of gloves—"

"We will not waver on this, *ma chère*."

"Bet it has poison on it," Reggie mutters.

"It does *not* have poison on it." Higgins laughs uncomfortably then pours himself a glass of water from the bottle of Evian on his desk. "It's cursed."

Reggie whips his head away from the Russian to glower at Higgins. "A who-where-what? A curse? You said curse. This thing here has a curse?"

How had she not known Reggie was this superstitious? "Calm down, Reggie," she says.

"Don't hold your hand up at me." Reggie scowls at her. "Lady, you heard the man. Cursed."

She shakes her head. "Higgins, if it's *cursed*," she puts the word in air quotes, "how— "

"*It-is-cursed*." Reggie claps his hands like Higgins. "The man said it's cursed. It's cursed!"

"Okay, it's cursed. I get it, Reggie."

"Clearly you do not, miss ma'am."

"Stop for a minute. Please." She takes a deep breath and shifts her focus to Higgins. "If it's cursed, how did it heal the lepers?"

"Because that is how the devil works." Reggie points a thumb over his shoulder. "Just ask him."

"Reggie!" She smacks the arm of her chair.

Reggie's mouth snaps shut, his expression one of a petulant child.

"Well, now, in fairness," Higgins takes a breath, "Reginald is not totally wrong there."

Reggie points at Higgins as if his finger is a skewer. *See?* his expression says.

She shifts in the chair, irritated. "Higgins, tell the story, please. The whole story."

Higgins winces then claps with the word, "*Well*...

"Apparently the lepers were healed and then may have, maybe..." Higgins pauses and holds up his thumb and index finger close together. "Just a little, little bit, just *un peu*..."

She throws up her hands. "Just say it."

"They may have murdered a little," Higgins rushes to finish.

Reggie's mouth drops open like when the whale swallowed Jonas.

"What do you mean *a little*?" she asks, watching Higgins closely.

Higgins sits with his lips rolled over his teeth.

"Answer the lady," Reggie says with a deep growl. "What do you mean by *murdered a little*?"

Higgins closes his eyes. "A little town nearby."

"They murdered a town?" she asks.

"Well, I have enjoyed this time with you all." Reggie straightens his waist band under his belly then mimics a tip of the hat. "Good day, Higgins. Good day, miss." He turns to the man in the corner, feigns another tip and says, "Satan," before heading for the door.

"Wait." Higgins rushes to block his way. "Wait just a moment,

Reginald, if you would. I would like one of our own security detail to accompany the item while it is out of the vault."

"I was worried you'd say that," Reggie mutters.

"Does it have a name?" She closes the lid on the necklace with a gloved hand and places the priceless piece in Higgins's safe. "Pieces like this generally do."

"I'm not sure." Higgins waves his hand to get the attention of the man in the corner, then points at the necklace. "What is name?" He waits a moment then repeats himself loudly, speaking slowly. "Name. What. Is. Name?"

"Saying it louder will not help him understand, nor will saying English words with a Russian accent." She reaches into her purse. "I have one of those translation apps on my phone."

"Oh, *moi aussi*." Higgins claps his hands twice before taking his phone from his pocket. "I use it when I travel to Paris," he says, seemingly to himself, then puts on his reading glasses and sorts the pages of his phone screen.

Reggie stares at Higgins, and his brows furrow. "I thought you spoke French."

She looks at Reggie, wide-eyed, and makes a cutting motion across her neck. *No*, she mouths.

Fortunately, Higgins is too preoccupied to notice.

"Ah, yes, here we go." Higgins holds up the device to his lips and says too loudly, "What is the name of the necklace?"

The phone beeps, then a female accented voice speaks in Russian. The three colleagues look at the guard expectantly.

"*Serdtse Romanovykh*," he replies in a voice like sandpaper.

"How do you even spell that?" Reggie asks.

"Well, I don't quite know, Reginald."

She sighs at her two colleagues. "Let him speak into the phone."

They look at the man, then the phone, then back to the man.

She *tsks*, takes the phone from Higgins, and walks to the Russian. She smiles, holds up the phone, and gestures to it with her hand.

He looks at her, his eyes still shrouded behind dark glasses.

A clap startles her and she looks back at Higgins. "What?"

"I said, *what-did-it-say*? We couldn't hear."

She looks back at the man. "I don't… I didn't hear..."

"*It-is-on-the-screen*," Higgins says with claps. "Just read it to us, dear."

The man takes her wrist in his hot hand, pulls the phone closer to his mouth and holds her gaze as he speaks.

The phone beeps before translating aloud: *The Heart of Romanov*.

She shivers.

"That's not such a bad name," Reggie says. "Hearts are good."

"Not all hearts are good, but the Romanovs' hearts probably were." She picks up her purse and hefts it onto her shoulder. "Unfortunately, that's exactly where they were shot."

~~~~~

After lunch, she sits at her desk and examines the necklace. The gloves she's forced to wear distract her, irritating her dry skin and tender scars. She wishes she had lotion, but she doesn't keep any with her, not even in her purse. The temptation to use it would be too great. Then she'd have to wash her hands before touching the jewelry which would, in turn, make her skin drier, unless the soap had moisturizers in it. She'd yet to find any such soap that didn't leave a film on her hands.

"Why does it have to be so dark in here? It's like a tomb. Can't hardly see Colonel Creepy over there."

She smiles at Reggie. He holds his hand out to shield his eyes from the light on her loupe headband.

"Oh, sorry." She pushes the headlamp/magnifying glasses to the top of her head. "Focal light is best. Any other light messes with me. Watch your eyes."

Reggie turns away as she repositions the loupe glasses.

"What are you doing?" he asks.

She looks up, and he again recoils. "You don't know what I do, do you?"

Reggie clears his throat and shifts in his seat across the desk from her. "Where do people even get chairs this small? These children's chairs? I can go upstairs and get adult chairs."

She turns on the desk lamp beside her, then turns off her headlamp and removes it from her face. "I need to stand up and stretch anyway," she says, then does just that.

"Okay, Reggie, whom I have known for years and know much about, including his anniversary, which reminds me..." The wood of the lower desk drawer creaks as she opens it.

Reggie smiles when she puts a small plastic bag in front of him. He opens it and pours a pair of sapphire earrings into his hand. "Mae will love them."
~~~~~

"Just pay me when you can pay me.

"Now, you wanted to know what I do." She stretches her neck and back, wincing with the pain. "I'm basically a counterfeiter. I reproduce items containing gems so that they can be displayed in museums."

"They aren't real?" Reggie is shocked. "The stuff in museums is fake?"

"Remember when I said I touched the Hope Diamond?" she reminds him. "Guess why. The insurance is cheaper for museums if they get a knock-off. Not that people would know. They don't generally get close enough to the display, and most people wouldn't know what to look for anyway. But my knockoffs are so good, people can get as close as they want. Without a jeweler's loupe," she points at the glasses attached to the headlamp on the top of her head, "they can't tell. Looks are deceiving, and deception is my livelihood."

~~~~~

The next day goes slowly with Reggie in front of her. She can't get lost in her work because he prattles non-stop. At first, she feigns interest. He tells her about Mae's reaction to the earrings and their romantic dinner. He even starts to tell her about *after* dinner, but he cuts off when she purposely shines her headlamp in his face and refuses to stop until he moves on to a different subject. When he speaks of sports, the weather, and the news, she does her best to ignore him.

He's still talking when it's time to go home, but his words don't register through the static of anxiety in her head. She hates this moment. It's the reason she comes early and leaves late. This time of day when the corridors are littered with people.

The elevator is crowded. She pauses to wait for the next, but Reggie's wake pushes her forward. The people inside fan out, and she steps into the void their shoes make.

The doors close, and her divided reflection comes together. She wants to look away, but she can't. The demarcated truth pulls her.

The warm light from above embraces the left side of her face with an ethereal glow. On the right, the light slips and shines on the satin licks of burned skin. To the west, she is beauty; to the east, she is beast.

She bursts through the doors before they open completely. Reggie calls after her, but she doesn't slow. She has to get as far from the elevator as she can. Now.
~~~~~

It's raining, but she hails no cab. She splashes through the filthy water on the sidewalk, hair sticking to her face, hot breath rolling out like smoke in the chill.

Under a coffee shop awning she stops to rest, looking out through the sheets of rain. She doesn't want to go home, doesn't want to partake in the after-work ritual of cooking, showering and sleeping. She wants to work, to stand in the void of concentration. In silence.

Jewel has ample food in his bowl. She has no reason not to turn back...

And so, she returns.

The night security guard looks at her, mouth agape. A puddle forms beneath her on the floor. He asks if she'd like some paper towels.

She doesn't respond. Instead, she raises her hands in surrender. He scans her and, after a cursory look into her soaked purse, allows her entry. She heads toward the stairs.

In-house security should be with her as she works, but she doesn't care. Where the Russian guard has gone, she doesn't know. All she thinks about is moving forward. The *clack-clack* of her shoes echoes through the empty hallway.

She enters her code at the door, and the lock opens. She walks to her worktable in the dark, turns on the lamp, and gasps. Her purse falls to the floor with a wet *thwop*.

In the spotlight of the lamp, the necklace waits.

She looks around the room, wondering who could have done this. Who could have entered into the third layer of the vault to retrieve the Romanov Heart. Only she and Higgins have access. In the event of their demise, only the makers of the vault could gain entry.

Beside the necklace are her tools. Someone has taken them from her drawer as if they knew she would return. Inexplicable, but handy.

The time is 6:30 p.m. She'll work for an hour of blissful silence—two at the most—then go home.

She wipes her wet hair back from her face, drops her soaking coat where she stands, and takes off her shoes.

Her chair squeaks as she sits. After smoothing back her hair a second time, she puts on her headlamp. The sketch pad and pencil she uses for notes are on her left, ready for her. She reaches for the necklace but remembers the gloves. Enough rules are broken for this evening. At the least, she should wear the gloves.

The desk shakes as she looks through her meticulously organized drawers. The gloves should be right there, first drawer. They aren't.

She sighs, sits back, and chews on her lip, thinking. Then she comes to a conclusion. Enough rules are broken for this evening. What's one more?

Despite the temperature of the room, the necklace is warm. She feels for the small heater beneath the desk with her foot. It's cool, hasn't been left on. With her big toe, she hits the power button and smiles at the comforting heat against her damp shins.

Loupe glasses in place, she continues her inspection of the necklace, stone by stone—no small feat. She estimates no less than one hundred gems. The diamonds graduate in size from the clasp to the climbing ruby roses slightly offset from the center. Each ruby is set at an angle, giving the roses dimension. Nestled between their petals, tiny diamonds rest as drops of water. Emerald leaves climb from the flowers up the diamonds.

It's the most beautiful thing she's ever examined. She can't help but pause her work and touch it to her lips. A sweet taste fills her mouth.

~~~~~

A sound startles her, and she sits up.

Reggie stands in front of her desk outside the lamp's glow, a formidable shadow with hands on his hips. "Have you been here all night?"

She rubs her eyes then looks around. "What happened?"

"You tell me." Reggie's voice is stern, and she imagines this is the same tone he used with Reggie, Jr. when he came home late as a teen.

"I... I don't... I don't know. I was walking home and then..." And then nothing. Or something. She's not sure. The memories are trapped in her head like inclusions in a gem.

She puts her hands on the desk to get her bearings and notices the steno pad glowing golden under the desk lamp. The first several pages are filled with notes and sketches of the necklace—her handwriting, her drawings. On the side of her hand, she finds the tell-tale, left handers' ink smear.

Reggie crosses his arms over his chest. "Tell me that you didn't
~~~~~

sleep here."

Had she? She doesn't know. Her body is neither sore nor stiff. There is no rainy-day ache in her hands where her scars...

Her *scars*!

She stands, and her chair careens across the floor.

Slowly, she turns her trembling hands palm up and back down, over and over, staring. Her face and her knees buckle, and she crumples to the ground.

Reggie runs around the desk. "Honey, what's wrong? What's happening?"

"I'm fine." *More than fine. Somehow.* "Leave me alone."

He plucks the radio from his pocket. "I need some—"

Without thinking, she backhands the radio, and it clatters across the floor.

"Why did you slap it like that?" Reggie stares at her like she's grown a third head. "What's wrong with you?"

"I need to go." She grabs her purse from the floor. "I just need to go."

"Well, here... take your coat, and put on your shoes!" Reggie holds her coat out, but she dives under her desk instead. "What's gotten into you? Talk to me."

"Shoes, shoes, shoes," she mutters, feeling around in the dark.

Her heart thunders in her chest, vibrating her bones, and she feels as though she will explode.

She needs to get away and think. Remember. Make sense of what's happening. She can't do that with Reggie hovering, Reggie questioning, Reggie...

"Dear glory, we can't see anything in here with just that lamp light." He flips on the overhead light, and the room bursts into incandescence.

She cries out, covering her face and turning the scarred side of her body away from him.

"Freeze," he yells. "Don't move."

Her breath catches in her chest. Why? What has she done? What does he *think* she's done?

She closes her eyes and swallows hard. Her breath rolls in gasps. She puts a hand on the desk and tries to slow her breathing.

"I said don't move," Reggie thunders.

A whimper escapes her. She closes her eyes and bites her trembling lips. "Please, please, just let me go home," she whispers.

A string of spittle escapes her mouth and dribbles down her chin. She doesn't bother to wipe it away.

"Stay right there," Reggie growls.

His shoes squeak toward her.

"I won't move. I won't," she whispers and raises her hands in surrender.

"Not you," Reggie booms. "Him."

In the corner of the room, as still as death, stands the Russian guard.

At least, that's who she thinks it is at first glance. He looks like the Russian guard, but as she studies him, she realizes it's not the same man. He's every bit as tall, but not as broad. He's still bald, but this man has a pointed goatee.

Reggie kneels to collect the radio and its broken bits. As he reassembles it, she and the Russian lock eyes, and that's when she notices he's not wearing dark glasses. Instead, bright eyes gleam under shadowed brows.

He smiles, raises a finger to his lips and hisses, "Shhhhhh."

~~~~~

She runs down the hallway on bare feet, her purse banging wildly at her side. She nearly slips twice running up the stairs to street level. The alarm blares when she barrels through the emergency exit.

It's still raining, but she doesn't care. She splashes through the city sidewalk murk and doesn't slow until she reaches her apartment building. People heading to work lurch out of her way and swear as she heads for the elevator.

Her keys jangle in her shaking hands and fall to the floor twice before she fits the correct one in the lock. She throws the door open, slams it behind her, and presses her back against it. The metal is cold against her wet skin, even through her clothes, sending a chill to her bones. Her shoulders quake.

A part of her wants to see, wants verification. The other part of her doesn't want to know. In her mind, it's far easier to think of herself as a monster than to look in the mirror and remove all doubt. Far less painful to assume the worst, than hope for anything else. Nothing has scarred her more deeply than hope. To some "hope is the thing with feathers that perches in the soul," but she's found it does so with talons, a curved beak, and impeccable timing, waiting for her heart to be full before it attacks.
~~~~~

She examines her hand again. The scars are there but only barely. The burned area remains slightly darkened, but now there are only minor puckers in the skin. It appears as though she was splashed with hot water rather than baptized by flames.

For a moment she continues staring and then, as if shoved, runs from the door to the bathroom.

Drawers and doors are jerked open then slammed shut. They are mostly empty. What little is in them, she pilfers and pushes around wildly searching for a reflective surface. She stands before the painting that hangs on the wall above the bathroom vanity. Picasso's *Girl Before a Mirror*. She'd hung it in irony. Now it taunts her.

Stripping her wet clothes off as she goes, she darts in and out of rooms, assaulting anything that could contain a mirrored surface. Closets are rummaged, boxes jerked down from top shelves, shoes kicked aside. Hangers rattle with fright as they are stripped. Cushions are lifted, pillows thrown, blankets whipped off the bed. At this point, she's no longer searching. She's punishing the apartment for not having what she hasn't allowed it to keep.

Finally, when the rooms are all but inside out, she leans against the wall and surveys her destruction. There's always the door of the microwave—its reflection is enough to assure her hair is in place every morning before heading to work.

Jewel ambles toward her, ears raised, a black sweater slung over his back. He pauses, looks at her with milky eyes, then huffs a complaint at having been caught in the crossfire of flying clothes.

She reaches her hand out for him to sniff. He licks it then quickly nips. His one tooth jabs between her pinkie and ring finger knuckles.

She pulls her hand back. "No biting, Jewel," she scolds. "You don't want to lose that last tooth."

He wags his tail and waits, his one fang sticking out.

She scratches under his chin, and he lifts his head to give her better access. The brass tag on his collar jangles. Completely happy, he falls to his side with a grunt and rolls onto his back. She lays down beside him and scratches his belly.

Her hand passes in front of his dog tag. Its reflection shows around the engraving in the shining brass. She leans forward. On the back of the quarter-sized octagon, there are no words, only polished metal. She closes her eyes and takes a breath, then counts to herself, *one, two, three.*

She opens her eyes and looks into the shiny surface. A scarless reflection stares back at her, but it's not her own.

Jewel yelps as she skitters across the carpet on hands and knees. By the time she gets to the bedroom door, she's gotten her feet under her. She dashes to the kitchen, grabs a knife, and presses herself against the wall.

Silence. She holds the butcher blade flat against her chest.

Movement in another room.

It's *him.*

He's coming.

The door was locked when she'd arrived home. She remembers unlocking it. Doesn't remember locking it after. Maybe he'd come in while she tore the apartment apart looking for a mirror. He must have. How many times had she passed him, looked at him without seeing him?

Tack, tack, tack.

She holds her breath and brings the knife away from her body. Where is her phone? She tries to think. It has to be in her purse, in front of the door. Had he stepped over it as he walked in?

Tack, tack, tack.

Please, no. Please.

Jewel lumbers into the kitchen. His claws *tack, tack, tack*ing against the tile.

She swallows a sigh and puts her hand out for Jewel. "Come, boy. Come."

With the sweater still clinging by a sleeve to his wiry fur, Jewel stops at her feet. He looks up at her and whimpers.

"Stay." Slowly, she walks forward, patting Jewel on the head as she passes.

The apartment is quiet. Before looking around the corner from the kitchen, she holds her breath. He's there. Somewhere.

"Come out!" Her voice echoes off the walls.

She sees her purse on the floor, the phone in plain view. Still holding the knife out defensively, she crouches quietly then crawls, eyes up, looking for him, waiting for him. Expecting him. She will kill him, she thinks.

But she's wrong. She couldn't kill anyone, and she knows it. She'll only threaten and hope it's enough.

Grabbing her phone, she inches back to the kitchen. Jewel huffs at her as she passes him on the cold tile.

She opens a large, low cabinet and positions herself behind it defensively, then attempts to open her phone.

It's dead.

Panic infests her. He will kill her. Why else would he be here? What did he want from her?

Jewel sidles up beside her and lies down on the floor, completely calm.

She sets the phone down and runs her hand over his head. For all of the dog's faults and disabilities of age, he is vigilant. If someone were in the house, he wouldn't be so calm.

Knife in hand, she walks quietly through the apartment. Her bare feet don't make a sound.

After closing the last closet door, she sighs, drops the knife to her side, and goes back to the kitchen.

She places the knife on the counter and puts her head in her hands. He was there. She could have sworn it. The new Russian. His long, pale face shone like ivory in the reflection on the dog tag.

"I'm losing my mind," she whispers.

She looks at her hand. As she does, she glimpses her face in the shining metal of the butcher knife. Slowly, she picks it up and turns her face to the light. Her chin trembles.

Impossible.

She grabs her phone and runs to plug it in. Why hadn't she thought of that sooner? The camera on her phone is a mirror!

After a moment, the phone beeps and powers up. She sits on the bed and looks. And looks. And looks.

~~~~~

Late in the afternoon, something wakes her. She's lying on her bed next to the phone. The camera is still open. She touches the side of her face and smiles.

Bang, bang, bang.

Startled, she sits up. She closes the camera app and sees fifteen missed calls.

Wrapping a robe around her, she hurries to the door. Reggie stands in the hallway, looking back and forth, rubbing his hands together. She backs away from the peephole and opens the door.

"Girl! I've been calling you all day. Are you okay?"

"I'm fine." She hides the side of her face where scars had been. "I'm just tired. Stress from the necklace got to me, I guess."

Reggie stands in silence. She glances up at him. His face looks hurt.
~~~~~

"I'm okay, really. I'm tired. I fell asleep as soon as I got home."

"You were there all night, weren't you?"

She nods, pulling her hair over the right side of her face.

"I don't like that necklace or that Russian." Reggie watches her closely. "Did he do something to you?"

She shakes her head. "I'm okay. Really. I'll be back in tomorrow."

"Higgins is worried sick. You never miss work."

"I'll call him; I promise. I just need some sleep. Thank you for checking on me," she says, then slowly closes the door.

Through the fish-eyed bubble of the peep hole, Reggie continues to stare, mouth slightly open. After a few moments, he rubs his head and walks away.

She sighs in relief and goes back to her bedroom. Jewel still sleeps on her bed. Reggie's visit hadn't woken him. He'd probably been worried about her when she didn't return last night, poor boy.

She edges her phone out from beneath Jewel. She'd taken twenty pictures before she finally fell asleep. Each a slightly different angle of her face. Some cropped and enlarged. Like her hand, her face shows a slight shadow of a wound. But only a shadow. The top of her ear is now a flawless arch with a full head of hair above it.

How? she thinks. *How did this happen*?

She scrolls through pictures of herself forward then backward. She scrolls one too far and sees a picture of the necklace.

The bed squeaks as she bolts upright.

That's it.

The necklace.

~~~~~

The next morning, she fixes a cup of coffee and looks through the pictures again, smiling, her face full of joy, her chest infested with hope.

She's rested and refreshed, despite a restless night. Thoughts of the necklace kept intruding like Reggie's constant chatter. At one point, she turned over and saw its shadow on the pillow next to her. When she went back to sleep, it waited in her dreams. This morning, she could have sworn she saw its shape swirling in the cream of her coffee.

She laughs. How silly. How fun. Is this the world she's been missing?

After another sip of coffee, she wonders how she will explain
~~~~~

her miraculous healing. Explain how a cursed necklace blessed her. Maybe she won't. Maybe she will just let people wonder or act as if this is who she has always been. *Scars? What scars? I have no idea what you're talking about. Are you feeling okay?*

Yes, that's how she will handle it. After all, who could understand? Only the lepers of Spinalonga.

What will life be like now that she's whole? Walking with her face to the sun. Dancing by the light of the moon. No more double glances from passersby, no more children pointing. No more talking to clients with her head turned awkwardly to the side. No more placating niceties from Reggie, Jr., who said only enough to keep his father happy.

No more hiding. No more beast.

Only beauty.

She sniffs back tears, still smiling, and tucks her hair behind her ear.

She runs her fingers over the top of her ear again, then along the side of her face. "No, no, no!"

Coffee lurches up in her throat. She coughs as she turns the camera on the phone to face her.

Her coffee cup shatters in the sink. Her phone hits the tile floor with a crack. *No,* she thinks. *It can't be.*

She holds her head in her hands a moment then pounds the kitchen counter with her fists. *This* is what happens when she hopes. *This* is what happens when that thing with wings perches in your soul—it shreds you.

She grips the edge of the counter and wonders what to do.

She picks up her phone and scrolls through the pictures. A glass shard from the cracked screen stabs into her finger. She winces and shakes her hand. Beneath a tiny smear of blood, she sees a picture of the necklace.

Yes, she thinks. There is nothing to wonder about. She knows what she has to do.

Yes. Yes. *Yes.*

The screen of her phone darkens. Light from the window behind her pours around her head, leaving her a dark, faceless reflection in the cracked glass. Her lips curl and her nostrils flare. The screen of her phone splinters again in her grip.

She's tired of being a shadow. Tired of hating the light. Tired of waking up every morning waiting for the sun to go away but dreading the night, because it will only lead to another morning. She's tired of being who she is.

But she won't be tired anymore.

Now she's awake. More awake than she has ever been. And she's going to stay that way.

She rushes to the bedroom to dress. If she hurries, she can make it to work before Reggie. No small talk. No pleasantries. No need for her to discuss what she can't quite explain.

She kicks around the clothing strewn on the floor until she sees what she wants to wear. She doesn't second guess herself, doesn't wonder if the outfit suits her without the luxury of a mirror to know for sure.

From now on, she will simply follow her gut. What she wants, she will take. And all she will take from now on is exactly what she wants.

No one will stand in her way.

~~~~~

The night guard is at the end of his shift. He's tired. His replacement, Reggie, isn't scheduled for another fifteen minutes. He half-heartedly waves the wand over her, doesn't check her purse.

Perfect. This is the man she wants at security on her way out. She has to hurry, though. Reggie is always early.

She taps her foot anxiously as the elevator slides down to the basement. When the doors open, she scurries down the hall. Her office is down one flight of stairs. Her shoes clap against each step with predatory speed.

She puts in her code on the door and the bolt slides shut.

Wait – the door was open. Had she forgotten to lock it? Yes, but that was yesterday morning. Surely Reggie or the custodians would have locked it before they left.

"Who cares," she mutters and runs inside.

Stops.

There on her desk, under the spotlight of her work lamp, is the necklace. It rests on a felt stand facing her. Waiting for her.

She advances slowly, then stares at it a moment before a sound from the corner startles her.

Movement.

She turns the desk lamp toward the corner and breath floods into her lungs.

The new Russian stares at her, a grin on his face. At least, she
~~~~~

thinks it's the same Russian from yesterday morning. Same height and goatee, but now he's thinner. He nods his head and smiles as he stalks toward her.

Her lungs feel paralyzed, only small breaths slip in and out of her mouth. She wants to run, but she also wants to stay.

He reaches out a pale, tendon-roped hand and picks up the necklace. "Take," he slurs, and holds the treasure out to her.

Their gazes lock, and she realizes it *is* the same man. There's no mistaking the fire in his eyes. The gleam that offers her the world.

She extends her hands, palms up, and he drops the necklace into them.

After putting it in her purse, she backs toward the door. The Russian stays, flashes her a crooked-tooth smile, and watches her go.

As soon as the workroom door closes, she dashes for the stairs. At the top, she runs into Reggie. Literally.

"Woah, woah." He holds her by the shoulders, so she doesn't fall. "Where you going to so fast?"

"I—I..." No words come to her. No explanation for why she's here, or why she's leaving.

"Well, I brought you one of those 'toe' cookies like you got me. They aren't bad." He's trying to be friendly, to cut through the awkwardness from the previous night. "You feeling okay, missy? You're sweating. And, honey, you've been acting a little strange—"

"I'm fine," she barks, then composes herself and says it again, "I'm fine."

"Okay then. Take this with you." He drops the small deli bag into her open purse. His face falls, and his brows knit. "What is that?"

"Nothing." She quickly turns her shoulder away. "I need to go."

"What are you doing?" he whispers hard. "No way that's a fake. You haven't had time."

"I'm going to work on it at home."

"You aren't *allowed* to work on it at home."

"Higgins said I could."

Reggie stands tall, face painted with hurt. He shakes his head. "Don't make me do this."

"Then don't."

"Girl, put it back."

She holds the purse tightly to her side.

"Put it back."

Her breathing quickens. *No one* will stop her.

Reggie swallows hard and grabs the radio from his belt. "I need back—"

She slaps the radio from his hand. It tumbles down the cement stairs, parts and pieces flying off, until it crashes into the wall.

"Again with the radio? That's it." He grabs her wrist.

"No!" She twists her hand out of his grip.

"What's gotten into you? You're acting crazy."

"It's mine, Reggie!"

He grabs her purse and pulls. "Just give me the necklace back, and—"

"You can't have it." She clings to the straps, teeth gritted.

Reggie's face is a thundercloud. So intimidating. Like yesterday with the Russian when he'd scared her so badly. Has he forgotten all she's done for him? About the earrings she gave him for Mae?

Mae... he probably wants the necklace for her. The ingrate. Well, she'll show him.

"I can't let you take it," he says, a final warning. "Don't make this worse than it has to be."

"You're the one making it worse," she says, and braces herself.

She times it perfectly. She waits until he pulls hard, then lets go of her purse.

The release sets Reggie a little off balance. He reaches for the railing, but before he's able to grasp it, she plants her foot in his stomach and pushes.

His eyes widen. His arms swim in the air as his great body falls backward. With the first impact, the air leaves his body with a grunt. The momentum carries his feet over his head, and he tumbles down the stairs until his head hits the landing with a wet *thunk*.

She stands above him for a moment in silence and watches as a ruby pool blooms behind his head. Tentatively, holding on to the railing, she steps down the stairs to retrieve her purse. The necklace is still in it, unscathed. She sighs with relief.

Reggie's chest moves with quick, shallow breaths. His eyes open, heavy-lidded and dazed. Bubbly exhalations sound from his slightly opened mouth as he struggles to breathe. Then, his eyes dart around wildly, fingers jumping as if sparking with electricity.

He is paralyzed, but not dead.

This is a problem, she thinks, looking over his body. It's easy enough to make his fall look like an accident. But where a witness lives, so does the truth.

She puts the purse on the ground and sits astride his chest. He's so large, her knees don't touch the ground.

"Reggie, I..." She stops and thinks. No, she won't apologize. Apologies are meant to mend broken relationships. There is no need for that. He'll soon be dead.

Also, for the first time in her life, she isn't sorry.

She opens and closes her hands, stretching her fingers then puts them around his neck. After a deep breath, she puts all her weight onto his throat.

There's a crackling noise, followed by a gurgle. Reggie stares at her, eyes open wide. His face reddens as his lips and eye sockets swell. Engorged veins raise and roll like fat worms on his temples. Spittle bubbles at the corners of his mouth as his skin turns amethyst.

And then, he stills. There is silence.

Panting, she persists a moment, feeling the hyoid bone fracture and crunch under the edges of her palm. With a loud inhalation, she stops. She rests her forehead on Reggie's to catch her breath. When she opens her eyes, they meet Reggie's lifeless gaze. Even in death, he still seems shocked.

She makes to sit up but wobbles. There's no leverage. Her hand goes out instinctively to catch herself. The sticky blood around Reggie's head causes her hand to slip, and she falls forward.

Groaning with disgust, she pushes herself up on Reggie's chest and holds out her soiled arm. Blood drips in viscous strings from her palm and the sleeve of her white cardigan.

"Gross." She slides backward down Reggie's body to keep the mess from further contaminating her.

Before standing, she wipes the blood off her sweater and hand on Reggie's clothing, then she untucks his shirt to clean between her fingers and around her nails. When she's finished, she sits back on Reggie's legs, tucks her hair behind her ear, and rests a moment.

"Okay then." She clicks her tongue in thought.

She'll need to dispose of the body and clean the scene. She visualizes the smear that will be left from dragging Reggie, if she moves him. But she can't. She's not strong enough.

At least, not alone...

Her workroom is dark except for the work light on her desk.

"Are you there?" she asks the darkness.

After a moment, footsteps sound from the corner, and a dark figure comes into view.

He stops by the light of her desk.

"I need your help," she says.

The Russian's goatee wriggles when he smiles.

~~~~~

It's been years since she's driven. She can't even recollect how long. There's no need to have a car in the city. But she needs one now. The more distance she puts between herself and the scene the better.

Reggie's keys jangle in her hand as she speed-walks from the emergency exit. How the Russian was able to disengage the alarm, she doesn't know. Doesn't care.

The small parking area beside the loading dock is empty except for Reggie's large sedan. She hopes she can maneuver it onto the street before the sun is up completely. Already, sunlight brightens the sky to her right and shines off the windows to her left. She looks up at the stacked floors of offices. No one can see her. The sun is too blinding, and she's in the shadows.

Even nature is on her side today.

Reggie's car is in pristine condition but old. There are no remote locks. She fumbles through his keys trying to fit each in the door's lock.

A car drives up.

Higgins. He too lives outside the city and shuns the subway.

"Pardon," he calls, getting out of his car.

Frantic, she fumbles through the keys faster. They hit the pavement with a clink.

"Hold there, hold." He trots awkwardly toward her, his briefcase hitting against his leg.

She doesn't turn toward him. Instead, she focuses on finding the correct key.

"This is a private parking area—oh!" He squints through the sun's reflection. "I couldn't see you, my dear. It's the proverbial hour of *entre chien le loup*. The hour between dog and wolf. It's the sun, you see."

He glances up at the office windows and quickly squints his eyes closed. He groans, then takes a handkerchief from his pocket. "Can't see a thing but shapes." He wipes the tears from his eyes. "Couldn't tell if you were friend or foe." The handkerchief is tucked back into his breast pocket.

"But here you are. *Just-a-dog*." He says the last three words with claps of his hands, then his expression turns to one of horror. "Not
~~~~~

that you're a *dog*. Certainly not. But here you are, and *bonjour mon cher!*"

He finally takes a breath. She can feel his eyes move over her and stop at the keys in her hands.

"What on earth are you doing in Reginald's car?" He pauses, presumably fishing his brain for an explanation. "Did he ask you to retrieve his coffee?"

Reluctantly, she turns to face him.

He squints at her from under the shield of his hands. "Good heavens, my dear, but you have blood on your face." He takes the handkerchief from his pocket. "Are you okay?"

"I'm fine." She grabs his wrist before he can wipe her face and procure DNA evidence.

An idea strikes her like a blow to the head: their meeting is evidence in and of itself. How inconvenient.

She sighs. "Come to my office. I have something to show you."

~~~~~

I-87 isn't congested beyond the city. Transferring her funds to an offshore account in the Republic of Georgia took less than thirty minutes. Combined with the time it took her to pack a bag and Jewel, she was in and out of her apartment in under an hour.

Before she left Higgins and the Russian in her office, she smashed her phone into bits with a hammer and left it on the desk. Higgins had nearly passed out at the sight. "Where are you going, *mon cher*?"

It was the last she heard him say.

It takes her about five hours to reach Montreal. From there she'll fly to England. She has enough cash. Her only concern is whether Jewel can handle all the traveling. He's not a young pup.

At two o'clock, she checks into a motel. She drives around and parks outside her room. Jewel sleeps in the backseat, his nose in her purse, the necklace between his almost toothless gums. She takes her overnight bag in one hand, then attempts to heft Jewel in the other. For a bag of old bones whose back only reaches her knees, the wire-haired mutt is far heavier than she remembers. She must be tired.

She puts her overnight bag in the room and returns for Jewel. When she attempts to take the purse from his head, he growls.

"Give me a break," she mutters and lifts the dog and bag together.

Having settled her few belongings and Jewel in the room, she
~~~~~

heads out, shopping list in hand. She passed a Walmart within walking distance on her way to the hotel. Fresh air and exercise are just what she needs to lift her spirits after the day she's had.

At the store, she buys a reloadable flip phone and credit card along with enough snacks and dog food for the flight.

On her way back to the motel, she pictures the long flight to England. Like a movie reel, she sees herself traveling with her geriatric dog. Getting stopped by customs and the attention it will bring. The inconvenience of it all.

Jewel simply can't go with her. This, she almost feels bad about.

Almost.

He's still asleep when she comes in. She closes the door quietly, sets down the bags, then puts her hand on his back. The covers she pulled over him are warm and move up and down rhythmically with the beast's breath.

In the morning, then, she thinks, and sighs. She can give them one last night.

By mid-evening she's called the airline and bought a single ticket. The light of the TV flashes off the walls of the room as she relaxes in bed. Thinking about her brilliant life ahead, she falls asleep, smiling.

A sound awakens her. She checks the room's alarm clock: 3:00 a.m.

"Ugh." She squints her eyes at the too bright TV. Fumbling over the bedside table with her hand, she finds the remote and turns the TV off.

Silence.

Except for the sound of heavy panting.

"Jewel," she says, reaching out. The other side of the bed is cold and empty.

"Okay, honey, okay. Let's go potty." She throws back the covers and sits up. She regrets not having killed him before bed to spare her this inconvenience.

Groaning, she stands then stretches her back.

"Come on, baby." She turns toward the sound of his breath. The room-darkening curtains are open. Light from the parking lot glows faintly through the privacy sheers.

A dark form sits in front of the window—the shape of her dog but the size of a wolf.

The animal stands. Light glints off the necklace dangling from its mouth.

"Jewel? Baby?"

The animal stalks closer.

She steps back, nearly tripping over her own feet. She reaches for the side table to steady herself and inadvertently hits the remote.

The TV ignites, and the room flashes with light.

Jewel continues forward, snarling.

"What are you?" she cries out.

Jewel barks, and the necklace hits the floor. Then he lunges.

The last thing she sees are his teeth, *all* his teeth, as they come for her throat.

END

THE BEASTS OF BLACKWELL
Abigail Falanga

Basilisks of Blackwell

Night cleared and hardened around Sir Basil without warning. He stumbled and collapsed to his knees, coughing at chill misty air. His cloak fell forward, obscuring his vision just as his sword slipped from his grip.

He groped for it first, swept aside his hood, gripped the hilt, and leapt to his feet, standing in a defensive posture.

What new devilment was this?

What sorcerer or foul fae had trapped him—?

His first clear glimpse corrected that thought. This wasn't the eerie Faerie-Land in which he had been trapped days without number. This was the ordinary, safe, familiar human world.

A silent, misty dale surrounded him; trees towered overhead, and somewhere nearby a stream chattered nonsense.

No sign of fae, good or bad.

No sign of anything or anyone. He was utterly alone.

Basil lowered his sword until the tip rested in the loam, breathing hard as if he'd been running or fighting instead of pursuing that cursed necrofae with calculated care.

Free.

He was free at last.

It wasn't a relief. He had been outside the normal world for so long that it seemed strange to him, alien and forbidding in its simplicity. Cold. Unwelcoming.

And yet... The trees were as familiar as beloved faces. The chattering stream sounded like a voice he knew very well indeed.

He was not merely free—he was home.

Basil raised the sword again, a chill running through his bones. His necrofae quarry made too much sense now—it was a basilisk, cruel and venomous—the bane of his ancestral land. That was the very reason why he had hunted it through the Faerie-Lands. It could not be permitted to escape. But now...

Home!

Basil scanned the valley for signs of the creature; it left a scorched trail wherever it slithered and its venom fell. Nothing. He sheathed the sword, far from reassured, and set off at a brisk pace over well-known paths toward the castle that had been his boyhood home.

His elder sister Rue had taken charge of the Blackwell lands when he had gone to war, and would still be there—strong and merry as ever.

And Jasmine…

The fair princess' face rose before him, a memory he had long cherished, though now she seemed vague and ephemeral as the moonlight on the mist.

They had grown up together from childhood, when she had first come to the Merimor court with her father, the new king, and he had come to join her brothers' companions at court. She was beautiful—a sight of dear loveliness as she came into her young womanly maturity. He had thought that one day he would take her as bride, bring her to the lands he loved…

And then war came.

So much had changed since then. He had seen her, of course, and knew that she was yet more beautiful than early youth had promised.

But he no longer knew her. No longer knew his home. He was separate and alone and wondered what had become of the others who had been exiled with him.

At least Rue would be waiting for him, ready to shoulder the responsibility he wasn't ready for yet…

The castle loomed against the stars over the trees sooner along the path than he expected. In fact, the trees were bigger and more tangled than he remembered—but memory itself was clouded and tangled.

Basil passed a hand over his face, feeling every haggard, sweat-streaked line of it, as if that could clear away the weariness and confusion.

He entered the open gates of the castle. Unguarded. No matter—he wanted no welcome.

And got none.

The courtyards were deserted. A solitary torch burned near the great hall. A passing serving woman gave him one glance, then hurried on with her head bowed.

Basil plunged into the great hall, his heart quailing as it hadn't even in the worst moments of war or the struggle against necrofae and foul magic. Before he could call for Rue, however, a door at the far end opened and a servant carrying a lit rush entered. Behind him strode a tall, dark-haired man, who stopped with a cry of surprise upon seeing him.

"Basil! By all that is holy…" He rushed forward to pull him into a close embrace, laughing heartily.

Basil returned a half-hearted smile. "Vedast! Yes, it is I. But what are you doing here?"

"What? Why—I'm your brother-in-law, man!" His former comrade-in-arms' face clouded instantly. He opened his mouth as if he would say something more.

"Rue married *you*?" Basil interrupted.

"It took some wooing—even after Lord Trevlyn suggested the match—but she saw reason in the end," Vedast smirked. "You've missed much, my dear old friend."

"Where *is* Rue?" He turned, a misgiving forming in his stomach like a shifting rock on a mountainside, as he plunged further into the building, calling, "Rue! Where—?"

"No, Basil, no." Vedast caught his arm. "You don't understand: Rue died, two weeks ago, and the child with her."

The rock slipped and the mountain crumbled.

"What?" Basil found his voice weak, and yet spoke on, refusing to believe: "Have I missed her by so little? She was always strong…"

"It's these foul basilisks. They've nearly overrun the lands. Rue encountered one while out on her daily walk not long before she fell, and the encounter was too much for her."

"Basilisks," he hissed. "Yet Rue was as skilled in fighting them as I. How…?"

"She was heavy with child. And there have been more of the damn creatures than ever hereabouts. Almost daily sightings. Anyone might be overwhelmed by an encounter."

Basil's hand tightened on the hilt of his sword, so that the familiar grooves of leather and metal bit against his skin. "I'll get them. I'll hunt them until their foul blood scorches the earth of this place—until the memory of them is void—until…"

He choked and Vedast pulled him to a seat, ordering the servant to fetch some ale.

"Not tonight, though," he urged. "It's late and you've only just come. Rest and hear the news. Make plans. Hear what we've already been doing. Then tomorrow, we can mount a mighty hunt!"

~~~~~

Days slipped by, one after another, in a haze of bewilderment, sleeplessness, loss, loneliness. Confusion after his release from the Faerie-Lands, separation from his friends and fellows left behind there, mad effort to find his bearings in the ordinary world and the grounds of his childhood, grief over his sister—all muddled together until Basil felt nothing but malaise and near-despair.

Basilisks, in greater numbers than he'd ever seen before—or even thought possible—had infested his ancestral land of Blackwell. He couldn't understand how Rue, who had the same responsibility he did to guard against them, had let the necrofae encroach so boldly—especially after he and Vedast found and destroyed two dens within easy reach of the castle. The only explanation he could think of was that Rue had grown fat and indolent, and resentment crept into his grief.

The farmlands and pastures had fallen into disrepair, as the people were driven away.

Few retainers remained. Their gladness at his return irked him, reminding Basil of his duty to them when he would rather have rested in quietness, peace, perhaps taking time to enjoy pleasures he had more than earned.

Ten years of war, from the time he was still a squire through endless, useless campaigns. Five years of exile in the Faerie-Lands for doing the right thing. Nothing to show for it—not even a warm welcome to rest and friends.

Vedast moved from the castle to his own house in the village.

Basil found the emptiness unbearable, hounded as he was by servants who seemed to only remember his youth without acknowledging or accommodating his new position as their lord. They were full of reminiscence and sadness over Rue—but had no imagination.

Settle down, they urged him. Rebuild, find a wife, father many sons, go no more to war.

He ought, he knew, to send for Princess Jasmine. If she'd waited for him. Though he didn't really care if she had or not.

In the nights and then the days between frenzied basilisk hunts, Basil went more often to the village and sought the company of
~~~~~

Vedast—loud, happy, and without a care, despite his mourning over his lost wife and child. It seemed easier to sit with him at the edge of the green, a cup of ale in hand.

He almost felt real, solid, present.

And there, nearly two weeks after his return, Basil saw a vision of great loveliness: a lady on horseback paused in her travels. Her dark hair coiled and coaxed, her deep violet eyes beckoned and soothed, her very presence felt like a cool breeze to his fevered heart.

Basil smiled and relaxed at last.

Bound for Blackwell

Jasmine slung the saddle over her horse, tightened the tackle, and then secured her bags behind it, running over their contents one more time inaudibly with her lips moving faster than her fingers. She'd packed them with care—her entire life reduced to three stout packs.

"Two gowns for summer, the blue wool for winter, extra chamise." Her fingers tugged at straps and flew at buckles. "Breviary, box of spices, the necklace Mother left me, a knife for fighting and another for secret. Candles and candleholder. The set of cups from the East. Two silken scarves, and three linen. The knit shawl…"

"Don't forget this!" Vicia stood in the doorway to the stable, holding out a thick and soft fur mantle.

"Oh—I knew I was missing something!" Jasmine slipped it around her shoulders and fastened the clasp. "Thank you."

Her stepsister half-smiled and her hands dropped thoughtfully to cradle her rounded stomach, her face clouded. "Are you *sure* about this, Jas? It seems a dangerous risk to take, going to a fate you can't be certain of, expecting never to return—*and* in the middle of winter?"

"I cannot *but* go!"

"We could send other messengers, in greater force this time."

"After none of the others have returned?"

Vicia groaned and laughed at the same time. "You see why I hesitate to let my sister walk into such uncertainty! No one has heard a thing from Blackwell in months; wouldn't it be better to make an expedition in force when spring has returned? You can go with them then."

"My mind is made up." Impatience clawed at Jasmine's limbs and she strained to see over the stalls to where the other horses were being prepared. "I can't wait for spring. Not with these dreams nagging at me!"

"You never were prone to dreams before..."

"Especially not vivid and urgent and inexplicable ones, as these are!"

"So," Vicia murmured, "you think there is something magical to these dreams?"

"I understand it as little as you do." Jasmine shrugged. "Why should I dream of Basil—and Basil in danger—after all this time? I had nearly forgotten him, and yet...!"

"Nearly forgotten him?" Vicia chuckled and said brusquely, "You were always *meant* to be with Lord Basil, ever since you were children, even if there was never a formal betrothal. You never forgot him for one single day, and I daresay he never let you far from his thoughts either."

Jasmine's face warmed in a sudden and embarrassingly uncontrollable flush and she turned back to the horse, saying with more anger than she felt: "Then he ought to have sent for me immediately he returned. And from the reports, others who were exiled in the Faerie-Lands have been released, so he *must* be back in our own realm! Back home, in Blackwell, where—where nothing has been heard for months. And—" She drew a sharp, quavering breath and remarked with surprise: "I guess I'm worried about him."

Vicia pulled her into an embrace. "Go, Jas. I know you must. But I will worry about *you*, all the same."

"You're going to say, 'Take care and only scout around to discover at a distance what has gone wrong.' But don't even think of asking it—I can't promise to."

"You are making this *so* much harder! If only you would wait a week, so that we could give you a proper escort instead of only two men and your maid."

Jasmine laughed unsteadily.

One of the men, Sir Theodoric, approached along the stable walkway and stopped just outside her horse's stall. "We are ready, my lady."

"Very well." Jasmine nodded. "Then let's make best use of the daylight: We leave at once."

Sir Theodoric bowed briskly, then turned and went back to the others with a curt command.

He was a big, battle-hardened, older man, nearly past his fighting days; while the other man, Matthew, was still a youth in training. Choices were slim, but with her maid Maggie, who could handle a sword with the best of them, Jasmine thought it likely they would get to Blackwell without too much trouble. *Afterwards,* however...

Vicia yanked her suddenly into another close hug. "I don't care what you say, I'm going to tell you to be careful anyway, Jas! I want to see you again someday, and soon."

"I'll try," Jasmine sniffed and gave her a quick kiss on the cheek.

Then she pulled away, mounted, and led the procession out into the winter dawn.

~~~~~

Battling thick snow, freezing winds, and roads made nearly impassable with mud proved the harshest challenge. The cold kept even those desperate enough to prey on others to their dens.

But the conditions grew worse the closer they came to Blackwell, until within the land itself they were buffeted by near blizzards day and night. They found refuge with cottagers three nights, and were warned not to continue lest they never find their way anywhere, ever. But the fitful sleep fostered by the relative warmth and peace brought only more dreams of Basil—in torment, crying out for help, somehow unreachable. So, pulled by the direction she felt from those dreams, she pressed onward.

"We can't keep going like this!" Sir Theodoric shouted at her over the howling wind. "Our horses will drop from exhaustion, if we don't freeze to death first. You know I would follow you to the worst hell, my lady, but this is a fool's errand that will only get us killed while achieving nothing. The fierceness of this persistent storm must be magical in nature!"

Jasmine nodded reluctantly and fought against the shiver that seemed to permanently rattle her teeth. "If we come to nothing by this afternoon, we—"

"Look!" Maggie's choked cry interrupted them.

She was with Matthew a little ahead on the barely discernable path, pointing up at something beyond and above the trees surrounding them.

Jasmine came alongside her and reined to a stop, then peered hard, shielding her eyes against the icy crystals driven by the wind.
~~~~~

At first, she saw nothing. Then, gradually, spires and towers emerged from the swirling fog, as if themselves made of cloud though they did not shift or dissolve.

"The castle!" she shouted. "Not far!"

They pressed on, though the glimpse of the castle soon proved a tantalizing hope more than anything else as it was lost behind the huddled trees. Jasmine nearly lost all sense of direction even as her hope and determination froze into numbness. She clutched at the reins, telling herself to follow Sir Theodoric's massive back, try not to look up from the shield of her hood, keep on—

"Ho there!"

The cry came as three lights sprang up before them.

Lanterns, and cloaked figures.

"Travelers! What are you doing way out here? Turn aside out of the blizzard before you drop to the roadside."

Sir Theodoric turned and followed before Jasmine had a chance to object, if she had any will to. In a moment, a small, firelit hall closed welcoming stillness around them. It was still cold, but out of the wind and a haven of warmth in comparison.

Gentle hands pulled Jasmine from her horse, unclasped the furs that were stiff with ice, led her to the stinging smoke of an open hearth, pressed something warm into her hands and sputtering down her throat.

"Lady Jasmine?" The familiar voice cut through the swirl of confusion and the pain of thawing, and Aldrich, one of the palace servants, loomed into view. "That *is* you! What are you doing all the way out here?"

"Why did *you* never return?" Jasmine demanded with an attempt at a smile. "We sent you to check on Blackwell's status more than a month ago, and here you are!"

"We can no more leave than we can reach the castle," Aldrich said tersely. "I arrived here half-dead in a storm worse than this one. It gets still and almost clement, if very cold, now and then, but every time I try to return the storm kicks up again. And there's no chance of getting to the castle!"

"Why not?" Sir Theodoric asked.

"It's as if a wall of icy spears surrounds it—I've made a few attempts at getting in myself, since it first fell several months ago," one of their rescuers answered. He was a large and very handsome man, with dark hair that glistened in the firelight as snow melted and ran off it. "I am Sir Vedast. This is my home, and you are more than welcome to stay here until the winter passes."

He smiled down at Jasmine with an appreciation that made her blush, as he brought forward a vast fleece and wrapped it softly around her.

"But what of the others?" she asked, sitting on the chair that he pulled forward to the fireside. "We sent three other parties of messengers, and have heard nothing else from them."

Aldrich exchanged glances with Vedast. "Why do you think I decided to stay here?"

"We found bodies in the snow the first time we tried going into the castle," Vedast answered, forthright but with his mouth pressed in a grim line. "Two men. That was all we heard of any messengers, other than Aldrich here."

"Winters aren't often this bad in Blackwell," Sir Theodoric mused.

"Not according to the village elders." Vedast nodded at some of the other men, still attending to the horses and talking among themselves.

"There must be some enchantment involved," Jasmine said.

"Could be. It's not my place to wonder about such things. There is an enchantress just outside the village, if you want to ask her. Magic's not my province—not at all."

"Perhaps we shall. But first—what news do you have of Lord Basil?"

"Basil? Do you mean—Rue's brother?" Vedast's face dropped into a crumpled frown as he passed his hand over it.

"Oh! Of course—I knew I had heard your name before." Jasmine reached forward to place a comforting hand on his shoulder for a moment. "You were Lady Rue's husband, weren't you? I am so sorry. We heard of her death; it was nearly the last news we got from here."

He nodded. "Yes, it was sudden and sad. But—what was your question?"

A stab of annoyed guilt at invoking something so obviously painful to him struck Jasmine, almost as hard as the sharp tingles in her hands and feet as they warmed. "Has anything been heard of her brother, Lord Basil?"

"The one who was exiled by the fae for breaking some rule, or some such?" Vedast rallied and met her eye, blinking rapidly. "No, nothing!"

"Oh..."

Jasmine felt more tired than she ever had before—struck and weary and useless.

"He may not have returned here." Sir Theodoric's voice seemed distant and hollow. "But even if he did, if it was during one of these storms, unprepared as he was..."

She blinked into the fire, stretching her fingers toward the flames until they trembled in agony as the heat seared away numbness. Think, think...

"We go on," she said at last, when her brain refused to work against what her heart knew.

"What?" Vedast leaned forward and snatched her hands away, gripping them close. He peered into her eyes and she couldn't look away. They were warm, comforting eyes, nearly convincing her to stay in their blue embrace forever. "Don't be mad, Lady Jasmine!"

"Lord Basil is in the castle; I am certain of it." She freed her hands and looked away. "I'm not giving up. We have come all this way, and it's not that much further, is it?"

"A few hundred yards up the street from the village. But—"

"Then we go at once."

"My lady," Theodoric said. "It is madness and folly—even death to approach the castle, especially in this storm."

"Does it ever lessen?" Jasmine asked.

Vedast shook his head. "Not really, but—"

"Then there is little point waiting. But," she glanced at their two younger companions, "Maggie and Matthew will remain here. Perhaps they can learn something from this enchantress. But I would be glad of your company, Sir Theodoric—at least as near the castle as we can get."

He nodded, reluctant but obedient, and before they had warmed too much, they set out again, wrapped well and carrying the heavy shielded lanterns. On foot rather than horseback, for their mounts were spent.

The struggle up the hill through the village seemed endless. With every step, the outline of the castle solidified—but that was the only thing that gave Jasmine any hope of ever reaching it. The storm increased in fury, until at last they could barely take another step against the bitter headlong wind.

"Stop!" Sir Theodoric's voice was barely audible, but he pulled at her arm. "This is it! The wall! No—further!"

He gestured ahead. Peering through eyes slitted against the onslaught, Jasmine made out a shivering, shifting mass of what seemed like icicles, except ever breaking up and reforming.

It was only yards away and, breaking away from him, she stepped with all her strength against the gale until she could touch it with outstretched hands.

How could she possibly...?

If this was magic, then the purity of her intentions must count for something.

"I have come for Lord Basil!" she shouted with every ounce of strength left in her.

As soon as the words left her mouth, they were lost in the furious wind. At the same instant, the shifting wall of icicles fell away before her and the storm turned to press against her from behind.

Jasmine fell forward, landing on her hands and knees, into sudden silence.

Blackwell the Beautiful

When she had caught her breath, Jasmine rose to her feet, clutching at her fur cloak against the chill. But—

It was warm as a gentle spring day. Beneath her boots was the soft green turf of a beautifully cultivated garden, tended plants on either side of a path lined with graceful marble statues of the kind the Romans carved long ago. Just ahead, stretching so high up that she had to crane her neck to see, rose a castle of breathtaking beauty. Its walls were pale gray and dotted with peaked and carved windows and arches; its spires and roofs were coppery green, and ornamented with gold.

There wasn't a sign of snow.

When she turned to look behind, the air faintly shimmered and shifted, although it looked as though the green hill sloped gently away toward the forest—without a sign of the village.

Nothing for it but to go into the castle.

Jasmine went up the path and through the open gates, her legs wobbly. There was as little sign of servants, retainers, or any other living soul as there was a gale blowing in the pristine blue sky. The castle was astoundingly beautiful, with marble floors polished to glassy perfection, soaring columns, intricate tapestries, carvings and furniture wrought to comfort and delight.

Yet no one to care for it.

"Hello!" she called. Her voice broke and was lost in the vastness of the place. "I have come for Lord Basil! Please—is there anyone…?"

Her legs gave out and she collapsed, exhaustion finally taking her.

~~~~~

Stone and marble. Hard and beautiful.

He roamed the corridors of the fair palace that had been his prison longer than he could remember, endlessly. Up and down flights of stairs, through halls and galleries, along battlements, past windows with vistas he didn't turn to see.

There was nothing *to* see.

There was nothing.

This was his prison, his existence, *him.*

He knew what he was. Even if the tearing claws at the end of crooked, fur-covered limbs didn't tell him, the reflection in the mirror was cruelly honest.

A monster.

Nameless, formless, terrible.

This loneliness was only right for such a thing as he was.

Isolated. Driven away, as terrors ought to be. The only living things he encountered—the necrofae basilisks that made daily incursions at the borders of his palace lands.

Roaming, onward, his growls shaking the walls, the only sound—

A cry.

Shaking, uncertain, wavering. Somewhere near the front of the palace.

Another trick?

Had the foul basilisks learned deception, too?

Or was this simply another torment of the curse?

He hesitated—but only a moment. Curiosity drew him, as it inevitably must. There was no use fighting it. There was no use fighting anything—even the basilisks he fought from mindless hate and rage.

The cry came again as he neared the gilded hall at the palace's main entrance. Then a soft thumping crash, then silence.

He followed his nose the rest of the way—mud, dirt, flesh, sweat, tanned hides.
~~~~~

There! A mound of motionless fur. An injured beast?

He cautiously approached the heap lying in the middle of a flagged colonnade, then rushed forward as he caught sight of a heavy glove.

Turning it over and shifting aside the furs, he uncovered a woman, pale as death and with a shallow cut across her forehead from striking a step as she fell. She was beautiful despite it. Soft golden hair fell across her shoulders, her eyes, even closed, were large and set wide above a slender nose in a round face.

He reached to touch her petal-soft cheek, then caught back his paw before he could do her more damage.

One touch of his claw would cut her, he reminded himself: His first instinct on smelling her blood was hunger.

Nonetheless—

As gently as he could, he lifted her, still wrapped in the fur cloak, and went quickly further back into the palace, calling for attendants.

They were there, always: Invisible and unheard, though he felt their hands and knew their ministrations when he was too tired or too despondent to drive them away.

Now, he needed them.

~~~~~

Numbness passed into pain, and then into curious ease and comfort.

Jasmine was aware of hands carefully tending her, stripping stiff clothes from her, wrapping her in warm and dry garments, placing her among cushions. Then the last feeling drifted away and she slept—she couldn't tell how long.

~~~~~

The first thing that struck her was the smell.

It was strong, green, summery—like roses and honeysuckle and jasmine, mixed with grass and mead. Most strange for the dead of winter.

She opened her eyes and discovered the source of the mead smell, at least. A silver goblet, richly decorated with opals, sat on a low table beside her couch, brimful of golden mead more sumptuous than any she had tasted in her life. She drained it at a draught, then sat up and looked around, feeling refreshed though rather sore.

A small fire burned on a hearth nearby, but large windows along one side of the room stood wide open. Beyond lay a garden bright with flowers and merry with birdsong.

"Impossible," she said aloud. "I couldn't have been asleep *that* long!"

She stood and took stock of her surroundings. The chamber was the richest and most beautiful she had ever seen, even on her incursions into the Faerie-Lands. Carved wood paneled the walls, carpets covered the floors, beautiful furnishings stood in every corner. Outside, a corridor hung with fine-wrought tapestries stretched in either direction, leading into rooms each different and lovely in their own right.

Curious. She had no doubt this was Blackwell Castle, but she had never heard of it being so beautiful—and people would speak of such wonders.

Puzzled, Jasmine returned to the room she had woken in, to find that in her brief absence a table had been filled with a feast fit to satisfy even the lustiest appetite. Fortunate, since the first delicious nibble told her she was famished.

A horrendous odor assaulted her as she was finishing, and she nearly choked on her last bite of honey cake. Next moment something approach, scratching and scraping on the tiles outside — something large, heavy, swift.

Jasmine leapt up, feeling for her sword, dagger—anything at all; only to find nothing but gown and belt.

She was stripped of weapons!

Whatever *it* was, it was at the door, feeling along the doorpost, claws winding around the frame...

Heart pounding, Jasmine snatched a heavy knife from the table and held it ready, casting a swift glance at the windows to see if any escape was to be had that way.

It entered.

A nameless monster, more than eight feet tall, crouching but upright on two hind legs, fur gray-brown and matted, claws extending sharp and terrible from cruel large paws. Its eyes flickered red, casting back daylight as if they burned with a light of their own. Glistening fangs lined its cavernous maw. Wide, silver-banded black horns rose proud, sharp, and crushing from its massive ugly head.

Jasmine recoiled, gagging at the stench, and fought to keep her hand steady as she raised the knife against it. She had to get out, get away—it would kill her for certain.

The monster crouched, hackles up, and snarled.

Its claws stretched poised for evisceration, and Jasmine

staggered backward from the death written in its eyes, stumbling against the couch.

But she paused, a breath coming between two lurching heartbeats, and lowered the knife a little.

Something in that snarl sounded like words.

She looked closer into the raging eyes, and gasped at what she saw.

They weren't flat and soulless like animal eyes—they were intelligent, their expression seething with anger but tempered with thought.

Jasmine steadied herself and straightened, breathing calmness and reason into her terrified limbs. "What are you?"

The snarl deepened, and for a moment she thought that either it wouldn't answer—or she was utterly wrong and it *could* not, and was nothing but an unthinking beast.

But then words formed within the growl, garbled at first, but then intelligible:

"I am lord of this place."

"The lord of…?" Jasmine's voice quavered and broke.

The creature rumbled something that sounded like "My prison and province."

"But," she tried again, "what of Lord Basil? Where is he?"

"Lord Basil is dead!"

Jasmine felt as if struck in the stomach. "No! He cannot be—I can't believe it."

"I killed him myself," the monster barked. It crouched lower, snarl deepening again. "What does it matter to you?"

"I love him," she said simply.

"There is nothing left to love."

"I *loved* him, then—once."

The creature watched her, motionless, for several long moments. Then it straightened a little and demanded, "How did you get in?"

Jasmine lowered her knife. A little. "I came to search for Lord Basil, thinking to find him here. When I said as much at the wall of ice, it—it opened somehow and permitted me through."

For several more minutes, the monster contemplated her, gradually rising from its crouch. At last, a low growl built into something like, "Hmmm…"

"I…" she drew a breath and ventured further: "I did not come to hunt you or challenge you in any way. If you truly killed Lord

Basil, then I suppose we are enemies; but I have no desire to seek retribution. I don't think I could threaten you at all, anyway, and only wish to protect myself."

"I will not hurt you," it said. "You will stay here."

"Stay? For how long?"

"Forever."

"Why?"

"I am lonely, and desire companionship," it snarled. "And the magic let you through. You—a human. A connection to the human world. The first in a long time. The last ever."

Staying was the very thing Jasmine most wanted. Whatever the monster said, she could not believe that Lord Basil was dead—not with dreams that brought him so close she felt she could touch him if she reached out in just the right way. He *wasn't* dead. And he *must* be held captive here, in his castle, by the magic that isolated it. And she must search and wait until she found him.

But best not let this monstrous lord know.

"I will stay, on one condition," she agreed with all the repugnance and horror she felt—and none of the relief: "If you can, release the Blackwell lands from the cursed snow and ice that entrap them. It threatens innocent lives unnecessarily!"

"It shall be done." It nodded slowly. "But the ice barrier surrounding this palace must remain, for worse would overrun these lands you speak of and all lives would be lost. Foul basilisks are loose on the grounds—and for this reason, you shall not leave the walls of the palace, if you value your life."

"Basilisks?"

"Necrofae of the foulest kind. Even if you are strong enough so that one look from a basilisk's eye does not turn you to stone, its venom will kill at a touch."

"I've heard of them, from old alchemical books." Jasmine shuddered, and finally set the knife on the table again. "Very well, I will stay, and remain within the palace. But—sir, what do I call you?"

"I have no name."

"You must have—"

"Nothing! Call me what you will."

"Beast, then. Will that do?" Jasmine shot back, goaded by fear and fury.

It growled. "You won't have to tolerate me much, but once a day I will have your company for the hour after you have eaten your evening meal. What is your name?"

"I am not fool enough to give that away so easily after relinquishing my freedom!"

"Beauty, then. Will *that* do?"

Jasmine flushed and bowed her head. "Whatever you like, Lord Beast. I—should not have spoken so hastily."

But when she looked up again, the monster was gone.

Be Bold

Though she saw no evidence of it, Jasmine did not doubt that the monster had kept his side of the bargain and released the icy enchantment on the land of Blackwell. It seemed less deceitful than most fae: what it said it meant, and that was that.

Assured that she had eased the countryfolks' plight, Jasmine proceeded according to what she had planned, and spent days searching the palace until she knew its every nook and cranny. It was wondrous and lovely, comfortable and filled with treasures and delights. But these soon bored and then galled her. It was a prison, as Lord Beast said: Delightful, but empty. Luxurious, but isolated. Keeping secrets behind a fair veneer, as if taunting her efforts.

Strangely, she dreamed less of Lord Basil now that she had come to his home; when she did dream of him, he seemed far off and more desperate than ever. She tried to call to him for guidance, but dreams were fickle and any response flew from her like trying to grasp a flame.

Only one phrase remained with her when waking: Trust not in appearances.

Well, then, she wouldn't.

The palace with its beauties was a lie. Lord Basil was *not* dead. And her beastly captor…?

Where he went during the days, she couldn't guess. Sometimes, she felt sure he roamed beyond the palace. She was sure by the injuries he came back with that he fought against the basilisks—and somehow survived. She didn't dare ask.

Night after night, he sat with her after her dinner and talked. He asked questions of life outside—doings at the court, regular life among the nobility and peasants alike, wars and diplomacy, social activities like marriage and death and birth.

As if he was genuinely curious, puzzled, interested.

And he never made any move against her, or threatened her. In fact, he seemed more considerate than most gentlemen, asking after her comfort and wanting to know whether she missed her family.

As weeks stretched on, Jasmine found Lord Beast's appearance less repulsive. She could even tolerate the musky, metallic, harsh odor he carried—almost. The raging savagery of his behavior that still showed itself seemed to be as much from bitterness as a manifestation of the animal he was.

Over time and as frustration grew at finding no sign of Lord Basil, Jasmine gathered courage and finally asked, "Can I learn to fight against the basilisks as you do?"

"As *I* do? No." Lord Beast scoffed. "You are delicate and soft as all humans, Lady Beauty, without thick fur or horns or claws."

"But surely ordinary humans *can* face them and prevail. There must be methods of it!"

He hesitated, glowering. "Yes," he replied at last. "There is a way."

"Then can you teach me?"

"Never!" he roared, and stormed off.

It surprised Jasmine, so she didn't bring it up again. But she was yet more surprised when Lord Beast led her the next week to an armory and shoved a spear at her.

"You should know how to defend yourself against the basilisks, at least," he said. "But never seek them out! Lovely young ladies have died by such foolishness."

~~~~~

Lady Beauty proved a quick study, for such a slight woman.

He had to conclude that she was trained in arms already, though she didn't admit it.

They went to the training yard that he had never visited yet somehow knew was there. There, he showed her the feints, attacks, defenses, moves that a human with hands, arms, legs, bare and defenseless skin could use against a basilisk.

He had his own methods. Teeth and horns, tearing claws and tramping—much more affective.

But the method of human technique came to him as easily as if he had trained in it.

Why…?

Within a few weeks, Lady Beauty was as skilled as she needed to be. More, in fact.
~~~~~

"Don't seek the basilisks out," he warned her again the final day of her training. "Never seek them."

She nodded, slipping her spear back into its rack and then pulling and retying her hair back from her sweaty neck. She seemed quieter than normal. He hoped she wasn't thinking of doing something stupid.

"I came here because of dreams," she said unexpectedly. "Far more vivid and real than most dreams."

What was this—an admission of weakness? A confidence? What was he to do or say?

He waited, and in a moment, she continued, blinking up at the sun: "I had a new dream, like it but different, last night. In it, a very beautiful woman came up to me and locked me in a golden cage. She was an enchantress—just like the one I heard about in the village before I came here into the palace."

Weakness. A rush of new information that was not new flowed at him.

"Are you all right?" Lady Beauty asked, her voice distant—but her hand very present, steadying his forearm.

"The enchantress—I remember her," he said. "In the village, across the green. More beautiful than any vision. She spoke to me, laughed at me, wooed me. We met in the woods, and again in the town, and again in the gardens, and again in the hall. She was everywhere. She bewitched me. But soon… I hated her—loathed the sight of her—could not turn away. She. Cursed. Me…!"

"How is this?" Lady Beauty drew back sharply.

"The palace—the ice wall—the magic of snow and storm." He choked, the knowledge nearly overwhelming the world he knew, for it was so very small. "It was all her doing."

"And Lord Basil…"

Her whisper was so faint that he almost did not catch it, even with his torturously sharp hearing. It enraged him, nearly overwhelming and driving back his new rediscovery. How *dare* she speak that name!

But her next words steadied him and brought him back.

Strange, how she always steadied and brought him back…

"Why?" she said. "Why would she curse you and this land?"

"Because I didn't care," he replied, and could say no more.

~~~~~

Jasmine fled as soon as she could get away to the large and
~~~~~

comfortably-appointed room that had been given her. She had to think—to understand.

Something lingered on the edge of her knowledge, which she couldn't grasp—didn't dare reach for.

Instead, she stuck with what she knew: For some reason, the enchantress in the village was responsible for this curse on Blackwell—and likely for Lord Basil's imprisonment. The enchantress had somehow brought the monster from the Faerie-Lands to guard the palace from within, while cutting it off from intrusion from without.

Really, it seemed very unfair to poor Lord Beast!

That *something* niggled at her again, but she dismissed it as impatiently as she discarded her training-dress. She couldn't think about anything else right now—she had to confront this problem and find some solution.

And the solution seemed to rest with Lord Beast.

It terrified her more than she expected. She still feared him, yes—after all, it would only take one good swipe of the paw for him to kill her. But more than that, they didn't *mind* each other anymore—he trusted her, and she detested the idea of breaking that trust or even demanding too much of it. But there was nothing else to be done.

She must venture from the palace to confront the enchantress.

So, how should she go about it?

The truth. It was time for complete honesty.

That evening, Lord Beast was moody and silent, as they walked through the cool dusk of the garden. But Jasmine gathered courage and spoke.

"I must leave the palace for a time, Lord Beast."

He barely glanced at her. "No. You agreed to stay."

"If all goes well, I shall be gone no longer than a day. You won't even miss me!" She tried to sound sure of herself. "I must go to the village and confront this enchantress that cursed you and this place."

"And if all goes ill and she curses you too?"

"It's a risk we must both take."

The monster faced her, brows lowered and horns glistening in the starlight. "I cannot allow it."

"The enchantress is the only one who can release the curse that binds you, so you should want this as much as I do," Jasmine reasoned.

"If you leave, you will never return."

"That's not true. I swear I will return—I must." She stopped, gripping her skirts in both fists to keep her resolve strong. "This is why I came, Lord Beast, and I must see my business through: I must know the truth of Lord Basil's fate, which you will not even speak to me of, and I must find where he is, alive or dead. Because of my dream last night, I am convinced the enchantress had a hand in it somehow. She must be made to undo it."

"What right have you to do this?" Lord Beast growled, a dangerous gleam in his eye.

"The same right that brought me here—old love and unspoken fidelity. Moreover, I am the king's messenger, sent to discover the welfare of this corner of his domain and the fate of his vassal. For I am Lady Jasmine, daughter of Victor and Lily-of-the-Valley of Nostermont, and princess by adoption of Merimor. What I have sworn to do, I will not leave undone as long as I have life in me."

Lord Beast shifted a sudden step backward, and an unreadable expression flickered over his face before a shadow hid him. Surprise? Shock?

"Allow me to go," she resumed after a moment of silence she couldn't interpret; "and I will do all in my power to return within a day. You have taught me to fight the basilisks if I encounter one. And I know how to approach an enchantress with due caution and respect. It should not be a perilous trip."

"Go."

The word was so low that she nearly missed it, and repeated; "Go? You allow me this freedom?"

"I have no intention of keeping you prisoner!" he snarled. "Go! Begone with you! Never return!"

She flinched away despite herself, but stood her ground. "No! I will return. I must, for—"

"For this Lord Basil?" he sneered. "Fool Beauty! He is gone and there is no getting him back."

"Nevertheless, I promise you that I will return before tomorrow evening."

Lord Beast huffed—a deadly growling sound. "If you return at all, it *must* be by tomorrow evening. Else there will be nothing left to keep me here. Death must find me; or banishment to other realms, which is the same as death in the end."

"I will be back before then—you have no need to doubt me."

"There is nothing for you here." He dropped to all fours and galloped away down the path, calling back: "Go!"

The Bewitchment

Jasmine stood at the end of the road from the front entrance of the palace, the shimmering wall of ice ahead of her. She wore a thick cloak and sturdy boots, and carried the hefty spear used against the basilisks as well as her sword and knives, which she had found in the armory. Best be prepared for whatever lay outside.

Did Lord Beast control the barrier? He seemed to be able to enter and leave, and had said that she could pass through—but was it within his prerogative to guarantee that?

No matter.

Jasmine extended her hand until her fingers felt the chill, semi-solid wall before her. Then she took a step forward, and—

With a jerking whoosh, she fell through the other side of the wall and hit the ground.

Instantly, the chill of winter replaced the balmy summer breeze of the garden, and drab, muddy browns filled her sight. It wasn't harsh snow and wind, and the green of almost-growth brushed the branches of the trees; but this was clearly a much different place from the enchanted palace.

Jasmine picked herself up, brushing mud from her hands, and retrieved the spear from where it had fallen. She hadn't gone very far down the road, however, before a startled cry greeted her.

"Lady Jasmine!" It was Sir Vedast, armed, with a heavy leather tunic and a spear of his own, but handsome and warm as ever. "Why! It is Lady Jasmine, whom we all thought lost to this world."

"Perhaps I was." She smiled, feeling disoriented from such effusive human interaction after so long with none at all. "But I'm here, for now."

"Thank the stars, you are!" Vedast pulled her into an embrace and then pulled her along toward his house with an arm around her shoulders. "Where have you been? In the castle this whole time? How have you stayed alive? Was anyone else in there with you?"

"Wait, and I'll answer all questions! But first I must know of my own people—Maggie, and Sir Theodoric and Matthew."

"All here still—the roads aren't passable yet, now that the thaw has melted the snow at last and made a mud puddle of the whole land. Maggie you will find with the other serving women of my house. Sir Theodoric and Matthew are out beating back the latest run of basilisks."

"What?" Jasmine pushed him away to look at him. "The basilisks are out here beyond the ice wall, too?"

"Not as bad as before it came and apparently trapped most of them, but yes."

"Lord Beast said they were confined within... But perhaps he doesn't know how bad they really are, or wished to shield me from the knowledge."

"Lord *Beast*?"

Jasmine nodded. "The monstrous guardian of the castle."

"Is *that* what has been keeping you prisoner within there all this time?" Vedast's face became dark as a thundercloud. "Foul thing! We must drive it away—never mind the basilisks. I'll summon the men of the town to form a storming party."

"No, no, don't be foolish, Sir Vedast," she chuckled. "It is a good, gentle, speaking creature, as trapped within the castle as I was. More, for he cannot leave to join living humanity as I am now."

He glanced at her suspiciously. "You have *sympathy* for the unholy brute?"

"I—" It was more than sympathy. It was something like camaraderie, friendship, even affection in a strange way. "Pity, yes," she said guardedly, "and I respect him and his dominion of the magical curse, as you ought to. When did the enchanted storm dissipate?"

"The same night you came to us and then disappeared. Why?"

"Because that was his doing—I agreed to stay on condition that the blizzard relent, for I wanted to search for Lord Basil as well."

"You're sneakier than I gave you credit for, Lady Jasmine!" Vedast guffawed. "Do what you like, and make it look like the enemy is getting what he wants, too, eh?"

"Something like that."

They had reached his house and she stopped outside on the path up to the door.

She pressed her lips together. "I don't have time to stay."

"What?" He clasped her shoulder again and drew her onward. "Nonsense! You'll need to wait for your attendants to return, at least, and get your things and your horses ready before you leave. In fact—you can't leave yet, not with the roads as they are. You'll get mired before you've gone a furlong."

"Leave? No—"

"Good!" Vedast sighed relief and leaned back against the wall under the eaves, where it was drier. "I'm glad that you don't intend to leave, Lady Jasmine. In fact," he suddenly looked as abashed as a schoolboy. "I've had time to think about this since you vanished. That was like a blow to me—another blow, grief after grief. But now that you are free, I thought, perhaps, you might stay with me. This house—I have plans of making it bigger, grander. Now that the castle is cut off, this land needs a new fortress, something more modern. And, with you, I thought..."

"Are you...?" Jasmine half-smiled and drew further away. "Are you proposing that we marry?"

"Yes!" Vedast looked so relieved that he nearly bounded forward. "I know I'm only a lowly knight, but just think—now that my wife and her brother are gone, the lordship of this place is vacant. The king will surely grant it to me if you ask, as your husband. The priest will marry us as soon as I ask him, and—"

"I haven't agreed, Sir Vedast."

"But you will." He smiled in a way that nearly toppled her heart over—trust, affection, admiration, assurance, all in an impossibly handsome package.

"I can't stay," she said softly. "I'm sorry, Sir Vedast, but what you suggest is impossible. For I am not a free woman; I have sworn to return to the castle by tonight."

"Sworn? Easily dealt with! Confess it to the priest and he will absolve you—anyway, everyone knows that the word of a woman is not worth much."

Jasmine stiffened. "The word of a woman? Sir Knight, I am a princess and a lady of the sword. If my word as a woman is worth so little, then my word as a queen's adopted daughter ought to count for something. Not to mention... I have promised this to someone I care far more for than you have given me reason to care for you."

"Not this Beast-guardian of yours?" Anger leveled Vedast's brows.

"Yes." She nodded, irritated into decision. "He's not all that bad, really, once you can ignore the stench. And he's done far more against the basilisks than you have, much as I respect your efforts and those of the villagers."

He was breathing short, heavy breaths through his nostrils and repeated, "The *stench*...?"

"Now," Jasmine said, settling her cloak and gripping the spear. "If you will excuse me, I must go find the enchantress you spoke of when I was last here, and see what she can do about lifting the curse."

Vedast let her go, which was more than she expected. She had angered him, insulted his boyish infatuation, crushed his self-assurance. Men in such a position did not forgive easily, as she knew all too well. But she was too impatient to see what he would try.

A village woman directed her to the enchantress' house, warning her to tread carefully and with respect.

Jasmine went briskly, but still the trip to the far side of the village where the forest touched the fields took longer than she anticipated. Mud sucked at her boots and dragged at her cloak, the wind picked up and cut to her skin, the spear seemed to grow heavier.

"Magic—just more stupid magic," she muttered. "Well, I don't care. I *will* get there!"

Then, finally, she *was* there; at the edge of a field rutted and thick with plowing, with a small house that seemed very drab for an enchantress' dwelling.

But the enchantress herself stood on the porch as if awaiting her, and she was anything but drab.

Jasmine gasped, and felt herself to be nothing but a weary, broken, dirty vagabond.

This woman—tall and dark-haired with nearly white skin and wide violet eyes—was more beautiful than anything she had seen. Lovely as a faerie queen. Something carved of marble and starlight and magic.

"Jasmine," she said, her tone enchantment itself.

"I—" Her voice sounded harsh and cracked. "I've come about the enchantment on the castle."

"Yes." The enchantress' mouth curved into a smile that betrayed cruelty. "And about Lord Basil, no doubt. Well, I would be a poor hostess if I did not invite you inside and offer some refreshment."

Jasmine followed her into a house that seemed humble still, though strangely lovely, and they sat opposite one another at a table. The enchantress made a subtle movement of her hand, and suddenly it was filled with a simple but delightful-smelling meal.

"No, thank you," Jasmine whispered.

"Don't be a fool," the enchantress laughed and bit into a tart. "You have been eating my food these four months now within the palace. It is a lovely place, is it not?"

"A gilded cage."

"Oh, yes. And worse than that—a slow death."

Jasmine drew a steadying breath and took a pastry. "But why? Why did you curse it and Lord Beast into being its guardian?"

"Lord Beast? What a strange name you have for him! Well—I cursed him because he did not care. I cursed the land and the castle especially because he did not care."

"And will you curse me because I care too much?"

"You? No, I will not touch you, Jasmine."

"I don't understand why you spare me and doom a whole land," Jasmine said. "But I must venture to be impudent in this request, because I have come to see what I can do in freeing it. In freeing Lord Basil, who I am convinced still lives and is trapped within the castle somewhere."

"Why should I, Princess?"

"For mercy, if for nothing else. Please, I beg of you, for the sake of my love—"

"What does love matter for anything?" The enchantress flared, fingers gripping her cup until the metal bent under the pressure. "Love is fickle and soon lost. Easily led astray, and won by a little beauty and wit—despite that appearances deceive."

Jasmine gasped a little at the words.

"What assurance do you have that Lord Basil loved you, that you seek to free him thus?" the enchantress continued.

"None. But we once loved each other, and for the sake of that bond I ask this of you. He doesn't deserve whatever imprisonment you have given him."

"Perhaps he does, though. Perhaps he is now as he always was—as he ought to be."

"Then," Jasmine repeated, breath shaking, "I ask again, have mercy on him, even if he doesn't deserve it. I will do anything to see him free."

"You will have to." The enchantress laughed again, relaxing and drinking her wine as if she had never felt anger. "*I* can do nothing. You are the only one who can break the curse!"

"What? But—how?"

"Oh..." Her smile grew even crueler. "By breaking your promises, being unfaithful to your love, and above all by never trusting appearances. Run along now, Princess—before I've had my fill of you."

Back to Basilisks

She was gone.

Jasmine.

The only woman he had ever really loved—gone. Lost forever.

And with Jasmine, the last connection he had to the world of humans. His realm. His home. The tenuous thread that he hadn't even missed before she came was broken. He was adrift, sinking, lost.

He staggered through the corridors and out into heartless sunshine, weakness sinking talons into him. The fae loveliness of the palace grew so sharp it stung him, and he turned down his gaze to what he was, to all he was now.

A monster.

The hiss and screech of basilisks alerted him and he bounded forward. At least he still had his rage!

At the edge of the garden near the ice wall—he stopped abruptly at the sight that confronted him:

A mound of writhing, slithering, clawing basilisks turned on him and charged.

Good. Let him meet death as he dealt it.

~~~~~

Jasmine reached the village far later than she wished, muttering curses and confusion under her breath. But then—more obstruction.

Seemingly the whole village had come out to greet her, talking, questioning, demanding to know how she had gotten out, if she was well, where she was going to stay. Sir Theodoric was there, looking grimmer and more battle-scarred than ever. Matthew too, scrawny but more muscled and grinning with satisfaction. Maggie embraced her closely and asked with an odd sidelong look if Sir Vedast really had proposed marriage to her.

Jasmine put them off with firm farewells, orders to go back to the court with full news, and commands to leave her to her chosen fate.

Then at last she pushed through and hurried up the hill toward the hazy outlines of the castle.

Vedast was nowhere to be seen, and she was glad of it.

She drew a deep breath, and stepped through the ice wall.
~~~~~

It threw her forward onto her hands and knees again. Before she could rise, something screeched very close ahead. Without thinking, she swung forward with the spear as she jumped to her feet and felt the tip impact something.

The screech ended with a gurgle and she jerked the spear away, looking around just in time to see more of the creatures headed her way. They slithered and jerked on scaled long bodies like a serpent or a dragon, but with rooster-like head, beak, cockscomb, and talons. Murderous wrath filled their empty eyes and sizzling venom dripped from their gaping and clattering mouths.

Jasmine dropped her cloak, drew her sword, held the spear ready—and fought for her life with all the skill Lord Beast had taught her.

It seemed only minutes later when at last there was silence and she was alone, slain basilisks around her.

Breathing hard, she looked around.

It was dark.

Light from the stars and streaming from the palace windows lit the garden, but it was just beyond dusk.

"No!" she cried. "No—no!"

Cursing herself for being late, breaking her promise, spending too much time in the village, everything—she took off at a run toward where she usually met with Lord Beast these warm evenings.

Surely he wouldn't die just because she was late? It seemed ridiculous, but misgivings sunk within her and she ran on through the twisting paths, calling to him.

At last! Ahead, there were sounds of movement—screeching and roars of battle.

Jasmine rounded a corner into a wider part of the garden, just in time to see Lord Beast gore two basilisks, toss them aside, then crush a final two more. And fall to the ground.

"No!" she cried, and began to charge forward.

"You're too late," someone said from the shadows nearby.

Vedast, wearing a dusky cloak, stepped forward smirking. His eyes glowed with a greenish tinge to match the basilisks, and he raised a hand as if in command. Three more of the necrofae slithered out in response.

"The basilisks are your doing!" Jasmine accused, realization and horror coursing through her. "But how? You are no sorcerer."

"Well," he shrugged, "I am a little. Enough to rule these

creatures. The enchantress gave me that power, along with a few other favors, if I helped her get established in the village. Something she wanted, for something I was more than willing to give. Convenient how that works out."

"Why?"

"I want to be lord of this place, and my wife impeded my ambitions. And then her brother showed up again, just when she was finally dead."

Lord Beast staggered to his feet and roared weakly, turning on him.

"Pathetic," Vedast mocked, and waved the basilisks forward at Jasmine.

She swung her sword and dispatched one, but weariness and bewilderment slowed her. They were almost on her when—

Lord Beast fell on them, rage and murder pouring from his savage teeth and claws and horns. In another minute, none were left.

He met Jasmine's gaze, eyes shifting from murderous fury into wonder and then regret.

And he crashed to the ground before her.

"Serves you right, Princess," Vedast called, retreating. "Your monster guardian is dead, and soon you will be too. And this was your doing, you know—you're the one who told me about the stench."

The basilisks obeyed Vedast. But if there was no Vedast…

Jasmine threw the spear toward where his back disappeared among the trees. There was a thunk, a cry, and then nothing. No sound, no motion, no basilisks.

Lord Beast moaned at her feet.

"No!" she gasped, and dropped down beside him. He seemed hazy, less-there than before. "Are you injured? Poisoned? Is there an antidote?"

"I am the antidote," he said with something like a laugh. "Too late… I am slipping away. You are free of me, Jasmine."

"I don't want to be. Don't give in—I'm back. I will never leave you again."

He shifted, and stretched one massive claw out, pointing at a place where two herbs grew beside each other.

"The antidote?" Jasmine jumped up, hoping against hope, and gathered a handful of each herb.

She pressed them against his massive chest, trying to look for injuries, hoping he would take it, or that the scent would be beneficial, or *something*.

He didn't move. But after several long minutes, he groaned: "Basil. You… came for Basil."

It was too late. She had broken her promise and he was slipping away. She leaned nearer against him, and found that tears streamed down her face. "I came for him, but I will not leave you. Please, *please* don't leave me! I don't care anymore—I can't lose you…"

The massive form stirred. "What do you care? I'm a monster. Loathsome. A stench…"

"A gentle monster. I love you for your goodness." Full knowledge of it came as she said the words and realized what they meant, and she wept fully, knowing her betrayal. And yet, it was right. It was the truth behind the appearance.

"You love… *me*? Savage? A raging beast?" The rumbling voice grew somewhat stronger. "But, Lord Basil… You came for love of him."

"Imprisoned here, somewhere," she said.

And a strange and terrible hope shot through her.

Vedast said that Lord Basil hadn't returned, but then spoke of him interfering.

She had seen no sign of other inhabitants in the palace. No one else, beside the cursed Lord Beast.

Could it be…?

"Rue!" she cried, clutching at the herbs. "And—basil! The antidote to the basilisks' venom. *You* are the antidote. You are—"

Jasmine reached out to grasp the Beast's pelt—and her fingers fell against skin.

Human skin. A human face. A solid human form.

The smell of basil and rue filled the garden in a wave, and a rush of light mist chased away darkness for a brief moment.

Jasmine collapsed backward, coughing and blinking. Then it dissipated, leaving darkness and the chill of an early spring night.

And the form of a man, just visible in the star and moonlight.

He shifted, groaned, stood.

"Jasmine?" he said. In a normal voice—a human voice. He reached out, pulled her up, clasped her close against his bare chest. "Jasmine! You have done it! I am free."

She laughed and cried, fingers brushing against his normal hair and beard and down his shoulders—then pushing him away. "And naked!" She laughed again, as he did.

He laughed too. "Better go inside."

They turned to the castle—and saw that it had changed. The uncannily beautiful visage it had presented had returned to ordinary stone walls and battlements—nothing special and in need of repairs in a few places.

"What…?" Jasmine began.

"The palace was more than half in Faerie-Land," he said grimly. "It kept me there, trapped—and all the servants who were in it trapped and invisible, too."

"Don't trust to appearances." She shook her head. "And I broke my promise to return in time to save you from slipping into it fully."

"But your love broke the curse after all."

"My love for you. I forsook my love for *him*—for Basil, as I remembered him, from all those years ago when we were young. Not really—I will always love him. But…"

"But you came to love me." He looked at her from eyes she remembered and knew very well, though grown older, harsher, kinder. "I may be free from that form, but I will always carry some of the monster inside me."

"And I love you despite it." She smiled up at him. "Even because of it. You are more than you were then, Basil; there is more *good* to you, even with the rage and change that years and war wrought."

"And I," he chuckled and then brushed her cheek softly, "I love you, Lady Beauty, and always have—and find you deeper and richer than anything I might have looked for elsewhere. I'm sorry I ever came near to forgetting."

END

THE HERO AND THE BEAST

K.M. Carroll

"I'm coming up on the place, now," Krissy Manchester said into her headset. "You can see it there, at the end of the street. It's quiet and spooky here, guys. Look, no cars. Empty houses. Dead trees. And in the distance, a creepy, mostly-abandoned mansion. With a villain inside."

Two thousand viewers were logged into her livestream. Krissy, also known as Silver Barb, wore a silver suit, a red cape, and boots, along with a mask that concealed her camera and microphone. Around her floated three bubbles full of water, each with a fish inside. Her power was conjuring and dismissing these globes, and she had built her entire persona around it.

Tonight, she was canvassing a gloomy, abandoned part of Indiana that had once been a summer village for the rich and powerful. Now it was nothing but abandoned buildings covered in graffiti, their windows boarded up, fancy yards overgrown with waist-high weeds.

But one house remained free of vandalism. This was the old Valiant mansion, built in the early 1900s by a land developer. The great-grandson of the family, Leonard Valiant, was suspected of running a crime ring, and had made his lair in the old house. Krissy didn't intend to take him down without backup, but she needed new content for her HeroTube channel. A little scouting around the Valiant mansion would intrigue her viewers.

She reached a wrought-iron gate with lions worked into the metal, and peered through. She panned the camera in her mask over the five gables on the mansion's roof, a huge front door, a wide veranda with its scattering of chairs and tables. Nothing moved, but one window on the top floor stood open.

"I'm going in," Krissy stage-whispered into her headset. She called her water spheres, positioned them like stair steps, and summoned big, heavy flounders to each one. She ran up the backs of the fish, her boots splashing in each bubble. The fish thrashed in protest, but Krissy banished them before they could escape their bubbles. She vaulted over the gate, made a perfect three-point landing with her cape settling gracefully around her, and set off up the gravel driveway.

"According to Heropedia," Krissy said to her viewers, "Leo Valiant has a metamorph power. He can increase his muscle mass until he's the size and power of a semi-truck. If he's also a villain, then ladies and gentlemen, this may be my last stream. We'll see if the rumors of his evil deeds are true." She climbed the steps to the front door, then detoured along the veranda, peering in the windows.

The mansion's interior was dim and dusty, with the indistinct shapes of furniture under sheets. Krissy peered about for signs of life, hoping that something might happen to liven up her stream. Instead, all she saw were depressing views of one more abandoned house in a dead neighborhood. If no villain awaited her, then this would be the most boring stream ever.

She circled the house until she found a side door. The knob turned. Smiling to herself, she opened the door. "Urban exploration beginning now," she said. "Definitely not breaking and entering. The door wasn't even locked."

"It doesn't need to be," said a voice.

Krissy looked up with a gasp. She had entered a gallery full of covered furniture with a dusty chandelier looming overhead. A staircase and loft overlooked the room with an elaborate carved banister. Looking over it was Leonard Valiant.

But she barely recognized him. The man standing at the railing was pale and thin, with his clothes hanging off his shoulders. His eyes were sunken, his hair long and stringy, and he held a glass of liquor in one hand. He looked as if the sight of her made him tired. For a second, Krissy gaped at him in dismay. He looked far older than his twenty-six years.

"Leonard Valiant?" Krissy said in her best hero voice, throwing back her shoulders. "I'm Silver Barb, and I'm here to end your villainous misdeeds!"

Leonard sipped his liquor. "Sure. Better leave while you can."

"Is that a threat?"

"It's a warning." Leonard gestured at the door. "It's still open. You have a chance."

At that moment, the door slammed shut by itself. Krissy jumped and whirled, her heart leaping into her throat. "Who's there?"

"Now you're stuck," said Leonard. "That was the ghost. Nobody leaves without his permission."

Krissy stood there, hands over her mouth. Then she strode to the door and grabbed the knob. An electric shock raced up her arm. She released the doorknob and leaped backward, shaking her fingers.

"How are you doing that?"

"It's not me," said Leonard. "I wonder why he locked you in here? You're just an annoying HeroTuber."

Krissy walked into the center of the gallery and glared up at him. "And you're a villain who runs a crime ring!"

"Am I?" Leonard blinked at her, then shrugged. "Believe whatever you want, HeroTuber. Try the windows. Maybe he'll let you out that way." He turned his back on her and walked out of sight.

Krissy checked her stream inside her mask. Five thousand viewers. Her chat was going crazy with people giving advice. Trying the windows was popular, but so was beating up Leonard. People also hoped to see the ghost. Krissy set out to explore the house, her heart beating hard.

Covered furniture filled every room. The kitchen was dirty, but the refrigerator had food in it—mostly microwave dinners. Every door and window refused to open.

"It looks like I'm trapped," Krissy said dramatically, standing in the middle of a sheeted ballroom. "But there was one open window upstairs, wasn't there? Don't worry. I can handle Leonard."

She summoned three globes of water with a red-bellied piranha in each. They escorted her through the house and up the stairs to the loft, where she had seen Leonard. There was no sign of him, but a door at the end of the hall stood open. She crept to it and peered inside.

Here she found Leonard sitting on a stool in front of an easel, paintbrush in hand. The room was packed with art books, disassembled mannequins, lights, vast collections of brushes, racks of paints, piles of canvas, and sketch paper. The open window was on the far side of the room, a fresh breeze blowing through. It almost carried away the smell of linseed oil and alcohol.

Leonard looked up. "Turn off your blasted camera. No filming in my studio."

"I'm trying to escape," said Krissy in a small voice.

Leonard shook his head. "You won't. The ghost will close the window if you try. Now, camera off."

"Going dark for now," Krissy said to her stream. "Stay tuned for updates!" She switched off her streaming mask and pushed it up her forehead. "Hey, Leo."

"Long time no see, Kris," he replied. "What, your channel is so starved for content that you come pester me?"

"I heard you were involved with organized crime!" Krissy retorted. "I couldn't believe it, so I had to come see for myself."

"Well, I'm not," Leonard said. "I'm a prisoner, and now so are you."

"Why?" Krissy exclaimed. "Even if ghosts existed, what could it want with you?"

"It wants me to paint it a picture full of beauty," said Leonard. "And I ... well, look at my art."

Krissy picked up the nearest sketchbook and flipped through it. Grotesque monsters. Robots. Evil faces. Everything was misshapen and deformed. She put the sketchbook down in disgust. She had gone to school with Leo Valiant. He had amused her and his friends with comic renditions of teachers, as well as cartoon characters and jokes. He'd left to attend art school and she hadn't seen him since.

"What happened?" she asked.

He hunched his shoulders. "I don't know. When Dad left and Mom died, I just ... didn't see anything funny anymore. I inherited this stupid mansion, and I thought I'd try to live here. Except it's haunted by some ancestor of mine. He's a real jerk. Wants me to paint him something beautiful, and I just ... can't." He indicated a wilted daisy in a vase that he had been trying to paint. But the canvas held only a dark brown blotch.

He pointed at her bubbles and piranhas. "See, that's more my style. Ugly fish with big teeth. I'd paint those any time."

"Piranhas aren't ugly," Krissy said. She banished all but one bubble, which she drew in to float above her cupped hands. The fish swam in circles, its gills gently pulsing. "They get a bad rap, but they mostly eat fruit and plants."

"Then why did you summon them?" Leo said with a smirk. For a second, he almost looked like the cute guy she remembered, and not the sad, wasted man he had become.

Krissy banished the last piranha. "Because they look good on stream."

Leo gave an ironic laugh. "Of course. You've turned so fake, Kris. You were always the nicest one. What happened?"

A surge of embarrassed indignation rose in her. "HeroTube is a full-time job. I make thirty grand a year off bounties. This is who I am, now."

"Sure," said Leo. "A fake persona for a fake person. It'll be a real joy being stuck in a house with you. Go stream your escape plans and leave me alone." He turned back to his canvas.

Furious, Krissy stomped back downstairs and tried the doors again. She was not fake! How dare he say that!

As she headed for the double front doors, she pulled her mask on and began streaming again. "I'm back, everybody. Still trying to find a way out. Sorry I can't show you the studio, but there's copyright issues involved."

She jiggled the front door's handle, then tried the deadbolt. Nothing would turn, as if they were frozen in place. As she eyed the hinges, thinking of taking them apart, a burst of cold struck her hands. A transparent figure emerged from the wooden door three inches from her face.

Krissy gasped and retreated, summoning a water bubble as a shield.

An honest to goodness ghost emerged from the front door and stood before her. He was a tall old man in an old-fashioned suit and coat, with a ruffled cravat at his throat. His face resembled Leo's, but craggier, and with a cold, shrewd light in his eyes. In one hand he carried a rose.

"Who are you?" Krissy said, hoping he showed up on her stream.

"I am John Marshall Valiant." His voice resonated, as if he were speaking to her from inside a much larger space. "You are no descendant of mine. Who are you?"

"I'm Silver Barb, superheroine," Krissy said.

The ghost laughed at her—a devastating, derisive laugh, like a man at a party mocking a mannerless child. "Is that your name? Or merely a title you have given yourself?"

"It's my persona," Krissy said, her voice quivering. Her whole body was shaking, but whether from fright or from rage, she couldn't tell. "I'm Krissy Manchester."

"That's more like it," said the ghost, flourishing the rose at her. "I assume you have met my thrice-great grandson, Leonard Valiant? Although he is unworthy of such a name."

"Yes," Krissy said through her teeth. "You're holding him prisoner."

"Yes," said the ghost. "Until he produces a painting of something beautiful. Or drinks himself to death. He seems set on the latter."

"Why don't you let him go?" Krissy said. "He wouldn't drink if he weren't so miserable."

"He was a drunk before he arrived," the ghost said. "He stared too long into the abyss. And now you are here. You cannot leave, either."

"Why?" Krissy burst out. "What'd I ever do to you?"

The ghost smiled, baring sharp teeth that weren't human. "You broke into my house, little girl. That's a crime in any age. You of the two identities and the glasses that allow others to see what you see. Until you decide which of you is real, my mansion shall be your home."

He faded like the Cheshire Cat, the smile lingering after the rest had vanished. His teeth weren't like a vampire's. More like an angler fish.

Still trembling, with heat racing through her, she checked her stream. The ghost must have appeared on video, because her chat was full of people screaming in all caps. If she spoke to her viewers, she would cry, so she ended the stream without a word.

Then she ran back up the stairs to Leo's studio. "I saw the ghost!"

Leo had covered his canvas in black paint. He'd stuck a paintbrush behind one ear, pushing back his dirty blond hair, and for a second he was almost handsome. Then he looked up, and the hollows in his face showed dark. "You did, huh? What'd he say?"

Krissy's control was breaking down. Her voice wobbled up a register. "I'm trapped here until I—until I figure out which of me is real." Tears overflowed. She pushed her mask far up on her head to avoid wetting it.

"Oh," Leo said. "That sucks." He gazed at her a moment, fumbling with the paintbrush in his hands. At last, he stuck it behind his other ear and rose from his stool. "There's a chair over here, somewhere. Come sit down."

He moved aside a stack of canvases and old palettes, revealing a worn sofa that still looked comfortable, despite multicolored paint stains.

Krissy sat down and tried not to sob aloud. "I can't stay here forever! If I can't work, I'll lose my apartment!"

"How do you think I feel?" said Leo, returning to his stool. "It's been eight months. I have a friend who buys me art supplies and food, but he has to pass me everything through this window." He pointed to a rope attached to a bucket that sat under the window.

Krissy buried her face in her arms and sobbed against the sofa's arm. Her terror and despair beat inside her like a bird's wings against a cage. This was stupid, and it wasn't fair. Ghosts weren't real. But she had seen one and spoken to one, and he had scary sharp teeth ...

Slowly her sobs quieted. She lay there against the sofa arm, her mind tracing the mansion's layout, seeking an exit the ghost might have overlooked. She turned her head to ask Leo about it, but lost her train of thought.

Leo was painting with rapid brush strokes, glancing at her now and then. The shape of a reclining woman on a sofa was taking shape on his black canvas, outlined in light from a window. "Stay there," he said softly. "Don't get up. Turn your head that way. Thanks."

"You're painting me?" Krissy said, interested and flattered.

"Your suit is silver and picks up the light," Leo said without looking up. "Incredible value grouping. I've got to try to capture it."

Krissy sat motionless, watching him paint out of the corner of her eye. Maybe this would be a painting beautiful enough for the ghost to let him go. The lines of it were certainly graceful and pleasing. The bright colors of her suit popped against the black background. He added touches of red for her boots and cape, then began on the way the light touched her hair. But when he got to her face, he painted a vague shape, then stuck his brush in a jar of turpentine with a disgusted growl. "You might as well get up. I'm done."

Krissy climbed to her feet and went to look closer at the canvas. "It's wonderful. You did it so fast! But what happened with the face?"

"I can't do faces," Leo said, taking a drink of cheap wine straight from a bottle.

Krissy watched him. "But you used to draw faces all the time at school. Cartoons, and—and what are they called?"

"Caricatures," Leo said, setting the bottle down. "Those don't count. I learned at art school how to draw faces for real. And I haven't been able to paint a single face since I got trapped in this stupid house. They all turn out like that." He jerked a thumb at a sketch book lying open on an end table. It was covered in screaming demon faces.

"You can practice on me," Krissy said.

Leo's eyes played over her face. "Maybe. Let your hair down."

Krissy pulled the tie from her ponytail. Her blond hair fell around her face in waves. She shook it out and gave Leo an inquiring look.

He smiled a little. "That's more like it. If you have to be stuck here with me, you might as well be my model."

~~~~~

Thus began a strange series of days with the two of them unwillingly living together in the haunted mansion. Krissy tried everything to escape from the house, but the ghost was always waiting for her. Leo accompanied her sometimes, grimly amused at her efforts.

He offered her any room in the mansion as her own. She selected one at the far end of the house, with blue and white wallpaper and a huge black bass mounted on the wall. She cleaned the room for a whole day and was pleased with the results. It gave her the itch to clean, so she tackled the kitchen, next.

Krissy summoned bubbles of soapy water and dipped a sponge in them, humming to herself. She was scrubbing the sink when Leo said behind her, "You're a wonder, Kris."

He leaned on the counter with a frozen pizza in his hands, watching her in fascination.

She gestured to her soapy orbs, which swirled with blue and green detergent. "I can call any kind of water, and anything that goes in water."

"Can you do coffee?" he asked with interest.

She nodded. "Hot water is dangerous, though. I have to draw that from hot springs, and it's more unpredictable. But it's a great weapon." She studied him. "Can you still use your power?"

He smiled and lifted a hand. His arm swelled and expanded, the muscles bulking out. It looked odd, the thin, unhealthy man with a huge bodybuilder arm. After a moment, he let it shrink to normal. "I haven't the strength to maintain it long. This kind of power has to work with what's already there, and the flabbier my normal body is, the harder it is to shift. Makes me hungry."

"The alcohol probably doesn't help," said Kris, returning to scrubbing.

"Probably not." Leo unwrapped his pizza and put it in the microwave. "Hey, you cleaned this, too?"

"Yep," Kris said. "Looks like you'd exploded a casserole."
~~~~~

"Ask me no questions, I'll tell you no lies," said Leo, grinning.

Kris scrubbed the kitchen and mopped the floor multiple times to remove layers of grime. Leo sat at the counter on a bar stool and watched her. They chatted as she worked. Leo asked if she wanted help, and Kris told him no, since mopping the narrow kitchen was a one-person job. Instead, they talked about their lives and interests. Leo had once been involved in the superhero scene, but from an aesthetic angle: he adored super suit designs.

"Remember Angelbow? I helped her make her suit," Leo said, doodling in a sketchbook. "The way the feather designs cross her chest and wrap around her back."

"I always loved her look." Krissy banished a bubble of dirty water and summoned a fresh one. "Did you ever post your designs anywhere?"

"I had an art blog," Leo said, sketching. "I stopped updating it when Mom died. I just ... lost my mojo."

"I'm sorry." Krissy sat back on her heels and gazed at him. "She was so nice. It's a shame."

"Yeah," Leo said, leaning his head on one hand. His gaze met hers for a moment, then flicked away. "I keep thinking I'm over it, but I'm not. Then Dad's lawyer calls me up and tells me that this mansion is mine, now. Dad was unloading assets to escape some tax thing, so he shoved this place on me. I dropped by for a look, and the ghost showed up and demanded a painting. I thought I'd whip one up and be on my way. Eight months later ..." He gestured to the kitchen. "Still here. Doubting my art. People saying I'm into crime or whatever. Must be when Louis brings me supplies. Pretty suspicious."

"For the record, I didn't think it was true," Krissy said, scrubbing the floor. "I was only trying to make an entertaining stream of this place."

"So, what's your beef, then?" Leo said. "You must have some problem or the ghost wouldn't have latched onto you."

"I guess ..." Krissy thought about it, sweeping her rag in circles. "I guess I've put so much of myself into HeroTube, there's nothing of me left. I barely have any privacy anymore. It all goes online to keep my view percentages up. So I guess ... I'm lost."

She looked up to see Leo frowning. "I understand that. It's sad, but that's why Dad left. He's a HeroTuber, too, and he could never separate himself from his persona. You ever watch Bonfire, the federally funded hero? That's him."

"I never liked Bonfire," said Krissy, scrubbing in fierce strokes. "There's something plastic about him, like he tries too hard."

Leo laughed. "That's Dad. He was like that in real life, too. I never really knew him."

Krissy rose to her feet, rubbed her back, and surveyed the floor in satisfaction. "Much better. Stay off this until it dries, okay?"

"Will do." Leo slid off his stool and gathered up his sketchbook. "I'm heading back to my studio. Coming?"

"Sure," Krissy said, rinsing her rag in the sink.

She followed him upstairs and flopped on the sofa. Leo set about transferring a sketch onto a canvas, marking its dimensions with dots. Krissy dozed off, watching him.

When she awoke, two hours later, the canvas had transformed. Leo was painting while standing, his brush at arm's length, applying precise, deliberate strokes, his palette in his other hand. He'd created a candid shot of Krissy on her knees with a sponge in one hand, her eyes raised to the viewer in a soulful gaze. He'd captured her likeness perfectly, conquering his own reluctance to draw faces.

Krissy lay still, watching, not wanting to break his concentration. Gradually, she became aware of the ghost. He stood behind Leo in his suit and cravat, his hands behind his back, watching intently. He was nearly opaque, only transparent around the edges. The longer he stood there, the more solid he became, as if he were drawing some virtue from the painting that empowered him.

At last Leo rinsed his brush and turned to the ghost. "Well, Grandpa?"

"Well done," said the ghost. "I believe that fulfills our agreement. You may go." As he spoke, doors unlocked with a chorus of clicks all around the house.

Krissy sat up, hope springing within her. "Me too?"

The ghost turned and pointed his rose at her. In his newly solidified hand, the rose was solid, too, a dewdrop clinging to the petals. "You remain here until you decide which of you is real." He turned on his heel and vanished in a swirl of smoke.

Leo and Krissy exchanged a despairing look.

"Here's what we'll do," Leo said, wiping his hands on a paper towel. "I'm going to find a priest I read about who does exorcisms. He's here in town, somewhere. I'll bring him back, get rid of the ghost, and you'll be free."

"How long will that take?" Krissy said. The thought of being alone in that huge house with the ghost sent cold creeping through her middle.

"I'll be back by tonight," Leo said. "Six hours, tops."

He left with the air of a man fleeing prison. Every door and window locked itself after him, ensuring Krissy did not escape. She stood at a downstairs window, watching as Leo vanished through the outer gate. He seemed to take all hope and cheer with him.

The mansion darkened around her. The ghost appeared at her side, smiling and showing his ghastly teeth. "Now, Miss Manchester, we will find out who you are."

Claws clicked on the wood floor somewhere in the house. Krissy spun around, hands to her mouth. Far down the main gallery, something moved: a huge black dog, its eyes glowing a demonic red. It growled.

Krissy considered running upstairs and hiding in her room. But a dog that size could break down her door in a few hours. She'd have to escape another way.

She summoned bubbles of the hottest water she could reach—water from volcanic vents on the seafloor. She conjured five, six, seven steaming bubbles, and all the time the dog paced toward her.

When it was ten feet away, Krissy hurled her bubbles. The boiling water splashed across the dog's face and sides. It yelped and howled in pain, shaking its head and pawing at its muzzle. With luck, she had blinded it. She dashed for the stairs.

Claws scrabbled on the floor. The dog charged after her, hunting by hearing and scent. She climbed halfway up the stairs, then made steps for herself out of flounders again. From there, she flung herself onto the huge chandelier in the middle of the gallery. The dog leaped after her, missed, and hit the floor with a grunt. It circled beneath her, its eyes still glowing, teeth bared.

Krissy crouched there, swinging back and forth, feet braced on the chandelier's iron frame. The crystals tinkled a chorus whenever she moved. The chain attaching it to the ceiling looked secure enough, for now.

Another dog emerged from the shadows, its eyes glowing red. Another joined it. Soon a pack of them filled the gallery, pacing about and watching her with unnerving growls.

"Leo will be back in a few hours," Krissy told herself. "I can last that long. Please. Let me last that long."

She pulled on her mask and activated her stream for company. Within minutes, curious fans joined her chat.

Krissy narrated an update to them. She explained about being trapped in the mansion by an actual ghost, and how it wanted a painting from Leo. "But it wants me to decide if Krissy is real, or if Silver Barb is real. I don't know how to answer. They're both me."

The chat filled with people discussing this, talking psychology and philosophy. Krissy watched it scroll by. She also watched the dogs. Some of them climbed into the covered furniture and jumped from there, trying to reach her, their teeth snapping. None of them lay down, like real dogs. What would happen when Leo came back? Would they attack him?

The chat began to wander from the subject, watching the milling dogs with her. Krissy would have to figure herself out. She mentally looked at herself, crouching on the chandelier with a cramp developing in her leg.

Some superhero she was. She was only a HeroTuber with amusing powers that looked good on screen. She had zero home life, no interests except her powers, no relationships except with other HeroTubers. At least Leo could paint and had drinking problems, things a real person struggled with. Krissy didn't even have those. Maybe, if she survived, she could work on rediscovering Krissy, and maybe explore having a life outside of Herotube.

Time passed. The afternoon waned toward evening. Krissy found a more comfortable position on the chandelier, growing hungry and tired, but she dared not leave her perch. Night fell. The batteries ran out in her streaming mask and her stream went off the air. Still Krissy waited, hoping and hoping that Leo would return with help. Hadn't it been six hours? Or longer? She was tiring. Below her, the dogs sat in a circle, their eyes fixed on her, waiting. It was only a matter of time before she fell.

The night wore on. Krissy dozed twice more, each time catching herself before a fatal fall. The chain holding the chandelier began to creak ominously. She summoned a bubble of cold coffee to keep herself awake. She summoned a salmon and dropped it to the dogs, hoping to distract them with food. But the animals didn't even look at the flopping fish. She finally banished it again, discouraged.

The dogs began leaping, one after the other, and snapping at her legs. They took turns, each one leaping from a different vantage point on the floor, or stairs, or furniture. Her adrenaline surged each time a pair of jaws lunged at her. All she could do was sit there and wait.

I've become the damsel in distress, she thought. *How humiliating.*

Near dawn, a crash at the front door startled her. Voices outside. Keys jingled. Leo's voice yelled, "Kris! Are you all right?"

"I'm trapped!" she yelled, hoping he could hear her. "Watch out, there's demon dogs!"

The dogs abandoned their jumping, ears pricked toward the entry. Half the pack trotted off to investigate.

Another crash shook the mansion and the doors caved in, torn off their hinges. Leo stood there in the gray dawn light, his body grown to massive proportions, bulging with muscle. His shirt and pants had torn, giving him a wild, frightening look. But to Krissy, he was the handsomest man who ever lived.

Leo sprang inside and tore into the demon dogs, who leaped at him, snarling and snapping. He threw them in every direction, fighting his way toward Krissy. They leaped for his arms, dragging him down, while others lunged for his throat.

They were going to kill him! Krissy drew a deep breath and began summoning a huge water bubble a few feet above the battle. When it was the size of a car, she called a vicious tiger shark to occupy it. Then she dropped it on the dogs.

The shock of cold water made the dogs release Leo. Leo gasped at first, then laughed. The shark thrashed on the floor, its jaws snapping. Several dogs didn't move fast enough to avoid the jagged teeth. Their howls and yelps split the air.

The other dogs, slipping on the wet floor, resumed their attack on Leo. But Leo grabbed the shark by the tail and swung it like a club, beating the dogs aside.

This was such a marvelous sight that Krissy shifted positions, trying to see better. One foot slipped through the chandelier's frame. A dog leaped and snapped his jaws on her boot. The jaws locked, and he hung there, jerking his head back and forth, trying to knock her loose. She shrieked, grabbing at the chandelier frame. The weakened bolt slid out of the ceiling another quarter inch.

The chandelier tore free and hit the floor with a terrific crash of shattering glass. Krissy's leg that had been in the dog's jaws took the brunt of the impact and her knee snapped. She screamed in agony. She couldn't disentangle herself from the metal and glass, and the broken glass slashed her every time she moved.

She looked up and saw the ghost standing there, staring down at her with red light in his eyes. "Save yourself, superhero."

Krissy summoned a bubble of boiling water and flung it at him. It passed through his transparent body and splashed on the wall behind him. The ghost laughed. He pointed at her and hissed. The dogs responded, charging through the broken glass, heedless of injury, to attack Krissy. She bent over, arms wrapped around her head, as their teeth tore at her.

Then Leo was there, beating them off her, punching and kicking, even as the glass cut his feet, too.

Behind him, a priest entered the house, carrying a crucifix and praying aloud, sprinkling holy water as he went. The dogs scrambled away from him. As the holy water touched them, the red light left their eyes. The ones attacking Leo and Krissy turned their ire on the priest, instead—only to be exorcised. They fled out the front door, whining.

Leonard heaved aside the remains of the chandelier and lifted Krissy in his huge arms. She was covered in blood, her clothes were torn, and her broken leg hung at an awkward angle. She sobbed in pain and relief. "Thank you, thank you! The ghost was trying to kill me!"

Leo turned and glared at the ghost of John Marshal Valiant. "You have no more power here, Grandpa. Get out of this house."

"My power was intended to help you," said the ghost with a grim smile. "You rediscovered beauty. And she has not only been repaid for breaking into my house, but she has discovered who she truly is."

The priest stepped up beside Leo and raised his crucifix.

The ghost smiled. "Yes, yes, I will go, now." His form blew aside in a mist that swirled into nothing. The rose fell to the floor. At once, the whole mansion became lighter, friendlier, as it had when Leo had been released. But this time, the ghost would not return.

Leo picked up the rose and handed it to Krissy, bending his head over hers. "Come on," he whispered huskily. "Let's get you to a hospital."

"Thank you, Leo," she whispered. "For coming back."

His face was inches from hers. She gazed into his eyes and saw the tenderness there.

"No more curses," he whispered. "No more booze. Only beauty from now on."

"Real beauty," Krissy replied through her tears, lifting the rose. "The kind that smashes down doors to save helpless women."

He laughed and carried her out of the mansion. "You're all the beauty I need."

END

HEN HOUSE

Deborah Cullins Smith

"I'm so bored, I could scream."

Janice tossed her golden hair in a backward flip with both hands. It was her signature move to show off the golden waterfall of curls and her fancy array of jewelry. This time it backfired. The prongs around a yellow diamond teardrop ring caught in her hair.

"Ouch!" She jerked to free her hair from the ring, and several strands left her scalp. She scowled at the ring. "I **told** Father I didn't want a raised setting."

Her brother, Jerrod, smirked as he shuffled a deck of cards. His hand-tooled boots propped on the tabletop, he leaned back in his chair with an insolence borne of privilege and wealth. Blond waves of carefully styled hair framed a handsome face, full lips twisting in a sardonic grin.

"Father knows best," he quipped.

"Oh, shut up!" Janice snapped. She smacked his feet off the table, and his chair tipped precariously. He caught himself before hitting the floor.

"Touchy, touchy," he murmured.

Their companions howled with laughter. Brian and Maggie, twins of the Macaw House, favored exotic silk tunics over white linen slacks. Their dark eyes glittered under the florescent lights of the lounge, the Bird Cage. Both teens carried themselves with the lethal grace of jungle cats—sleek, beautiful, and potentially dangerous.

"Keep wearing your shiny baubles and soon you'll be bald," Maggie gasped, her giggles rippling between her words.

"Maybe I'll just reach over and rip your hair out—with both hands." Janice glared across the table.

Maggie leaned forward, a dare in her eyes. "Maybe you should try, little princess."

Brian and Jerrod reached out and eased their sisters back from temper's edge.

The doors to the lounge opened and Jerrod groaned at the sight of the black-clad Owls. Edward and Jonathan strode toward their table, their black knee boots clicked against the tile floor. Owls were the peacekeepers—both on their home world and aboard the airship, *Hope Rising*. The massive space-faring vessel was the newest product in exploration. While their home world struggled from depleted resources, many of these ships had been sent out to find new homes, new sources of life for their wandering clans. The Owls kept order in society. The main challenge for them had been the undisciplined behavior of the children of Hawk House and Macaw House. Edward and Jonathan spent more time watching these four teens than the rest of the ship combined.

Hawk House was the wealthiest and had been the apex of the ruling class for centuries. Stanton Hawk had headed this project and brought his children along, partly because he had hoped to teach them some sense of responsibility for their future and partly because they couldn't stay out of trouble for more than a few minutes at a time.

Macaw House had made their fortunes on the beauty of their rich islands. Tropical paradises made perfect vacation spots for the world's wealthy. Too perfect. Soon condos and elaborate villas had encroached on the natural beauty of their islands. The wildlife had been hunted to the point of extinction. Even their House sigil—the Macaw—was endangered. Saving as many species as possible from the home world was the order of the day.

The Crow House gave the world the intelligent classes—scientists, architects, physicians, and those who could use their brains to preserve their people. Victor Crow was the head of his House aboard the *Hope Rising*. An egghead supreme, he lived in his laboratories with his pet crow, Archie, and his two sons, Matthew and Michael.

The last House was Hen House. These were the farmers and the keepers of cattle and poultry. Hens were their greatest commodity, providing both eggs and meat. They were humble people, not given to violence in any form, but they were necessary to the survival of this society. No one else knew the intricacies of growing food or caring for the animals like these gentle people did. But the Hen House was scorned by the Hawks and Macaws, a cause of much social friction.

As Edward and Jonathan approached, Jerrod groaned and flipped his cards in the air, scattering them across the table.

Brian leaned back in his chair. "Well, well, well. What brings you to the Bird Cage?"

Edward planted his feet and folded his arms across his chest. "Lunch time. But it's always a good idea to make sure you children aren't disturbing the peace."

"Children?!" Janice bristled. She leapt to her feet. Scanning the room, she glared at the few patrons and the waiters. "Who would dare to call the Owls on us?"

Edward and Jonathan exchanged amused glances. Jonathan's left hand landed on Janice's shoulder. He turned her slightly to face the bar. He pointed with his right hand.

"See that camera?" He shifted her again. "And that one over the door? We monitor this entire ship. All the time."

Janice jerked away from his hand. Her face was sullen as she sat with a huff.

Edward shook his head. "Just take it down a notch, okay?"

The teens scowled and rolled their eyes at the Owls. Jonathan would have liked to knock their heads together, but Edward sighed and shook his head. It wasn't worth the paperwork.

The Owls walked over to the bar and spoke to the barkeep for a few minutes. The door slid open and Victor Crow entered, his large black bird, Archie, perched on his shoulder.

"Lunch time, sir?" The barkeep greeted him genially, pausing in his conversation with Edward and Jonathan.

Victor's sons, Matthew and Michael, followed behind him. Matthew stood head and shoulders above his father, a handsome, athletic young man. Michael, seventeen, was younger and far more dedicated to a good time than to science. His face lit up when he saw the teens at the table.

"Hey, guys!" he said, darting away from his father and brother.

Janice rolled her eyes. "They'll let just anyone in here," she muttered. She still struggled to untangle the long blond strands of hair from the prongs of her ring. "Rrrrrr!" She shrieked in frustration as she threw the ring across the room.

"Shiny!" squawked Archie as he sailed off Victor's shoulder in the direction of the discarded ring. "Shiny! Shiny!" He sailed up to the metal ceiling struts with the ring in his beak.

"My ring!" Janice screamed.

Michael laughed. "Well, in all fairness, you did throw it away." But the adoring gleam in his eyes belied his flippant words. Brian and Maggie smirked at one another. Michael's crush on the beautiful Janice was obvious to everyone on the ship. He wore his heart on his sleeve, and right now the poor boy was almost giddy with the joy of finding the teens just waiting here in the Bird Cage for his lunch break!

Jerrod cast a worried look at her. "Father paid a fortune for that ring, Janice. If you lose it to a bird..."

Archie plucked the hair from the ring, holding it with his talons and pecking with his beak. "Mine!" he shrieked. "Mine!"

"It's **mine**, you stupid bird," Janice screamed.

Victor strode forward, Matthew and the Owls close behind him. "Here now! Archie, come down here. What's all this fuss?"

"Your bird has my ring and I want it back," Janice hissed.

"Mine!" squawked Archie, dropping shredded hair from his perch.

"Well, he's giving you back your hair," Maggie murmured. "That's a start."

Janice kicked off her stiletto pumps. Bending down, she picked up one and chucked it at the crow.

"No!" shouted Victor.

Jonathan grabbed her arm before she could throw the second shoe.

"That's enough," he ordered.

Edward stood at Victor's side. "Can you get your bird down, sir? We don't need more trouble here."

Archie squawked at Janice, flapping angry feathers.

"Archie, come here," Victor urged, reaching into his pocket for a handful of corn. Spying the treat, Archie flew down and landed on Victor's forearm.

"I, Brian of Macaw House, will retrieve your ring, fair lady." Brian made a quick grab for the ring and was rewarded by a sharp beak to the knuckles. "Ouch!" he cried, jerking his hand back.

"Terribly sorry, young man, but that is not the way to retrieve something from a crow," Victor said testily.

"How about we make crow stew, then retrieve the ring from the gravy?" Brian retorted.

"Dreadful, nasty bird," she muttered. "He should be blown out of an airlock."

"Nonsense!" Victor scolded her. "Crows are highly intelligent. Far more intelligent than people, I can assure you."

Victor reached into his left trouser pocket. But rather than grain, this time he held a sculpted emerald stone. He held it up, letting the light catch the facets.

"Mine!" screamed Archie. His beak grabbed the stone, eager to reclaim his treasure. The ring slipped from his grip, and Michael caught it before it hit the floor.

Turning to Janice, Michael bowed with a grin. "Your ring, m'lady. That's my dad's best trick to get Archie to cooperate," he added.

Janice glared at Victor and Archie before turning to Michael. "My hero," she murmured. Michael missed the sarcasm in her voice, but Brian and Maggie did not, and they giggled behind manicured fingers.

Matthew groaned. His little brother was just foolish enough to let this go to his head. Giving his younger sibling a smack on the back of the head, he turned to follow his father. "Let's go, Michael. We'll take lunch in the lab."

"I'm going to hang out here for a while," Michael said, rubbing his head. "I'll come to the lab later."

Matthew stopped in mid-stride. "You have projects to wrap up, Michael."

"I know, I know," Michael said with a grin. "I'll be back later."

Matthew sighed and returned to the bar to order lunch to go.

"So!" Michael said, plunking down on the sofa next to Janice. "What are you all doing with your afternoon?"

They stared out the windows at the vast space before them. It had seemed like an adventure when they boarded, but now time stretched out in an endless stream of mind-numbing boredom.

"Let's go to the Aviary," Maggie said. "That horrid black bird made me long for our beautiful Macaws."

"You know we're not supposed to disturb the birds," Brian said with a sigh.

"Who's disturbing? I just want to see them." Maggie's voice held a sultry note that was not lost on the boys.

"And I want to see our hawks," said Janice. She turned her charms on full blast in Michael's direction. As expected, he took the bait.

"I can get you into the Aviary," Michael said with an offhanded shrug.

His heart beat wildly when Janice took his arm and turned on the 300-watt smile. Michael reveled in the smooth texture of her skin, the shimmer in her eyes. Janice Hawk was the most beautiful woman in the universe!

Dazzled by the sultry look in Janice's eyes, the star-struck youth never saw Jerrod roll his eyes, never noticed Brian and Maggie hiding their laughter as they looked everywhere except at Janice and her starstruck hero.

~~~~~

They trooped through the upper decks, past agricultural rooms filled with beds of grain and vegetables. The Crows had done remarkable things with hydroponic gardening to feed their colonies on the long voyage. There were even two sections of fruit trees. Though the scientists of the Crow family had invented the methods of space farming, it took the Hen family to coax the seeds to grow and produce. Stout men worked among the plants, pruning and snipping, harvesting the best produce and planting seeds to keep the crops replenished.

Janice sniffed. "Hens! Such boring people. Why did we even allow them on board?"

"Are you going to sully those lily-white fingers in the dirt, princess?" Maggie snickered.

"If Crows can create all of this," she waved her hand to indicate the temperature-controlled room filled with light to mimic the sunlight of their world, "...then why can't they also tend the crops?"

"We tried," said Michael with a laugh. "There's just something extraordinary about the Hen people. They have a way with plants, animals, birds. Everything thrives in their care. Besides, we do have a few more important things to deal with in the lab," he added, excusing her dismissiveness. She'd never had to study the way he had—to earn a place of respect. Her position was given from birth.

"Are you saying they use magic?" Brian hooted in derision. "I thought you scientists were the brainy ones!"

Michael's face reddened. "It's not magic," he protested. "But it is—"

"Yes?" Jerrod prompted.

"Unexplainable," Michael finished. "Hey, we didn't understand it either. But it's like each of our houses has something to offer. And we need each other to survive out here. Father says we have to have the Hens, or our food sources won't last."

"What?" Jerrod exclaimed. "You don't really believe that, do
~~~~~

you?"

"Are you Hawks going to grow our food?" Maggie's temper flared. "If Michael says we need the Hens, then it must be true. No matter how… awkward they look."

"Maybe the Macaws could try their hands at farming," Jerrod said. "I think Brian would look cute in those overalls."

Brian dove at Jerrod and they wrestled briefly with each other. Brian mussed Jerrod's hair amid Janice's mock shrieks.

"Dude! Watch the hair." Jerrod laughed.

"Hey!" A short man with snowy whiskers stomped toward them. "What are you doing here? Take your rough play elsewhere."

"Says who, little man?" Brian asked, thrusting out his chest and flexing his muscles.

"Must I call the Owls?" The little man's voice squeaked as Brian grabbed his shirt collar.

"Do you know who we are?" Jerrod asked.

"I do." The voice came from behind them and carried a deeper timbre. They whirled to face a tall, gaunt man of ancient years. His eyes burned with an intensity that knocked a bit of the cockiness out of the teens. His bronzed skin lay in wrinkles beneath long gray hair bedecked with a variety of feathers.

"I am Gravant. And you are trespassing."

"That's a macaw feather!" Maggie cried, pointing to a long blue feather beside the man's left ear.

"And that's a hawk feather!" Janice exclaimed. "You've dared to steal feathers from our House sigils?"

"I. Do. Not. Steal." Gravant's words marched from his lips and the floor quivered with his intensity. "We care for your birds as we do our own. When they shed feathers, they are presenting us with gifts. I wear these to honor all Houses aboard this vessel. You would do well to remember that, younglings."

"Younglings?" Brian blustered. "Younglings? Did he just call us…?"

"Let's go, guys," Michael urged. Gravant made him nervous. Michael remembered the day that Gravant first appeared at their lab on the home world. Their experiments had all ended in failure until Gravant appeared and offered his services. Whatever power the old man possessed, it wasn't wise to cross him.

"Go," Gravant said with a grim smile. "Visit your birds. See how well we care for them."

The teens moved toward the Aviary door. Gravant's voice froze them at the threshold.

"But **do not** disturb the hens."

"Come on." Michael pushed them all through the door before they could protest.

"Who is that guy?" Jerrod demanded as they stomped down the long hallway toward the Aviary.

"I'm telling Father." Maggie pouted. "When he finds out how that old man treated us, he'll send his flayed body out of an airlock."

"What is your fascination with airlocks?" Brian asked.

"I prefer the old ways," Janice said. "Long ago, when people crossed our forefathers, they were beheaded."

Maggie laughed. "Wasn't that a children's story? Something about a queen who cried 'off with his head' every few pages?"

"No!" Janice retorted. "It's from the history of the Hawk House. Our people have never tolerated insubordination—or rudeness—from other Houses."

"Really?" Maggie's voice became steel and ice. "Well, little princess, do not think you will take my head unless you want a knife in your heart."

"Hey, hey, hey!" Michael protested. "Enough with the ancient warrior stuff, ladies. We're supposed to be more evolved than that, remember?"

The girls sulked while their brothers threw harmless punches at each other. Michael was beginning to wish he'd stayed in the lab. Matthew constantly chided him for trying to be friends with the Hawks and the Macaws. But he needed companions his own age.

Or so he had believed until today. Then Janice smiled that perfect smile. He felt ten feet tall when she turned her charms in his direction. That she would mock his puppy-love adoration behind his back never crossed his mind.

Brian finally broke the silence. "What do you know about this guy, Michael?"

Michael felt a chill of apprehension. Father always said that what happened in the lab stayed in the lab. Idle speculation could get him into a lot of trouble. And yet… Janice's eyes fixed on him, and he wanted to tell them anything that kept her within his proximity. But where would he have to draw the line?

"Well," he began slowly. "He's something of a mystery."

Jerrod snorted derisively. "In other words, you know nothing."

"Hush!" Janice scolded. "I want to hear what Michael has to say. He'll tell us." She laced her arm through his and molded her body to his left side.

"Not much is known about Gravant," he began slowly. "We were still trying to come up with a way to transport our livestock through space safely, but the stress was too much. Cows stopped giving milk, calves died before they could be birthed, hens stopped laying eggs. And the plants! They just wouldn't grow. Nothing was working."

"And you guys are supposed to be the smartest guys on the planet?" Brian snorted.

"Yeah, well, we were trying. What was your House doing?" Michael shot back.

Maggie gave her brother a push and a withering look. "So, what did you do, Michael? Whatever it was, it obviously worked." She took Michael's right side, and snuggled closely. The effect of both girls on the Crow lad was intoxicating.

"One day, this old man comes down from the High Mountains," Michael said slowly.

Shut up now, his conscience said.

But with a girl pressing against him on each side, that little voice dulled and Michael continued.

"He asked for my father at the gate to our laboratory. They were about to send him away..."

Michael remembered the storm clouds that had formed funnels over the lab, darkening every window and whipping the cedar trees about like saplings. When they rushed outside, Gravant had seen them and shouted, "Silence!" to the storm. The clouds had cleared immediately. Struck dumb, the guards had let the old man walk past, too afraid to try to stop him again.

Gravant had bowed to Victor.

"I have come to assist you in your quest," the old man had stated. "But it must be done exactly as I tell you."

"Perhaps," Victor had said. "That depends on how you intend to help us, sir?"

Gravant had pointed to a particularly woebegone patch of garden. It had been sadly neglected and overgrown with weeds as they had struggled in the lab to perfect gardening under space conditions. Gravant murmured some words in an ancient tongue and sprinkled a powder from a small pouch on his belt. Before their startled eyes, the plants straightened, blossomed, and bore fruit within minutes. Weeds withered, providing mulch for the healthy plants.

Victor had led Gravant toward the lab, his eyes wide. The old man had paused in front of Michael. His dark eyes twinkled amid bronze wrinkles.

"You will want to harvest those vegetables. We'll need their seeds in the days ahead. Don't be wasteful, young man." As he strode away, he added, "That's what has been wrong with mankind. You have grown wasteful."

His words had left Michael uneasy. 'You' have grown wasteful? Was he not part of 'mankind' as well? But Michael could not relate that part of the story to his friends. They would never believe him anyway. Not even his beloved Janice.

~~~~~

"Well," he coughed and regrouped. "Father did let him in, and Gravant showed us some amazing... er... adjustments to our equipment. Within... months... all the kinks had been worked out. He brought in the men of Hen House and here we are." Michael gulped. He'd almost slipped and said 'days'. And the Hen people had been slated to be left behind, an order direct from Stanton Hawk and the Macaws. When Gravant had heard, he threatened to leave them to starve on the voyage.

"Fear of those who are different or special can lead to frightening consequences, Michael," Victor had told him.

Just seeing Jerrod and Brian with his own father today was reminder enough. Let them believe Gravant was a strange old man with feathers in his hair. It was better that way.

They stepped into the Aviary—and gasped!

"I thought all our birds were being kept in metal cages!" Maggie whispered. Lush bushes and trees surrounded them with blossoms the size of a man's cupped hands. Birds flitted in the treetops. Macaws in bright blues, reds, and golds screeched at the teens.

"How did you do this?" Maggie asked, her eyes bright. "It looks just as our islands used to be—before the hotels and casinos and condos came. It's exquisite!"

She flitted from one corner to another in the steamy warmth of the jungle climate. Spinning in circles, with her arms raised, she laughed with pure joy. Brian's face reflected the same awe.

"It's all about climate control," Michael said. "Each habitat is
~~~~~

geared to the creatures who live in it. We just had to find the right conditions for each of them."

Michael coaxed them from room to room. Crows filled a habitat of fir trees. They spied wolves, foxes, and other species of animals largely seen only in zoos these days. Owls filled a densely wooded room. Rabbits and mice rustled in the underbrush. An owl swooped down and snatched up a mouse only a few feet away. Wild hawks circled above, their cries shrill.

He led them to a cozy little nook off the hawk enclosure. Huge cages housed Stanton's special collection of trained hawks for hunting expeditions. Janice and Jerrod spoke softly to their hawks through the bars of the cages. Clearly, they were unhappy, even as Michael explained the difference between wild hawks and domesticated ones. The tamed birds would be no match for the wild hawks who had never known captivity.

"That's it," Michael said lamely. Somehow the tour of the Aviary, which had begun so well, had fizzled toward the end.

"No," Jerrod said. "We haven't seen the hens yet."

Michael's head shot up. "**No**!" The hawks flapped their wings in agitation. "We can't disturb the hens. If they quit laying eggs, this entire ship will have us..." He tried to think of an apt punishment.

"Blown out of an airlock?" Maggie offered with an impish grin.

"Exactly!" Michael said. "I'm rather fond of the air inside this ship myself. We can't disturb the hens."

"Hey, Brian," Jerrod said thoughtfully. "Back in ancient times, didn't people fight their chickens? Like contests? Last chicken standing won."

"Ye-e-e-ah..." Brian drawled. "But I think that was cock fighting with roosters, not hens."

Michael paled. "You can't try to fight them. If we lose the roosters, we could lose the whole flock."

"Oh, we won't fight them to the death," Jerrod said. "We'll just give them a chance to rough each other up."

"**No**!" shouted Michael. "You can't do it. I'll yell for help if I have to."

"Okay, okay," Brian said. "No fighting. We get it, Michael. We just want to see them. And riling *you* up is entertaining enough." He winked at his sister and they burst into laughter.

Michael knew there was no way this could turn out well, but he also saw no way out.

"Keep quiet," he warned sternly.

"Hey, you're the loud-mouth in this group," Brian said with a chuckle.

They stepped through the next door into a rural farmland setting. Chickens milled about, pecking at grain in a dirt yard. Janice stepped in chicken droppings and her stiletto slipped beneath her. She grabbed her brother's arm and recoiled in disgust.

"Ugh. Let's just leave," she whispered to Jerrod.

Maggie laughed and several of the chickens flapped their wings, drifting away from the teens. "Oh, poor little princess! Did you soil your glass slipper?"

Brian watched the birds with dark mischief in his eyes. "Hey, Jerrod," Brian whispered. "Watch this." He crept up to a cluster of hens and yelled "Boo!" as he jumped at the startled birds. The poor hens scattered in fright.

"Look at that one run!" Jerrod howled, pointing to a red-feathered hen.

"My money would be on that brown speckled one," Janice said, pointing at a fat bird who almost lifted herself off the ground in her distress.

"That's it!" Jerrod exclaimed, snapping his fingers. "Let's race them."

"What?" Michael cried. "**No**!"

"Yeah!" Brian jumped at the idea. "We'll each choose a hen, then we'll race them to see who can run the fastest."

"What are you doing in here?" A small man with gray sideburns and dark overalls shook a stern finger in their direction.

"We're busted for sure this time," Michael groaned.

"We're just having some fun with your chickens, Hen-man." Jerrod's arrogance rose at the sight of the little man. "I'm the son of Stanton Hawk. Our money paid for this vessel, which means I'm the boss. We want to race your chickens."

"You shall **not**," the little man squeaked. "Titles mean nothing here. You are trespassing and you must leave. Now!"

Jerrod's fist connected with the little man's face and he fell among his feathered charges.

"Hey!" Michael shouted. "That's uncalled for, Jerrod."

Janice turned on Michael. "No one speaks to my brother that way!" She took a swing at Michael and fell into a bucket of feed. Chickens flew at the young people, furious at the abuse to their keeper, as well as the disruption to their yard. Michael recoiled in shock at her sudden change from adoring to outright attacking him.

"Ack!" Janice screamed as feathers caught in the lace of her tight pants. Jerrod kicked at one of the angry hens and received a few pecks in the shin for his efforts. Janice tried to dislodge the feed bucket from her backside and succeeded in toppling it over on herself. A big red hen pecked at her head, removing a chunk of scalp with her hair. A grey and white hen snagged the lace on her clothing, tearing holes in the delicate fabric.

"Stop it!" Jerrod screamed. Two fat hens had tripped him, and a third one pecked at his hair and his ears. Michael looked on helplessly, unsure who to help first. The hen house was in chaos.

Brian and Maggie grabbed Michael.

"Come on! Brian said. "We have to get out of here. They've gone crazy!"

"We are so fried if they catch us here," Maggie groaned.

Michael pulled away. "I have to stop them. Go! Go!"

Maggie and Brian bolted back the way they'd come.

Michael turned and screamed at Jerrod to stop. Jerrod paused long enough to punch Michael in the face, then he turned to chase down the hen keeper. Michael sprawled in the dirt. He shook his head and rose. Running full tilt at Jerrod, he hit the older boy in a tackle that sent them both rolling in the white bird droppings.

"What are you thinking, Jerrod?" Michael cried.

"I'm thinking that these people shouldn't even be on this ship! I'm thinking the strong survive and the weak don't. I'm thinking you should stay in your lab, Crow."

Fog rolled across the room with a crack of thunder.

"Oh, no..." murmured Michael. "He's coming."

Jerrod turned in circles, ready for an attack. "Who's coming?"

Janice screamed and vanished.

"Janice!" Jerrod screamed. He turned to Michael, his face a mask of pure panic. "What have you done to my sister?"

"N-n-nothing," Michael whispered. "It's n-n-not me..."

Jerrod vanished.

~~~~~

By the time the Owls burst through the doors, Michael sat on the ground by himself.

"I tried to stop them," he whispered as Edward knelt beside him.

"I know, son," Edward said gruffly. "But you shouldn't have
~~~~~

brought them here to begin with. It was a disaster waiting to happen." He turned to Jonathan. "Call the physician. We'll need some bandages to patch up the damage."

"That will not be necessary."

They all turned and watched Gravant stride across the hard-packed earth.

Edward rose to his feet and bowed his head respectfully. "Master Gravant! I assure you, sir, that we will catch the ones responsible for this and they will be punished."

"I am dealing with them myself, Edward Owl," the old man said sternly.

"But, sir, it is a matter for the law..." Edward protested.

"This is Hen House territory, and I am more than capable of meting out appropriate punishment." Thunder rumbled behind his words and his eyes crackled with lightning.

Several other Hen men approached. Two of them helped their bruised brother to his feet, dusting him off. The others leaned down to pet the hens and smooth ruffled feathers.

"Taught them a lesson, didn't you, my girl?" one Keeper muttered to the red hen.

Gravant's eyes examined Michael, looking beyond the shame-faced boy with a bloody nose to the heart that squirmed beneath his gaze.

"This shall be your punishment. You shall come here to tend the hen house morning and evening for the remainder of the voyage." His voice rang with authority. Then he softened. "Your heart is good, young man, but you need to learn the humility of service."

Edward nodded his agreement. Then cleared his throat. "About the Hawk children, Master Gravant..."

"They are well and shall remain so," Gravant said, his voice once more rumbling with authority. "But they will remain here with us. You may tell their father that they will be well cared for."

Edward and Jonathan exchanged anxious glances. That would not please Stanton Hawk, but they had no recourse. Gravant would not be crossed.

Gravant's lips twisted into a grim smile. "If Stanton Hawk wishes to debate their punishment with me, he's welcome to come here to the Hen House to discuss the issue." His eyes narrowed.

"We'll explain, Sir," Edward said carefully. "Hopefully, that won't be necessary."

~~~~~

Michael's encounter with his own father was scathing. Every minute would be devoted to his studies from now on; free time was a thing of the past. Michael agreed with every word his father spoke, remembering the haughty anger on Janice's face. He had suddenly seen her disdain for the rest of their shipmates as somehow beneath her station.

"What was I thinking?" He shook his head. "I must have been totally insane, Matt. She'd never love a Crow. What chance did I ever have with the daughter of Stanton Hawk?"

"Cheer up, little brother," Matthew said with a sardonic smile. "It could have been worse. You could have actually married the little princess **then** discovered what a witch she was."

"Thanks a lot," Michael muttered. "As if that would ever happen anyway. You should have seen the way she looked at me. What do you think Gravant did with her? Do you think she'll be okay?"

Matthew grunted as he smeared ointment on the cuts on Michael's face. "I don't think there is anything that old man could do to her that wouldn't be considered her just desserts at this point. No one is going to be pleased when they find out that egg production is down for today. Those two will be better off if he keeps them confined for a few days."

Matthew helped him clean up and gave him some ice for his face. He spent time alone in study, then a couple of hours beside his father at their workbench making up for the time he'd wasted with the other teens.

A communication on his father's beeper sent Michael back to the Aviary for his evening with Gravant. He raked the yard, moving gently among the hens. They really were beautiful birds. Michael marveled at the variety of colors. Then he spotted a yellow-feathered bird off by herself. She ruffled her feathers, shaking and agitated. She refused to mingle with the other hens and kept herself apart. A large spot on her head looked like feathers had been ripped out. A claw mark had been treated with a thick ointment but looked raw and sore.

"That one is new."

Michael jumped at the sound of Gravant's voice.

"She hasn't quite settled in yet. But she will." The yellow hen squawked at him and put as much of the yard between herself and the old man as possible. She left behind a yellow feather with curly
~~~~~

wisps on the tips. Michael's fingers shook as he picked up the feather, remembering soft white hands rippling through blond curls.

"The other one will make a good rooster," the old man added. "Good for the flock." He chuckled softly. "And you'll take care of them until we land."

"S-sir?" Michael gulped.

"Don't ask, young man." Gravant laughed. "Those other two will behave without their ringleaders to stir the pot. And Edward Owl will enjoy the peace and quiet." He turned and strode from the room, still chuckling to himself.

Michael gasped in horror. He tried approaching the yellow hen, carefully easing himself lower to the ground. He inched closer and knelt near the corner where she had hunkered.

"Janice?" He whispered as he reached a tentative hand out to stroke her head. "I'm so sorry. I had no idea this would happen."

The hen squawked and flapped her wings, her limbs trembling. The other hens cheeped at her and pecked any time they came within range. But she shrieked at them, flapping wildly, and they retreated, cackling among themselves.

Michael shooed the other hens away gently, careful not to touch any of them. He eased closer until he knelt before the little yellow hen. She jerked forward two steps, and Michael picked her up gingerly in his arms. He felt her body tremble against his chest.

"I'll take care of you, Janice. I promise," he whispered.

She squawked again, more insistently. Somehow, he knew what she wanted.

"I can't change you back," he said. "It's not within my power. All I can do is take special care—**ouch**!"

He released the indignant little hen and clutched his chin. Blood seeped through his fingers.

One of the hen Keepers waddled toward him, pulling a handkerchief from his overalls. He tsked as he pressed it to the young man's face.

"Hold that in place until the bleeding stops," he said. He thrust his chin toward the yellow hen cowering in the corner. "She's not happy with her lot. And you—" he leveled a finger at Michael, "will not give her any special treatment. Let her learn to be one of the hens, just like all the rest. It'll do her good." He started to turn away, then he muttered, "Maybe."

Michael still knelt in the dirt where Janice had pecked him.

"But she is special!" he cried. "She's special to me!"

"Oh, really?" the little man said, facing him again, one eyebrow raised. "Why?"

"She's... she's beautiful," Michael gulped. "And she's graceful and ... and..."

"Hmph," the little man snorted. "Beauty never lasts, young man. You might as well learn that now. Once her looks fade, what will hold you together? Her kindness? Her patience? Her goodness of heart?" His voice grew more sarcastic.

Michael swallowed hard. In his mind's eye, he saw Janice flinging her sharp-heeled shoe at Archie, her face twisted in anger. He saw her arrogance when Maggie threw little verbal barbs at her. And he saw her face twisted into that ugly snarl when he had tried to stop Jerrod from hurting the hens.

The Keeper saw doubt flicker over the young man's face. "Just tend the hens, boy, and forget the Hawk. She'll never be good enough for a Crow. You can do better than a princess with hen feathers in her hair."

Michael rose from the dirt. He gave the little hen one last sympathetic smile, but she turned away from him, bristling with anger.

"What am I supposed to do?"

"Finish raking the yard first, then feed the hens," said the Keeper, thrusting the discarded rake into one hand and the feed bucket into the other. "**All** the hens," he added sternly. "No preferential treatment." Then he turned and headed toward the coop to gather what few eggs there would be from the agitated hens.

Michael raked the dirt, careful not to disturb the hens in any way. They moved from his path, clucking among themselves. When he'd finished, he scattered the feed among the chickens, stepping carefully around them as they pecked and strutted. He tossed a few handfuls into the corner where the yellow hen quivered indignantly. She turned her beak from the offerings.

"She'll eat when she gets hungry enough."

The voice of the Keeper made Michael jump.

"Come on, boy," he jerked his head. "There's work to be done. Now we need to tend the roosters. We only put them in the hen coop for a few hours every morning and again in the evening. We'll release them in here, then clean their cages. Easier to do it that way."

Michael wondered if one of them would be yellow in color.

Jerrod would probably not give him a very warm welcome, if he was indeed in that pen! With a sigh, he turned to follow the Keeper out of the Hen House.

~~~~~

Michael continued to assist in the Hen House. Stanton Hawk tolerated the absence of his children for all of two weeks before he sought out Gravant and demanded that his children be returned at once. The conversation was epic—and quite one-sided.

"Gravant," Stanton bellowed, striding across the Hen House, his tunic billowing around his knees and scattering the hens in a flurry of feathers. Gravant looked up from his conference with the Keepers. Michael's mouth fell open, then he studiously applied himself to raking the yard—and trying to be invisible.

"You have kept my children imprisoned long enough. I want them back now." He gave Gravant his most imperious stare. Gravant merely raised an eyebrow.

A small yellow hen clucked nervously at Stanton's feet, but he kicked it away, disgust etched on his sharp features. A ghost of a smile tugged at Gravant's lips.

"I'll keep them away from your … precious hens, if that's what concerns you," he continued. "They'll stay in their quarters with brief forays to the Bird Cage occasionally, but they will not be allowed to enter the animal enclosures again. You have my word."

Still, Gravant remained silent.

At that moment, the doors slid open and Edward Owl entered. He sighed and shook his head, knowing the situation was going south fast.

"You cannot keep my children caged up like one of your stupid birds!" Stanton bellowed at Gravant, his face turning red. The little yellow bird clucked and pecked at the hem of his tunic. Stanton shrieked at her, "Get away from me, you filthy fowl!" He kicked a feed bucket, which slammed into her and sent feathers flying.

"Hey now!" The Keeper protested, his voice squeaking as he scurried over to pick up the little hen and cradle her to his chest. She quivered there for a moment before squirming, a signal she wanted to be released.

"This is no concern of yours, Hen-man, so kindly keep your opinions to yourself. I want my children back." Stanton's disdain was palpable, undisguised class hatred.

Edward started to speak, but Gravant raised one hand and he
~~~~~

fell silent.

"Mistreat these hens again and they may decide that you can do without eggs for the rest of this journey, Mister High and Mighty!" The little man quivered with indignation.

"How dare you talk to me that way!" Stanton exploded.

"How dare YOU!" The Keeper said, his voice rising. "Every human on this vessel is worthy of respect, especially those doing the work required to keep humanity alive. Aside from your money, I see you contributing nothing to this venture. Maybe you should keep a civil tongue in your head, Stanton Hawk, or you may end up sharing quarters with your off spring for the duration of this trip."

Michael peeked up at Gravant and noted that, though the older man was frowning, he looked suspiciously like he was trying very hard not to bust out laughing! Michael had never seen Gravant laugh, but he seemed to be enjoying Stanton Hawk's discomfort enormously. He also displayed a sense of pride in the tiny Hen man who knew his place in this world and in the work that needed to be done, and he was pleased to see the Hen people standing up for themselves.

It's about time, Michael thought. *They've earned some respect. They work harder than anyone else on this floating space tub.*

Stanton finally noticed him and pointed a shaking finger in his direction. "You! You're that Crow boy that got my children in trouble! Where are they?"

Michael looked helplessly at Gravant.

Stanton advanced toward Michael and reached out to grip his lapels. He shook Michael only once before Edward stepped between them and broke his hold.

"That's enough, Stanton!" His voice brooked no nonsense. "Michael did his best to diffuse the situation with Jerrod and Janice that day. Their own actions got them in trouble. His actions earned him the duties of cleaning out cages for the rest of the trip. Not an enviable job, if you ask me. So, unless you want to take over those duties for him, I suggest you leave the boy alone."

"You dare to speak to me—" Stanton's eyes bulged in anger.

"Yes, sir, I dare." Edward's voice was steel. "I'm expected to maintain law and order on this vessel. That means **all** citizens, including you. Laying hands on this young man while he's doing his job is assault and battery. Shall I ask if he wants to press charges against you?"

Stanton quivered with rage. He whirled to face Gravant again. "I want to see my children immediately. Bring them out here right now. I demand it. I DEMAND IT!"

Gravant stared at him impassively for a moment, then very calmly uttered one word—"No"—before turning to walk from the room.

"COME BACK HERE!" he shrieked as the little yellow hen danced around his feet once again.

"Time to leave, Stanton," Edward said, gripping his arm and pulling him toward the exit.

"Not without my children."

"Not going to happen today."

"I want my children!"

"Stanton, I can escort you to your quarters, or I can escort you to the brig. Which would you prefer?" Edward's voice had grown cold enough to freeze the sun.

"How dare you!"

"How dare I?" he asked. "Really, sir? How dare you? Are you really saying you are above the law? In the last five minutes, I've seen you verbally assault three people, one of whom made the food supply possible for this venture, another who keeps that food supply cared for, and another who is not only the son of our leading scientist, but is also doing manual labor because of trouble brought upon him by your son. On top of that, I've seen you abuse a bird that helps supply this expedition in eggs, a food source. And I've seen you physically assault one of the afore-mentioned people. That's enough charges to lock you up indefinitely. Now I've tried to treat you with the respect due your station, but my patience is waning, sir."

Stanton's eyes narrowed. "We'll see about this." He stalked from the room.

Edward gave Michael a lop-sided grin and followed the angry father from the room.

"There, there, my girl," the Keeper crooned to the little yellow hen. He held out a handful of grain to her. "Imagine having to put up with a father like that—OUCH!" The hen pecked his fingers and scurried to the far end of the coop, her feathers fluffed up in angry ruffles. Michael tried not to laugh, but failed. "She pecked me!" The Keeper looked at Michael with shock on his bearded face.

"She's a feisty one, sir," he said. "And you did say we weren't going to give her any special treatment."

The little man huffed. "I was only trying to be nice after her father actually kicked her away. But maybe the action was not unwarranted after all." He turned and shook a finger at her. "Just see if I offer you a special treat again, young lady."

The hen quivered and her feathers ruffled again as she clucked loudly.

~~~~~

Michael heard later that the leaders of the houses gathered in the Bird Cage to hear Stanton Hawk's grievances. He ranted and raved for thirty minutes about the injustices being heaped upon his children by the heathen Gravant. Then he ranted about Edward Owl and his "threats" against his own august personage and the unfairness of it all. Edward bore it all with graceful forbearance. When the floor opened, the general consensus was that the ship had been a far more peaceful place with the Hawk children incarcerated—wherever that might be—and that they would all be dead or dying without the Hen people and Gravant. So, they should all be a little more thankful and a lot less judgmental if they intended to survive. With no one to so much as sympathize with his plight, Stanton was forced to withdraw, wrapped in whatever shredded dignity he could muster.

He tried once more, a month later, to retrieve his children. Edward accompanied him that time. The answer was still no, but he was assured that his children were healthy and thriving, and that their punishment was in no way taxing upon them mentally or physically. When Stanton asked to at least see them, Gravant again said no, and walked away.

After that, Stanton remained in his quarters. Rumors circulated that he had aged terribly from the ordeal. No one dared to challenge Gravant after that. Not that there was any reason to! The inhabitants of the vessel thrived on the food grown by the Hen people and Gravant. And they had so many new chickens and turkeys, they were able to give up a few for an enormous feast at the halfway point in their voyage and again close to the end of the journey. They were always careful not to choose the little yellow hen or the proud yellow rooster though.

And the months flew by.

~~~~~

Michael entered the Hen House for the last time. A flock of fluffy chicks cheeped and chirped at his feet, vying for his attention. He bent down and gave them each a gentle stroke, speaking softly to them.

"One would think you actually like these creatures."

Michael looked up to see the Keeper leaning on a rake, a merry smile beaming through his beard.

"Guess they kind of grew on me," he said sheepishly. He stood, brushing the feathers from his knees. He was taller now, and his voice was deeper. Michael had done a lot of growing up on this trip, and much of it had occurred because of his time in the Hen House. Not only was he fond of the animals he had cared for, but he genuinely liked and respected the Keepers who had trained him along the way.

"We thought your father might keep you in the lab today," the Keeper said, "but I'm glad you came back one last time. It's only right that you should be present today."

Michael tilted his head, a puzzled look on his face. "Why is…" His voice trailed off when the door slid open and a familiar figure appeared. She was still blonde and beautiful, but thinner than she had been the last time he saw her. She wore paper slippers and carried her stiletto heels in one hand. Her hair was combed, but hung in limp strands rather than the beautifully sculpted curls that he'd last seen.

"Janice!" Michael's eyes lit up, though not with the adoration he'd once had.

She cut him to the quick with a withering look. "Still hanging out with the bird people, Michael?" she asked in that condescending tone only a Hawk could convey. "Guess some people will never grow up."

"That's the truth," the Keeper muttered.

Michael smiled at her. "Nice to see you, Janice. I'm sure your father will be glad to have you back."

Janice rolled her eyes and ignored him. Michael glanced at the Keeper and saw him shaking his head in disgust.

He was right! Michael thought. *All those months ago, he hinted that she would never change, and he was right. Wow. Guess I really did dodge a bullet.*

"Come on, Jerrod!" Janice huffed impatiently.

She stalked toward the exit door. Jerrod appeared in the coop entry. His hair was slightly disheveled, and he was leaner, but seemed as fit as ever. His eyes lit up when he saw Michael, and he approached with his hand outstretched.

"Hey, man! It's good to see you, Michael. I was hoping I'd get a chance to say good bye." He grasped Michael's hand firmly and shook it. Then suddenly, he pulled Michael forward into a one-armed hug and patted him firmly on the back. Michael was startled, but responded to the warmth he felt coming from Jerrod.

"Good to see you too, Jerrod," he said. "I mean, good to see you like this."

Jerrod laughed. "Yeah, you've been 'seeing' a lot of me these past—has it been months? Seems like forever, but birds don't do too well with time!"

"Yeah, several months," Michael said. "About a year and a half's worth."

"That long?" Jerrod marveled. "Well, I wanted to thank you, Michael."

"For what?" Michael was truly bewildered.

"You could have really taken advantage of the situation," Jerrod said with a wry grin. "I mean, a human has a big advantage over a rooster. You could have been pretty vindictive."

"Hey, those spurs were nothing to mess with," Michael said with a laugh.

"You know what I mean," Jerrod said. "You could have exacted some pretty harsh payback. But you didn't. Took me awhile to appreciate that, but I did come to realize a few things. I just wanted to let you know that I appreciated the way you took care of us. I think I learned something about being a better man by watching you, Michael. At least I hope I did."

"Enough, Jerrod. Let's go." Janice's tone could have sharpened iron.

Jerrod rolled his eyes. "Guess some things didn't change, huh?"

"Guess not." Michael's smile was rueful.

"Don't pick up that torch again, man," he whispered, leaning in closer. "I hope you're older AND wiser."

"I believe I might be," Michael whispered. Then he returned to conversational volume. "Good luck on the planet, Jerrod."

"You too, Michael. I hope to run into you now and then." Jerrod clapped Michael's shoulder, then hurried off to join Janice.

"So, you did learn your lesson," said the Keeper. "I just hope you remember it."

"Well, there *is* this gorgeous girl. One of the Owls. Beautiful brown eyes, dark wavy hair…" Michael's eyes took on a dreamy haze.

"Oh brother! Here we go again!" The Keeper tossed his rake to the ground in exasperation.

Michael burst out laughing, as he reached down to pick it up. "She's a very nice lady," he added. "Very kind and sweet—at least as far as I've been able to determine."

"You mean you don't know? After over a year on this ship, you haven't figured it out yet? God, give us strength to endure this boy," the Keeper wailed.

"Well, you **have** kept me pretty busy, you know."

The Keeper stopped and stared at him for a moment. "Yes, I guess we have at that."

Michael laughed again, and he grabbed a bucket to help with the feeding of the chicklets and the hens for the last time aboard the ship, *Hope Rising*.

END

SHADOW OF THE CINCHONA GROVE

Cassandra Hamm

Navarro is home today, which means my life will be miserable.

I kneel next to a flowering qantuta. The sun beats against my shoulders and neck, sure to leave burns—but none as deep as words can leave.

I brush my fingers against the petals, focusing my *magia* on this specific plant. It sends me traces of contentment and warm flashes of its surroundings, including myself. Still, I check the crimson tubing on the blossoms, as if my touch could trigger some hidden malady.

Really, I'm just avoiding walking toward Gobernador Navarro, who lingers by my papá on the other side of the garden.

"This patujú looks *pathetic*." Navarro gestures to a shrub. He wears his human skin today, which I much prefer to his caiman scales. "Are you a jardinero or not? Get on with the healing, Verdoro."

I resist the urge to roll my eyes. *We only just got here.*

Papá is much more civil—which is why he tells me to let *him* handle interactions with Navarro. Probably for the best. "My apologies, Gobernador. I will tend to it now."

"Good." Navarro glares down his long nose at Papá. "Antiguan diplomats are coming tomorrow. This garden must be spotless."

"*Sí*, I understand." Papá dips his head.

I crush a blossom in my fist. The qantuta sends me fury and flashes of my hand wrapped around its pink petals. Releasing my grip, I transmit images of an extra watering. Its wrath calms as its petals bounce back to their original shape.

The plants have always spoken to me. Some Verdoras can control a plant's growth; some can heal their maladies, like my papá; others can bind curses and blessings in the leaves. But I receive the mental images and emotions of those nearby.

Nothing compared to *animales magia,* I know. Every Animalo and Animala in Paloma loves to remind me of that.

"Why aren't you working?" Navarro's low voice is much closer than before.

My head snaps up. Navarro stands over me and the qantuta, his lips curved in a severe frown. He has the same thick eyebrows and strong chin as Manuel but nowhere near the character. Or so I thought.

The surrounding plants send images of sun-speckled fallen leaves. I cling to the soothing transmissions and try to forget the fact that Manuel hasn't spoken to me in a month.

"Verdora!" Navarro snaps.

Doesn't he know my name by now? I lift my chin with all the dignity I can muster. "I was examining this qantuta, señor."

"And what did it tell you?" Frown lines etch into his forehead, almost like scales.

I draw back from the grayish green leaves. "That it's fine."

"Then why are you lingering here?"

Words catch in my throat. His eyes have grown flat and hard like a caiman's.

"Remember that there are others with *verdores magia* I can employ. Ones who are actually *useful."*

I shrink back. The words cut almost as deeply as his son's.

"I'm sorry, Rosa," I hear Manuel say in my mind. *"But you're just a Verdora."*

Navarro stalks away, his brightly colored poncho flapping behind him like a banner. He moves toward his castillo, whose white stone walls stand far above any of the others in our tight-knit community.

The qantuta sends me its experiences—the warmth, the sunshine, the rest. I exhale, focusing on that bit of happiness. At least the plants won't abandon me.

Papá beckons me closer. I stand, my legs wobbly, and cross the cobblestone path. The nearby patujú's down-turned flowers are a paler pink than they should be, its stalk thin and frail.

Papá will fix it. He always does, no matter the cost to himself.

"He won't let you go, Rosa," Papá says. "You're a good jardinera."

Yes, well, I was a good friend to Manuel too, and look where that got me. "I can't heal plants like you, Papá," I say in a low voice. "All I can do is talk to them."

"*All* you can do?" He shakes his head. "You say that like it isn't incredible."

I sigh. It's not that I don't love communicating with plants. It's just... sometimes I wish I had healing gifts, like Papá.

Still, at least I know what I'm capable of. Hortensia, my older sister, is still trying to figure out her *magia.*

"Without you, I don't know what's wrong with a plant," Papá says.

"Other Verdoras speak with plants too," I mutter. "So there's nothing stopping Navarro from hiring them."

Glancing around, Papá lowers his voice. "Please don't refer to him so casually, Rosita. Especially since..."

I know; my position is precarious enough as it is.

I brush the patujú's withering petals. Its reply is weak, a few flashes of me and Papá and a slight tingle of pain. "*Ay ay ay,* this poor patujú!"

"Rosa—"

"We really need to get back to work, Papá." I glance around the garden. It seems so empty without Manuel chasing me through the rows.

A new image forces its way into my mind—a young woman backed against a tree, cornered by a jaguar. It repeats from different angles, sent by dozens of different plants until I want to scream.

That woman is my sister.

"Rosa?" Papá grabs my hand.

"It's Hortensia." I squeeze my eyes shut, trying to focus on the surroundings instead of the beast trying to eat my sister. The cinchona grove isn't far from here, and the clearing behind the jaguar seems familiar.

The plants must be desperate if they're sending me messages from this far away.

"What's happening?" Papá's brow furrows. "What are the plants telling you?"

"I have to go." I squeeze his hand. None of the other jardineros would be of any use, and I don't want them losing their jobs because of our family's problems anyway. "You stay, Papá. One of us needs to keep our job."

Then I bolt through the garden, dodging qantutas and rosebushes and wondering how I can possibly save my sister.

Papá's magic is just as useless as mine in defensive situations. But at least I can pinpoint Hortensia's location.

The plants continue bombarding me with images, showing Hortensia shifting away from the tree and the jaguar following her.

But it doesn't attack.

Could the creature be an Animalo? It does look larger than an average jaguar. But why would an Animalo corner Hortensia?

Whatever the case, I can at least distract the beast so Hortensia can get away.

I enter the cinchona grove, sticks snapping beneath my boots, and try to remember if I've seen the shriveled rosebush at Hortensia's feet. Nothing comes to mind.

Please keep her safe, Díos. I push my body as fast as I can. The plants' incessant communication hammers against my skull, the pictures blurring together until I can barely see my surroundings.

Yes, I know *Hortensia is in danger! Can't you be more specific about where she is?*

A distant growling catches my attention. I hurry toward the noise, vines and branches whipping at my face. The voices are getting louder, clear enough for me to hear—

"You wouldn't hurt me!" Hortensia's high-pitched voice rings out through the forest. "You wouldn't *dare.*"

I dart around a tree and nearly plow into the jaguar.

It's just as the plants showed me—my sister's sharp-boned face, as regal as ever despite her predicament; the jaguar I almost ran over, stocky and short-limbed.

He turns his massive head. His snarl should have made me scream, but I'm too focused on the eyes I've pined over far too many times.

"Why are you threatening my sister, Manuel?"

He doesn't say anything. As if he doesn't recognize me.

Something shrivels in my chest, like the rosebush at Hortensia's feet. After all our years of friendship, Manuel still won't acknowledge me?

"Rosa?" Hortensia frowns. "What are you doing here?"

"The plants have been screaming at me for the past ten minutes."

Her eyes soften. "Thank you for coming, Rosita. But everything is *bueno.*"

"Then why is Manuel attacking you?" I fold my arms over my chest.

Manuel shakes his head vigorously, rosettes rippling and tail lashing. I flinch despite myself at the sight of his long, curved teeth.

Just because he can turn into a jaguar doesn't make him a beast.

Still, I've never seen him so animalistic.

His eyes focus on me as a frown curls his black lips. "Rosa?"

I scowl, ignoring the way my heart has been racing. Pretending that I wasn't just scared for my life. "So *now* you decide to acknowledge me?"

The plants have stopped sending me their frantic messages. No more transmissions bombarding my head, thank Díos.

"Sorry." Manuel's voice is low, almost a growl.

It's the first time I've seen him in a month, and I already want to run away. I ball my hands into fists to keep them from trembling. "What's going on, anyway?"

"Nothing, Rosita." Hortensia skirts the dying rosebush and joins me. "Manuel and I were just talking."

Right. *That's* why the plants were sending me terrified messages.

Why is Manuel in his animal form in the first place? He prefers his human skin.

Unless I never really knew him at all.

I hook my arm through Hortensia's and tug her away. I know what the plants saw. I know what *I* saw.

Manuel was threatening my *hermana*. And I have no idea why.

Hortensia won't tell me anything; I know that. She thinks being twenty years old makes her so much wiser than me at eighteen. But whatever the case, I don't want her anywhere near Manuel.

"*Adiós,* Rosa," Manuel calls after me.

I don't look back.

~~~~~

"You didn't have to leave work for me, *hermanita.*" Hortensia's words pierce the silence of our walk home.

I trudge along the path, kicking up dirt. The surrounding plants send me images of falling raindrops and leaves soaking in sunlight, but nothing eases my mood.

Seeing Manuel tore something inside me, reminding me that things will never be the same between us.

"Rosa, really. You know Gobernador Navarro won't be happy —"

"He's never happy."

"Still, you shouldn't aggravate him. You don't want to lose your job."

"What else could I have done?" I glare at Hortensia.

She clicks her tongue. Her linen dress is stained, but it's nothing
~~~~~

a good scrubbing won't fix. "You worry too much."

"Then why won't you tell me what happened?"

"Because you don't need to know everything, Rosita." She pokes my nose, as if I'm still a little girl.

I scowl and start to take the dirt path toward home.

She grabs my arm. "You need to return to work. If you don't go back until tomorrow..."

I really don't want to see Navarro right now. Not that I ever want to see him, but right now is *not* a good time.

"Rosa."

The gobernador's castillo looms in the distance, white-walled and intimidating. I wouldn't mind never returning, but we need the dineros.

I love being a jardinera, working with the vast variety of plants in the gobernador's *jardín* and learning their hurts and voices. But I don't know if I can take Navarro's disdain one moment longer.

Hortensia tucks a curl behind my ear. "Don't let Manuel ruin your life."

"You're not an Animala, Rosa." Manuel's words echo in my ears. *"I'm sorry. My padre won't allow it."*

I focus on the simmering coal in my chest instead of the tears that want to fall. How *dare* he act as though our years of friendship never happened? So what if we can't be together? That's no excuse to stop talking to me.

I'll be mature about it, even though he isn't. Instead of hiding in the woods, I'll keep showing up to work and being a functioning citizen.

"Fine. I'll go back." I gently shove her. "Now, what are *you* doing away from work?"

Her grin is just as forced as my own. "Ah, yes, back to the wash."

If only she could finally figure out her *magia*. Then she might not be stuck as a laundress.

She squeezes my hand. "I'll see you at home, Rosita."

~~~~~

I think I'd rather face a jaguar—a *real* jaguar, not an Animalo—than an angry gobernador.

"Who gave you permission to leave early?" Navarro looms over me.

The other jardineros pretend not to see the confrontation, but Papá abandons the rosebush he was healing to come toward us. His
~~~~~

eyes are wide, his steps full of fearful energy.

I subtly shake my head. He shouldn't have to face Navarro's wrath because of me.

"You think working for me is something to laugh at, Verdora?" Ridges cut into Navarro's cheeks.

I flinch, but the marks smooth out into his normal brown skin.

"I'm sorry, señor." I force out the words in the politest tone I can manage. "I shouldn't have left without your permission."

"*Obviamente.*" His eyes flash, sharp as a caiman's bite.

"I'll make it up to you, señor. I can work as late as you need—"

"You think I need you?"

I focus on the nectar-filled blossoms of a nearby patujú. Its contentment flows through me, smoothing away the words I shouldn't say.

"I can make sure no one hires you. Is that what you want?"

I look up. His teeth have grown long and sharp, and scales reform on his face. I resist the urge to back away.

He balls his clawed fist. "You won't ever work in a garden again!"

Fear clamps my throat shut. If he lets me go, no self-respecting citizen will hire me.

"Please, señor, give me another chance." I blink rapidly to dispel the tears. "I promise I won't disappoint you."

His coal-dark eyes study me, like a caiman perusing a juicy meal. I try not to squirm.

Díos, please, have mercy on me!

"I'll give you one chance, Verdora." The ridges recede from Navarro's skin. "This garden had better be spotless for the diplomats tomorrow. One complaint and you're gone."

I swallow hard. "*Sí,* señor. I understand."

Only after he leaves am I able to breathe again. The tears take that as permission to fall.

Papá crosses the distance between us, crushing me in a hug. I cling to him for only a moment before pulling away. I don't want to give Navarro another reason to let me go.

"Is Hortensia all right?" Papá asks.

"*Sí.* She's at home now."

"What happened?"

I shrug. "She won't tell me." I decide not to mention that Manuel was the one who attacked her. That would cause more questions than

I can bear—and I don't want to see Papá's eyes crinkle with pity.

Honestly, I just don't want to talk about Manuel.

Before he can ask me any more questions, I say, "You'll have to ask her when you get home. Maybe she'll talk to you." I crack a smile so he won't pester me anymore.

When he looks back at the garden, my smile disappears faster than a jaguar killing its prey.

"I guess we're in for a long night," he says.

"Not you. Just me. *I'm* the one who ran off."

"You think I'll leave you here alone?"

"Hortensia seemed pretty shaken by the whole jaguar thing," I lie. "She needs you more than I do right now."

His eyes search mine. "I suppose you're right. But I don't want to leave you."

"I'll be fine, Papá. This is my mess."

Technically, it's Hortensia and Manuel's fault. But my answer seems to satisfy Papá.

"If you're sure." He brushes a kiss against my head. "Remember, what's happening here is *not* your fault."

"It actually is—"

"Yes, you left without permission, but if Gobernador Navarro were kinder to those of us with *verdores magia,* you wouldn't be in this position."

Navarro has always been a *burro,* but Manuel is good to me and my family, even though we're just Verdoran workers on his padre's plantation. I remember how he used to communicate with the plants through me, how we'd laugh at the simplicity of plant life and wish our own lives were that easy.

He used to love the plant side of nature as much, if not more than, the animal side. But maybe his padre rubbed off on him more than I thought.

"I really need to get to work before Navarro comes back. I don't want to give him another excuse to hate me." I say the words with a smile, but Papá's brow wrinkles anyway.

I hurry toward the nearest plant—a rosebush—before he can coddle me. The gentle pressure of the plant's thoughts is soothing. Its wilting leaves brush against the ground, and sure enough, it sends me the image of a water pitcher.

With a sigh, I get to my feet. I'm going to need a lot of *agua.*

~~~~~
~~~~~

Papá is long gone by the time I hear the noise. The darkness combined with the fact that it's been me and the plants for so long makes the slight rustling sound like a scream.

Setting down the water jug, I mentally reach for the plants. They transmit images of an animal slinking among the night-darkened rows.

"Manuel?" My hands tremble.

A shadow detaches itself from the darkness, framed by waving plants. "It's just me." Manuel's voice.

I exhale. "What are you doing here?"

"It's my family home." The words have a strange edge to it.

"Fine, be vague." I stand, strangely off balance.

He steps closer. His rosettes undulate with each movement, and moonlight turns his tawny fur silver. The air feels charged, like a storm getting ready to break.

"Showing off?" I say.

He cocks his head.

"Your *magia.* Feeling proud of your jaguar skin, are you?"

Something wild flashes in his eyes.

My skin prickles. I'm alone with the boy who threatened my sister. Why haven't I run away screaming?

"Rosa, I need your help."

"What could you possibly need from *me?*" I snap. "I'm 'just a Verdora,' remember?"

He flinches.

"Manuel, I really like you." The words play in my head, as hard as I try to push them away. *"I have for a long time."*

I remember the silence. The heat that flooded through my cheeks as I realized he didn't feel the same way. How stupid I felt for bringing it up and replacing our camaraderie with awkwardness.

"It'll be easier to show you," he finally says. "Please."

Something in his eyes and tone compels me. It's the old Manuel—not the one who removed himself from my life, but the one who made me feel seen and valued.

I spread my arms wide. "Lead the way."

His black lips curl into something like a smile before he pads away, claws clicking against the cobblestones. I follow, ignoring the way my heart is thumping.

It's not like I could do much else in the garden, anyway. I can figure out what's wrong with the plants, but I don't have healing *magia.* Without Papá, I'm useless.

So really, what could Manuel want from me?

We exit the garden and head away from the castillo—good riddance—toward the cinchona grove. I barely have time to wonder what's going on when Manuel halts.

"This would be faster if…" His voice cracks. It sounds strange in his jaguar skin. "Would you be willing to ride on my back?"

My heartbeat stutters. You don't *ride* Animalos. They're humans, not beasts of burden.

Things must *really* be bad if he's willing to humiliate himself like this.

"I just… I don't have a lot of time." His dark eyes meet mine. "So if you're willing…"

"If—if you really want me to," I stammer.

He nods.

My lips part, but no words come. Exhaling, I slide my legs over his back. He smells like fallen leaves, different from his musky human scent.

"Can I…?" I clear my throat.

"Sí."

I grip his ruff with shaking fingers, wishing he wore his human skin. Maybe I would know how to talk to him.

"Are you ready?" His torso rumbles beneath me.

"Yes," I whisper.

He takes off. At first the movement is relatively gentle, his body shifting from side to side, but as he gains speed, the bouncing turns to lurching. Yelping, I dig my knees into his sides and clamp my arms around his neck to keep from tumbling off. His paws thunder against the ground, crushing grass and fallen leaves.

I'm going to die, I'm going to die, I'm going to die!

The wind softens as Manuel slows his pace. His gait evens so I can sit up. My heartbeat continues to race as I look around. Cinchonas rise around us, their bark ominous in the limited light. Is this the same clearing from earlier?

Flanks heaving, he pads up to a rosebush. The dying rosebush.

My brow furrows as I slide from his back, my boots touching the forest floor once more. Then, Manuel beside me, I kneel next to the bush.

The once-pink blooms are dry and discolored, the stalks drooping. I brush my finger against papery petals that crackle with *magia.* And, strangest of all, I don't sense anything from it. No flashes of emotion or glimpses of its surroundings.

Plants inherently trust me. Why is this one different?

Frowning, I turn to face him. "What's wrong with it?"

"That's what you're supposed to find out."

"You mean you don't know?" I arch an eyebrow.

His tail twitches, stirring the grass blades. Is it just me, or are his eyes starting to turn blank, as though he is becoming more beast than man?

It's only Manuel. He would never hurt you.

My fingers tap against my leg. "I can't heal plants, Manuel. You *know* that."

"I know. But you can find out how to fix it."

I have so many questions. Mainly, why does he care about a few dying roses?

Roses that don't speak to you, I remind myself.

I clutch an unblemished blossom to help me focus on the bush, then stretch my consciousness toward the plant, only to meet a wall.

Frowning, I push against the barrier, but it holds firm, as though the plant *wants* to keep me out. As if it were made to keep me out.

This is the work of a Verdoro. A much more powerful one than me.

"I… I don't know what's wrong."

"You can't speak to it?"

I don't understand his tone, not without facial expressions to accompany it. Seriously, why hasn't he shifted yet? Animalos can change from one form to another without breaking a sweat, just as I can hear the plants without even trying, though I use touch to help me focus.

I used to know him so well. He was the boy who shifted into his jaguar form when people teased me for my *magia.* The boy who wanted to know about the plants' inner lives. The boy whose smile felt like a balm from the hot sun.

Now I don't even know what to say to him.

"Rosa?"

I jump, pushing my thoughts back to the task at hand. "Sorry you brought me out here for nothing."

He sighs, giving me a glimpse of his fangs. "I really thought you'd be able to figure it out."

"Sorry," I say again.

"Don't be. It's not your fault she—" He bites back his words, pain flashing across his face.

A blossom withers right before my eyes. A petal drifts to the jungle floor, settling against the grass.

My muscles go rigid. I can't breathe, can't *think.*

"Please don't ask." He closes his eyes. His chest heaves up and down. "I've told you too much already."

"Why? Because I'm '*just* a Verdora'?" My jaw clenches.

His mouth opens, then closes. He looks away.

"My padre… you know what he's like." His words ring in my ears like a mosquito that just won't leave me alone. *"If I was with a* Verdora, *he'd never speak to me again."*

"Never mind. Forget I said that." We're not here to talk about that awkward conversation. We're here to figure out what is going on with this bush.

I reach again for the plant, sending messages of kindness. Instead of earning the plant's trust, my efforts slam against an invisible barrier. No return messages come, only an eerie blankness.

I turn my thoughts to the plants around the bush. It's difficult sometimes to get them to pin down a specific moment, but I send them images of the strange bush, and they give me images in return—

A shadowed figure, a hood shielding their face, moving long, slender arms. The bush shivers as if touched by the wind.

A Verdoro—or, if Manuel's slip is any indication, a Verdora. Then I notice who is behind the woman.

A boy kneels on the ground, his moonlit face full of anguish, his mouth gaping in a wail.

I know that chin. I know those eyebrows.

My eyes pop open. "What does this plant have to do with you?"

Manuel's tail lashes again, harder this time. "Stop asking me questions."

"You mean…" I bite my lip. "You actually *can't* talk about it? The Verdora won't let you?"

The silence is answer enough.

"*Cielo,*" I whisper. "Did she place a *curso planta* in the leaves?"

When Manuel meets my gaze, the raw pain in his eyes cuts me to the core.

My lips tremble. Is this a *curso muerte*—a death curse? Is that why he's so desperate for me to figure out what's wrong? When the plant dies, does *he* die?

But I can't ask him that. He won't be able to answer.

"There's nothing you can do, Rosa," Manuel says.

Nothing except find the original Verdora. Only she can break the curse.

Why didn't the plants warn me when this was happening? They told me Hortensia was in danger, so why not when Manuel was being *cursed?* Does the Verdoran *magia* interfere with their communication? Maybe their transmissions were blocked.

His jaw tightens. "Rosa, let it go."

"No! I have to figure out what's wrong."

The plants around me transmit red-hot flashes of fear and images of me confronted by a jaguar. As if they think I'm in *danger.* From *Manuel.*

"You *can't,*" Manuel snarls. "I should've known you wouldn't be able to."

There's something wrong in his eyes, something blank and cold. His muscles bunch, as though he's about to pounce. The burning coal inside me dims, replaced with a hard knot of panic.

Is it because of the curse? Because this is not the Manuel I know.

Maybe that's why he's been avoiding me. Because he's changing into something *other,* something *else.* Something inhuman.

His nostrils flare as his claws dig into the ground. I edge backward, my skin prickling.

"I'm going home," I say.

His tail flicks back and forth, and he bares his teeth.

I flee, ducking under branches and vines, my heartbeat thump-thump-thumping. But I don't hear any pounding pawsteps or growls, just a faint, confused, "Rosa?"

I don't stop.

~~~~~

"I thought you were never going to come home."

Hortensia is sitting cross-legged on her bed, hand hovering over a potted plant, when I walk into the room we share. Papá was already asleep when I trudged inside, so I can't help flinching at my sister being awake.

"I guess the gobernador forgave you," she says.

I flop onto my own bed, my legs burning from the effort of gripping Manuel's back. "You could say that—but he also made me stay until the garden was *perfecto.*"
~~~~~

Hortensia grimaces, pulling her hand away from the plant she was… I don't even know what she was doing with it.

"Burro," she mutters. "At least you still have a job."

"I know." When I close my eyes, I see the shriveled bush and Manuel's broken eyes. *If he dies…*

Hortensia's eyes soften. "What is it, Rosita?"

The whole story spills out—Manuel coming to me in the garden, the moonlit ride, the rosebush with the Verdoran curse.

Her lips press in a tight line. "You went with him in the middle of the night? As a *jaguar?"*

"Really? *That's* what you're focusing on?" I groan. "My *amigo* is cursed!"

"I thought you said he wasn't your friend." She cocks an eyebrow. "Remember what he said about you being 'just a Verdora'?"

"I know." I cover my face with a pillow. "But… he could be *dying,* Hortensita."

"I doubt he's *dying."*

"But he's cursed!"

"Not all curses bring death." Hortensia's feet hit the ground. The dirt muffles her steps. Her hand closes around my arm.

Reluctantly, I remove the pillow.

She gazes at me with such affection and sorrow I want to look away. "Leave him behind, *hermanita.* He's not worth it."

Tears seep from my eyes. Hortensia wipes them away, her thumbs soft against my cheeks.

"Get some sleep." She kisses my forehead. "The gobernador won't be happy if you show up to work dead on your feet."

I slide beneath the blankets. Hortensia blows out the candle, plunging the room into darkness.

I mentally reach for the plant at our bedside, hoping for comfort. Instead, murkiness surrounds it like a fog. What *was* Hortensia doing to that plant?

Sometimes I forget she's a Verdora. Her work is in washing, not gardening, since she hasn't quite pinned down her magical strengths. Is she experimenting with plants, still trying to discover exactly what she can do?

I should be grateful I at least know my strengths. That's more than some can say.

But I can't help but feel I failed myself, somehow, by not being able to speak with that rosebush. As if I was proving Manuel right—I really *am* just a useless Verdora, unworthy of marrying into the gobernador's household.

If he dies... A knot forms in my stomach.

I dream of falling petals and gravestones.

~~~~~

The Antiguan diplomats spend a lot of time in the garden. A *lot.* Honestly, the gobernador should've given Papá and me a day off, but when I mentioned it, Navarro said Papá needed to be around to help if things went wrong—and that I needed to be around so he could fire me on the spot.

Add that to the fact that I keep wondering if the *curso muerte* overtook Manuel in the night, and let's just say the day is a bit more than I can handle. Only the soothing images from the plants around me keep me from vomiting.

"How late did you stay last night?" Papá murmurs as we watch the diplomats move through the verdant garden. Navarro wears his brightest smile as he engages them in conversation.

I can't believe that man runs our village. Well, I guess I *can;* his confidence and charisma are enough to keep our people trusting him. But I wish they could see that the caiman isn't just a skin he wears on occasion; it's his true character.

"Rosa?" Papá prods.

"Late," I mumble. I'm not about to tell Papá about Manuel's visit, not after the way Hortensia reacted.

"I should've stayed."

"No, I'm glad you went home." I squeeze his hand, then indicate a nearby qantuta. Its petals droop just slightly. "That could use a burst of energy."

He kneels and sends a healing rush through the plant's leaves, making the red shine like rubies, and gets out of the way before the diplomats walk by. At least we're invisible, unmeriting of *any* attention, good or bad. That is, until something goes wrong.

"The garden looks nice," Papá says.

I shrug. It could be better, but at least the diplomats haven't complained. I wish they would just go inside the castillo so I don't have to worry about losing my job.

"It's an honor to have you here at our humble village—" Navarro cuts off mid-sentence, his eyes fixed on something in the distance instead of the diplomats he was addressing. His face drains
~~~~~

of color.

I follow his gaze and see a jaguar. My heart leaps. *He's still alive!*

One of the diplomats flinches away from Manuel. Do they not have *animales magia* in Antigua?

"My apologies." Navarro clears his throat. "If you would return indoors for a moment? I need to deal with this Animalo."

You mean your son?

The diplomats nod and say a few polite words, then turn back toward the castillo. Manuel pads closer, just breaching the garden.

I weave my way through the rows, my boots lightly crunching the soil. I need to see his eyes, need to know somewhere within, he's still human.

"Rosa?" Papá says.

I turn and hold a finger to my lips before continuing through the garden.

No one will notice. After all, I'm just a jardinera.

Once the diplomats are inside, Navarro closes the distance between him and Manuel. His hands are balled into fists. Manuel blinks at his padre.

"What are you doing here?" Navarro's hiss is just loud enough for me to hear. "I told you to stay away until you can get" —he gestures to Manuel— "*this* under control."

My eyebrows knit together.

"I can't break it." Manuel's voice is a low rumble. "So I wanted to see you one more time before..."

My legs buckle. I catch myself on a nearby stalk. Fortunately, the Navarros are too embroiled in conversation to notice.

He is *going to die.* My throat clamps shut. *How could this happen?*

Other Verdoras work in the Navarros' garden. Maybe one of them cursed Manuel to punish Navarro for the way he treats us. But why wouldn't they just curse the gobernador? Why go for his son, who has always been kind to us?

My mind rushes back to the present as I realize I've missed part of the conversation. Now, Navarro says, "You were already dead to me."

The pain on Manuel's face makes me want to wrap my arms around his furry neck, hang on until every ache is gone. If I could take his pains, I would.

But this is something I can't fix.

A nearby patujú sends me enough clarity to realize that I'm

standing much too close and the conversation is over. I back away as Manuel meets my gaze, his broken eyes searing into mine, and lopes away.

Navarro swears, his hands morphing into gray-brown claws. It takes everything in me to keep from tripping backward. Instead, I bend over the nearest plant and study the lines on its gray-green leaves, trying to calm my breaths.

I look up as Navarro tears a qantuta out of the ground. Soil sprays into the air, spewing across the pristine cobblestones. He flings it across the garden, flattening another plant.

I flinch. The diplomats are here. They'll complain. And then he'll fire me, even though it was *his* mess.

Manuel is going to die, *and you're worried about a job?*

Navarro whips around, his claws dirt-stained. He meets my gaze with beady brown eyes and bellows, "What are you looking at?" He stomps toward the castillo.

My hands won't stop trembling.

Papá comes up behind me, tentative. "What did they say?"

I shake my head, unable to speak. All I know is that I need to say goodbye to Manuel. I can't let things end like this.

"I have to go," I choke out. Then I'm running, my boots clattering against cobblestone, ignoring Papá's shouts.

He won't come after me. He is too afraid of losing his job.

But no job is more important than my best friend.

~~~~~

I'm almost to the clearing with the dying rosebush when I spot a figure making its way through the woods. Despite the sunlight creeping through the canopy, the cloak hides the figure's form.

I press myself against the nearest cinchona, drawing from its strength and sturdiness. Is this the Verdora who cursed Manuel?

The Verdora continues on, heading in the direction of the rosebush. My breath comes in shallow gasps. If I try to warn Manuel, the Verdora might see me.

At least the plants haven't sent me frantic messages yet, so Manuel must still be alive. But why haven't they warned me about the Verdora? Is it because the Verdora's *magia* blocks their communication?

I creep through the cinchonas, reaching out to the plants around me, but they don't show me anything suspicious. All I can do is hope I reach Manuel before the Verdora ends him.
~~~~~

A twig snaps beneath my careless boot. The Verdora turns, her hood slipping to reveal a familiar brown face.

Something in my core turns cold and hard. Brow furrowed, I step into the open. "Hortensia? What are you doing here?"

"Rosa?" Her long-lashed eyes widen. "I thought you were at work."

I bite my lip. "I was. But then…"

"Did Navarro let you go?" She wrings her hands.

"No." I try to make sense of Hortensia's presence. Why is she in the cinchona grove, especially garbed so suspiciously? I can't help but remember the Verdora who tormented Manuel. Hortensia fits the image perfectly.

I shake my head. Surely another cloaked woman would look just like her.

"You should be at work," Hortensia says. "If Navarro finds out you left—"

"I need to find Manuel."

She flinches. "Rosita, I told you, you need to let him go! Is that so hard?"

She's been encouraging me to stay away from Manuel for the past month. Is it because of sisterly concern or because she doesn't want me to know what she did to him?

Could my sister have placed the *curso muerte* on Manuel?

"Rosa." She takes my hands. "What's wrong, *hermanita?*"

I remember how Manuel had her cornered, how she said, *"You wouldn't hurt me."* Killing the one who curses you brings the curse to its completion. I'm sure Manuel knows enough about Verdoran magic to be aware of that. But would he have tried to hurt her if he thought it would break the curse?

My stomach threatens to expel the salteñas I ate this morning.

"Rosa?" Hortensia's tone borders on panic.

I withdraw my hands. "What are you doing here?" I repeat.

Her eyes flick in the direction of the clearing with the dying rosebush, then return to me. "I was just… practicing with some of the plants—"

"Making *cursos plantas?*"

Hortensia's eyes stretch wider than I thought possible. She takes a step back, then another. "Why would you say—?"

"You cursed him." Tears sting my eyes. "You cursed Manuel."

Her mouth opens, then closes.

"Hortensia, how *could* you?" I clench my fists, my throat almost too tight to force out words.

"Because he didn't care!" Her voice cracks. "He broke your heart and *didn't care.*"

Any words I might have said die in my throat. Is she saying... she cursed him for *me?*

"You were so distraught." Tears sheen her eyes. "I couldn't stand seeing you like that—broken, yet *defending* him. Even though he placed himself above you time and time again."

"He didn't—"

"Defending him even now!" Hortensia shakes her head, making her curls bounce. "Even though you weren't important enough for him to defy his father."

The words plunge deep. Suddenly I'm back in the garden in the soft sunset, confessing the feelings I'd hidden for three years, only to see Manuel freeze up. I swallow the lump in my throat, trying to shut out the words *"You're just a Verdora."*

Hortensia lifts her chin. "All he cared about was *animales magia.* So I made it all he would ever know."

"You."

The snarl, more animal than human, comes seemingly from out of nowhere. I whip around, searching the dappled forest for life.

Navarro steps into a patch of sunlight. Though his body is shaped like a human, his face is covered in scales.

What is he doing here? Why did he leave the diplomats?

He points a clawed finger at Hortensia. "*You* cursed my son."

I stiffen.

Hortensia steps back, shaking. "Sir, I... I didn't..."

I clear my throat. "Gobernador Navarro, shouldn't you be with the diplomats?"

"I told them I had a family matter to attend to." The guttural growl goes right to my bones.

Of course, he has as much right to be angry with Hortensia as I do. But he wouldn't *attack* her. Would he?

Navarro moves closer. His irises are blown out of proportion. "You ruined his life!"

Hortensia opens her mouth, then closes it. The panic in her eyes makes me forget my anger.

This is my *sister.* I won't let the gobernador hurt her, no matter what she might've done.

I hurry in front of Hortensia. "She was just trying to protect me, señor, so calm down. We can talk about this. I'm sure she'll lift the curse if you—"

"I won't be *calm!*" Navarro's lip curls, revealing pointed, jagged teeth. "My son is lost to me. Because of that Verdora!" From his lips, the title sounds like a curse.

"I'm sorry, señor," Hortensia says in a small voice. "I shouldn't have—"

"You will pay for what you've done, Verdora."

His body thickens, his limbs shortening. His clothes tear as his skin forms gray-brown ridges, and he drops to all fours. His face lengthens into a snout, teeth protruding over his lips, and his eyes push to the side of his head. A tail sprouts from his backside, tapering to a thin, ridged point.

A caiman. A full-scaled caiman. I back against a tree, my heart pounding in my throat.

He's your boss. He wouldn't hurt you or Hortensia.

But Navarro crawls forward, jaws bared.

A scream tears from my throat. Hortensia grabs my hand, and we stagger away, tripping over the plants I love. Their images pound against my brain until I can't see where I'm going. I trip over a protruding cinchona root, pulling Hortensia down. The breath whooshes from my lungs as we hit the ground.

Hortensia struggles to her knees. My vision flickers, but I can still see the plant in front of me—the rosebush. Its leaves are curled and gray, and its petals have almost all fallen. Only a single pink petal remains untouched.

Soon, Manuel will die.

"Rosa, get up!" Hortensia cries, dragging me to my feet.

I wobble and turn my head. Navarro is almost upon us—

A snarl, guttural and thick, cuts through the air as a shadow surges from the trees and crashes into Navarro. They roll through the dirt and grass, crushing weeds and wildflowers, and rest in a patch of sunlight.

Tawny fur and midnight-black rosettes. *Manuel.*

I allow myself only a moment of relief. His time is almost up.

I turn back to the bush. The only remaining petal wilts far too quickly to be natural.

"Do something!" I scream over the sound of yowls and bellows.

"I can't lift a curse that fast!" Hortensia's hair is tangled, matching her wild eyes. "And he doesn't deserve it!"

"No one deserves to die like this!"

"Die?" She recoils. "What do you mean?"

I frown. "You placed a death curse."

She gapes. "A *curso muerte?* What kind of person do you think I am, Rosa?"

My cheeks fill with heat.

"I just made it so he would be forever trapped in his animal form. A *curso muerte, ay ay ay!*"

Now I know why he didn't shift when he came to ask for my help. He *couldn't.* It wasn't to make me uncomfortable or prove his superiority.

I exhale, my shoulders suddenly free of a load I wasn't aware of carrying. Then the petal detaches itself from the rose and floats to the forest floor.

"No!" I kneel next to the fallen petals, scooping the dry, thin pieces up in my hands. The sounds of battle grate against my ears. "It's not too late, right? You can fix it, can't you?"

"The curse is complete, Rosa." The blood drains from Hortensia's face. "He's a jaguar now."

I whip my head toward the sound of crashing and snarling. Manuel tears into Navarro's torso, slicing through scales, and Navarro's jaws close over Manuel's leg, piercing to muscle.

And Manuel's eyes... I see only a glimpse, but it is enough. The boy I knew is gone, replaced by a mindless beast.

I lunge at the bush. Thorns slice into my fingers. Yelping, I cradle my hand to my chest.

Hortensia joins me on the ground, her hand resting on my shoulder. "Rosita, please, calm down," she says over the noise. "I'll try to lift the curse—"

"Gracias, gracias!" I cry.

"—but I don't know if it'll help." She touches a shrunken leaf and closes her eyes.

I can't bear to watch either her or the battle, so I stare at the blood dripping down my fingers. The plants are no help right now; they're screaming in my head, sending fear and images of the Navarros' mutilated skin.

"There!" she says.

The rosebush is restored, new leaves and blossoms uncurling right before my eyes. I turn back to the battle.

Manuel has his father pinned and thrashing. His dark eyes are wild, animalistic, devoid of humanity, and his jaws hover over Navarro's head, ready to crush his skull.

"I'm so sorry, Rosa," Hortensia whispers. "I was too late."

I can't lose him! I close my eyes and reach for the rosebush before me, prepared for the thick wall—but the bush is free and entirely blank. No memory of the past days. Nothing that could help me.

Panic claws at my throat. My eyes find Manuel's wild ones, and without thinking, I send my mind toward his.

His mind is gnarled and tangled, like the forest at night, more complex than a plant's. I push through the mist, mentally screaming his name. The farther I go, the more I feel like a capybara being hunted by a jaguar—every movement a gamble, every breath a beacon.

Then I see the beast—a shadowed thing, massive and consuming, with grasping tendrils and a gaping hole for a mouth. Is it the jaguar inside him? Or is it what his consciousness has become, now that he has lost his humanity?

No—his humanity *must* be here, somewhere in the darkness.

The shadow moves closer, its form clarifying into that of a jaguar. Then it pounces, its shadow-skin pressing against me like icy vapor. I can't move, can't flee.

"Manuel!" I say through chattering teeth. "It's me, Rosa! Please, I know you can fight the beast—"

The shadow-beast pins me, its jaws hovering over my throat. I gasp, my breaths shallow. Then a dark tendril wraps around my mouth, strangling what else I might have said.

But maybe I didn't need words.

I send memories—of his gentle smile, his quiet laugh, his knowing eyes. How he defends me against bullies and pushes me to be better; how he makes me feel seen and known.

The jaguar growls, its hold loosening just barely.

I continue, releasing memories of him chasing me through the garden; of hugs that I never wanted to end; of laughter that filled the air and released our burdens. The plants lend me their strength, transmitting feelings of joy and bliss and protectiveness, as though they too want to see Manuel human instead of beastly.

The shadow-beast twitches, giving me more freedom to move. But I don't need to move—I just need to deliver the final blow.

Love pours from me—fierce, undying, overwhelming love for

my best friend, my protector, my person.

The jaguar shudders, emitting a strangled noise. Then something else steps from the mist—the figure of a boy, indistinct and glowing.

"Leave," Manuel says.

The beast shrieks, withdrawing from me. I gasp for air, rubbing my throat. My skin is cool where the shadows were.

Never have I been able to immerse myself so fully in someone's mind. It feels *real,* even though I know it isn't taking place in the material world.

"I am a man, not a beast," Manuel shouts. "I am a *man!*"

The shadow dissipates with a piercing scream.

I pull myself from Manuel's mind and find myself gasping on the ground, my vision blurred. I close my eyes and press my face to the ground, drawing from the steadiness of the plants surrounding me.

"Rosa?" Hortensia shakes me. "What happened? Are you all right?"

I open my eyes. The restored rosebush swallows my vision, vibrantly pink. I melt into Hortensia's embrace.

"Where did your mind go?" she asks.

"Into Manuel's," I say softly.

She pulls back, studying me. I touch my throat, wondering if the shadow-beast left bruises.

"But he's not a plant—" Hortensia says.

"I know." Apparently my *magia* isn't just limited to communicating with plants. What else am I capable of?

"*Cielo,* Rosa! He—" Hortensia's voice catches. "He's a *man!*"

With a gasp, I turn. Manuel and Navarro lie on the forest floor, both human and naked. I look away, cheeks hot.

Does this mean that the curse is broken? Did Manuel really banish the jaguar? Or are they both *dead?*

My mind races. Maybe when Manuel sent the jaguar away, he destroyed himself. What if my meddling ruined everything?

"Manuel?" I force the words through my choked throat. "Are you…?"

"I'm here."

I slump, my heartbeat slowing to its normal pace. *He's alive.*

Hortensia unfastens her cloak and tosses it, the thick garment thudding against the grass. "I'm sorry, Manuel." Her voice wobbles.

"I just wanted to protect my sister."

"I know," Manuel says.

"Give me that!" Navarro hisses.

"She gave the cloak to me, Padre." A gentle rustle, presumably Manuel putting the cloak on.

I can't help it. I look.

Black curls brush the nape of Manuel's thick neck. Though he's not much taller than me, his stocky build turns him into a giant. Hortensia's cloak shrouds his muscular frame in shadow, and the raw rage and need is gone from his eyes, replaced by weary awareness.

"You brought me back, Rosa." Manuel's cheeks are streaked with blood. "I can never thank you enough."

Tears fill my eyes. "Is the jaguar…?"

"Gone." His smile brightens his entire face. "No more *animales magia.*"

I cover my mouth, my entire body shaking.

"There must be some mistake," Navarro says. His clothing is in shreds, just barely covering his form.

Scarred, I jerk my eyes back to Manuel, who is shaking his head.

"You're sure?" Navarro says.

"As sure as anything in my life," Manuel says. "No more jaguar clawing at me, begging to get out."

"That's unacceptable." Navarro's lips pinch. "You must regain it."

I hold my breath. I can't lose Manuel, not to his padre. Not again.

But Manuel says, "No."

"No?" Navarro's eyes narrow. "Did you just—?"

"I did." Manuel lifts his chin. "You aren't who I thought you were, Padre. You tried to *kill* Rosa and Hortensia—your own citizens!"

Navarro's mouth clamps shut.

"You can't control me anymore, *Gobernador*. Go back and entertain those Antiguans while they still respect you."

Navarro sputters, reaching for his neck as if to adjust his tattered shirt, then drops it. He backs away, wary but hard-eyed, like a predator abandoning difficult prey. "You will not speak a *word* of this. You hear me?"

Manuel meets his gaze, unflinching.

Lip curling, Navarro stalks into the grove and disappears. Good riddance.

One thing is certain—I am never working for him again. I'll be seeing his toothy jaws in my nightmares.

"I'm so sorry, Rosa." Manuel's voice breaks.

I whip my gaze toward him, suddenly breathless. The furious coal inside me has dissipated, replaced by… I don't know what. But it's deeper than what I felt before when I confessed my "undying love" to him. Still, I say, "You should be."

He winces. "I know. I should never have shut you out."

"You shouldn't have," I agree.

"I thought my padre wanted what was best for our people. What was best for *me.*" His jaw tightens. "Clearly he doesn't."

I suppose family bonds can be blinding. I glance at Hortensia and sigh.

"I knew he would be upset if I… if we…" He looks away, then clears his throat. "I shouldn't have put him above you, Rosa. I'm sorry. And you're not '*just* a Verdora.' You're my best friend, and you always will be."

The words soothe the ache inside. What he did was wrong—just like Hortensia—but I know them both. They mean what they say.

I take his hand. "I forgive you."

"Thank you." His smile starts to mend the tear between us.

Hortensia wraps an arm around my shoulders, squeezing. "I should go find Papá," she murmurs. "Let him know you're all right."

"I love you, Hortensita," I say.

Her smile is warm and full. Then she slips through the trees.

Now it's just me and Manuel. I bite my lip as I stare at his haggard, blood-stained face.

He just fought his father. Almost to the *death.* I can't even imagine how he feels right now. And here I am, making him grovel.

"What are you going to do about your padre?" I ask.

"Tell the truth." Manuel exhales. "The people need to know."

"But then… you won't be the gobernador's son anymore. You've already lost your *magia*--"

"I don't care." He takes my other hand. "I'd rather our people have a leader who truly cares about them. Maybe one who doesn't over-value *magia.*"

I know I need to stop staring into his eyes, but I can't. "You're a good guy, Manuel," I say softly.

"Not as good as I should be." His sorrow melts something inside

me. "But I'll make it up to you, Rosa, I swear."
I smile. "You already have."

END

DAMSEL IN THIS DRESS

Cindy Koepp

Angie Neer set her hammer aside and inspected Morgrim's gauntlet. The dent over the back of his knuckles still glared at her, but it'd probably hold well enough. She checked her skill limit displayed in the top left of her vision. At Level 6, she had sixty total skill points, and repairs to everyone's armor had taken fifty-five of them. She could probably risk one more repair attempt on that dent, but if she exceeded her limit, she'd damage the item. Not worth it. What she'd done would do for today.

She added the gauntlet to the box of armor pieces she'd worked on this evening before cleaning up the station she'd borrowed in the tinkerers' workshop. Like Grandma always said, "Never leave a place worse than you found it." Besides, if she did a good enough job tidying, the NPC in charge of this area would refund part of her fee.

After discarding metal shavings in the recycle box in the corner of the room, Angie picked up the box of armor parts and exchanged nods with the NPC who ran the place.

"Thanks for cleaning up!" The NPC's voice was just a little too cheery to be real, but she preferred that to the dead monotone of the previous version.

Upon stepping out of the workshop and into the crowded foyer, Angie paused to let her eyes adjust to the dim light of the Guildhall. It wasn't lit to the same noontime brilliance as the tinkerers' workshop, and the dark wood paneling only accentuated that. The pictures of the game's development team hanging on the walls added a brighter element, but the room's ambience could suck the joy out of her day.

On the way through the growing crowd, Angie glanced at the Stats cogwheel next to the system clock in her vision. "Inventory."

A transparent 5x5 grid appeared across her vision, showing the first twenty-five objects in her endless backpack. As usual, the locker numbers note she needed was in the first box. When she focused on the note, the grid faded as the transparent scroll unrolled in front of her.

By now, she'd have hoped to have had everyone's locker number memorized, but every day, she still needed the reminder.

Focusing on the world around her dismissed the note and inventory screen as she walked into the locker room. Rows of metal lockers filled the space. When logging out, whatever players had equipped went into the locker. That way, tinkerers in the party could come in early and fix the damage caused during the previous adventure. Having a tinkerer in the party meant lower repair costs.

A myriad of other tinkerers scrambled around the rows of lockers restoring their party's equipment. The way they huffed and puffed, they had to be running out of time. This daily phenomenon was silly, really.

Sure, gear in lockers automatically equipped when the player logged in. Otherwise, the player would have to don whatever it was manually. Not a big deal, but some players threw a full-on toddler tantrum if everything wasn't just so. The team she'd started with had been like that, which was why she'd jumped at Morgrim's invitation to join his team.

Playing on a developer's team meant they had extra responsibilities and obligations, but the perks were nice, and Morgrim, a stocky, dark-haired dwarven warrior, had assembled a no-drama group.

Angie went to each teammate's locker and deposited their repaired gear. She slipped on her chain mail—now with fewer damaged links from last night's fracas—and returned the empty box to the stack near the door.

On the way out of the locker room, she glanced up at the system clock. Her team would arrive in about ten minutes for tonight's session. Plenty of time for her to get her equipment sorted.

When she passed the stairs to the tower, she caught a glimpse of Leif Etree, her tall, elf teammate in green studded leather armor, running up to the observation area at the top. After using his herbalist skills to prepare elixirs every evening, he used his elven eyesight to recon the area they were going to. Most of the time, that bit of long-distance snooping helped them plan strategies and avoid trouble. Once in a while, he'd catch issues that Morgrim needed to address in his admin role.

Angie let him do his job without interference and headed down the hall to the space Morgrim reserved for them to gather and chat before setting out. The furniture was all wrought iron with floofy gray cushions. There were a couple of armchairs, a sprite stool, and a very sturdy loveseat that could handle even Morgrim's bulk. The pictures on the wall showed some of the developers who used this room alongside their characters. She still had a hard time visualizing Morgrim as a middle-aged, clean-shaven cowboy type. The gruff dwarf with a beard just fit him so well. Even his primary account was a dwarf, but a redhead in that case.

She settled into the gray armchair and snuggled into the dark gray afghan draped over the side as she sorted her inventory. Only the first few rows of slots were static. The rest shuffled into a new order every time she added or removed something. She preferred weapons and tools at the top and everything else at the bottom. If she focused on an object when she reached in, it would jump to her hand, but sometimes she needed to get to things—like the locker number list—when her hands were full. And sometimes, she just liked to do things a bit Old School.

Honestly, she could probably clear out some of the flotsam in her inventory. When would she ever need a quarter-vial of red dye, for example? Doing a proper dye job on even the smallest object took half a vial. She had long ago fully embraced her inner packrat, so the vial stayed in her inventory. Someday, she might actually need a quarter-vial of dye. What for was anyone's guess, but without a doubt, if she chucked it, she'd need it the next day.

The door opened revealing Morgrim in his Level 5, dark-haired dwarf-with-a-permanent-scowl persona.

"Good evening, Angie." He flexed the gauntlet. "Thanks for the repairs."

"Glad to do it." She smiled. "How was your day?"

He rolled his eyes and flopped into the loveseat, which creaked ominously. "Spent half the day cleaning up the red tape from last night and dealing with customer service complaints from the night before."

Red tape from last night, she understood. They'd been called upon to deal with a group of Level 7s and 8s sniping low-level players outside of the player versus player zone. Stopping them had been hard, but even victory gave Morgrim some mopping up to do to prevent the jerks from just regrouping and doing it again. He'd mentioned dropping the ban hammer on the other party, which meant a mountain of paperwork.

"The night before? More problems with the glitched AI?" She

leaned forward with her elbows on her knees. "Something to do with the guy passing out cheat codes?"

"Nah. Cut and dried. The usual 'just kidding' excuse. We told him to go joke around elsewhere." Morgrim leaned back in the loveseat. "Those noobs we had to rescue? They had a choice of either forfeiting their characters and starting over or doing chores. They chose to start over."

Angie shrugged. "At Level 1, I would've, too."

"Right. They'd only completed the tutorial. Made sense, but they found out through a chat board that the other parties who took cheat codes got away with a reprimand. So, they filed a complaint." Morgrim sighed.

"Those other groups didn't use the codes, though. We got to the warden in time to lock them out." Angie rolled her eyes. "Big difference between taking codes and using codes."

Morgrim pointed at her and nodded once. "You got that right, and that was the company response, along with a reminder that we would have been within our rights to ban them altogether as the user agreement says. That shut them up pretty quick."

"But that still meant paperwork." Angie sat back.

"Yep, and plenty of it." Morgrim's scowl deepened.

"Maybe tonight we'll get a break from admin duties." Angie leaned her elbow on the arm of the chair and her chin on her palm.

Morgrim smirked. "We will. I took an opportunity to remind everyone that developer's parties should receive no more than 20% admin duties. Our group plays five nights a week. Two nights in five is 40%, so barrin' an absolute, server-wreckin' problem, they're supposed to leave us alone for the rest of this week and all of next."

Angie smiled. "Good. I don't mind helping but—"

Morgrim held up a hand to pause her. "Y'all are volunteers. Would be different if you were on the payroll, but you're not."

The door opened and Gemina slipped into the room and closed the door, then leaned against it. The four-foot-tall, skinnier-than-a-bean-pole sprite had short blue hair and blue wings that contrasted weirdly with her orange eyes. "Oh! Do not go out there."

Angie chuckled. *Her typical greeting most nights.* "Why?"

"Group of noobs are talking trash about Morgrim. They're all—" She scowled and lowered her voice. "—'Teach that stinking dwarf a lesson.' Only they didn't say 'stinking.'"

"Bet you a root beer float it's the noobs from the night before last." Angie blew out a breath.

Morgrim rolled his eyes. "No bet."

"On the bright side, the prude filter still works." Gemina waggled her eyebrows. "Hey, where's Leif?"

"When I saw him, he was headed up to the tower." Angie glanced up.

The party chat icon appeared in the corner of her vision. Only team members could instant message each other.

"Oh! That's gotta be a note from Leif!" Gemina perched on the sprite chair.

As Angie focused on the icon to open the message, Morgrim pushed off from his loveseat and stood. "Let's go. They stopped talking."

The message opened into a transparent text box. "Hey, those noobs we rescued from the swamp? They're here and causing trouble. They just pulled weapons. Don't suppose I can bash heads?"

Angie sighed and dismissed the note. Morgrim led the way out with Gemina floating over his head. Angie trailed behind.

At the Guildhall entrance, they found Leif at the foot of the stairs deflecting pitifully weak attacks with his staff and ignoring openings to smack the noobs into next week. The crowd of other adventurers had left them a wide space and shouted encouragement to Leif to get him to strike back.

Morgrim drew a deep breath. "That's enough o' that." His voice carried well, and the background noise faded to nothing. He glanced up. "Best if you back up a bit, sprite."

Gemina nodded and fluttered down the hall. When she landed at Angie's side, Angie pointed at Gemina's blue hair.

"Right. Helmet." Gemina reached into her bottomless belt pouch and withdrew a helmet that matched the rest of her blue leather armor.

"You know, it'd auto-equip if you left it in your locker." Angie leaned closer.

"Yeah, but I lost the last two that way." Gemina secured the chinstrap. "No idea how, but poof! Gone."

The noob party ahead looked different from the folks they'd rescued from the glitchy AI, but the names were the same mess of lower and capital letters, numbers, and symbols.

"You want to fight players, go to the PvP zone. This ain't it." Morgrim frowned at the nearest noob, a Level 1 sprite herbalist.

"We lost all our money and items!" The sprite squeaked planting his hands on his hips and narrowly avoiding stabbing himself with his own dagger.

"You were given a choice of restarting or doing chores at City Hall to make amends for using cheat codes. You chose to restart. So, yes, you lost everything and started over. That's how these things work. This was all explained to you earlier." He jabbed his finger at the sprite. "You regrettin' that now? Tough. You want to take it out of my hide? Go issue me a challenge in the PvP zone. Right now, Leif is perfectly in his rights to press a charge against you for attacking him in the Guildhall. That'd be your second offense in a five-day period. That gets you banned. You want that?"

The party sheathed their weapons and grumbled.

Morgrim nodded at Leif. "You got the right to explain this to them clearly if you want it."

Leif shook his head. "No harm done."

"That's fair." Morgrim mimed brushing them off. "Y'all skedaddle. The next time you have a beef with someone, take it to the PvP zone. Y'hear? Now get!"

The noob party shuffled off, muttering. Goose honks, cow moos, and other farm animal noises coming from them suggested they were using some language deemed not suitable for the game's All Audiences rating.

Morgrim shook his head. "Some people's kids." He blew out a breath then smiled, only looking more strained for the effort. "Shall we?"

Angie nodded. "Let's."

She followed the others out of the Guildhall and out to the road leading to Trierluk Forest.

Gemina, clad in blue leather that matched her blue wings, fluttered over Morgrim's head. Leif, a tall elf herbalist carrying his wooden staff, stayed with Angie. A kind gesture, she knew, because she was the weakest fighter in the group. He meant to protect her if the going got suddenly rough.

"All right, sprite. Remind us of the quest." Morgrim glanced up at her as much as his plate armor allowed.

She zipped ahead of them and flew backwards while pulling a slip of paper from her belt pouch. "According to the quest note we nabbed from the job board three days ago, this is a damsel in distress quest. A lovely bride-to-be vanished, and we're supposed to secure her safety. Details are available at the castle."

"'Secure her safety?'" Leif's brow furrowed. "Not rescue her or return her to the castle."

Gemina shrugged. "That's what it says."

"That's an odd way to phrase that." Morgrim snorted.

Angie leaned closer to Leif. "There will be a reason it's stated that way."

"Likely." Leif nodded. "Can't imagine what that'd be, but that has to be deliberate."

They reached the vine-covered arboretum that marked the entry into Trierluk Forest. The warden, a massive Level 20 NPC who stood as tall as Leif and as muscular as Morgrim, stepped to one side as they approached. Yesterday, the purple flowers on the arboretum had hissed at everyone to warn them off while the region was on lockdown; but today, they sounded like tiny trumpets as everyone walked through.

"Y'all wanna wander the forest and pick up some XP or stick to the quest?" Morgrim glanced at each of them.

"Nope, can't wander first. The quest had a five-day time limit when we picked it up three days ago." Gemina held up her fingers to match her words.

Leif nodded. "We can wander after we complete the quest. I've been looking forward to this after two admin days."

Angie shrugged. "I'm with you guys."

Morgrim pointed his hammer down the path. "On to the castle."

Since they'd cleared this low-level area ages ago, they wouldn't be attacked on the road—respawn timers on the monsters were only active away from the beaten path—which gave Angie a chance to admire the fun scenery created by the game's art department.

Many of the trees had humanlike faces and struck poses like they'd been frozen mid-action. A couple appeared to be holding rackets on opposite sides of a hedgerow with a yellow butterfly that constantly flew from one racket to the other. Another appeared to be stirring a pot on the stove. Another seemed to be walking.

When they passed under the massive oak tree halfway to the castle, the silly attitude of the scenery turned more sinister. Now one tree seemed to chase another with an ax. A grove of spindly trees looked like they were reaching with clawed hands. Several appeared to be screaming.

Leif shuddered, and Angie wrapped her arm around his back.

Morgrim had once told a story about this particular area where some knucklehead named Fritz had corrupted the AI and turned it into a haunted house gone wrong. Morgrim had gotten there in time to rescue Leif from the demented skeleton Fritz had turned into.

He smiled at her. "I'm okay. Not a fan of this art, but—" He shrugged.

"I know what you mean." She patted his back and stepped away.

They arrived at the castle and strode across the drawbridge, Morgrim's bulk rattling the timbers with each step.

A spindly guard who didn't look sturdy enough to fight off a stiff breeze, blocked their way. "State your business."

Gemina fished the quest description from her belt pouch and showed it to him. "On a quest."

The guard stepped aside. "You'll find His Highness in the drawing room."

Inside the gate, they passed through a garden of barking dogwoods, meowing cattails, and fire-breathing snapdragons.

The double door stood open. A sign in the foyer had arrows pointing to the drawing room, the kitchen, the throne room, and the dungeon.

"This way." Gemina fluttered down the indicated corridor.

"Get it right next time!" A man's voice echoed from down the hall.

Moments later, a servant in a simple, gray tunic and pants rushed past with a covered tray.

"Oooo, someone needs an attitude adjustment," Gemina whispered.

Morgrim hefted his hammer. "I just so happen to have brought my attitude adjuster."

When they entered the room at the end of the hall, transparent hands floating around the room got to work sketching their portraits on the wall. Transparent amethyst purple drapes filtered the sunlight into shifting patterns that flickered around the room. Angie stepped in front of Leif and blocked the way. "Might be best for you to wait out here."

He squeezed his eyes closed and turned away. "Definitely. Thanks."

Angie waited until he was further down the hall to make sure he wasn't going to have any problems. The poor kid got migraines from unsteady lighting. She still recalled having to abort their first mission as Morgrim's party because of guttering candles in a dark room.

Angie waited until Leif was further down the hall, then joined the others.

Morgrim and Gemina stood in front of a muscular man with a very strong, square jaw, dark hair, and blue eyes. He was dressed in Medieval court finery and lounged on a deep purple sofa while explaining the quest.

"—no sooner started planning for the glorious event than she disappeared. I've sent five parties to rescue her, and none returned. If you return her to me or bring me evidence of her demise, I shall give you each two gifts." The prince adjusted the bulky gold and gemstone chains draped around his shoulders.

Movement drew Angie's eye to the wall where the ghostly hands had drawn her, Morgrim, Gemina, the prince, and an unfinished version of Leif.

"We'll see what we can do to find her." Morgrim hefted his hammer. "Any clues to who took her where?"

The prince rolled his eyes and huffed, muttering something about "useless questions." "Her mud boots, trousers, a couple shirts, and her favorite dress are gone, so I assume they took her to Tocksiturdle Swamp." He bolted to his feet and clenched his fist. "Just find her!"

Gemina flew backwards a few feet, but Morgrim met his scowl with an even deeper one.

"Watch it, Bub. I got no patience for rudeness." Morgrim glared. "We'll find the lady. You just keep your hair on."

He spun on his heel and strode out with Gemina close behind. Angie stayed long enough to see the ghostly hands erasing their artwork, then jogged to catch up.

"Sorry, Leif." Morgrim patted Leif's back. "The art department swore to me they'd fixed all the lighting issues. I'll tell them to go rare on it again. Can't have players droppin' for migraines and seizures."

"I appreciate it." Leif nodded.

Gemina gasped. "That's why you stayed in the hall. I forgot that flashy stuff makes your brain go all wiggly. You okay?"

"Angie stopped me before I got more than a glance. I'm all right." Leif smiled at her.

"All part of the service." Angie's cheeks warmed.

They backtracked through the forest, across the town of Newburgh, and out to the decaying stone path where the warden marked the entrance to Tocksiturdle Swamp. The warden stepped aside as they approached the Level 5-10 area and let them pass without comment.

Gemina flew backwards and looked at Leif. "So, any likely prospects from your snooping?"

He nodded. "I found a little house. Actually, more of a duplex. There were two humans, a dwarf, and an elf walking around, but neither of the ladies seemed to be a kidnap victim."

"Maybe she's confined in the house?" Angie squinted and tipped her head to one side.

"Stockholm syndrome?" Gemina tapped her cheek.

"Could be. Play it by ear when we get there." Morgrim pointed down the path. "Lead the way, Leif."

"And remember, we haven't cleared Tocksiturdle, so the road may not be safe." Angie rested her hand on the hilt of her short sword.

"Yeah, so don't swat any wisps." Gemina watched one of the tiny light spheres buzz by.

Morgrim smirked at her.

She held up both hands palm out. "That was a reminder for me. I didn't know what it was. I know better now."

Angie winced. Last week, their first brief trip into the swamp had them running for the exit after Gemina had batted one of the little lights with her hand, thinking it was a fly.

The stone path from Newburgh faded into the muddy swamp. Angie pulled her double-decker crossbow out of her backpack, where it never should have fit, and loaded both bolts. The tweaks she'd made to it earlier should have fixed the problem that kept throwing her aim off, but she didn't plan to try shooting in the direction of one of her teammates until she could confirm her improved accuracy.

As they walked past a frog on a lilypad, its tongue shot out and stuck to the edge of the quiver on her belt. When the frog pulled on the quiver, Angie braced against it, but her feet slid.

The head of Morgrim's warhammer landed on the frog with a sickening squish and the frog's tongue let go. An inventory screen popped up above the frog's corpse, showing a bizarre assortment of items, including a large sword.

As per their usual procedures, Morgrim stuffed everything into his endless backpack. His superior strength meant he had the encumbrance points to spare. They'd sort and sell later.

"May be best if you archery types take out frogs before we're in range." Gemina flew higher.

Angie joined Leif on the front line. "I've got the right side. You've got the left?"

Leif nodded once. "You got it. I'll help you spot them, but you get to take the shot."

"Thanks. I need the practice." She looked back at the squashed frog. "Weird that the frog waited for the last person before it struck."

"Lowered guard means better odds." Morgrim hefted his hammer.

"I liked them better playing leapfrog and doing synchronized swimming." Leif switched his staff for his bow and nocked an arrow.

They passed the fork in the trail where they'd turned off during the rescue mission, but Leif directed them straight.

Every few yards, another frog appeared on the side of the road. So far, they'd all been on Leif's side, and he skewered them with an arrow, usually on the first try. Morgrim looted them as they passed.

"There." Leif nodded toward her side of the road.

Angie squinted and leaned forward. "Where?"

"Fifteen feet ahead. Just his face visible through the cattails." He couched the arrow and pointed. "There."

Angie tracked his direction and spotted the beady little eyes. "Got 'im."

She raised her crossbow and took aim, then pulled the trigger. Instead of kicking up like it had been doing the last few nights, it kicked straight back into her shoulder. The bolt slammed into the frog.

Above and behind her, Gemina shrieked. "Leif!"

Something splashed in the swamp water.

In a single, fluid move, Leif nocked the arrow, stepped back, turned, and aimed.

In the same moment, something behind Leif moved. Angie spun, located another frog, and shot the second bolt from her crossbow. She missed the frog she was aiming at but hit a different one that popped up behind it. One of Morgrim's hatchets sailed in and nailed the remaining frog while three of Leif's arrows whiffed from his bow.

Angie turned the crank that would reset her crossbow and loaded two more bolts while a couple more arrows and a hatchet dispatched more frogs.

"Another one! Big bruiser," Gemina called and pointed.

Angie followed Gemina's direction. "Boss frog." She took aim and triggered the top bolt.

The boss frog dodged then hawked a loogie that fell short and landed on a lilypad that sizzled and smoked.

"Boss frog shoots acid." Angie took aim and shot the lower bolt.

The bolt hit the frog, but it hopped closer. Angie crouched to give those behind her a clear shot, then set to reloading her crossbow. A blowgun dart, a hatchet, and two arrows sailed over her head.

The frog spat another glob of acid at them, landing it on Angie's gloved hand. She quickly stripped off her glove and dunked it in the swamp water before she set it aside and shot both bolts. One of her bolts hit at the same time as Leif's arrow, and the frog was a goner.

Angie started reloading.

"I don't see anymore," Gemina said.

"Good. Everyone okay?" Morgrim started looting frogs.

Gemina growled. "I hate wet armor."

"Aside from that." Morgrim knelt by the boss frog.

Gemina sluiced water from her sleeve. "I wouldn't call that insignificant."

"Angie, did you get some of that frog spit?" Leif flipped his bag open.

She held up her glove. The hole with blackened edges glared back at her. "Armor caught it."

Morgrim rejoined them. "Well, these gloves look intact." He held up a pair of serviceable brown leather gloves.

Angie set her glove aside and selected Inspection from her skills menu. The label appeared above the gloves. "+2 Dexterity."

"Upgrade for you." Morgrim looked at the others. "Objections?"

Leif shook his head. "Fine by me."

Gemina nodded. "Agreed. That'll help your aim and your tinkering."

"Thank you." She stripped off her other glove and tucked the old pair into her backpack—never know when she might need a bit a leather to quick-patch Gemina's or Leif's armor—before donning the new set.

"Onward!" Morgrim aimed his warhammer down the path.

Around the curve, the path forked again. Leif veered to the right then slid to a stop as a flock of wisps buzzed by.

Gemina gasped. "Psycho fireflies."

"Don't bug them; they won't bug you." Angie watched them zoom past.

"Say, Leif, can you make psycho firefly bug spray?" Gemina grinned.

He chuckled. "Find me a recipe, and I'll see what I can do."

"I'll keep an eye out."

Morgrim snorted. "Frogs were cute and all, but I expected more trouble. Five other parties have failed."

Angie glanced back. "Trouble might be at the destination."

"True."

As they traveled, more frogs popped up at intervals, and wisps zoomed by singly or in groups. Finally, they stepped out into a clearing.

The single structure looked like two houses glued together, the "duplex" Leif had mentioned. A raised garden grew several plants in various stages of their life cycle, and frog legs cooked over a fire.

A human woman came out and froze. She had dark hair and eyes and a red tunic and gray pants tucked into boots. The name tag over her head read, "Freida Goh."

She heaved a sigh. "Missy, Guda, Whet! He sent more of them."

"Seriously?" The door of the other house opened and another human woman, this one a strikingly gorgeous blonde, stormed out, followed by a stocky dwarf. The woman's name tag said, "Missy Persun," and the dwarf was dubbed "Guda Frent".

A male elf, tagged "Whet Lanz," stepped into the clearing. "This has to stop."

The blonde, flanked by her three friends, stormed over. "You can just tell Prince Sir D'Fied Enzane that I'm not coming back!" Her emphatic gestures caused her clothing to shift, revealing old bruises that were a little green around the edges.

Angie's stomach soured. This might be just a game and the woman was an NPC, but she'd volunteered in a battered woman's shelter for a while in college, and bruises like that were common enough.

Leif fished a red healing elixir from his bag. "Here. This will heal your injuries."

Missy looked away. "I'll be fine."

He stepped forward and held it out to her. "I know, but this will help."

"Your loving fiancé did that?" Morgrim growled.

She accepted Leif's elixir but didn't use it. "Yes. I didn't like the wedding dress he picked out for me."

The other woman snorted. "Dress. That wasn't a dress. It was barely a bikini."

Gemina tensed until she trembled. "OOOooo! That beast!"

Morgrim nodded. "And now we know why the other parties failed."

Angie nodded. "And why we're going to blow it, too."

Missy uncorked the elixir. "He'll just send another party and another and another." She chugged a couple swallows, which mended all hurts, and then handed it back. "Thank you."

Leif nodded and returned the vial to his bag.

"So, we need to convince him that sending more rescue parties is no good." Gemina tapped her chin.

Morgrim hefted his hammer. "I know one way to convince him."

"Yeah, and then you'll spend the next couple weeks in a dungeon for killing the prince." Angie frowned. "Even though he deserves it."

Gemina held up one finger. "I got it. We have to kill Missy."

Guda stepped in front of Missy. "Over my dead body."

"Not for real, you noob." Gemina rolled her eyes. "The quest didn't say we had to take her back to the castle. It said we have to secure her safety. We have to make him think she's dead. Then there's no point to sending more 'rescuers.' Get it?"

Morgrim nodded. "I do like how you think, sprite."

"Do you have something he'd recognize as yours? Preferably something you might've been wearing. Shirt, pants, dress, something." Gemina fluttered forward and landed in front of Angie.

Missy sighed. "My favorite dress. I brought it with me. You're going to ruin it, aren't you?"

"Sorry." Gemina winced. "If anyone's got another way to make him think you're dead, I'm all ears." She smirked. "Well, not literally. That would look funny."

Guda turned to Missy and clasped her hands. "It's for the best, honey. When we get enough money put aside, we can commission you a new one."

"All right. I'll get it." Missy trudged back to the house.

Whet, the elf, glanced toward the trees. "I'll catch us a frog. We'll need blood."

"Wait!" Angie reached into her backpack and withdrew the quarter-vial of red dye. "This needed a purpose. I think this qualifies."

Leif chuckled. "You still have that?"

Angie shrugged. "I'm a pack rat."

"Good thing you are."

Missy returned with her dress. Freida took her back inside while Guda dragged the dress through the mud, strategically applied the red dye to it, and created a few well-placed tears that would be fatal if they had been created while the dress was on.

Guda held it up and then looked at Whet. "Think that'll do?"

"With the right story, it'd convince me." Whet clapped the dwarf on the shoulder.

Morgrim added the dress to his inventory. "Leave it with us. We'll set Prince Knucklehead straight."

Angie joined Leif on the front line again, but since they were reversing their inward route, they encountered only the ubiquitous wisps and an occasional frog. No acid spitters and no toxic turtles. They'd have to go further in or further off the beaten path to run afoul of the poisonous turtles of remarkable size. A challenge for another time.

The trip out of the swamp, through Newburgh, and across Trierluk Forest to the castle took less time than the outbound trip. The gate guard directed them to the drawing room again, so they left Leif in the hallway where the migraine potential was nil and went on.

Knowing her storytelling skills were minimal at best, Angie drifted back to let Morgrim and Gemina take the lead.

They entered the drawing room, which busied the ghostly hands with drawing their likenesses. The prince sat in one of the armchairs with a curvaceous young lady on his lap.

"Well, isn't that the picture of a deeply worried fiancé," Gemina muttered.

"I don't see my darling Missy with you." The prince shooed his lap ornament away, then stood.

Morgrim pulled the tattered and stained dress from his backpack. "I'm afraid we have terrible news, Your Highness." He held up the dress. "Is this your bride's dress?"

He came closer and leaned in to inspect it without touching it. "Yes, I believe so. Where was it?"

"Deep within Tocksiturdle. Found it in a critter's lair."

"Bones everywhere," Gemina interjected.

The prince returned to his seat. "So, you're saying she's dead."

"I can't see how else. We barely made it out ourselves," Morgrim offered the prince the dress.

He grimaced and waved Morgrim back. "A pity, really. I was so looking forward to our wedding."

"Our condolences," Angie said.

The prince blew out a breath. "Well, not the result I might've wanted, but I can't fault you if she got herself eaten by a monster. I promised you two gifts each. Go to her bedroom. Select your things. Now go."

Angie paused on the way out to watch the hands erasing their sketches. Morgrim stuffed the ruined dress in his backpack as they collected Leif and returned to the foyer. There, the sign sported a new arrow directing them up the stairs, where other signs eventually got them to the exact room.

They stepped into a room that appeared to have been visited by two typhoons, a Cat 5 hurricane, and a modest tornado. The canopy bed was bare and the bedsheets and blankets had become an impromptu carpet. Most of the contents of the wardrobe were in a jumbled pile in the corner. The drawers in the dresser were partly open and the clothing within had formed a still waterfall.

Gemina spun midair. "Wow. Housekeeping has had the millennium off, huh?"

Angie closed the door. "What say we pick out eight things and take them to her?"

"I say we stuff everything we can into our bags and take it all to her." Gemina spun and took in the room with a wave of her hands.

"Then spend some time in the dungeon. We're only allowed eight things." Leif picked his way over to the wardrobe.

"Nuts."

"Okay, ladies, help a guy make selections. What are eight things a gal might want to have?" Morgrim walked to the dresser and opened the small box on the top. "Jewelry's gone."

"That figures. His Incredible Irritatingness probably already snitched anything of monetary value." Gemina fluttered over to the wardrobe to help Leif with the clothes. "Fortunately, sentimental value probably doesn't sell for much."

Angie piled the bed linens on the bed and came across a quilt with intricate hand-stitching. "A quilt would be special, a reminder of whoever made it for her."

"Okay. There's one." Morgrim rooted through the dresser. "What's this?" He withdrew a carved box and flipped the lid open. "Hair clips?"

"Definitely. She has gorgeous hair." Gemina held up a dress, shook her head, and handed it to Leif.

Angie stuffed the quilt into her backpack and opened the nightstand drawer. Inside, a well-worn book with a lock was the only occupant.

"A diary." She held it up.

"Good. So that's a quilt, a diary, and a jewelry box with two hair clips. Three to go." Morgrim counted the objects off on his fingers.

Leif picked up a dress. "Similar to the one we messed up."

"There you go. Two more." Morgrim held up two fingers.

"Comfy PJs?" Angie suggested.

He stepped away from the dresser. "Didn't see any, but I skipped the top drawer when I came across skivvies."

Angie strode over and rooted through the top drawer until she found a nightgown and stuffed it in her pack.

"Here. A good shirt. She probably needs that more than another dress." Gemina tucked it into her pouch.

Morgrim quietly counted on his fingers. "That'll do. Let's go make the gal's day."

Angie followed the others out. They were well outside the castle when Gemina tapped the top of Morgrim's helm.

"All right. Spill. We can't just let Prince Wacko back there get away with hurting girls and being a world-class jerk. Can we?"

Morgrim glanced up at her. "Dunno."

"So, we don't get to give Sir Beastliness his well-earned reward?" Gemina planted her hands on her hips.

"This is a new quest sequence that I wasn't involved in, but even if I knew, I can't tell you that, sprite." Morgrim shook his head.

She mimed pinching something small. "Just a hint?"

Morgrim shrugged. "We'll find out in due time."

"'In due time.'" She crossed her arms over her chest. "Well, he better get his dose of karma."

Angie nodded. "I'm sure he will, Gemina. In the meantime, his chief victim is safely away with friends who clearly love her."

"Yeah, in a swamp while Sir Jerkface is living in the lap of luxury." Gemina huffed. "It's not fair."

"No, it's not, but better happiness in a hovel than despair in the castle." Leif nodded once.

She drooped a little. "Yeah, I guess you're right. Still stinks, though."

They left Trierluk Forest and headed for Tocksiturdle Swamp.

END

CURSE OF THE ROSES
Kaitlyn Emery

Moonlight sifted through the branches above Pierre. He should have stopped for the night in the last town. Curse his folly. He had been away from home for so long trying to find work, all he wanted was to see his children. He thought he could make it if he cut through the forest, but somewhere along the path he must have made a wrong turn.

Claudius flicked his ears back and forth, listening to moonlight serenade of the crickets, his hooves providing a steady beat. Fog thickened as they came upon a creek cutting through the landscape, the spires of a castle visible in the skyline beyond.

Pierre wouldn't be able to find the path home until morning with all of these shadows. His fingers felt numb from the cold. If he didn't seek shelter soon, he would have to contend with the elements. Plus, with the small bit of money he carried home with him, he could not afford to be raided by bandit in the night. The castle was his best bet for hospitality. If nothing else, surely they would allow him a place in the stables with Claudius out of the cold.

Icy water splashed beneath Claudius as they crossed the creek, water rising till it lapped over Pierre's knee. Climbing their way out of the ravine, Pierre looked for signs of the castle, keenly aware of the water stiffening his pantaloons in the cold.

Where was the castle? Why had he not come across any lights to help lead them to shelter? Perhaps coming this way, through the waters, had been a bad idea. His children were at home, waiting for him. He should have just pressed on and tried to find the way home.

His wife's death had nearly crushed his children. What would they do if he left them as well, penniless and heaped with debt? The fog thinned a bit, exposing a wall of stone. Ah! He must be close to the castle. Pierre followed the curve of the structure, leading him deeper into the forest.

Claudius grew restless beneath the saddle.

"Easy boy." Pierre offered a friendly pat. "We will be there soon."

Like magic, the fog pulled back, revealing a castle rising from the shadows towards the sky, surrounded by an imposing wall. Strange that so large a castle would be so far from civilization.

Pierre dropped down from the saddle and tested the gates. They opened without a sound. "See, boy? We have found shelter at last," Pierre said as he closed the gates behind them.

Pierre noticed the lack of sound in the dense atmosphere. There were no chirping crickets, no owls calling to one another. Just silence. Eerie silence.

His boot crunched as he stepped forward, causing Pierre to realize there was a fine layer of snow carpeting the ground. Snow? He had not noticed any snow along his travels. Spring was almost upon them. What sort of sorcery was this?

Claudius planted his feet, refusing to move forward. "Come, Claudius." Pierre encouraged. The grinding ache in his bones from his bad leg, aggravated by the cold, made him leery of walking the long path towards the castle on his own. But Claudius would not budge.

"Fine," Pierre sighed, leaving the horse. He was safe from predators within the walls of the castle grounds.

Pierre pushed forward, ignoring the hairs standing on the back of his neck as he crept along the winding driveway. Bloom-laden bushes grew in the shadow of the castle, clawing up the walls and into the stonework, as if trying to choke out the life from within. Not a petal withered from the cold, or vine discolored by frost. Enchanting. They were the only sign of life in the dreary landscape surrounding them.

Massive stairs led to the door at the entrance of the castle. It was more than three times Pierre's height and equally as wide. The aged wood looked as if it had been standing for more than a century.

His breath pooled in the air as he lifted the heavy, gilded door knocker and let it fall. In the stillness, the sound was jarring. No one answered. Nothing stirred.

Pierre could hear the crunch of his clothes hardening against his skin. With a deep inhale he tested the latch. Soundlessly, it opened.

"Hello?" Pierre called as he opened the door. "I mean you no harm. I lost my way in the woods and need a place to stay for the night." The moonlight was the only light in the interior.

"Hello?" Pierre called again. Down the hall, the light of a chandelier slowly came to life. "Hello? Is someone there?" Pierre walked towards the newly lit area. A sweeping staircase at the end of the entrance led up to a second floor towering above him in the shadows.

A creak to his right drew Pierre's attention to an opening door revealing a crackling fireplace. A chair sat before the fire with a small table laid out for a single meal. Pierre looked for his host, but there was no one. Pierre entered the room. Steam rose from the Florentine-patterned teacup with sugar crusted palmiers and canelés on the matching saucer.

Pierre waited for the master of the house to return to his meal, hopeful that an introduction and explanation would smooth over his trespass.

Drawing closer to the fire, Pierre observed the room and tried to calm his nerves. Colossal portraits hung on the walls of the spacious room with tapestry curtains draped across one side, complimenting the fresco painted ceiling. A pendulum clock trimmed in gold with hand-painted designs on its face sat upon the marble fireplace, alerting Pierre to the lateness of the hour.

The hearty aromas of boeuf bourguignon and potatoes dauphinoise escaped from beneath the domed plate covering on the wheel tray that was still untouched. For the first time, Pierre's stomach growled, making him realize how hungry his travels had left him. Eyeing the food, Pierre inched closer, lifting the linen off the small basket sitting on the silver dining tray to reveal baguette slices. His mouth salivated, and the gnawing in his stomach grew.

His stomach won over his nerves. Glancing around, Pierre bit down, the crunch of the perfectly crusted bread chasing away his lingering doubts. Beside the tray, draped over the velvet armchair, was a fur-lined robe and beaded slippers atop the footrest.

Pierre realized he had stopped shivering, but was now thawing before the fire, dripping water onto the lavish rug beneath his boots. Perhaps the master of the home had seen his approach up the long driveway to the house and set out these items for his comfort?

"Hello," Pierre called to his invisible host, peeking back out into the hall. Curious that the master of the home would not want to be seen, but with such hospitality, who was Pierre to judge the eccentricity of his host? "Thank you!"

Returning to the room, Pierre removed his clothes and wrapped himself in the robe before settling into the lush chair and delightful meal. With a full belly and his velvet-shod feet resting upon the footrest before the fire, Pierre drifted off, grateful for the hospitality he had been shown.

The next morning, Pierre awoke to thin sunlight drifting in from behind the curtains. Beside his chair sat his clothes, dried and neatly laid out for him, and a tray of coffee and golden-colored croissants with fig jam. His slippered feet carried him across the room to the window. The world beyond was still covered in snow, roses hanging from vines draping over the windows and partially blocking his view. Claudius remained by the gate, waiting for him.

After eating, Pierre dressed and made his way out of the castle, calling a thank you to the empty house that had cared for him through the night. The extensive roses throughout the grounds were even more beautiful in the daylight as he made his way down the stairs and onto the snow-covered grass.

Glancing back, Pierre noted many of the windows had been boarded up from within, the invasive climbing roses overtaking them. It was a wonder the master of the home did not trim them back. Although perhaps it would be a shame to tame roses of such beauty.

His wife loved roses, to the point they named their daughter after them. Rose shared the same love for her namesake as her mother. He knew Rose thought of their old gardens back home, and the trellis she loved to sit under. She was too kind to mention it to him, but he caught her more than once trying to coax rose seeds to life in the dirt behind their hovel, but the soil would not accept the grace of such a treasured flower.

Pierre checked the saddle on Claudius, musing over how far he had fallen from being a wealthy merchant. It was a simple thing to miss a rose, but when so much had been stripped from you, it was perhaps the simple things you missed most. The beauty of these roses far surpassed any that had grown back home. Surely one bloom in all this vastness would not be missed.

Leaving his horse's side, Pierre walked towards one of the stone walls leading up the castle stairs, roses clinging to the inhospitable structure. He marveled over their rich red color. They were enchanting.

Pierre plucked a rose from the vines, a thorn piercing his flesh as the delicate stem snapped. He drew back in pain, dropping the flower at the same moment he heard a vicious growl.

"You know not what you have done, old man."

~~~~~
~~~~~

A heaviness settled over Beau. There they were, wrought iron gates overgrown with twisting, thorn-ridden roses entangled through the bars. Just like father had said when he returned home, ranting about a beast and inevitable death if he did not return to live out his servitude.

The forest had not seen snow for many months, but just on the other side of the gate the ground was covered. The infamous roses that brought him there, the color of velveted blood, were defiant of the winter frost.

Beau patted Claudius to reassure him before sliding from the saddle. Like it or not, they must enter the forbidden grounds. For father.

The massive gates opened without a touch, as if expecting his arrival. The snow crunched beneath Beau's boots, but oddly left no tracks.

Roses clung to everything- statues scattered throughout the gardens, walls built up around the grounds, even the castle itself. It was beautiful, in a wild and unruly way. He had never seen such beguiling blooms in all his life, not even in his mother's garden.

Beau shivered from the wind and drew his threadbare cloak closer. How did roses survive such cold temperatures? It defied the laws of nature.

The castle appeared abandoned, yet still charming and unique. Peacocks perched on either side of the stairway with their slender necks held high, watching him, flashy tails a stark contrast to the snow.

"You are not Monsieur De La Cour." The voice grated on his nerves like a rake over barren soil.

"No, Madame, I am Beauvais De La Cour, his son. I have come in his place." As Beau turned to face her, predatory green eyes rimmed in black lines with white fur outlining them met him and chilled his soul. He wasn't sure what he expected based off his father's description, but the creature before him was neither animal nor woman.

Fangs pointed upwards between dark lips. Large ears outlined in black with long tufts on the ends of the same color rested among the dark curls piled on her head. What should have been skin was covered in short, tawny fur with a cream-colored ruff coming over her shoulders and down her chest. Dark spots mottled her arms and up the unusual curvature of her nose and cheeks, more like a lynx than a human. Whiskers sprouted from the dots lining her muzzle.

He knew he had been staring too long when the monster's lips curled slightly, as if she was contemplating a snarl. Quickly, he looked away.

"I sent your father home to put his affairs in order. Why did he send you in return?" Her voice was as cold and biting as the piercing wind through the garden.

"My father is old, Madame—"

"Mademoiselle."

"I—I'm sorry?"

"My title is not Madame."

"I see. Forgive me, Mademoiselle…?" he paused, waiting for her to give her name.

"Beast."

Beau could feel his eyebrows furrow. "That cannot be your name, Mademoiselle, surely?"

"It makes no difference."

"But—"

"A Beast!" She hissed, her voice burning like ice.

Beau swallowed his gut response to press further. "Mademoiselle Beast, I have come in place of my father. He is old and sustained an injury from war that never healed. I fear servitude could kill him. My sister and I have already lost one parent, it would be cruel to lose both."

The Beast's features remained blank. "Many children lose two parents. That does not garner them special treatment or pity."

Irritation pricked Beau's tongue, but he swallowed it. He was here to protect Father. He couldn't afford for her not to accept his trade. "I am a young man and stronger than my father. It is a servant you require. I would be superior in this regard."

The Beast arched her whiskered brow, but otherwise her expression remained vacant. He could tell she was shorter than him, but somehow her intimidating demeanor made her more imposing. "Very well," she said, before retreating towards the castle.

"Wait!" Anger bit the back of Beau's throat as he watched her leave, and with it came words that strained to be unleashed.

She stilled, the train of her gown matching the backdrop of roses trailing the stairway.

"You demand lifelong servitude for taking a single rose? The crime does not match the punishment."

The Beast spoke with her back to him. "I have no need of your services. You are here to uphold the debt of your father."

"What debt could you require for a rose?"

This time the Beast turned to face him; her lips pursed in as thin a line as her protruding fangs would allow. "If you have not noticed, Monsieur De La Cour, this castle is enchanted. It is the roses that keep that enchantment alive within the walls of my castle. Your father chose to take that which was not his, and because of his action enacted the same enchantment that holds the inhabitants of this household prisoner upon himself. You may do as you like. The gate opens freely to all who come and go from this house. But know that if you leave these grounds, the enchanted blooms will require atonement and your father will die. It is the curse of the roses that require eternal imprisonment, not I."

And with that, the beast swept up the stairs and into the castle, out of sight.

~~~~~

Weeks passed before Beau saw the Beast again as he settled into his private chambers in the south wing of the house. Within the walls of the giant castle, it was easy to avoid the reclusive mistress of the home. But that hadn't stopped him from exploring the grounds or acclimating himself to his new surroundings. Had you described to him weeks ago that he would be living in a castle without the hustle and bustle of his father's busy household, he would have thought that life sounded boring, but his time in solitude had proven to be quite different than he imagined. The castle was full of mystery and opportunities for exploration.

Early on, Beau realized the castle ran like clockwork. Though he never saw another living being aside from his horse and the magnificent, crested peacocks that roamed the grounds, he noticed that the gardens and the castle were maintained in optimal condition. Somehow meals that would rival the king's table were prepared throughout the day and left for him, stables were tended, fresh linens placed, fires kept cheerful and roaring, and any other detail, no matter how small, was cared for. He had concluded that whatever enchantment held the castle hostage must have made the men and women of the household invisible as well. It seemed such a silly thought, but he would have said a beast in women's gowns roaming through a castle would also be a silly notion. Strange seemed to be his new way of life.
~~~~~

The Beast held true to her statement that he was free to do as he liked. He roamed the halls and rooms at his leisure. When he desired fresh air, he would bundle up in the fine clothing that had been provided for him in the armoire within his bedchambers and roam the gardens. Sometimes he would walk Claudius through the winding pathways. Other times he would stroll through the maze of rosebushes that converged into a center garden where iridescent peacocks would lounge around a bubbling fountain filled with the most unusual and colorful whiskered fish.

It seemed odd that the fountain would continue to flow, despite the eternal snow covering the grounds. He had noted hints of spring just outside the gates, yet snow remained within the walls of the castle grounds. Sometimes more snow would fall, adding a magical feeling to the air, yet never adding more accumulation.

At first, he enjoyed puzzling over his environment, exploring the many splendors of the castle, and surmising the backstory he had invented for the bewitchment of the place. But as time drug on, the grounds began to feel monotonous, and Beau grew tired of never interacting with another soul.

Until now, Beau had avoided the east wing because the Beast dwelled there. He could hear her moving from time to time, and once caught a glimpse of her at the top of the grand staircase. It seemed odd to him that she did not venture beyond this section of the home. She never came to dine in the great hall. Not once had he seen her within the gardens for fresh air. With all the boarded windows she could not possibly get much sunlight within the walls.

Beau decided if he had to go one more day without hearing another voice besides his own, he would go mad. Plucking up the courage to deal with the displeasure of his fellow housemate, Beau began to explore the open areas of the east wing, hoping half-heartedly to run into the creature that ruled over the castle.

Like the other wings of the castle, there were many private bedchambers, which Beau avoided so that he did not intrude on Beast's personal quarters. Unlike other wings of the castle, this one held a wine cellar and ballroom that looked like no one had darkened its doors for years. The small chapel near the courtyards was a new find, as were the dungeons that thankfully appeared unoccupied for decades.

Beau's favorite discovery, however, was the large study. Stone and glass swirled together in intricate patterns across the floor. At one end of the study was a glass wall overlooking one of the many rose gardens. In the middle of the glass wall was a beautiful chaise lounge, almost matching the blood red roses on the other side of the glass barrier. Lining the walls were portraits of varying sizes and depicting many different people.

A magnificent oak desk and velveted chairs framed the opposite side of the room from the rose viewing. A small, gold leafed easel was displayed there, exhibiting a small, but ornate portrait frame. Delicate vines spiraling along the frame's edges with cloisonne roses dropping down over where a portrait should have been. Instead, the metal backing was empty.

What an odd thing to display a handheld portrait with no likeness inside. Beau walked towards the empty frame, almost drawn by some invisible pull. Beau reached out to inspect it, but a loud noise down the hall startled him, drawing his attention away from the frame and out into the hall.

Across the foyer from the study was an arched door with multicolored light peeking beneath its frame. When Beau tested the doorlatch, it yielded under his touch with a soft groan.

Multileveled bookcases were carved into the walls and inlaid with contrasting ornamented designs. Sunlight streamed through the stained-glass dome ceiling, letting in beautifully prismatic light and casting a magical glow within the circular walls of the room. To his right a winding staircase led to the open second level, the intricate iron rail the only barrier between the spaces.

His eyes followed the curve of the room. He wanted to reach out and touch the soft leather covers. So many titles intrigued him.

The sound of someone clearing their throat startled Beau, drawing his attention to the furred creature oddly curled in one of the fireplace chairs. Twitching ears, a deep scowl between protruding teeth, and wrinkled nose told Beau the Beast was not excited to see him.

She wore a corseted gown that draped across her awkward figure. The fluted sleeves lay in stark contrast against the spotted fur covering her arms. Great clawed feet were tucked up into the chair with her, and the end of a black tipped tail peeked out from the hem of her dress. It was an odd combination to see someone so fashionable yet seated in such an improper and cat-like manner.

"Good morning, Mademoiselle Beast." It felt odd to address her like that. He wished he knew her name.

She stared at him for a moment, whiskers alert, before dropping her eyes back to the fragile pages of her book. "You may enter."

The irony of her words was not lost on him, but she spoke without a snarl, so Beau took this as acceptance of his presence. Turning towards the beautiful spines resting within their cubbies, Beau walked towards the first row of books he could reach, letting his fingers caress them as he scanned the titles written by writers he admired. Each of them had a place of honor upon the shelves.

Before his father had lost the family fortune, Beau had access to the best tutors. His mother placed great importance on the education of both her children and spent many nights discussing the works of authors and philosophers with him. These conversations had helped shape him into the man he had become, giving him an appreciation for other cultures and ways of thinking.

After his mother's death, Beau continued to seek comfort within the minds of the authors they enjoyed together. He had not realized until now just how much he missed that.

Beau risked a look at the Beast as he fidgeted with the gold band around his finger. Her eyes followed his every move from behind her book, expressionless. He returned his gaze to the leather-bound beauties, keenly aware of her stare.

Above the fireplace hung a large portrait. Curious, Beau moved towards it. Green eyes captivated him, alive and bright with their intensity. Dark tresses curled around the girl's face and down her back, the escaping wisps the only sign of imperfection, if they could be called that. She was a beauty beyond compare, and the pride in her countenance indicated she knew it. Settled among her curls was an entwined crown of golden leaves and brilliant gemstones resembling flowers.

From the corner of his eye, Beau noticed the Beast stiffen. An odd reaction, he thought, but he did not want to get kicked out of her haven, so he returned to the shelves, removing one of the books. He stood before the Beast. "May I be seated?"

The Beast raised an eyebrow but maintained her composure before nodding. Beau sat, repositioning the decorative pillows before settling into his story. They sat this way for hours, the light shifting through the glass above the only indicator that time had passed.

A soft click of the opening door roused Beau from his story sometime later. A small push tray of tea wheeled into the room, set between them, and then a few moments later the door closed again.

Unphased, the Beast proceeded to take her tea with unusual dexterity for such large paws before returning to her reading.

Beau glanced from the tea tray, the door, and then at the Beast. He did this several times before closing his book, leaning forward, and plucking up the courage to speak. "Are they invisible?"

The Beast looked up as if surprised he was speaking to her. "Yes." She replied before dropping her gaze back to her book. "A blessing because I don't have to see the look of horror on their faces. A curse because until your father came, I had not seen a soul in many a year."

Beau nodded. He could see her point. He'd been here mere weeks, and already the isolation was maddening. He couldn't imagine being alone for years. Glancing around, he attempted another vein of conversation. "I haven't been to the east wing before today."

With mild irritation indicated by the flick of her tail, the Beast glanced back up from her book. "That would be why I haven't had the displeasure of having you invade my sanctuary until now." Her words were dry, but they held no bite. She returned to her book and repositioned herself in her chair, as if to convey she was done conversing.

Beau was not deterred. He was starved for conversation. She was the only companion available. "Stories have been my means of escape for years as well."

With a huff the Beast snapped her book closed and turned towards him. "They are my only remaining link to the world outside these walls. Now, what will it take for you to leave me in peace?"

Beau smiled. Her displeasure reminded him of a riled kitten, back arched, squeaking out a small hiss between its fangs. The image was hard to shake and brought him much amusement, disarming whatever fear he may have brought with him into the room. "You can start by giving me your name."

The Beast narrowed her eyes. "I already told you—"

"Mademoiselle, you and I are the only inhabitants within this castle that can see and speak with one another. While I love the companionship of my horse, and the extravagant birds you keep, it is tiresome to only partake in one sided conversation. Should you and I not try to make this curse under which we suffer more bearable?"

A few sputtering attempts to respond caused the Beast to go

silent for a moment, regaining her composure. "You are a very forward boy."

"Hardly a boy, Mademoiselle. I would wager I'm similar in age to you, if not older."

"Only because the enchantment keeps me trapped in a perpetual cycle of agelessness."

His eyebrows rose almost to his hairline. "You mean you have not aged since the day your curse was enacted?"

The Beast nodded.

Beau fidgeted under her tragic gaze. "And… and how long have you been under its spell?"

Her eyes trailed across the library, looking beyond what he saw. "A hundred and five years."

As shocking as the statement was, it also made sense. A castle off the beaten path where a forest had grown to hide it over the years. Roses with vines as thick as his arm growing everywhere, as if they had been there for hundreds of years. And then the realization that he too was trapped within the timeless nature of this curse added a level of dread to Beau's situation.

With a deep breath, Beau locked eye contact with the Beast. "Would it not be better to spend the next hundred and five years having someone else know your name?"

For the first time, the Beast's features softened. Her furry brows pulled towards one another and for a few moments they sat in silence. "Rosalee." She finally spoke, meeting his gaze. "My name is Rosalee."

The irony of a curse trapping a creature whose name literally meant rose garden was cruel. "Thank you, Rosalee. My sister's name is Rose. It seems you two have something in common."

Rosalee nodded thoughtfully, as if accepting this information about his life before coming to live at the castle.

"My family calls me Beau," he offered.

Rosalee was silence, gazing off into nothingness while Beau contemplated what to say next.

"Do you eat dinner regularly?"

"No, I go out and hunt my prey before devouring it with my teeth and drinking the blood of animals." Her tone was razor sharp as she glanced over at the teacup beside her.

Beau blushed. "No, I didn't mean— Of course you eat regular food. What I meant to say was—" he recollected himself and took a deep breath. "Would you care to join me in the dining hall for dinner this evening?"

~~~~~

"Isn't this a nice change of pace to taking your meals in your bedchambers?"

Rosalee looked up from her first course, tongue suspended over the bowl of cream soup she was lapping. "I am not convinced at present."

Beau smiled. He had grown fond of Rosalee's dry, feigned disinterest in life. "Well, if we are to be trapped for hundreds of years together, perhaps we should learn to make the best of things and form a camaraderie."

"We will not be trapped for hundreds more years."

Beau cocked his head. "Beg pardon?"

"The curse is coming to a close." She stated simply, taking a corner of her cloth napkin and dabbing at her lips. It was odd to witness the mixture of human and animal qualities mingling together in her habits.

"The vines choke out more and more of the castle every day. At some point they will overtake everything that lives within these walls, including myself." Her voice was cold and precise, as if she were talking about the weather and not her impending doom.

"And by overtaking, you mean to say—"

"That I shall die. Yes. But have no fear, I do not think you shall suffer the same fate. Who knows, perhaps by my death you will be freed."

While the idea of returning to his family was a welcomed one, her future death was not. "Can the curse not be broken?"

"Can and will are often two different questions. It can be broken. It will not be broken."

Beau waited for her to share more. "And that is because...?"

The next course came out, served by invisible servants, and Rosalee dove into the pheasant with relish. After a while she noticed he was still waiting for an answer. Huffing, she cleaned a leg bone with her teeth and rolled her eyes. "To love the unlovable."

"Is it a riddle that must be solved?"

Dropping the bone upon her plate with a clatter, Rosalee intertwined her paws and leaned forward in her chair. "Perhaps we should discuss something else. Like you. Why is it you incessantly twist the ring on your finger? Did it belong to a lady you left
~~~~~

behind?"

Beau glanced down at the simple gold band that encircled his pinky, absently spinning it around his finger. "It was my mother's. One of the few things left to me after my Father's ship went down in the ocean and we had to sell most of our possessions to pay off debts from the loss."

Rosalee eyed the empty plate before her as the servants brought desert to them. "I am sorry."

"She was terribly ill towards the end. It was a mercy she did not have to suffer under the burden of our family shame. We could not have provided her the same level of comfort in her dying days otherwise. How about you? I assume you have parents?"

"They died a long time ago."

"I'm sorry. You must miss them."

"You cannot miss those that never wanted you to begin with."

This statement, spoken so factually, surprised Beau. "I don't understand."

"It is a blessing to have parents that love and care for you. Not all children are afforded this. My own parents could not be bothered with a female child. They had tried for years to produce an heir, but none came. I was a nuisance left for the servants to care for in my parent's many absences. When I came of age, they sought to be rid of me and strengthen their alliances with foreign dignitaries. Plans were made for my eventual marriage, but the curse altered things. After my…" Rosalee glanced down at herself. "Disfigurement." She indicated with a wave of her paw. "My parents returned to the castle once. Packed what they wished to take with them, and never returned."

What would it be like to grow up without the love and protection of parents? How difficult it must be to learn one's place in the world without a guiding force to steer one through life and maturity.

"Perhaps something befell them, and they were unable to return?"

Rosalee shook her head, curls shifting around her tufted ears. "No, I had ways of learning their whereabouts. They enjoyed their life away from here until old age took them."

Silence fell for a moment before Beau summoned the courage to ask the question he had been wondering since his arrival. "How were you cursed?"

Perhaps Beau was wearing Rosalee down under his stream of questioning. She only hesitated a moment before turning her gaze on him. "Growing up I was given everything I wanted. My servants loved me in their own way, but they were also my subjects and thus feared the wrath of a child's desires. One night, when the snow was falling, an old beggar came and asked for housing. When the servants brought her before me, I asked what she had to offer in return for my generosity. She offered me a portrait frame..."

Rosalee looked towards the windows covered in wood planks, as if seeing beyond them. "It was unlike any frame I had ever seen, but it held no likeness... she told me it needed no likeness, for it contained magic. I took the mirror from her, asking if the magic could free me from my impending marriage. She told me it could not, but she could, for a price. When I was close enough to smell the stench clinging to the witch's garments, I threw her out of the house, back into the cold, because of the disgusting creature she was. She demanded I return her portrait, but I refused."

"The frame that rests in the study," Beau offered, thinking back to his discovery earlier in the study.

Rosalee nodded. "I learned that day things are not always as they seem. Coveted beauty can enact a terrible curse. The witch I scorned cursed me for stealing all she had when I had so much to offer in return. I would pay for my disgust by turning into a monster. The portrait frame was left as a reminder of all I had lost."

"She cursed you for taking all that she had...which is why the curse fell upon my father when he stole a rose after being given so much..."

"You miss him, don't you?"

"Yes, more than I could say. He and my sister. I worry about them. Father's injury from the war causes him more pain with age. My sister is still young, penniless with no dowry. Much of the hardships of life will rest upon her."

Rosalee focused on the empty dessert plate before her, her paws resting on both sides of it. "You took care of them, didn't you?"

"I did. And I thought I was taking care of them by coming here in my father's stead. But now that I am here... now that I know this curse is one of isolation and not of servitude... I wonder if it would have been better for my family had father come and I remained at the farm to tend to things in his place. I worry about them both."

"I am glad you came to stay." The words were spoken so softly

Beau wasn't sure he actually heard them correctly. But before he could ask, Rosalee stood up, pushing away from the table and walking towards him. "If you could see your family again, would you?"

"Of course, but I thought that was impossible?"

Rosalee motioned for him to rise. "Come with me."

They walked, past the formal staircase, the ornate train of Rosalee's ballgown whispering against the floor behind her. Opening the doors to the study, she motioned for him to be seated upon the chaise that sat before the rose viewing. Even in the moonlight the flowers glow with radiance.

"The roses here are quite stunning."

Rosalee walked to the desk, her padded paws noiseless. "They become a rather offending flower when they have overtaken everything else that used to grow in your gardens." She stopped before the easel displaying the ornamented frame. Gently lifting it from its stand with a grimace, Rosalee returned and sat down beside him before offering it.

"What is this for?"

"The witch did not lie. The frame does contain magic. It allows the viewer to see beyond what is in front of them. A loved one. The beauty of spring. Whatever you wish to see it will reveal to you."

"I don't understand—"

"Hold it in your hands," she said, her soft furred paws taking his hands and placing the mirror within them. "Think of your family and stare into it."

Her eyes sparkled with unshed tears and pierced his soul. Her features seemed so much softer in the moonlight as she sat there, holding his hands within hers. What she was saying seemed absurd.

"Look," she encouraged.

What did he have to lose? Stranger things had happened in the past months. Beau searched within the frame, his own reflection peering back at him through the metal backing. As he continued to stare, thinking of his father and sweet Rose, the glazed finish began to warp and ripple with iridescent colors swirling together before revealing a clear image of his family. A live portrait within the for sides of the frame.

Father sat by the fire, his features worn, Rose curled beside him reading from one of Mother's books. Beau had never seen her without a smile. Even after their mother's passing, even after their lost fortune. But now her features were drawn and sad.

"Are they well?" Rosalee asked, breaking his concentration.

Brushing back a tear, Beau replied. "Yes. They seem healthy…"

Rosalee nodded. "I shall retire now. Feel free to use the library whenever you'd like. It will not bother me."

Beau rose with her, offering her back the magical frame.

"Keep it. It is a gift," she said.

Beau felt warmth spread in his chest, unsure how to process the gift she had just given him. "I- I can't. It is yours."

"It is a reminder of all I lost in the world beyond my gates. It drove me mad seeing my parents happily living in our summer home, moving on while I endured my curse alone. They never gave a second thought to their child… The mirror has been a millstone around my neck. Perhaps for you it can be a blessing."

Beau cleared the lump in his throat. "Thank you, Rosalee. You will never understand the gift you have given me. Thank you, for everything."

She didn't seem to know how to respond to his emotions, so she left without another word, the clicking of her claws against the floors the only sound between them.

~~~~~

Days bled into weeks. Beau's small world began to feel smaller as life remained unchanged. Every day the grounds were still covered with snow, and every week the roses continued to invade more and more, curling into windowsills and twining through the boards. The beautiful vines felt more like a net tightening its grip.

One morning, while in the west wing, Beau noticed a draft coming from one of the rooms. Opening the door, he found that the rose vines had busted through the boarded window, glass shattered across the floor. Further investigation revealed adjourning rooms crumbling under a solid carpet of roses. The curse of the roses had claimed the gardens. It seemed they intended to take the house as well. After that day, Beau tried to rid his mind of the haunting image by avoiding the west wing.

Beau lost track of how long he had been a resident of the castle. Every morning Beau took his meal in his room, rode around the grounds with Claudius, and spent his afternoons perusing the world of literature, often seated beside Rosalee in the library. Their conversations became more frequent— the only respite from the monotony of life. At dinnertime, he would accompany Rosalee to the
~~~~~

dining hall for their meal before retiring from one another's company later in the evening. But every night was the same. Beau would enter the study and stare into the empty portrait, longing to help ease the hardships of his family.

"What is that you are reading?" Rosalee asked one day.

Beau glanced down at his book, unsure. He had not paid attention when he grabbed it off the shelf. Turning the pages was more a distraction for his occupied mind, the words lost on him. "Ummm..." he lifted the book to show her the title.

"A Study on the Finer Points of Provincial Dance," Rosalee read aloud. "I used to enjoy dancing a hundred years ago."

Beau paged through the book, noting the step-by-step layout of the refinement and skills required of many popular dances. "I imagine the ballrooms in the castle saw quite a bit of frivolity in their day."

Rosalee smiled, leaning over the arm of her chair to look at the images within the book. "Yes. Mother was always throwing a ball. Sometimes multiple in one week. It was the one social function I looked forward to. A chance to meet interesting people..." her voice trailed off as she set her whiskered chin within the palm of her hand, gaze drifting.

Beau noted the sadness in her dark rimmed eyes. Over time he had grown accustomed to the oddity of her features. The large furry ears sprouting from her skull no longer shocked him, the furry ruff around her neck seemed natural, and he found the way her wet nose twitched curiously whenever she caught a whiff of food to be endearing.

"Do you miss it?"

His words snapped her out of whatever dream world she had fallen into. "I do."

Rising from his chair, Beau stretched out his hand. "May I have this dance?"

Rosalee's brows drew together in confusion.

"Surely in this curse we can find some moments of comfort and happiness." His words were as much to reassure himself as they were her. "Come, join me."

Taking his hand, Rosalee stood, unsure. They began, slow at first, Beau reacquainting his body with the movements ingrained in his memory from childhood. His mother had taught him how to dance. It was one area of his tutoring his mother insisted be hers.

Beau and Rosalee moved back and forth to invisible music, swaying and circling around stacks of books and furniture. Beau had never liked dancing, but here, in this place, it felt right. There was no judgment, no expectation from other partygoers. It was just he and Rosalee, together within the walls of his imaginary ballroom. A smile spread across his lips and he looked at the woman in his arms.

Rosalee kept her gaze downcast, long lashes veiling her eyes. A softness had overcome her as she glided across the floor. Refracted light shifted across her dress, shimmering beneath the dome of the glass ceiling. The fabric rustled softly from their movements, keeping time with the clicking of her claws upon the floor.

She must have felt the heat of his gaze. As she lifted her eyes to meet his, he felt an odd sense of belonging sweep through him. The emotion jarred him and instead of turning right, he went left. As he realized his misstep he tried to overcorrect and stumbled over a stack of books, sending them to the ground in a tangle of limbs with Rosalee landing on top of him.

They came face to face, inches apart, her whispers standing at full attention. Shock rimmed Rosalee's eyes in white while all her muscles stiffened against him. Her response seemed almost animalistic. She drew back, scooting across the floor away from him.

Beau gently helped her up, holding her hand before she could pull it away from him. "Rosalee…" She looked as if she might bolt like a rabbit at any moment. For the first time, Beau noticed how fragile she was. She still saw herself as an animal, not a creature worthy of love and kindness. "Rosalee. When I see you, I don't see a beast."

Her whiskered brow rose into a wrinkled forehead. "Then what is it you see?" She whispered.

He smiled, brushing his fingers against the furry softness of her cheek. "I see so much more."

She pulled her hand away from him, and Beau was unsure if he had upset her or not. Without saying another word, Rosalee left, Beau's heart aching with her departure.

Rosalee did not join him at dinner, only further causing Beau concern. Did he say something that hurt her? Everything had been so perfect, such a happy moment.

After he finished his meal, there was still no sign of Rosalee, so Beau retreated to the study early. He took the frame in his hands and sat before the rose viewing; the charm of the gardens now lost on him. As the swirls of magical current parted beneath his gaze, Beau noticed that there was something wrong. Rose was wringing her hands, pacing back and forth before a closed door. His father was not present, and the fireplace seemed low. In a few moments, the door opened, and a doctor stepped out. Rose rushed to him, concern etching her features.

Beau cursed the witch for creating an enchanted frame without sound. Maybe that was the point. Pictures don't talk. Or maybe the lack of human voice was another cruel act meant to drive Rosalee mad? It was driving him mad!

The doctor left, and Rose entered the bedroom slowly. In the bed was his father, coughing, a fevered flush across his pale skin. Rose looked terrified. She tried to offer him a bowl of broth, but his father pushed it away with a weak shake of his head.

He was ill. Wasting away in the bed, feeble, like his mother had. Perhaps dying. What a burden to have to bear alone. What would become of his sister? He would lose his father, never able to assure him of his love. He had come to this castle intent to keep his family safe and he had failed. Tears stung his eyes, escaping at the corner of his lids.

Padded footsteps entered the room.

"Beau? Is something wrong?" Rosalee's voice wrapped around him like a blanket. She came up beside him, stretching out her paw but drawing back before reaching him.

"Yes." He said, brushing at his eyes with his sleeve. "My Father is sick. I don't know if he will make it. And my sister…" Rose would be out on the streets. She would have nowhere left to turn. Worse, she would be taken advantage of by men in her compromised state. And he would be here, locked in a rose entwined castle unable to do anything. The thought of his family's suffering, and the weariness of his isolation from the world came together in a wave of overwhelming grief for all he had lost. Beau's chest caved in on itself as he muffled a sob.

"You should go to them," Rosalee said softly.

Beau hid his tears in his hands. "I can't. You know I can't."

Sitting down beside him, Rosalee took his hand, removing his mother's ring from his finger and sliding it onto her own. "I have now stolen that which belongs to you. You are free from the curse of the roses. Go to your family. When you are ready, you can return to claim your mother's ring."

Beau stared in disbelief. Could his curse be broken so easily? He looked at the golden ring now circling her smallest digit and then into her eyes. Pain tightened the corner of her eyes. She would be alone. Again.

"I will come back to you, I promise." He said, taking her paws in his hand.

Rosalee tried to smile and nod, weakly. She was putting on a brave face for him, but he could see the weight of her isolation resettling on her shoulders. "Take the portrait frame with you. It was a gift. May it remind you of the time we shared. I will have the servants send you with a cart of provisions you can hitch to Claudius to help your family."

"You are a gift, Rosalee! I must go, quickly, but I will come back. I promise."

And with that, he left her alone, the cursed flowers her only company.

~~~~~

Beau stayed in a constant state of busyness upon returning home. There was so much to set right from his absence. When he left the castle, Rosalee did as promised and attached a cart of provisions to Claudius. Beau learned that it carried food to stock the pantry, bedding and clothing to protect from the elements, and bags of gold to pay a physician for constant care and tend to the many needs of the household. It was a constant reminder at home of how much Rosalee had changed his life.

Once his father's fever broke, Beau tried explaining to his family that he had not escaped but been freed. He told them the curse of the roses and the witch who cursed Rosalee. At first, his family did not believe him. It was easier to imagine her a villain than a creature treated cruelly by the world. But as time went on, and the family blossomed from the relief provided by the castle, they came to feel empathy for the creature trapped within the rose-covered castle.

Beau would often talk about returning, but his father protested. The mistress of the castle freed him. Beau's place was with his family, not her.

In Beau's absence, food and money had become scarce. They had fallen behind, and the garden would only produce cabbages, an item that did not fetch a good price at market. Beau began to strategize new ways for the household to bring in money with the purchase of a milk cow. His father was steadily growing stronger and the
~~~~~

household began to flourish again. They were comfortable and happy together in their modest little cottage on the outskirts of the village and near Rosalee's forest.

It was all Beau could have hoped for, but in his heart, emptiness remained.

"Is Father in bed?" Beau asked as he prepared the fire for the night while Rose sat down in the rocking chair near him.

Rose nodded, winding a ball of yarn from the basket beside her. "Yes, he is well."

"Good," Beau said, poking at the fire and staring aimlessly into the embers.

"Are you?"

"Am I what?" Beau asked.

"Well. Are you well, Brother?"

"Of course," he replied. "Why wouldn't I be?"

Rose tapped her foot softly with every rocking motion. "Because you have lost your heart."

"I don't know what you mean."

"Yes, you do. I wanted you back so badly, brother, but I did not know that coming home would cost you so dearly." Rose stood up, replacing her yarn work in the basket. "Father wishes to keep you because he cannot bear the thought of you held captive for his crime. But your heart is still held captive, Beau. Your Rosalee has afforded us a foundation upon which we can build a life. But there is no life here for you so long as your heart remains with her."

Placing a kiss upon his cheek, Rose departed for bed, leaving Beau alone to wrestle with his thoughts.

That night, Beau tossed back and forth in fitful sleep. His mind wandered through dark castle corridors, seeking light amidst the shadows. Darkness covered all. He searched and searched, but there was no life within the walls he had come to view as home. Outside, the moon shone sickly, wind howling past him.

A spectral figure stood within the dream world, the first sign of life. Dark curls trailed down her back. She walked the grounds, alone.

Beau followed, her ethereal dress of gossamer trailing behind her in the wind. She drew him into the rose maze, fingers trailing over the blooms as she weaved within the twists and turns of the hedges. He chased her, sometimes losing sight for a moment before catching a glance of her dress as she turned the corner.

Beau tried to call out to the girl, but he found he had no voice within this world. She seemed familiar, like he had met her before but couldn't place it. As the dense foliage pressed in on all sides, he plunged further, always following the girl. She kept moving, quickening her pace as she broke through an opening. Beau came to a halt. The girl stood, winds swirling her dress around her pale legs, hair whipping past eyes green like the grasses of spring, yet full of sorrow and tears.

He recognized her as the girl in the library portrait, but her eyes were Rosalee's. She was in pain. Beau tried to reach for her, but she stayed outside his grasp. Sadly, she looked towards the fountain shaded under the massive weeping willows that littered the maze. The waters had frozen into thick ice cascading down towards the basin. In front of it a single rose lay, not red like every other rose in the garden, but white. Beau reached to pick it up, petals cold and lifeless, falling from the bud at his touch. Entwined around the stem was a golden ring.

Beau awoke with a shudder, flying out of bed. Was it a dream or a vision? Tearing through his armoire he pulled out the magic frame. He begged and pleaded to see Rosalee, but all he could see was the shadowed rose maze.

Saddling up Claudius, Beau rode hard towards the castle, fearful of what he might find. The journey felt like forever as Beau plunged through the forest, pushing Claudius harder and harder. Using the mirror to help guide him through the twists and turns, Beau felt relief when the castle rose in the skyline.

Something was wrong. Thick vines wove through the gates and barred his entrance. How, in the space of a month, had this happened?

Leaving Claudius tied to a tree, Beau scaled the gates, thorns ripping at his cloak and biting into his gloves. As his feet hit the snow-covered ground, he took off running towards the maze, noticing the various garden statues had crumbled beneath the powerful jaws of the rose vines.

Beau was grateful he had memorized every twist and turn of the maze in his many months of isolation. The ground beneath his feet had become more treacherous during his absence. Sinister vines grew like roots warping the ground, intent on causing a fall. Vines tore at everything, ripping stones out of place and crumbling parts of the castle beneath their grip.

He ran and ran until he came up short in the center of the maze. There, where the white rose in his dream had lain, was Rosalee, but not as he had left her. Roses and vines ripped at her flesh and closed her within its snakelike embrace. The life was literally being choked from her. She strained for breath, her chest heaving against the thorns.

Dropping to his knees, Beau ripped at the vines, fearing he was too late. Why hadn't she run from the vines? Why had she just let the roses overtake her? Blood splatters stained the snow beneath her body where the thorns had pierced her flesh.

"Rosalee, please!" He begged for a response as he loosened the vines from around her upper body. She was cold. So very cold as she lay there, usually perked ears limp and fur crusted with blood, eyes dull and unblinking.

"You... you came back." Rosalee wheezed through her parted lips. Rose petals and thorns clung to her fur.

"Don't you dare die on me!" he cried.

In a weak voice, barely audible, she bequeathed the castle and all therein to him. "Bring your family to live with you," she whispered, her breath sending a puff of white vapor in the cold air.

"No!" He cried, drawing her into his arms as best he could. "We belong together! You are the only person that makes me feel whole. Rosalee!" His voice broke. "Rosalee?"

He stroked back the curls from her face, his tears falling on her furry cheek and freezing on his own face as he placed a kiss upon her dark lips. She no longer fought for air. "I love you, Rosalee." He whispered against her mottled fur.

There was a cracking sound, like ice breaking. A bright light emanated from Rosalee's body as a gust of wind, strong enough to swirl the snow around them pulled at her body. He tried to hold onto her, but she was ripped from his grasp by the storm, vines snapping. The world whirled around him. Flashes of light sparked, causing Beau to shield his eyes as he saw stars.

An explosive thunderclap caused his ears to ring before the winds died down, replaced by the sound of moving water. Hesitantly, Beau removed his hand from his eyes, only to wince from the powerful moonlight streaming through the trees and caressing the green grass beneath his knees.

Startled, Beau scrambled to his feet, whipping around and taking in the sights surrounding him. The willow trees were no longer draped with snow, the white replaced by pink flowers clustering down their limbs. The fountain sprayed water in jubilation while the breeze carried the fragrance of honeysuckle and cherry blossoms.

Flowers of all different assortment decorated the garden surrounding the fountain. The rose-hedged walls that once held the cursed red blooms now displayed a collection of red, pink, yellow, white, and variegated blossoms.

And there, in the center of everything, was a girl with dark curls and a simple gold band around her finger. Her white dress draped over her shoulders, iridescent peacock feathers adorning her.

"You loved the unlovable." She whispered.

"You were always lovable. You just didn't know it." He closed the gap between them.

"You came back."

"I'm sorry it wasn't sooner." He let his fingers brush back a curl from her face as he gazed into her green eyes, gleaming with life.

"I forgive you if you promise to stay with me. Freely this time."

Beau smiled, cupping her cheek. "I want you to meet my family."

Rosalee dropped her gaze. "What if they don't like me…"

"They will love you! Like I do…"

She looked up at him, her eyes smiling. "And I love you."

Beau felt his chest tighten. "Who would have thought a stolen rose could bring me such happiness."

Rosalee entwined her fingers through his. "You know, I grew to hate roses… The curse made me sick of them. Now… no flower is more beautiful."

END

DAUGHTER OF THE BEASTLY BEAUTY

Michelle L. Levigne

'Na wanted nothing more than to be considered ordinary.

Average.

Normal.

Impossible. She lived in an enchanted castle, for one thing.

There were no human servants in the castle, just very efficient breezes. Because of various curses flung at her parents over the years, since they took up their full-time occupation of curse-breakers and enchantment-smashers, working for such a notorious couple could be dangerous. Having no other people in the castle was no hardship, because the breezes could do almost anything. Whip up a gourmet feast in no time (without an accompanying chorus of disembodied voices and instruments, fortunately). Create a ball gown that five neighboring princesses would have fought to the death over (which was why 'Na had no playmates most of the time, as she was growing up). And most important, handle the cleaning of the castle and tending of the garden when the lord and lady were away on some new mission. Which was most of the time.

The breezes also made very good nursemaids, from 'Na's parents' point of view, at least, because they could be everywhere, instantly. That made it hard for her to get away with anything. That also made it nearly impossible for the occasional vengeful sorcerer or faerie queen to wreak vengeance by stealing a child with so much magical potential. Being the daughter of the Beastly Beauty and the Dis-enchanted Prince sort of guaranteed there would be strong magical hijinks in her future. Or maybe the more accurate phrasing was that she was doomed to it.

'Na grew up in the library, when her parents weren't home. Mostly because of the lack of people to talk to. The breezes were wonderful servants, but decidedly disappointing when it came to conversation. Fortunately, 'Na's magical potential awoke early, allowing her to learn to read before she learned to walk. Until she learned enough self-defense spells to safely leave the protections built into the castle walls when she was alone, 'Na spent most of her days, and many nights in the library.

She still spent most of her time in the library now, even though she was self-sufficient and more than able to defend herself. The library, the gathered knowledge and magic suited her. She especially loved the quiet, except when the magic-filled books got their feelings hurt through neglect. Or they had temper tantrums when different spells woke up too much and got into arguments over which was more powerful. Then it was best to retreat to one of the gate towers and daydream until the storm and whirlwind of torn pages settled down. 'Na grew extremely adept at putting books back together, and creating new looks for them when the bindings split or the covers wore thin

She could only name a handful of people, in history and currently alive, combined, who had the upbringing and life that she did. So 'ordinary' and 'average' moved farther away from her grasp every year.

And of course, there was her name. 'Na was short for Belladonna. Her parents gave in and saddled her with the name because it was the only one that more than three dozen allies could agree on. They knew the value in not irritating people who could snap out curses while sneezing, especially slightly disgruntled faeries and enchantresses. It didn't matter if that happened on purpose or accidentally. Best to live on the defensive. Especially when 'Na was young and easily snatched up by pixies or eagles, or able to slide through the tiny, momentary tears that often appeared in the fabric of reality. One of the hazards of living in such a heavily enchanted castle, full of magical books. And of course, the growing hoard of magical objects, beneficial as well as inimical, that her parents collected through the years. Some were souvenirs, and others were brought home to the castle to keep them out of the hands of idiots and villains. All that collected magic had a tendency to thicken the atmosphere and make magical accidents even more probable.

And, of course, push 'ordinary, average, and normal' even farther away from 'Na.

This moon, being ordinary and average was even more impossible.

Her seventeenth birthday was approaching. Actually, her birthdays, plural, because she had been born at the stroke of midnight. Her parents always celebrated on both days, and took all the usual magical precautions, just in case. Being born at midnight had a tendency to leave her open to twice as many of the usual, expected magical curses for someone of her pedigree.

Her parents were away on another disenchantment mission, and because of the very touchy nature of this pivotal birthday, they hadn't taken her with them. Best to leave her within the defenses of the castle, just in case. For all any of them knew, enemies made through the years could have left all sorts of curses around the countryside surrounding the castle, sort of an obstacle course to maneuver through, time-triggered for her birthday.

And second ... there was a somewhat patchy, bedraggled, arthritic bunny scowling up at her from the threshold of the castle gates, old bloodstains visible on his massive front teeth.

'Na couldn't name a single enchanted prince or princess or poor-but-deserving maiden who had a wannabe vampire bunny for a playmate and sometimes-guardian. Another step away from the realm of ordinary.

Well, at least she wouldn't spend her birthday alone. The housekeeping breezes and the talking books really didn't count. They weren't able to plow through an entire banquet table of goodies, when she was in the mood to do some comfort eating. For hours on end. And what was the fun in doing that all alone? So this visitor, despite arriving so wretchedly early in the day, was rather welcome. At least, 'Na hoped so. Fang didn't show up anymore unless he needed help.

"So, Fang, you're back." She leaned against the doorframe and rubbed her eyes to get the sleepy-grit out.

Among his other qualities, Fang had the amazing ability to arrive at the crack of dawn, leap up, and pound the door with his hind feet hard enough to sound like an entire troop of soldiers. 'Na had awakened from a sodden sleep, her brain tangled with dreams full of portents and complaints, and seriously considered throwing something vile out the tower window on whoever had woke her up so early.

Fang hopped backward and looked around, his left ear curving down in a question mark and his right ear pointing into the castle.

"Mom and Dad are gone on another curse-breaking quest." 'Na sighed. "Out of the castle, out of the enchanted forest, out of the kingdom."

The left ear drooped in disappointment. Fang had been her

mother's sidekick back in the days when the Beastly Beauty had terrorized the enchanted forest. His right ear curved into a sideways question mark, and twitched, pointing down the road away from the castle.

"No, I couldn't go with them this time. Complications." She shrugged and stepped back. "Coming in?"

Helping her parents with disenchantments and curse-breaking was usually interesting, if not always fun. People had a tendency to ignore her, which was lovely most of the time. Usually because they were so busy gawking at her parents. 'Na didn't have their reputation, so she hid behind it. She rather enjoyed the fact that her only "reputation" so far was for being supremely organized, the perfect support staff, and her prodigious memory. If her parents needed to look up the history of a country or royal bloodline or haunted castle or curse, they asked her before they went to the library. That and an enchanted bag of unlimited capacity, and who needed a cast of thousands to handle the never-ending task of making the contents of the library and the magical items treasure room behave?

Several times over the years when Fang showed up at an inopportune time, 'Na had considered putting him in the bag of unlimited capacity. Just to get him out of the way. The only downside to that option was that he would still be there, preserved, only a few seconds having passed in his perception since she put him in. Plus, Fang was wickedly smart and he would know what had been done to him. Unless she managed to put him to sleep before she shoved him in?

Both Fang's ears drooped and he sniffled and turned to give a glare at the rising sun. A whiff of smoke rose from his bedraggled fur, and he glared at it. If power of will was all that was required, Fang's entire body would have burst into flame at the touch of sunlight. However, that wasn't all that was required. Now, 'Na understood what brought the old, battle-scarred bunny to her door so early in the morning.

"Well, come on in," she said with a sigh, telling herself to be grateful he hadn't come in the middle of the night. Fang lived like he was allergic to sunlight, most of the time, to prepare for the role he had been longing for all his unnaturally long life. "Let me guess. The vampires threw you out again?"

Fang sighed and hopped forward, a little more crooked than the last time he had come back to the castle to mope. And grumble. And drown his sorrows. And wait for 'Na's parents to plead for some understanding on the part of his adopted tribe.

The housekeeping breezes swirled around to greet Fang, pick him up, and carry him up to the tower room kept waiting for him. The vampire tribe got fed up with his bloodthirsty curmudgeonly attitude about once every fourth moon. He made them look bad, they said.

"Well, what do you expect, looking like a toy that should have been tossed onto the refuse fire about twenty years ago?" 'Na muttered. "You're not good for their dignity and reputation. Charm is all they have going for them."

Fang was far enough ahead of her as she trudged up the stairs to the top of the tower, he didn't hear her. It was always wise to grumble about Fang outside of his hearing. Those front incisors of his kept growing. While he had gained quite a reputation as a wood carver in the effort to wear down those vicious weapons of his, he wasn't above some punitive nibbling and gnashing if he got irritated.

However, 'Na's grumbles gave her an idea. She waited to propose her plan until the housekeeping breezes had finished their routine of scrubbing Fang and feeding him. And then scrubbing him again. He refused to eat anything that wasn't red, in his old age. The juicier the better. Which explained why a second bath was needed.

"If you're plump and cuddly and big-eyed again, maybe they'll beg you to stay and ignore your more drippy aspects," 'Na said. "After all, you're a bunny. Not a rabbit. Not a hare. Not a coney. A bunny. Look like one again."

Fang tipped his head to one side as far as his arthritis would allow and waggled his mangy eyebrows, clearly saying, "How are you going to manage that one?"

"This is the enchanted library castle," she said with a toss of her head. "Among all those anti-spell and anti-curse and anti-enchantment books, there has to be an aging spell or mange-ifying spell or something that would make someone look as worn and lumpy as you. So, we work it backward and make you young and plump and fast again. Cuddly enough, the vampires will beg you to join the tribe again."

Fang's eyes narrowed, then they lit up with that manic fire that had once been a near-constant state for him, back when he and 'Na's mother had been young. They had built a manic reputation, mainly to drive away that slithery, pompous, self-righteous Prince Ruprick who was determined to tame and marry her. That reputation had brought a certain adventurer into the kingdom, to try to capture the Beastly Beauty of the forest. 'Na's parents got their happily-ever-after, to some extent, and Fang finally got his invitation to join the vampires. The only downer was that Prince Ruprick became King Ruprick XI.

The kingdom certainly hadn't gotten their happily-ever-after, because every Ruprick was like the one before. Still, didn't Fang deserve to have his dream, even if only partially? As if he heard her thoughts, the old, bloodthirsty bunny intensified his questioning look, very clearly doubting her dedication to the plan, or perhaps her ability to carry it out.

"All right," she said, punctuated with a sigh. "I know how many books are in the library, and how long it might take to find the right spell and work out how to do it backward. But look at it this way, what do you have to lose? We'll make you cute and cuddly and a fair damsel magnet once again, Fang. I swear, or my name isn't Belladonna."

~~~~~

'Na adored the library. Her parents loved books almost as much as they loved each other, and whenever they had a chance on their frequent rescue missions, they brought books home. It really was amazing, and a little depressing, how many castles were out there with cobweb-festooned and dust-covered libraries that many of their occupants didn't even know were there. They gladly gave wagonloads of books to their rescuers. One of 'Na's jobs, as she learned to read and write, was to organize the books. She recorded how many and which books came from which beleaguered nobleman or down-on-his-luck wizard. She organized the books on the shelves by topic. Then she kept several journals to sort the books by kingdom, by author, and even by the magical entities associated with the various stories or spells. Such as giants, elves, faeries, shapeshifters, dwarves, goblins, pixies, talking beasts, and so on.

For fun, she figured out the ratio between number of books from each source, and how soon her parents had to ride out to rescue that book-donor yet again. 'Na was sure that somewhere out there was a formula relating to loss of knowledge and decreasing amount of reading time each year, and the frequency of utterly stupid, avoidable mistakes. Often repeated mistakes. Such as activating or
~~~~~

re-activating, or falling into yet another malign spell. Or irritating the wrong enchanter or magical being. Why? Because those clumsy, oblivious oafs didn't recognize the very clear warning signs. Which they should have learned and remembered from the first time they needed rescuing. Or the fifth time. Or the twentieth time. Or lessons their parents or grandparents should have learned and passed on to them.

For instance, recording their memories and warnings in books. Which they most likely had done, but those books had been neglected, discarded, or given away.

The collected intelligence and protective measures encompassing the surrounding fifty kingdoms increasingly lay in the growing library of 'Na's castle. Fortunately, the castle's enchantments automatically expanded the library to accommodate the wagonloads of books brought in every year.

'Na inhaled with pleasure, like she always did when she stepped into the library. Nothing more invigorating and full of potential than the aroma of paper, dust, leather, and magic-infused ink.

Fang snorted.

"Yes, I know it's a mess. I'm in the middle of reorganizing. I decided I needed to group books by type of enchanter and their specialties. Or maybe by geography and the alphabet. I'm still experimenting. There is far too much repetition, if you ask me. I've actually found several dozen titles that are multiple copies. Can you imagine how important those books have to be, to have those ink-stained, nearsighted monks make more than one copy?"

Fang snorted again. He wasn't impressed by the wealth of knowledge. He couldn't possibly be irritated at the mess of stacks of books everywhere, blocking the aisles between the half-empty shelves. No one who got as dusty, mangy, bedraggled, and blood-spotted as Fang cared about messes. Except perhaps pride in *making* enormous messes.

He stopped snorting when 'Na settled down at the central worktable and consulted the master directory she had been compiling since she was five years old. He hopped up on the table and leaned close enough she felt his hot breath on her arm. As long as he didn't try for a snack, she didn't mind. There was something comforting in having someone else warm and alive in the castle while her parents were away. Housekeeping breezes and enchanted kitchen equipment and self-filling wash basins and larders were all well and good, but even a bookish girl got lonely once in a while.

~~~~~

Two days later, 'Na and Fang had read through the thirtieth book with a possible spell and discarded it. She sighed and got up to put the book on the shelf where its fellows would join it when she finished her reorganizing. Then she stretched her arms to the ceiling and bent over backwards, stretching. Her stomach twisted and growled loudly enough to get an impressed, wide-eyed look from Fang.

On cue, the library doors swung open and the housekeeping breezes swirled into the room with a large tray of lunch. Tucked in among the bowls of radishes, strawberries, tomatoes, hot peppers, rhubarb, and a steaming venison pie, was a glistening, pink, sparkling cake. Magic shimmered all around it, sending up streamers of light that formed blurry words and numbers.

'Na tripped over a pile of books when she got close enough to see the number seventeen, repeating over and over.

She muttered curses in forty-two different languages in the thirty-six seconds it took to force her feet to navigate the obstacle course stacks of books. The tray hovered by the central table. Of course, it didn't stay there. The library's protective spells usually prevented eating within its precincts. 'Na followed the tray out into the hall, where the housekeeping breezes had thoughtfully set up a table with a place setting for her and a ramp for Fang to get up to the other end of the table. He hopped eagerly behind her, and nearly didn't need the ramp to reach the tray when it came to rest on the table. His mangled nose twitched, and he hopped as close to the cake as he could get without landing in one of the bowls of his lunch. He did have some manners, after all.

"It's my birthday already," 'Na muttered. "How did that happen?"

"Happy birthday, dearest." Her parents' voices came out of the swirls of rainbow shimmers surrounding the cake, taking turns talking. "We're so disappointed we can't be there with you today, but we know you're very well capable of taking care of yourself on such a momentous day. You don't need our protection. Not like the dozens of numb-witted princesses and their alarmist parents who take such extreme measures that they bring on the curses they're trying to prevent. Nothing like a simple pair of thick gloves to prevent so many pricking curses. But that's beside the point. Please
~~~~~

take simple precautions. We know you'll stay in the castle. No need to remind you. But just to be safe, don't let any visitors in. Don't go digging in the garden. Don't eat anything the breezes don't give you, and don't help yourself to the replenishing larders. Just in case someone nasty manages to access the other end of one. Tuck yourself up nice and safe in the library and enjoy the peace and quiet. You'll pass your seventeenth birthday safely. When we get home, we'll have a jolly celebration. We found Smedley on our way here, and Uncle Milrose thinks he finally found that fire repression spell, so Smedley can come back to live with us. You'd like that, wouldn't you, dearest?"

"Yes, I would like that very much," 'Na whispered. She looked around the library, and for once didn't wince when she glimpsed the dark corner that was still charred. Smedley, still a baby at the time, had set two bookcases on fire. Entirely an accident, and should have been entirely preventable. But she had only been four years old herself, and it never occurred to her that dragons equaled fire at inconvenient times, and fire and ancient books didn't go together.

"We love you, dearest, and we're so disappointed, and quite frankly, irritated that we can't be there with you. A girl of your heritage is almost certainly doomed to having something momentous happen on her seventeenth birthday. Be careful. We know you are, and you make us so very proud. We'll see you as soon as we fix this numb-wit's problem for the umpteenth time. If he had a tenth of your intelligence and common sense, he wouldn't keep bringing this wretched curse on himself. Well, we mustn't grumble, and you have a cake to enjoy. We love you, dearest. Happy birthday."

The sparkles faded and the housekeeping breezes lifted the plate with the cake and set it on the table directly in front of 'Na.

"I wish ..."

'Na paused and didn't quite hold her breath, waiting for the castle to react. Or for something or someone outside or inside the castle to react. She had learned somewhere between her second and third birthday that it simply did not pay to make even the mildest, most harmless, or even the most helpful of wishes inside the enchanted castle. Centuries ago, some wizard or enchanter had tried to bend the wish-granting magic of the castle to his will. He wasn't even evil, but simply frustrated and trying to take a shortcut. He had bent it all right. According to 'Na's father, instead of harnessing the magic to his will, he had given it ***self-will.*** The castle granted wishes as it chose. It never gave the exact wish someone made, no matter how specific they were when they voiced the wish.

Even worse, the infected area of warped wish-granting was spreading out from the castle. On last tally, a frustrated stepfather half a league away from the castle had shouted, "I wish you would grow up," to his dimwitted stepson. The irritating snot had grown upward, but hadn't matured a jot. He was at last measurement ten cubits tall and still growing, perhaps a finger's thickness every moon.

Considering the doubly tricky circumstance of this being her seventeenth birthday, 'Na feared that even thinking her wish, for someone with a face and voice to share the cake with her, might be enough to trigger the quixotic magic of the castle. And not in her favor.

Despite loving him dearly, even when he was curmudgeonly, Fang just didn't count. Playing charades to interpret the semi-sign language of his ears could be irritating at times. She wanted someone who could talk, maybe even sing a birthday song for her.

"Thank you, Mummy and Da-dear," she whispered, knowing her parents would hear her.

All in all, perhaps it was for the best that they weren't together on this landmark, if-anything-can-go-horribly-wrong-it-will birthday. Somewhere out there, some nasty wizard, enchanter, sorcerer, hedge witch, or seer had awakened on the wrong side of the pallet. If her parents were here with her, the gathering magic potential might be enough to get the grump's attention. Chances were, the grump would be in a bad enough mood to try to take advantage of that surge of magic. Because of course, this was her seventeenth birthday, and that meant trouble.

Before she could ask, a knife appeared, hovering in the air over the cake. The housekeeping breezes cut her a large slice, enough to put her into a sweets-induced haze for the entire day. 'Na chuckled and thanked them. With her venison pie in one hand and the plate of cake in the other, she headed for the stairs to sit in the gate tower. Looking out over the countryside, 'Na could relax and indulge in daydreaming while Fang buzzed through his very red lunch. She figured she had at least two hours, as he slept through his after-lunch haze, before he would want to get back to work.

As a bribe, she left the remainder of the cake for him to devour. If she was lucky, he would sleep for the entire afternoon, likely covered with frosting and three different flavors of preserves in between the delicate layers. She would have peace for the remainder of the first day of her birthday.

The sound of hooves clopped on the wide road leading up to the castle gates. She heard it before she got to the top of the stairs and stepped into the tower room. 'Na muffled a groan in an enormous mouthful of cake. From the crackling sound underneath the heavy hooves—at least two horses, large destriers—she guessed the castle's decorating magic had turned the pavement into seashells this week. She thought that was a nice touch, and wondered for a moment, while she took another huge mouthful of cake, if the castle had done it because she liked to go to the seashore and collect shells. She was more than willing to believe it was aware and paid attention to its inhabitants. Her parents agreed with her. It was always wise to treat anything magical with respect and courtesy. Even if there was no real evidence, other than a growing list of coincidences, that a magical object or creature or building was aware.

'Na took another mouthful and peered out, staying as much in the shadows of the tower room as she could. She chuckled, nearly sending some frosting up her nose. Yes, she had been right. Not just seashells but rainbow stripes. Very nice touch.

"Thank you. Lovely," she whispered to the castle, then swallowed, wiped her mouth, took a deep breath, and stepped up to the tower window and into the light.

Of course, the overdressed prince and his liveried companion didn't look up as they approached the closed gates of the castle. Weren't princes taught properly anymore about the necessity of asking questions as they went through unfamiliar territory? What idiot approached a castle, much less an enchanted castle with a growing reputation, without preparation of some kind? In this case, simple common sense said to check for guards in the towers of the gate. Especially a closed gate, with a sign that warned not to irritate the occupants or the dragon sleeping under the threshold. Granted, the dragon had moved out decades ago, when he outgrew the chamber, but 'Na's father had left the sign. It had effectively kept away the peskier visitors who didn't have enough magic in their blood to sense there was no dragon to worry about. Smedley was supposed to take up that job someday, when he learned to control his fire.

No, wait. 'Na had grumbled too soon. The companion looked up. A little late in her opinion. The time to check the windows and arrow slits and boiling oil portals in a castle was at the far end of the long path leading up to the gates. Not just a few horse lengths from imminent disaster and injury.

The companion reined in his horse and stood up in the stirrups and bowed. The prince noticed a few seconds later and yanked hard, making his horse snort and dance sideways a few steps before coming to a halt. He looked around and frowned at his companion, then when the young man stood up again and looked up at the tower window, the prince looked up.

"Ah, greetings, lovely maiden." He cleared his throat and bowed, but not half as deeply as the companion. He dropped back down into his saddle, earning another snort from his horse.

Is he always this inconsiderate, or is he having a bad day? she asked the destrier.

The big gray warhorse snorted and tossed his mane, then whinnied, *Huh? Well, that's a surprise. Guess the older cobs in the stable were right. Powerful enchanters live here.*

No, just grew up soaking in magic. It's an occupational hazard, my father says.

No, he's not so inconsiderate. The warhorse tossed his head. *He's just in a bad mood. His father has ordered him to win the hand of the girl who lives here.*

Oh, bother. Why?

Because the king couldn't win her mother. Humans have such stupid ideas and goals, the horse said, stomping and dropping a pile for emphasis.

'Na snorted and muffled a chuckle of agreement.

"Do I have the pleasure of speaking to the lovely maiden, Belladonna?" the prince said.

"Who told you she was lovely? How do you know she isn't a beast like her mother was? Or maybe she's a musclebound bully like her father?" 'Na wanted desperately to disappear back into the shadows before she burst out laughing. She did love playing with the misconceptions of the people of the surrounding countryside. Too many half-truths had sprung up around her parents in the years since they had shattered each other's disguises and broke several minor curses on the kingdom. And yes, frustrated Prince Ruprick's ambition to rescue the rumored lovely maiden being held prisoner in the castle by the Beastly Beauty.

"I've heard about you—"

"How do you know I'm the Lady Belladonna? Isn't that somewhat presumptuous, thinking the first girl you encounter, before you even step through the gates—which I'm not going to open for you, by the way—how do you know the first girl is the one you're looking for?"

"Pardon us, Lady Belladonna, but we did take steps to prepare for this interview," the companion said. He had finally settled down into his saddle again.

He means he did all the preparation, the destrier said. *Lovely boy. Courteous to all the animals and servants. The king was smart enough to assign him to the prince when they were both still on leading strings, when his seers said he was wise beyond his years. Hoped he'd be a good influence on the prince. And he is. Most of the time.*

"We know there are no visible servants in the castle. Just housekeeping spells. Your lord and lady parents crossed the border four days ago on another mission of mercy. Perhaps the timing isn't good, or polite, since some could construe evil intentions, approaching you without your parents present—"

They learned your parents were gone after they were halfway here, the companion's horse filled in. *Should have heard them argue over whether it would help them in their mission or they'd be rude.*

"Your timing is exceedingly bad. I just received advice from my parents not to let anyone into the castle today or tomorrow. Come back in three days, and we can talk," 'Na said.

Why? the companion's horse asked.

It's my dratted, tricky seventeenth birthday, that's why.

"Congratulations, Lady Belladonna," the companion said, standing and bowing again. "Best wishes to you, and safety from evil intentions on this momentous day."

"Eh? What?" the prince said.

"We will go back to the inn at the crossroads and wait, and then if you will permit us, return in three days to celebrate your birthday with you. Safely," the companion added, with a crooked smile and another bow.

"Wait. How do you know—" 'Na gasped, half in shock and half in delight. "You can speak the animal common tongue? You heard what we were saying?"

"I didn't intend to eavesdrop, but Fleetfeet here," he affectionately slapped his horse's neck, "makes it easy to hear when I'm riding him. Something about our friendship over the years, working in partnership. And ... an unfortunate soul-switching curse incident, when I was ten or so." He shrugged and his grin turned slightly embarrassed.

"He took the curse in my place," the prince said. "Would it help that we brought gifts?"

"Gifts from strangers and those hoping for favors are usually fraught with pitfalls and tangles, as well as future problems and obligations both sides might rue," 'Na called down to them. "Let's start all this over again in three days, shall we?"

"Of course. Thank you. Please forgive the interruption," the companion called.

"What are your names, by the way?"

"This is Prince Ruprick, and I am Ambrose Fitz." He bowed again, then turned his horse.

The prince's horse turned before the prince could tug on the reins.

"Happy birthday, Lady Belladonna," the prince called back over his shoulder as the two men rode away. "We will see you in three days."

"Not if I can help it," she whispered, and stepped back into the shadows again.

There went her quiet time of daydreaming and indulging in her cake. She had quite lost her appetite. Even knowing she had narrowly avoided a disaster, thanks to her parents' warning, she couldn't repress a shiver of premonition. It was barely past noon. She had more than thirty-six hours left of her tricky, potentially disastrous seventeenth birthday.

When she went back down into the hall, she found Fang had finished his red lunch and went on to devour more than half the remainder of the cake. He was asleep where he had tumbled off the table, and onto the flagstone floor. He snored, drooling from one side of his crooked mouth, and his fur was still sticky with smeared frosting. She contemplated her chances of disaster, then decided she wasn't in a good enough mood to be cautious. She summoned a housekeeping breeze, which dumped massive amounts of water on Fang until he was thoroughly rinsed off, and awoke. To her disappointment, he didn't respond with the hoped-for irritation and argument, maybe even attempts to knock her flat and jump on her face. A fight would have been just what she needed to work off some of the knots threatening to form in her belly. And perhaps frighten away a few malevolent spying sprites or other tiny minions of magical enemies.

They returned to the library to continue the search for the spell that would rejuvenate him and earn him readmission into the society of vampires. He squelched when he hopped crookedly the few dozen steps down the hall behind her. 'Na supposed she might regret losing out on all that cake. She could request all the sweets and delicacies she wanted for her dinner tonight, but it wasn't the same thing as receiving a treat she hadn't asked for or anticipated.

Fang waited until they were back in the library before pointing with his left ear toward the gate and curving the right ear into a question mark.

"Who was I talking to?" she guessed. He hopped up and down for yes, scowling at her a little. She supposed he had appointed himself her guard since her parents were away. What part of birthday cake and its implications didn't he understand? She was seventeen today. Some independence and freedom, and adult responsibilities were implied.

Granted, her birthday was a trigger point for magical folks to try to skim off or harvest the inherent magic that swirled around any girl on her seventeenth birthday. Whether she had magical parents or not. Whether she lived in an enchanted castle or not—or come to think of it, a castle, period. What part of "enchanted castle," with all the implied protections, didn't Fang understand? She was safe, and quite honestly, she wouldn't have left the castle even if her parents hadn't warned her to stay inside until her doubled birthday had passed. Company, yes, she was grateful. Musty-smelling and bedraggled self-appointed guardian, not so much.

'Na went back to work looking through the books while she told Fang about Ambrose and Ruprick. She wondered if she should have expected the prince to come to win her. It was a matter of pride to succeed, since his father hadn't tricked her mother into marrying him. His father had most likely sent him to take advantage of the magic and vulnerability of her birthday. What did it say about the prince that he had apparently forgotten that detail? Well, King Ruprick hadn't caught her mother, and the son certainly wasn't going to trap or persuade 'Na.

The story didn't take long, and 'Na put the two visitors out of her mind minutes later. The frustrating task of tracking down just the right sort of spell to help Fang rejuvenate required all her attention.

Frustrating was the operative word, she decided several hours later. She looked up and sneezed at the dust she raised from closing a book that had sat ignored on the shelf far too long. The book was so sleepy it hadn't even tried to bite her fingers when she picked it up, in retribution for leaving it un-read for so long. She tried to calculate how much time had passed by the angle of light coming through the shutters on the tall windows. Another sneeze, and she made a mental note to ask the housekeeping breezes to dust the library more often. Books grew irritable and sometimes uncooperative if they got too dusty.

Then she looked around and sighed at evidence that Fang had gotten extremely frustrated before he wore himself out and fell asleep. Judging by the number of pages strewn across the floor, several books had taken the brunt of his temper. Maybe the vandalism was why the last few books she had flipped through had seemed particularly reluctant to cooperate.

"Very sorry," she told the library, and repressed a wish for the housekeeping breezes to show up and pick up all the scattered pages. That wouldn't help her, and would just mix up the order of the pages even more. She had to do it herself, if she had any hope of putting the books back together close to their original state. She had to develop a plan.

It's enough to make me wish for enough eyes to read four books at a time, and enough hands and arms to hold those books, she mused, after filling her hands with torn pages and one gnawed wooden book cover.

Her words whispered through the library, with that particular resonance that meant a magical artifact, somewhere in the castle, had awakened and listened. It didn't matter that she hadn't actually *said* those words. Listening didn't require ears, after all.

Drat it!

"No, no, no," she moaned. "I didn't mean it! Can you hear me? I did not wish for— " 'Na bit her lip and then her tongue, to keep from adding to her trouble by speaking the wish aloud. Just in case the wrong magical thread was listening to the wrong part of what she refused to say.

"Oh, Fang, you have gotten me into so much trouble," she whispered, and stomped over to the little room off the library her mother referred to as the infirmary. It held everything she could possibly want or need to repair those ravaged books. The sooner she regained the good favor of the library, the better. She was going to need all the help she could get to withstand whatever warped version of her thoughtless wish was going to slap her once she stepped out of the confines of the library.

Come to think of it, maybe she shouldn't leave the library until her parents came home. All the spells to keep magic quiescent would shield her, and the breezes could tend to her needs, including clean clothes and washing water and other necessary items of life. There were plenty of cushions to make herself a comfortable bed. She would just have to persuade the library to allow some food to come in. She would rearrange the bookshelves to create sufficient open space between her washing and eating area, and the books.

That was what she would do: stay here in the shelter of the library until she figured out Fang's rejuvenation spell, as well as how to ward off the spell waiting to pounce when she left the library.

Come to think of it, if this was the "doom" destined to fall on her for her seventeenth birthday, a coming-of-age test of sorts, it wasn't so bad. There were far worse ways to spend her birthday than locked in a library. Even if she was locked in the library with a curmudgeonly, threadbare vampire bunny.

Within fifteen minutes, she found the page with the spell that had made her wish audible. 'Na seriously considered not putting that page back into the book, but only for a few seconds. There was half of another spell written on the back of the page, and she couldn't be so cruel to whoever would come to the book next, by depriving them of what might be the most important part of that spell.

~~~~~

Crash!

The sound reverberated through the castle. That ridiculous iron suit of armor on the third floor by the balcony door had fallen to pieces and was rolling around the flagstone flooring. 'Na staggered halfway to her feet before her eyes opened. The angle of the moonlight told her it was somewhere between ten and eleven. She had only been asleep maybe twenty minutes.

Third floor balcony. Her father had put that suit of armor there as an early warning signal, in case anyone tried to enter the castle without permission. Every defensive spell had a weak point, the "seam" where everything came together. A wise man made sure he knew where that weak point was, and had backup measures in place to catch whoever tried to slide through. One backup anchored the
~~~~~

weak spot on the third floor, to wear out the intruders with the climb up there, and hopefully discourage them from trying. Obviously, whoever had just fallen through the balcony door, tripped on the ankle-high threshold, and knocked over the armor, was hard to discourage.

"Hello? Lady Belladonna?" A rich, tenor voice that hinted at hours of elocution lessons rippled down the central staircase. "Very sorry about the mess. You really shouldn't leave armor sitting in front of doors. It makes a ghastly noise. We have stands for our armor at my father's castle. Helps keep the pieces together. Would you like me to send you one or two?"

His father's castle. Of course. Prince Ruprick had decided to prove himself by breaking into the enchanted castle. What part of "come back when it isn't my birthday" didn't he understand?

Fang woke up from the bed he had made for himself in the rib cage of a tough old ram the housekeeping breezes had brought him for dinner. He snorted and shook his head, whipping his ears around and scattering bits of raw meat and fragments of blood that had dried into his fur.

"I don't suppose you want to deal with him?" She smiled at the thought of the prince coming face-to-face with a decrepit, blood-streaked bunny coming out of the shadows into a streak of moonlight. The clash of impressions might be enough to send him running.

Fang grinned, saluted her with a flick of his right ear, and bounded across the floor of the library. A housekeeping breeze swirled past 'Na and hurried to open the door for him. She thought she caught a whisper of a chuckle in the air. Of course, they would appreciate this late night, uninvited guest being terrified by Fang just as much as she would. Especially since the breezes would have to put the suit of iron armor back together. Maybe she should take the prince up on his offer of a stand or two? Then again, those handy alarms would be ruined.

She followed Fang to the doors of the library and made sure she stayed back a good five steps, so she wouldn't make the mistake of stepping out of the protective spells. After all, she still had nearly twenty-six hours until her seventeenth birthday was officially over. Just to be careful, in case she tripped and rolled, she took two more steps back.

"Aaaaaaaah!" a tenor voice shrieked and echoed through the

central column of the castle. Then the sound of something large hitting the wooden railing of the stairway crashed and undercut the echoes of the shriek. More thuds. Yelps and oophs and what sounded like metal hitting the wooden stair treads and the railing.

"No. Please tell me he didn't," a warm, baritone voice groaned, to 'Na's right. A moment later, Ambrose stepped into the moonlight coming through the windows where the housekeeping breezes had pulled back shutters. Probably in anticipation of what 'Na had just deduced was happening.

Ruprick tumbled down the stairs from the third floor, bouncing down several steps at a time, ricocheting off the railing at just the right angle to keep himself going, down the multiple turns and landings of the stairs.

"Oh, very sorry to disturb you, Lady Belladonna," Ambrose said, with a little startle as he turned to look at her. "When I realized Prince Ruprick had snuck away from the inn, I tried to catch up with him, to stop him. He had some fool notion—" He winced at an especially loud yelp-bang. 'Na hoped that meant Prince Ruprick had hit his particularly hard head. "Some fool notion of coming and keeping you company, protecting you on your most sensitive birthday. Happy birthday and many blessings on you, by the way."

"Thank you." She caught sight of movement at the first landing between the ground floor and second floor. Just a few more yelps and bangs and thuds and tumbles, and Ruprick would be on the ground floor.

"I was hoping to stop him before he broke in on you. He's very good at being charming while being totally overbearing. I promise, he has the best intentions, but there's quite a bit of weight on him to be a hero."

"And twice as much on you, cleaning up all his messes?" She caught herself just in time before she put her foot over the library threshold. What was it about Ambrose that made her want a closer look at that crooked smile, those laughing eyes? Those laughing, intelligent, apologetic eyes. And that voice ... he could read to her for hours, and she wouldn't mind how boring the book was.

Get yourself together, ninny. Deal with the intruders now and—

'Na sighed as Prince Ruprick tumbled down the last few steps and sprawled, *splat,* on his back on the flagstone pavement, with his heels on the third step. Then a small shadow erupted out of the shadows filling the stairs. Fang leaped down from the railing of the landing between first and second floor, mouth open and displaying his bloodstained teeth, ears flapping vainly in an attempt to fly, limbs spread and his claws extended.

Ruprick shrieked and leaped to his feet. He took one step, then tripped over his untied boot laces and tumbled straight at 'Na. She sidestepped out of the way. Ambrose raced after him, with Fang bringing up the rear.

"Very sorry," Ambrose said as Ruprick disappeared into the library, shrieking. Fang thumped and banged in crooked leaps right behind him. "He figured, lady in enchanted castle, seventeenth birthday, he has a duty as the crown prince to protect you."

"I was fine as long as strangers stayed out of the castle!" 'Na gasped, realizing she had stepped out of the library. She darted over the threshold, back into safety. She didn't feel any sort of magic activating, but somehow that didn't make her feel any better.

Oh, that's right, because a stranger was *in* the library, her most secure sanctuary and shield. Sighing, she followed the sounds of thuds and—was that the low rumbling waterfall sound of books falling out of shelves? What was that idiot doing?

No, it wasn't the idiot, it was the delusional lunatic chasing him, bouncing from bookshelf to bookshelf, trying to fly and then land on the Prince's back. And missing multiple times.

"Fang! Leave the nice prince alone!" 'Na picked up her feet and ran, following her ears, with Ambrose right behind her.

"Fang? A three-headed monster, by any chance?" he asked.

She giggled, which was hard to do when she was trying to follow her ears and run and turn corners without running into any of the bookshelves. They were tall, anchored to the floor and the ceiling, but with her luck—because yes, this was her seventeenth birthday—the bracings and anchors would break and she would have a domino effect of one bookcase falling and knocking the others down.

"No, unfortunately. A three-headed dog is a little easier to control. This is a demented bunny that is upset the transformation into a vampire stopped with a larger gap between his extra-long teeth, and a taste for raw meat."

"Ah. You really do have bigger problems than me."

'Na had to agree. The crashing and banging had settled in one place—the book infirmary. Fang had chased Ruprick into the room and was currently chasing him around the table. Actually, Ruprick was the only one going around the table. Fang had the intelligence to leap up onto a long table in the center of the room and just hop from one side to another, only taking three steps for every twenty the panting, red-faced, sweating prince took.

Until Fang hopped crooked and landed sideways on the book 'Na had been mending. It skidded out from underneath him, straight at Ruprick, and hit him in the chest. It burst apart, scattering all those pages 'Na had spent so much time sorting back into proper order. She had saved sewing the pages into bundles and gluing them into the spine for later.

Ruprick stopped short, and the look of dismay on his face over the destruction of the book made 'Na like him just a little bit. At least he had some proper priorities. Fang gathered himself and leaped straight into the swirling cloud of papers, scattering more. Worse, he smeared them with blood as he twisted and kicked and snatched at papers, trying to swim through the storm to get at Ruprick.

"Fang! You stop that immediately or so help me I will forbid you entrance into the castle. You'll never get the regeneration spell and you'll remain exactly as you are! Do you hear me?" 'Na stomped into the final swirl of the pages. Spits and crumbs of magic stung her face and bared arms. It figured. The agitated activity was enhanced by the outrage of the half-repaired book. She caught hold of Fang by his right foreleg and right hind leg. Half-dried blood smeared her hands. He writhed, trying to break free, and slid across the front of her shirt, smearing more blood. 'Na flung him across the table and promised herself she would find a spell that turned Fang into a vegetarian again. This was simply going too far. Obviously, the table manners spell her mother had tried weaving around Fang the last time he created havoc in the castle had worn off. Why couldn't he have been bitten by a werewolf instead of a vampire? Werewolves were so much easier to tame, and he would only be a raving bloodthirsty imbecile a few nights out of every month.

"Very, very sorry," Ruprick mumbled, staggering back and nearly knocking over the small table with the book mending supplies on it. He caught himself in time, but ended up with a handful of pages. "Please let us help you?"

"Yes, please. What is the most important thing to do right now?" Ambrose said, resting a hand on her shoulder.

Just like her father would do when 'Na was about to explode. Eagerness, excitement, fury, it didn't matter. However, Ambrose didn't have quite the healing touch of her father.

Quite the opposite. A funny little thrill raced through her, which didn't combine well with the fury swirling up from her belly. It collided with the smell of blood Fang smeared on her, and the realization that quite a number of pages had stuck to her. All that work she had done repairing the book had been wasted. Ravaged magical books were exceedingly touchy and prone to twist spells sideways. They often lashed out at the person trying to help them.

"Here, this is interesting. What's this word?" Ruprick peeled a page off his hand and turned it around, mouthing the words on the page.

"Don't you dare even read any of that, much less aloud!" She snatched the pages from him. "With my luck, you'll trigger the worst possible spell. And on my birthday, too! Do you know how touchy things are on a girl's seventeenth birthday? Especially if she lives in an enchanted castle? With invisible servants? And she has magic in her blood because both her parents were enchanted? And with a partial curse hanging over the whole family because the king—" She pointed at Ruprick, who looked suitably chastened. "Because the king had a hissy when my mother chose my father instead of him. Because she didn't want to be stuck with the possibility of turning into a stepmother to a prince who is rumored to have been cursed at birth." Again, she pointed at Ruprick, who paled and took two steps back, again nearly running into the supply table.

"His Majesty is very sorry," Ambrose said. "Look on the bright side, it's nearly eleven. At midnight, your seventeenth birthday is over." He dug in the pouch slung across his chest.

"You'd think it would be that simple, but no, I have to be doubly careful, because I was born at midnight. That means I have to act like I have two birthdays. Just in case someone manages to curse one day and I pick the wrong one to relax."

"As I said, the king is very sorry about the whole misunderstanding with your parents."

"I'm very glad she was kind enough not to want to be a stepmother," Ruprick offered. "I liked the pretty lady, but my nanny and nursemaid warned me. Stepmothers always start out nice but then there's always some royal curse hanging around that everyone has forgotten about. They always seem to glom onto stepmothers and turn them rotten. I've told my father a thousand times he's better off being a grieving widower. It's a better public image, than worrying a second wife will go psychotic on him. First she turns herself into a widow again, then she goes after the rest of the royal family to secure her throne. I really ought to do a scholarly paper on—"

"Ru, that's enough." Ambrose finished digging in his pouch and brought out a round, glistening red box, neatly cut in half, with a hinge and a clasp made of gold and emeralds.

"Is that a red pearl?" 'Na caught her breath, fascinated by the fact that it was big enough to be a target in lawn bowling.

"A gift, lovely lady, as a peace offering from my father," Ruprick hurried to say. "He wanted to send some protection, as well as re-open a relationship between your parents and this castle and the throne."

Fang thumped repeatedly on the floor, nearly slamming 'Na's foot with his. She looked down at him and he emphatically shook his head. His eyes were so frantic they had lost their usual reddish tint and looked more like his original blue. He was afraid. She had never seen him afraid. Usually because he was so passionate about something, he didn't have the time or energy to be afraid.

For her?

Well, duh, a red pearl was an especially chaotic, unpredictable magic. Add to it being sent as a gift from the king who had tried to seduce her mother and have her father locked up as a criminal. It could be a trap, presented as a gesture of peace and offering her protection. If the king had really been sincere, he would have tried to make peace years ago. Unless this was a last-ditch effort to get control of the enchanted castle back into the royal family, by tricking her into marrying his moronic son? Well, maybe the prince was *slightly* less moronic than she first thought. After all, she had a good idea of the kind of pressure he was under. But what was so hard about listening when someone said not to come back for three days? What kind of a friendship or alliance or whatever he was hoping for could they have if he started out by lying and ignoring what she said and wanted?

Nope, not going to happen. A bad foundation was worse than no foundation at all.

Plus, she was angry with herself for being tempted.

"Sorry, not going to touch that. Not until after next midnight, when my birthday is officially over." For good measure, she clasped her hands behind her back, because she really did want to hold that red pearl. Maybe there was a spell on it to make her want to touch it? She noticed Ambrose was wearing gloves. Then she took a step back.

"Oh, of course, but don't you want to at least see it?" Ruprick stepped up and swooped the red pearl out of Ambrose's hand.

"No, thank you. What I want to do is put this book back together before it gets any more infuriated at being in this state. I want to go back to bed and sleep safely through the next eight or ten hours. Which means I want you two out of here. My parents specifically told me not to let strangers into the castle."

"Technically," Ambrose said, bending over to pick up pages, "you didn't let us in. We're trespassers."

"Any curse aiming to latch onto me won't pay attention to fine points like that. Don't you two imbeciles know anything about enchanted castles and enchanted bloodlines and spells and the trouble you can get speaking the absolutely wrong—" She stopped with a gasp as a chain as light as thistledown and as bright as sunrise and as cool as a morning breeze in spring slipped over her head.

Amazing how she could feel and know all those characteristics before she even looked at the necklace that idiot prince had just put around her neck. That was the nature of enchantments, of course.

Oh, botheration, it was an enchanted chain. Not what she wanted to see or feel or encounter right now, thanks very much! If there was a charm in there to make her fall in love with that imbecile prince, she was going to wish she did indeed have four very strong arms, to punch him across the room. And how about four heads with very sharp teeth, to terrify him if not take four quick, deep bites where it would do him the most harm and her the most good!

"Ru, weren't you listening?" Ambrose snarled. "I'm sorry, Lady." He reached out to grasp her arm and help her stay upright, because her legs felt oddly wobbly and ready to fold, and she leaned far to one side. "He means well, but my job is to do all the reading and interpreting and understanding of magic. He's usually too busy learning all the physical, sweaty parts of being a prince."

"I wish there were fifty leagues between me and well-meaning idiots!"

'Na gasped as the pages clasped in her hands buzzed and stung like she had plunged them into a pot of nettles.

No, it wasn't entirely the pages. Blue-black hair sprang out of her hands and spread up her arms like incoming tide.

Then the blue-black turned to pink and golden sparkles that

filled her eyes, blinding her. The only thing that stayed solid was Ambrose's hand on her arm, gripping tight, as they both tumbled through one of the corridor dimensions. Then they changed direction and spun down a swirling well of sparkles, to land hard and flat on cobblestones, in moonlight. She landed on top of Ambrose, on her side. She had to fight to focus and see where they were, because suddenly there seemed to be four of everything. The first detail she could make out clearly, by focusing until her head hurt, was a signpost, lit by two feeble, guttering lanterns. It proclaimed she was at the trading town of Crossroads. So named because it had been built up around a major crossroads.

Fifty leagues exactly from the enchanted castle.

Ambrose gasped and his chest heaved, and she looked down at him. There were four of him, all staring up at her, his eyes wide and his face growing paler with every heartbeat. Then his gaze traveled down his arm to his hand clutching her arm. Except suddenly she seemed to have two arms on that side of her body. Or was that eight, since she could see four of everything? Why could she see four of everything?

"Lady Belladonna?" he wheezed.

"Who else did you grab—oh." Now she was hearing four voices, but how could those raspy snarls be her voice? They were paired baritone and bass. She looked down at her arm again. Her shirt was in shreds and she certainly had more muscles than she had before, and all that blue-black hair. "What do I look like?"

His mouth moved and he couldn't seem to speak. She supposed he needed to breathe, which meant she needed to get off his chest. She slid off and stood up—not four legs, fortunately, but she seemed to be stretching her favorite pair of trousers uncomfortably. Thank goodness she had gone to bed in her day clothes instead of a nightshirt. Although bare legs would certainly be more comfortable right about now. Yet she was so much taller now than when she had gone to bed, maybe her nightshirt wouldn't cover enough?

Why was she wasting time thinking of things like that? She had just been turned into a worse beast than her mother had ever shifted into during her foul moods and rages against oppression.

The door of the tavern, the only building with light seeping through the shutters this late at night, banged open on the far side of the moonlit town square. Light and people carrying torches spilled out into the square. A man bound with ropes writhed as he was carried along, aloft in the grip of the angry, shouting, jeering crowd. A pungent wave of odors rolled out with him. The nose-stinging scent of sour beer and bad whiskey. The charred tang of tobacco. The pong of sweat in dirty clothes and unwashed bodies. The cloying sickly-sweet stink of terror.

Well, it made sense that if she had four times the vision, then she had four times the—

"No, oh no," 'Na groaned, with four voices, as her four hands touched her four faces. And found her four noses that certainly felt like wolf muzzles.

Yes, four times the smelling sensitivity. What did she look like?

"That's Melvin the monster hunter." Ambrose yanked hard on one of 'Na's arms.

"They're going to hang him, aren't they?" She could almost laugh at how easily she jerked herself free of his grip. She had thought Ambrose looked rather strong. Of course, now that she was standing up straight, she towered over him by a good two heads in height. Her shoulders were certainly twice as broad as his now. Wide enough to support four heads. It helped to be able to look in four directions at once. Somehow, she would have thought she'd have a headache, seeing with four sets of eyes.

Why was she wasting time on such details?

"If they don't burn him at the stake. Now come on," he whispered urgently, and yanked on her arm again.

"But I like Melvin. He's a braggart, and I doubt— " 'Na gasped as somehow Ambrose yanked her off balance and she staggered backward with him.

"He's a monster hunter who hasn't brought back even a boar's ear for the last five years, much less tusks or poisoned talons or any other proof that he's killed a monster." Ambrose pulled harder, and she ducked down, hunching her shoulders as he did.

There was something compelling about the way he kept looking behind them and seemed rather worried. Maybe worried for her? She rather admired a man who was in an unsteady situation and thought about other people instead of focusing on himself. Of course, how many heroes did she get to encounter, with most visitors to the castle being of the "Oh, save me, please save me, I made the wrong bargain/choice/married into the wrong family/insulted the wrong brute," variety?

"But shouldn't we help him?"

That was definitely her parents' influence speaking through her now. They could afford to be heroes, and they firmly believed that all their magical gifts and training gave them an obligation to help others. Even if they weren't exactly deserving. Even if they were utter selfish ninnies who deserved the terror they were suffering at the moment.

So why was she in this mess, when she hadn't done anything wrong?

Oh, that's right—because that ninny of a prince put an enchanted necklace on her and frustrated her to the point she forgot herself and spoke a wish. A stupid wish. On her tricky, pivotal, dangerous seventeenth birthday!

All right, so maybe a little of this was her fault.

"Lady Bella—"

"Please, you're seeing me at my worst." She chuckled. It was a pleasantly rough rumbling kind of laugh, rather than the alto tones of a stream over pebbles she had worked so hard to develop. She couldn't stand girls who giggled and sounded like out-of-tune wind chimes. "Call me 'Na."

"'Na, pardon my saying, but you're a monster. No offense intended."

"Oh."

"I'm sorry. That was rather blunt."

"No, that's ..." She picked up the pace and took the lead, heading away from the village. She flinched every time her four sets of sharp—monster-sharp, monster-sensitive—ears picked up sounds like windows or doors opening and closing and footsteps.

Ambrose proved rather clever at skulking through shadows and staying out of sight. That implied he had lots of practice in this sort of thing. Most likely getting Prince Ruprick out of trouble. 'Na hunched over and let him lead while she digested the situation she had almost blundered into.

Melvin was an older man, rather pathetic in some respects, who made his living telling tales of his many monster hunts. Bragging, to be quite blunt. He had been a mentor of her father's long ago, long before her parents met, so Melvin had been a guest at the castle from time to time. He had never once shown a trophy from his many hunts, and now 'Na had to wonder if he didn't have any to show because he never really had any.

Her mother had warned Melvin a few times that it would be

wise to let others tell his stories, and quietly fade into the shadows while he still had his head on his shoulders. Hadn't her father mentioned a few close calls, where people had gotten upset about the lack of proof of his prowess in monster hunting? Maybe the people of Crossroads had gotten tired of his bragging. Or more likely, tired of how he expected to be honored and given free food and lodging, based on heroic deeds from years ago.

The worst thing she could have done was march into the town square to stop his hanging, or whatever other punishment was planned. She was new to her monster shape. How would she be able to fight to defend herself, much less rescue Melvin? In fact, what good were her multiple arms and heads to her? She didn't even have talons, and while a test of her teeth with her four tongues revealed they were pointed, they weren't really fangs, were they? Just sharp.

"All right, I think we're safe. We can stop and think. Figure out how we got here." Ambrose led her into a little shelter a few steps back from the road.

Her eyes adjusted quickly enough to see the wooden cover over a low, round structure of stones. This was a well. For all she knew, it had enough magic that the locals had built a shelter over the well to appease whatever faerie or magical being had showed a fondness for it.

"We got here because it's my seventeenth birthday and I wished for fifty leagues between me and well-meaning … well, what does that say about you, that you got dragged along? You're not well-meaning?"

"Or I'm not an idiot, at least." Ambrose nodded, glanced once at her, then settled down on the well covering. Not quite facing her.

"I was staying in the library where the spells to restrain stray magic and the effects of unwise words couldn't touch me. I was planning to stay there until my parents got home and they could undo … oh, no." 'Na spread her arms and really looked at herself. Then she laughed.

"What? Undo what?"

"I made an unwise wish that I could read multiple books at once. Any wish made in that dratted castle can be fulfilled, whether spoken aloud or not, but never quite in the way you expect."

"That necklace probably was stronger than the protective magic in the library," he said, and gestured at her neck.

"Enchanted? I was really hoping I was wrong." She managed to reach up with only one hand, rather than all four, and rubbed at the delicate chain.

Ambrose nodded. "To grant a wish and protect the wearer." He looked around. "I wouldn't call lobbing us fifty leagues away from the castle within the definition of protection."

"We could be in a much worse situation. There are any number of truly vile towns and swamps and bogs and ... well, enchanted castles have a tendency to attract the wrong sort of folk, and creatures, and buildings and doorways into Faerie. Crossroads might very well be the nicest, tamest spot for us to land."

"How did I get brought here with you? I promise you, Lady—'Na." He grinned and nodded, mute apology. "I promise, I really am well-meaning, even if I do hope I'm not considered an idiot."

"I'll wager one of those pages ... Oh, doubly no." She looked all around them. "I know we both had pages sticking to us. All that blood Fang was spraying around. There has to be a spell on one of them. Or it's just that wretched book, punishing us for getting it torn apart again. And blood on its pages. Magic books can be rather vindictive. We'll never get the spells reversed if we don't have all the pages."

"You stay here, I'll—"

"Can you see in the dark?"

"No."

"You don't dare light a torch."

"No." He sighed and his shoulders slumped.

"I can see in the dark incredibly well right now. Almost like it's full daylight. We need to work together."

"You're right. Although I don't like putting you at risk. You're in this mess because I didn't do a good job of restraining Ruprick." He got up and took a step out of the shelter.

"Please, Ambrose, don't be too good to be true."

He laughed, and immediately muffled the sound behind his hand.

They found six pages dropped on the roadside, going back the way they had come.

Unfortunately, the seventh and eighth pages had been picked up by the night breeze and lay in clear view, tinted orange with torchlight, on the cobblestones about ten paces from the edge of the crowd. Melvin sat on a platform, leaning far to the right, sweating and pale, and visibly shuddering. All his attention focused on the two men who stood on the platform, arguing with each other and the crowd. 'Na's eight sharp ears twitched, picking up all the bickering back and forth, the demands for different punishments for Melvin—hanging, burning at the stake, and the water test. It was no test, but just a lame excuse for tossing him in the nearby pond and letting him drown. Why did no one ever consider that someone who failed the water test wasn't magical, which meant they were innocent of the accused misuse of magic?

"Stay here," Ambrose said.

He stepped out of hiding and into the open, into the torchlight, before she could respond. Not that she was in the mood for arguing or taking foolish risks.

Except that Ambrose, for all he was a servant and companion of a prince, was dressed far too well for this town, or this angry, drunk crowd. The minute someone turned around and saw him, his fancy clothes would catch their attention and probably their ire. People who were willing to rough up a silly old braggart in the middle of the night were exactly the kind of people who would resent a well-dressed stranger. Especially someone with—she strained her four sets of eyes and found what she was looking for—yes, especially someone with the very visible rampant bear crest of King Ruprick on his vest and his belt pouch.

To put it mildly, none of the Rupricks had ever been popular.

Please, please, please, don't—

Of course, since it was her tricky seventeenth birthday, that meant the response to anything she wished was going to be the exact opposite. She would wager anything, the ridiculously dainty necklace around one thick, hairy throat only had one wish embedded in it, and she had used it up getting them here.

"Hey, who are you?" the snarling, bilious man on the left shouted from the platform. He pointed at Ambrose, who straightened up with the first page in his hand.

"Sorry. I dropped some papers when I was here earlier." Ambrose nodded politely to several people, tugged his forelock and bowed to several women, and with cool aplomb walked up to the second page and bent to pick it up.

"He's here to rescue this fraud!" the second man on the platform shrieked. Followed by a loud belch. 'Na smelled the stench of beer belch from thirty paces away.

"I don't even know him," Ambrose protested. He raised his

hands. As if that would prove his innocence?

"What's that in your hands?" a man standing close to him shouted.

He didn't need to shout, because the crowd had grown quiet in ripples moving out from the platform and from the people directly in front of Ambrose.

"Just some papers." Ambrose lowered his hands.

"What's on them?"

He hesitated. Not good. 'Na knew he couldn't confess the papers were pages torn out of a magic book, but he didn't have a ready story, and that—

"Get him!" a woman shrieked.

Ambrose turned and ran. Smart.

He didn't run straight back to where he had left 'Na hiding. Even smarter.

She was grateful. No wonder he had been chosen to keep Prince Ruprick out of trouble. He was clearly a fast thinker as well as a fast runner. Very smart choice, and her last glimpse of him was Ambrose tucking those crucial torn pages inside his coat. Very smart man. She decided she liked him.

Fortunately for her, the people in the square were drunkenly stupid. Everyone ran after Ambrose. The two snarling men from the platform jumped off and tried to get ahead of the others.

They left Melvin behind, with no one to guard him. Granted, he was tied up hand and foot and didn't look like he could move if he got to his feet again. As 'Na debated her options, Melvin whimpered and finished sliding over, and hit the platform on his face.

She crossed the square in a few running leaps. Very nice, her extra-long legs were especially springy and agile. She leaped up onto the platform. Melvin blanched, but he had the integrity not to beg for mercy or shriek, and he didn't close his eyes. He did lose control over his bladder, but she supposed he had been drinking heavily not long ago, which explained how he had gotten into this mess in the first place.

Multiple sets of arms, exceedingly long, were useful for carrying a man the size of Melvin. He didn't look quite as imposing and strong and athletic as he had been in his glory days. And most important, those long arms made it possible to hold him far enough away, his wet clothes didn't rub against her.

"What are you going to do with me?" he wheezed.

"Saving your worthless neck, you old badger," she said, once they were out of the town square. She made sure she headed at a wide angle away from the direction Ambrose had gone. 'Na just hoped that once she had untied Melvin and set him on his way, she could find Ambrose. Common sense told her they needed to be together to put things right.

"What did you call me?" he said, after choking and gasping.

"What does it matter?" 'Na blurted, remembering just in time that Melvin was the worst sort of gossip. "Old Badger" was the nickname her father had for Melvin. How many people had called him that over the decades? With her luck, only her father had. And while Melvin could be an idiot, he was clever enough to guess who she was. Once he sobered up.

To add insult to injury, if he knew who she was, he would claim an obligation between them, as her father's oldest and dearest friend and wise counselor. None of which was true, and her father would collapse laughing at the very thought. That wouldn't matter to Melvin. He would insist he had a moral duty to accompany her on her quest to break the curse. Meanwhile, he would take advantage of the monstrous form she was in to protect him from enraged townsfolk, and anyone else they met along the way. Bottom line: Melvin likely didn't know how to spell *moral duty*, much less what the words really meant.

Once she was sure they were far enough away from Crossroads, she could set Melvin free. If she was lucky, she could run fast enough on these doubly long legs of hers she could escape him and find Ambrose. There were several iron-clad rules of spells and curses, and one of them was that all the pieces there at the beginning had to be there at the end, or there was no cure. She needed Ambrose. With her bad luck, she needed Prince Ruprick too, which meant she had to get back to the castle before he fled, probably in another misguided and well-meaning quest to help her. And probably in the wrong direction. Oh, well, at least she would be able to smell which way he went.

Yes, this was indeed turning out to be just the kind of seventeenth birthday she had not been looking forward to.

"You're a monster," Melvin said, once she had set him on his feet and propped him against a tree while she worked on untying the ropes wrapping him in a cocoon.

"Glad to see your eyesight is still good."

"Why are you helping me?"

"Just because someone looks like a monster on the outside doesn't mean they are on the inside. And just because someone looks like a faerie princess doesn't mean her heart is. As you very well know, Melvin." She gave an extra hard tug on the trailing end of the rope and the knot unraveled itself. She gave a satisfied sigh and stood back as the loops unspooled, pooling at his feet.

"Yes, I do indeed." He blushed a little and sighed. "Young folks today have no respect for us old-timers who made the world a safer place for adventuring. So safe and boring, no one believes that such creatures once existed."

"The monsters aren't gone, you ninny. They're in hiding."

"Where?" Melvin drooled a little and he went to his knees. "Please, lady monster, whoever you are, please tell me? Just an ear, a claw, a new trophy every few moons would make life so much easier for me."

"Yes, where?" Ambrose said, stepping into the clearing where they had stopped. "This one is a location spell," he said, before 'Na could ask, and waved one of the retrieved pages at her. "The writing is still glowing, and according to my granny, who had more than her fair share of magic, that means the spell is still active. I asked where you were, and it brought me to you. I imagine those idiots are running around in circles, trying to figure out what happened to me."

"Clever." She grinned at him. Melvin blanched. 'Na wished she knew what she looked like. Probably she had bared her teeth, all four sets, and they were even sharper and longer than she had guessed.

Maybe she should take some time before breaking this curse, to find out how to regain this shape again. It would be very handy chasing away annoying peddlers and traveling elixir salesmen. What part of "enchanted castle" didn't they understand? It was implied that the inhabitants of said castle had more magical elixirs and other potions and powders and rings and scarves and mirrors and other claptrap than they could use up in a century.

Then what Ambrose had said really registered. She held out her hand—well, at least she had learned to only hold out one, instead of two on that side of her body. Ambrose handed over the pages and she studied the words, glowing in a pale greenish-gold.

"Can you take us back home?" she asked, and pressed the index fingers of three hands on the writing. It flared a lovely emerald green, which she took to mean yes. "Well, that will certainly save us some traveling time."

"Wait," Melvin said, when Ambrose stepped up to her and held out a hand to clasp one of hers. "Please, make an old man's retirement years a little easier?"

"You want to go monster hunting, in a closet dimension, where you're the odd race out?" 'Na shook her head.

"Go out in a blaze of glory." Melvin grinned and struck a cocky pose.

"Every good deed helps in the quest to break a curse, my old granny always said," Ambrose added.

"Yes, and often every good deed gets some sort of punishment, to teach people to mind their own business," she snapped.

Still, she did like Melvin, and Ambrose had a point. With her luck, someone in the magical auditor's office would point out that she had brought some of her problems on herself for not being hospitable and for being so exasperated with the mentally deficient. Ruprick and Fang both qualified. Helping a bumbler like Melvin, whose best days were behind him, would count in her favor. She might need all the bonus points she could get.

"Very well." She tipped all four heads back and looked at the moon. It was probably closer to midnight than eleven now. A shudder ran through her. "There's always a codicil relating to time in these tricky spells. Either I need to get back to the castle by midnight, or by dawn, or by sunset, or the curse is set in stone. And of course, chances are very good the book that explains all of it is one of the books Fang ripped apart in his temper tantrum. And now it's angry enough to warp everything."

"Then let's get back by midnight." Ambrose stepped back and bowed, gesturing out of the clearing. "Which way do we go, and how long will it take to get there?"

"We don't have to actually go anywhere. Closet dimensions are just a step sideways."

She tucked the pages in her shredded pocket, then thought better of it. Working magic with hands she wasn't quite used to yet would be tricky enough, without any lingering residue from the violated pages of the magic book. She handed them back to Ambrose, then gestured for him to step back while she walked around Melvin, weaving a magical tether in the air around him. When they were joined to her satisfaction, she wove a timer spell into the tether, to break the link between them but leave the connection with the closet dimension tied to him. Melvin had the sense to hold perfectly still and not ask any questions.

Ambrose also had the sense to keep quiet, but the wonder in his eyes made her feel jittery after a few seconds. He walked a slow circle around them, watching what she did, until she felt something tighten in the air, and suspected that he had done it—circling them three times. Was that going to help, or hurt?

No way to know except to try.

Tearing a slit in the fabric of the curtain between dimensions was easy, despite her claws being blunt. Well, of course they were blunt: she had asked to be able to read multiple books at a time, which meant her claws were good for turning pages, not shredding things. That gave her a good idea of how precise the magic was, even if it was quirky. In seconds, she had a door sliced open, caught the tether between herself and Melvin with two hands, and stepped through.

Ambrose came with them. He looked a little startled as they slid sideways down a narrow, dark corridor lit by the energy of their souls, so definitely he didn't know what he had done, circling them. Just what she needed, a novice who would probably ask questions at absolutely the wrong time.

Yet Ambrose didn't. He kept quiet, he kept up, and he looked more interested than stunned or appalled. That was always helpful when visiting the corridor dimensions, because there was no telling who was watching. There were those who might get offended by some honest fear or a bit of revulsion when things weren't quite what the visitor expected or hoped.

"Here we are." 'Na caught hold of Melvin's hand to press it against what looked like a door made of gnarled, mossy, mud-stained oak. His handprint glowed for a few seconds. "You can find your way back here now any time. The tether will hold the slit open enough for you to get a hold on it and pull. Just be careful not to spend very long here, and always smooth the edges down flat on the flap when you leave."

"So the monsters don't escape?" Melvin asked, his voice and body quavering with eagerness.

"No, so you don't let in a draft. They're all older than you and they catch cold easily. You don't want them all dying off from sniffles and sneezes, do you? That's why they're living here, away from the weather." 'Na bit back a sigh and a comment about lack of common sense. She had to show mercy and kindness while she was here, or the auditors might make it harder to break the curse. While this current form of hers would indeed be very helpful in reading multiple books and doing multiple chores, she rather liked the body she was born with, thanks very much.

She waited for Melvin to find the latch on the door and pull it open and step into the closet dimension. He grinned at her like a little boy about to open an unexpected solstice feast gift, and that was all the thanks she needed. Which was good, because the old fool didn't thank her. He hurried through the door and it thudded closed behind him.

"Do we go that way?" Ambrose said, pointing further down the corridor.

"What?"

"I recognize this, from when we were yanked from the castle." He shrugged, and handed her back the pages.

"You saw, when we were tumbled head over heels and inside out and dumped out on Crossroads?"

"Granny taught me to see sideways."

"Uh huh. You're more useful than I thought." 'Na scanned the pages, found the right side of the right page, and pressed her fingers against the writing. "Home, please?"

The corridor whizzed past around them and the floor dropped out from under her feet. She stumbled and landed crooked so she almost fell, at the foot of the stairs, with the library door on her left. Ambrose caught her and held her upright until she regained her balance.

"Thanks."

He just nodded, then flinched.

Her ears twitched as a wailing shriek assaulted all eight of them. Well, that was one fear answered. Ruprick had not left the castle.

"Fang! Leave him alone! Come out here right now and help me gather up all the pages of that book you mauled. We don't have much time." 'Na pounced on several pages fluttering across the flagstone pavement. Ambrose headed in the other direction, snatching up pages. He was awfully handy to have around. He didn't have to be told what needed to be done, and he could figure things out without asking a dozen questions and wasting time. And yes, she had to admit, he was a little decorative. Not that she had had much time to notice. 'Na wondered if this was one of those unavoidable parts of the curse of her seventeenth birthday—noticing things about boys and men she had been able to ignore up until now.

Fang came hopping out of the armory, a bouquet of pages caught in his mouth. He delivered them to her and headed out, hopping and snatching at pages and bouncing off the walls. 'Na hurried and tried not to pay attention to the ticking of a silent clock in her blood, telling her how close she was to midnight.

"Hello? A little help would be very much appreciated," she called to the housekeeping breezes. "Could you find all the stray pages and help me assemble them? Get them into proper order, if that's possible?" 'Na bit her lip to keep from adding that time was of the essence. The housekeeping breezes didn't do well under pressure. Sometimes they got so excited about special events, they became miniature tornados, which just achieved the exact opposite of the hoped-for effect.

Ambrose joined her in the book infirmary with the covers of three books and a heavy armload of pages clasped in his arms. 'Na swallowed down a moan that would likely turn into a shriek. How could Fang have torn apart more books in the short time she and Ambrose had been gone? Or had Ruprick done it? Probably tossing books at Fangs in self-defense. That was a very bad excuse, but what could she expect from someone who had Ruprick XI for a father? Why couldn't he have picked up a few good points from Ambrose, at least?

"How long have the two of you been together?" she asked, as she spread the mangled book covers out on three different worktables, and started roughly sorting the pages. Fortunately, the books were different sizes, so that would help.

"Me and the prince? Oh, since we were little chaps. With a few interruptions." He shrugged. "Our mothers were good friends, and when that whole foolish battle between the faerie godmothers and the minor magicians flared up, of course they're going to target the royal family. Queen Epsibellah hid Ruprick with us."

"Not long enough to do him any good, I imagine."

"Hmm, maybe not." He shrugged and they shared a thin smile. "Oh, very sorry." He stepped back as a housekeeping breeze yanked a handful of pages out of his hands and spun them across the room to another table.

"You don't frighten easily. I like that."

"Spend as much time as I do in the court, dodging all the rivalries and feuds. And all the power players who spend two-thirds of the kingdom's budget on spells and charms and counter-curses and defensive orbs and whatnot ... this is a rather relaxing way to spend a few days, by comparison."

'Na laughed, and she suspected from the pleased twitching of his lips and the slight flush in his cheeks, that was what he had been hoping for.

"Very sorry to have made such a mess of your birthday, Lady—'Na." He nodded to her, silent apology.

"Well, it could have been a lot worse."

"How?" His voice cracked a little.

She laughed and shook her head. There wasn't much time left, and she needed to focus all her attention on fixing the three books. She dearly hoped that simply having all the pages together inside the covers, with glue and binding thread at hand, would be enough to satisfy the requirements of curse-breaking, and meet the midnight deadline.

"Oh, there you are. Where were you?" Ruprick said, his voice a little thick, either having damaged it from shrieking or weeping. He didn't sound sulky, and 'Na decided that was a point in his favor. He cleared his throat. "Can I be of some help?" Another cough. "After all, I did make some of that mess." His footsteps grew louder as he approached the door of the infirmary.

"Try all of it?" Ambrose said without turning around.

"The rabbit was the one—"

"First of all, he's a bunny, not a rabbit. And second, you threw books at him," 'Na said, turning around.

Ruprick shrieked. To his credit, while he blanched, he grappled for the sword at his waist (which made her wonder why he didn't try to use it to defend himself against Fang) and leaped into the infirmary. "Ambrose, step back—"

"That is Lady Belladonna, you ninny," Ambrose snapped. "You did this to her, just like you made a mess of her library and knocked down the suit of armor. Because you decided you knew better. You broke into her castle and you broke the one rule her parents gave her to avoid enchanted trouble on her birthday." He winked at 'Na, with his head turned so Ruprick couldn't have seen it. Then she noticed that he didn't say what that one thing was, and the prince didn't ask.

Babbling apologies, Ruprick stumbled the rest of the way into the room. He detoured around Fang, who was pace-hopping from one side of the infirmary to the other, and helped by the simple expedient of staying out of the way. Ambrose told him to be quiet and make himself useful, and pointed at a spot between the supply table and the worktables. Ruprick shut up, clamping his teeth together fast enough they clicked, and took up the spot.

"How much time do we have?" Ambrose asked, as the last page fluttered into place in the last mangled book. The housekeeping breezes lifted the covers and folded the books closed. A soft, rosy-golden glow enfolded all three books. "Is that a good sign?"

"A very good sign." 'Na felt a little breathless. "Hello? Whoever is listening, I'd like to thank you for answering the wish I didn't really mean to make. It was more thinking aloud. I really do think it's much wiser to use the shape I was born in, so if you could turn me back to my original form, my original number of heads and arms and hands and such, I would be ever so grateful. Umm ... I know you were trying to help, being my birthday and all, but ... well, considering the number of people we have to deal with who come here for help, it would be kinder on their nerves and probably safer for me if I look like an ordinary girl again." She looked around, hoping for a ripple of rainbow light, a harp chord, some kind of response. "Thanks very much all the same."

Fang hopped over to her and landed heavily on her foot. She looked down at him and he wrapped his arms around her ankle.

"Hello? I'm Prince Ruprick and I should apologize too. For making a mess of things. It's just so dratted tricky nowadays, being a royal, what with all the ..." He blushed and shrugged, and 'Na looked over to see Ambrose giving him a scolding sort of look. "Sorry. I'm a ninny, just like he said. I really am sorry for making such a mess of Lady Belladonna's birthday. Is there something I can—"

The first solemn, deep bong of the clock striking midnight shuddered through the castle. 'Na gasped as a tiny stab in her gut warned that yes, this was the deadline. If they had satisfied the unknown requirements of the counter-curse, she wouldn't know until the last bong—and then it might be too late.

The second bong vibrated in the floor of the library. The housekeeping spells swirled around her, warm, comforting embraces.

"Is there something more we can do?" Ambrose asked. 'Na shrugged.

"It's a curse. It's a damsel in distress, under a terrible spell. Turning her into a beast." Ruprick's face lit up and he snapped his fingers. "How else do you break a curse like that?"

Third bong.

Ruprick hurried to 'Na, went down on one knee, and caught hold of one of her hands. Then blanching a little, he took hold of another hand. "Lady Belladonna, will you do me the honor of becoming my wife?"

Fourth bong.

"That's what started this whole stupid mess!" Ambrose blurted. "I doubt that trapping her into a marriage neither of you want is going to fix anything."

Fifth bong.

"But that's always how the beast curse is broken or the maiden is released from foul enchantment. The maiden agrees to marry the beast, the prince kisses the princess."

Sixth bong.

"Well, I'm not a princess, so it probably doesn't count," 'Na retorted.

What if she was wrong?

Would it really hurt if she agreed to marry the prince?

Seventh bong.

But what if she agreed and the spell broke and she was returned to normal—would the spell settle in again if she didn't marry him in a reasonable amount of time?

What was a reasonable amount of time, when it came to princes and broken curses? He wouldn't expect to carry her off to his castle at dawn and rush her through a romantic, hurried, heroic wedding, would he?

Eighth bong.

With her luck, his father was already arranging the wedding feast, positive that no one dared say no to him or his son. Even though her mother had certainly said no to him.

On principle alone, 'Na wanted to say no.

"You're right, you're not a princess, you shouldn't have to put up with that kind of life." Ambrose stomped over from his worktable. "Sorry, Ru, you're my best friend, and as your best friend, I have to tell you, you aren't good enough for her."

Ninth bong.

"Well, what do you think we should do to rescue her? True love's kiss?" Ruprick shrieked.

Tenth bong.

"There's no way either of you can say you're in love with me, or I'm in love with you." 'Na choked on a bit of semi-hysterical laughter. "Not after what we just went through. Not in just a few hours."

Eleventh bong.

"How about the possibility?" Ambrose caught hold of her shoulders, pulled himself up a little higher, closed his eyes and aimed for the far right head and mouth. He kissed her.

Nothing happened.

Twelfth bong.

He opened his eyes, and she could almost have laughed at the desperation and panic in them. Ambrose moved left and kissed the next mouth, while the bong still reverberated in the air. 'Na brought in the next head and caught hold of him, and their teeth sort of clashed in the third kiss.

She held her breath and he leaned in hard against her, holding on tight as he kissed her fourth mouth and the bong died from the air.

The shimmering of sound from a dozen whispering chords turned her bones to jelly. She shuddered and fell, pulled off balance. Ambrose wrapped his arms tight around her. They hit a bookcase crooked and went down and somehow, she got his hip in her belly and the air knocked out of her. She tasted blood and rolled off him, blinking the last of the magical sparkles out of her eyes. She wasn't quite sure if her lip had been cut or his.

"Umm ... it worked?" Ambrose said, his voice shaky.

"Yes, I think it did." She laughed, just as shaky. Yes, that was her own laugh again. Funny, how she had missed the sound of her own voice.

The housekeeping breezes swirled around them, leaving trails of sparks, and magically replaced her shredded shirt before she realized how chilled she was. Fang hopped over and jumped on 'Na, bouncing in glee, until he went crooked and landed on her stomach. She *ooph*ed, breath knocked out of her again.

"So ..." Ruprick stepped over and offered his hand to help her up. She ignored him and climbed to her feet, braced against the bookshelf. "Does that mean you won't marry me?"

Before she could come up with an answer that wasn't a dozen repetitions of no, shouted at the top of her lungs, the castle doors banged open. Lights rippled to life throughout the castle. The housekeeping breezes sounded like tornados as they raced away to greet the returning lord and lady of the castle.

"Ask my father," 'Na said, and gladly ran to welcome her parents home. She muffled a giggle, seeing how Ruprick's face blanched. He was a ninny, but not so stupid that he didn't know what kind of a reaction he was going to get from her father. There was no love lost between the lord of the enchanted castle and King Ruprick.

Her parents caught her between them, holding her tight. They apologized for not coming faster, but there was a travel spell that kept trying to take them the wrong direction. 'Na saw Ambrose and Fang hurry Ruprick out of the castle, through the open gates, into the engulfing darkness. Of course, her parents had felt the magic activate, and detected when quite a few malevolent spells set up around the castle and surrounding countryside were triggered. Her mother said the reverberations from all that nasty magic felt like a rubber ball tossed into a pit full of mousetraps. Her parents had quite a few things to say about various rivals and slightly insane friends who had played such unfriendly tricks on their daughter's seventeenth birthday.

They compared notes and deciphered whose spells had been involved, and 'Na had told them everything that had happened to her, while her parents unpacked. Then they went down to the library to finish repairing the books. The housekeeping breezes filled the great hall with a feast. Filling their plates, they settled into a nest of floor cushions next to the hearth, to lounge and eat.

"Not a bad birthday at all," her father commented. "Considering what could have happened. The disasters waiting to fall on you."

"Starting with being betrothed to another Ruprick. There must be a curse attached to that name," her mother added, with a shudder. Then she blushed and her eyes sparkled and she chuckled. "So, how did you like your first kiss?"

"Please ..." her father murmured, and shook his head, gazing up at the vaulted ceiling. "Well, there's no remedy for it, is there? When will we meet this lad?"

"We are not betrothed, we are not courting, and it certainly wasn't true love's kiss," 'Na protested.

"No," her mother said, shaking her head, "but the codicils of the magic wouldn't have worked if there wasn't the *possibility* that someday, it could be."

Those words rang in 'Na's mind when she finally went to bed, halfway to dawn. She was surprised she slept at all. Especially when

Fang came bouncing up to her room and gave her a big-eyed, sorrowful look of apology. He shivered like a drowned kitten until she finally gave in and told him he was forgiven. Then he wrapped his mangy, skinny front legs around her leg, hugged until she thought she had lost all feeling in it, and curled up to sleep at the foot of her bed.

Just after dawn, while everyone else in the castle was still asleep, including the housekeeping breezes, 'Na crept out of her bed. She got dressed and went to her perch in the gate tower. She wasn't exactly sure why she felt the need to go there, until she climbed the stairs and could see over the sill of the tower window. There was Ambrose, coming up the path. He looked like he hadn't slept since he rushed Ruprick out of the castle. There was just enough time for him to have gotten the prince home, then turned around and come right back. If he raced and pushed his horse to the point of collapse. When he tipped his head up and their gazes met, he smiled, and she couldn't have stopped herself from smiling back even if she had wanted to. Which she didn't. She thought she rather liked smiling back at Ambrose.

"I don't suppose it's safe for you to leave the castle, since it's still technically your birthday," he said. "Would it be safe for me to come inside? Or I can sit here and we can talk, if you prefer."

"It's never really safe inside this castle, but I think you can handle it." She gestured for him to wait, and hurried back down the stairs.

END

Meet Your Authors

K.M. Carroll is happily married to her high school sweetheart and they have seven children. Her other superhero fantasy books are available on her website, kmcarrollblog.wordpress.com. [Deborah's notes: Ms. Carroll is too modest! She not only has the After Atlantis and the Vid:ilantes superhero fantasy series, but she also has two Draconic Mysteries, the young adult Puzzle Box Trilogy, and the Regency Shifter Series in Historical Paranormal fiction.]

Kaitlyn Emery was obsessed with dragons and fantasy at a young age. When she grew up, she learned reality was darker than anything she read in a book. Through writing, she learned to cope with the world around her and find a voice in fiction. Kaitlyn has written short stories for various magazines, Flash Fiction for Havok Publishing, and been published in multiple anthologies including Havok Season One Rebirth and Havok Season Three Sensational. She has also written her own children's book, The Dragon Ate My Nightlight. You can learn more about her writing and other creative endeavors at her website, kaitlynemery.wordpress.com.

Abigail Falanga may be found in New Mexico creating magic in many ways—with fabric, food, paper, music, and especially with words! She's loved fantasy ever since playing out epic adventures of swords, fairies, and monsters with her siblings, and loved sci-fi since her dad's stories around the dinner table. More than two dozen of her flash fiction stories have appeared through Havok Publishing and been featured in three Havok anthologies. She's also been published in Cracked: Anthology of Eggselent Chicken Stories, and is the editor and publisher of Whitstead Christmas: A Speculative Anthology. Busily trying to launch approximately five hundred novels into the world, Abigail has released A Time of Mourning and Dancing, the first in The Floramancy Archives - of which The Beasts of Blackwell is part.

Lisa Godfrees is the Operations Manager and a daily editor for

Havok Publishing (gohavok.com), a flash fiction ezine and bi-annual anthology. More than twenty of her short stories have been published online and in anthologies, and she's the co-author of one novel. Read or listen to some of her stories for free at https://www.lisagodfrees.com/stories/. Lisa also serves as the Director of Operations for Realm Makers, a faith-based community for fantasy and science fiction fans (realmmakers.com).

Cassandra Hamm is a psychology nerd, jigsaw puzzler, and hopeless romantic who is usually lost in another world. She fell in love with Latin America during a college missions trip to Bolivia and can't stop writing Latinx-inspired stories. Her work also appears in other anthologies, including Stories that Sing, Bingeworthy, and Sensational from Havok Publishing; Warriors Against the Storm; and Faces to the Sun. She is often found reading fairy tale retellings, especially if they're middle grade, and her favorite fairy tale is Rapunzel.

Carla Hoch is the author of the Writer's Digest book Fight Write: How to Write Believable Fight Scenes and proprietor of the award winning FightWrite™ blog. She is a Writer's Digest author and instructor and regularly teaches workshops on the mechanics of fighting for writers as well as the craft of writing fight scenes and a writer for Black Belt Magazine JiuJitsu. Carla is a Brazilian jiu-jitsu fighter with training in nearly a dozen fighting styles. She lives just outside Houston, Texas with her family and host of mammals.

Originally from Michigan, **Cindy Koepp** combined a love of pedagogy and ecology into a fourteen-year career as an elementary science specialist. After teaching four-footers - that's height, not leg count - she pursued a Master's in Adult Learning with a specialization in Performance Improvement. Her published works include science fiction, fantasy, and GameLit novels; a passel of short stories; and a few educator resources. When she isn't reading or writing, Cindy is currently working as a tech writer, hat collector, quilter, crafter, and strange joke teller.

On the road to publication, **Michelle Levigne** fell into fandom in college and has over forty stories in various SF and fantasy universes. She has a bunch of useless degrees in theater, English, film/communication, and writing. Even worse, she has over 100 books and novellas with multiple small presses, in science fiction and fantasy, YA, suspense, women's fiction, and sub-genres of romance. Her training includes the Institute for Children's Literature; proofreading at an advertising agency; and working at a community newspaper. She is a tea snob and freelance edits for a living (MichelleLevigne@gmail.com for info/rates), but only enough to give her time to write. Her newest crime against the literary world is to be co-managing editor at Mt. Zion Ridge Press and launching the publishing co-op, Ye Olde Dragon Books. Be afraid … be very afraid.

Lyndon Perry is a writer, dad, and preacher from central Kansas. He actually likes decaf coffee, herds cats on the side, and enjoys travel and hiking with his family. He also runs Tule Fog Press, an indie publisher of mystery, thriller, fantasy, science fiction, and more at TuleFogPress.com.

Stoney M. Setzer lives south of Atlanta, GA. He has a beautiful wife, three wonderful children, and one crazy dog. He is the author of the Wesley Winter trilogy, and he has also written a number of Twilight Zone-like short stories with Christian themes. His works have been published in such online magazines as Fear and Trembling and Residential Aliens, as well as a number of anthologies.

Kristiana Sfirlea is the author of the darkly whimsical MG fantasy novel Legend of the Storm Sneezer, a finalist of the international Wishing Shelf Book Awards. Her short stories, featuring clueless zombies, undercover werewolves, and grumpy ghosts, have been published by Havok and included in numerous anthologies such as Havok's Rebirth, Stories that Sing, and Sensational. She dreams of the day she can run her own mobile bookstore. Learn more about Kristiana at www.KristianasQuill.com, on Facebook @KristianasQuillBooks, and on Instagram and Twitter @KristianasQuill.

Deborah Cullins Smith has contributed to the anthologies Light at the Edge of Darkness and Underground Uprising, as well as publishing her own collection of short stories called Ominous Tales Vol. 1. In 2019, she released her first full-length novels in the Hippies trilogy—Shroud of Darkness: Book 1, The Birth of the Storm: Book 2, and Victoria's War, Book 3. All three came out over the summer and fall in honor of the 50th anniversary of Woodstock. In 2020, she took a leap of faith and joined Michelle Levigne in the publishing co-op, Ye Olde Dragon Books. Ms. Smith is the grandmother of twelve and loves nothing more than a rousing tea party with a table full of children.

C. S. Wachter lives in rural Lancaster county, Pennsylvania, with her husband Joe, one German Shepherd, and three cats. She and Joe have been married for more than forty years and have three sons, one grandson and one granddaughter. Ms. Wachter earned her degree in Performing Arts and English Education from Rowan University in 1975. She compares developing a character's perspective to preparing for an acting role. As a life-long lover of books, she has read and enjoyed a variety of genres. However, after reading J. R. R. Tolkien in middle school her favorite has been, and remains to this day, Fantasy with a Christian perspective. Website: https://cswachter.com/

MOONLIGHT AND CLAWS

In Fall 2021, Ye Olde Dragon Books will launch the first of our **Classic Monster Anthologies**, and we're beginning with a tried-and-true favorite—**Wolfman!** He's monstrous, he's tragic, he's the guy next door—until the full moon brings out the worst in him. But we don't want the wolfman that's been seen over and over in movies and literature. (much as we may love him!) We want fresh new approaches. We want you—to use our favorite phrase—to turn the story on its ear!

What are we looking for? (besides 1,000 to 5,000 words?)

Comedy.
Tragedy.
Creepy.
Romantic.
Tear-jerker.
Heroic.
Giggles.
Modern.
Futuristic.
Historical.
Sentimental.
Shudders and shrieks
Steampunk

In other words—anything and everything under the Moon!

Thrill us, chill us, make us laugh, make us cry, scare us into sleeping with a nightlight on until the new year. We want your best inventions. Go back in history, leap forward into the future, take us into steampunk universes. (If you mention Larry/Lawrence Talbot, it better be just in passing!) Take us someplace new and exciting, and you'll land a spot in this anthology!

But most of all— ***have a howling good time.!***

For information, check out the Anthologies page at ***www.YeOldeDragonBooks.com***.

The submission window will be short, and we're aiming to release in October.

But WAIT!
Before you go ...

Start brainstorming **RAPUNZEL**.

That will be our theme for the spring 2022 Fairy Tale Anthology.

What fun can you have with "lady in a tower"?

Once the Wolfman has been set free, we'll have details and dates and deadlines for Rapunzel. So keep checking the Anthologies page.